Triorion: Abomination

Book Two

L. J. Hachmeister

Copyright © 2012, 2015 by Source 7 Productions, LLC
www.triorion.com

First Edition*

This is a work of fiction. All names, characters, events and situations portrayed in this book are products of the author's imagination. Any resemblance to actual persons or events is purely coincidental.

All rights reserved. No part of this book may be used or reproduced in any manner whatsoever without written permission, except in the case of brief quotations embodied in critical articles or reviews. Please do not participate in or encourage the piracy of copyrighted materials in violation of the author's rights. Purchase only authorized editions.

Cover art and design by L. J. Hachmeister and Nicole Peschel
Illustrations by Melissa Erickson, Jeremy Aaron Moore, Jacob Mathews and Michael Webber

Source 7 Productions, LLC
Lakewood, CO

Novels by L. J. Hachmeister

Triorion: Awakening (Book One)
Triorion: Abomination (Book Two)
Triorion: Reborn, part I (Book Three)
Triorion: Reborn, part II (Book Four)

Forthcoming

Triorion: Nemesis (Book Five)

Short Stories

"The Gift," from *Triorion: The Series*
"Heart of the Dragon," from *Dragon Writers*

A Note from the Author

Since the release of *Triorion: Awakening,* I have been asked many questions about the series, most of which I think are answered in one way or another in the books, but one in particular I think is worth a dedicated answer: "Where and when did you think up this story?"

This story has haunted me since I was seven or eight years old. Despite school, life, jobs, and other commitments, I've never been able to get away from it, even in my sleep. I had to tell this story. It wasn't until I completed the main part of this series in August of 2012 that I finally felt like I could breathe again.

None of it was easy. My first draft of *Awakening* was cringeworthy at best. But I kept at it, and after countless drafts and many bottles of ibuprofen later, I felt like I had something presentable.

Why is this important? Because I believe we all have a story inside us that needs to be shared. It can be daunting. I know much of my early writing was flat and forced. There was a lot to be afraid of. However, somewhere in the whole writing process I started to have faith my characters, and all of a sudden their world opened up to me.

But my "where and when" isn't as important as your "where and when." I hope that reading my story will inspire you to write your story. It will require a great act of trust on your part, for each character you write about will be a small—or perhaps large—window into your soul.

I hope you at least give us a glimpse.

For Amneris Castro
my Wa

Triorion: Abomination

PROLOGUE

Before they could get down to business, the two Scabber Jocks toasted with their favorite drinking song:

"The sun may rise deep underground
The air may stink of rot
My food is full of maggots
But this is all I got
The dead may roam the wasteland
And the sky may burn and blister
But I have my drink and I have my gun
And I have my bad-assino *sister."*

Bossy stood on her tip toes, her head barely reaching the middle of Agracia's sternum. "So, we got something?"

Agracia held up the letter just out of reach, knowing full well what the result would be. A swift kick to her shins cut her in half, allowing Bossy to pluck the letter from her fingers.

"Holy *chak*—" Agracia nursed the sore spot on her shin as she reached for her pint. Little consolation could be found; her glass held only a few sips left of the orange-colored brew.

"Barkeep, jeezus, ya sure know how to keep a lady happy," she shouted above the blister-rock playing over the radio.

The barkeep ignored her and continued his conversation with another patron. Save a few lonely fools, the bar was nearly empty as a thin ray of simulated morning light filtered through the slatted shades.

Agracia shrugged. "Eh, that's life, yeah? Gotta help yourself out 'cause nobody else will."

Her black eyes darted from one end of the bar to the other as she chewed on the end of her unlit cigarette. The barkeep remained occupied, and the other patrons were fairly soused. *This isn't the most dangerous part of town, but I can't be careless.*

Before her nerves could best her, she dunked her hand in and out of the cooler, nabbing herself and her companion two bottles of beer.

"Gimme one," Bossy muttered as her fingertips traced the words on the letter. She couldn't read very well, but Agracia didn't feel much like helping her out. The kid was smart enough that she'd get the gist of it.

Agracia nudged the bottle over to her, and Bossy, as always, didn't care to hide her prize. Biting the cap off and spitting it over her shoulder, she resumed deciphering the letter.

The letter was stamped as if it came from the Mars colony, but Agracia knew better. Stamps and tracer heads could be forged. But whoever had written it had taken some time crafting it, perfecting every line with telltale Scabber vernacular, even choosing the right ink and recycled newspaper to write on, so she knew it couldn't be one of the local Johnnies trying to lay a trap. *This is somebody else. Some chump who's studied me, knows my territory, knows what I'm capable of.*

Bossy let out a belch. "Trick. Dumb. Let's throw it out and get wasted over at Hamasuka's. This joint sucks. There's no way I could get drunk enough to do any of these losers."

"You should slow down. You ain't even legal yet," Agracia said, taking the letter from her.

Bossy raised an eyebrow as she tipped back her bottle, chugging the rest of it. "It ain't like we gonna be around tomorrow, remember?"

Agracia gave a half-salute and tipped her own bottle back, downing the entire thing.

Grumbling, Bossy slammed her bottle on the nearest table. "So, you gonna tell me what you think, or am I gonna get drunk without you?"

Agracia hoisted herself up on a barstool, finally drawing the barkeep's attention.

"You gonna pay for that kid, or am I gonna have to call the *chakking* Dogs?" he shouted.

"Jeezus," Agracia said, pulling out a crumpled dollar and wadding it up. "All that huff and no puff. You're lucky we even passed through."

She threw the bill at the barkeep, thrilled to see his anger turn to frustration the second he realized she'd paid in hard cash.

No, I ain't no ordinary Scabber, she thought, watching his face turn red.

"Don't think I won't throw you the *chak* out," he said, stabbing his finger at her.

"Relax and we can all have a good time," Agracia said, unafraid of his empty threat.

Thrilled at the prospect of a fight, Bossy produced a ball of 20-20 and tossed it back and forth in her hands. The barkeep eyed the explosive, muttered something under his breath, and resumed his previous conversation.

"*Chakking* townies," Agracia said.

Disappointed, Bossy slung the 20-20 back in her belt and crossed her arms low across her chest, making her breasts pop out.

How'd a young kid got such a nice rack? Agracia thought, eyeing her own flat chest. With a sigh, Agracia continued their discussion. "So, you're right—it's a trick. What else you know, or do I have to spell it all out for you?"

Bossy let out a belch. "You're buying the rest of the night—"

"Morning," Agracia corrected.

"*Morning*, if I get this, alright?"

Bossy dug into her shirt pocket and popped out the lollipop she had been working on for the last two years. The extremely expensive designer candy, made by the scientists who tried to save Earth's last resources, could theoretically last a decade, but given that it was never out of her mouth unless she was drinking, Agracia was surprised it had lasted this long.

"This ain't local. This is a big contractor. No Scabber would really write like this."

"Right language. English. Right words. What's up?" Agracia said.

Bossy's nose wrinkled. "It *stinks*, is all. Smells like a trap. Nobody offers this much money to dig around the wasteland. Ain't nuthin' there no more. Any artifact that be worth finding is gone."

"Yeah, maybe. Maybe not, though. So?"

"It's a piece. There's more to this. I bet we're two Jocks in a dozen tribes that was set up for this kind of a job. We don't know enough."

She nailed it. Agracia smiled. "I wish you weren't such a *chakking* expensive date. We don't have enough cash left for food and booze."

Bossy rearranged her pigtails back under her cap and snorted. "Like that's ever stopped you. Come on, you're not getting soft on me, are you? Gonna make me do *all* the work around here or what?"

Agracia rolled her eyes and shoved Bossy out of her way as she made for the exit. "Don't fool yourself. You ain't that cute no more.

I do all the work around here."

"Watch your back, kid," the barkeep said as they exited the bar and into the subterranean street. "There be bigger fish than you out there."

Agracia didn't even bother retorting. It required too much effort, and she had to concentrate on finding food and supplies for the proposed job, especially since Bossy wasn't in the mood for work just yet. If they took up this contract it meant a trip to the surface, and she didn't have the coin to repair their radiation suits or buy the weaponry necessary to handle the dangers of the outside world.

But someone must have known about her knowledge of Old Earth—how she knew the surface better than anyone else, how she had survived for years traveling through the maze of underground Pits—to seek her out for this kind of mission.

"You're seriously considering this job?" Bossy said, shielding her eyes as the yellow sun crept higher into the video skyline above the main street. The artificial sky was supposed to make life underground a little less dismal, but Agracia didn't think the townies gave a rat's *assino* about it. Life in the Pit—any Pit—was just that.

"Yeah, what else we gonna do?" she said, stretching out her neck and arms. "I'm sick of the biz down here. Besides, they're offering 2,000 for this in hard cash. We do our own research, we play a little hard to get, and we turn it into ten. Eventually you'll get it."

Bossy twirled the lollipop in her mouth. "You still owe me the rest of the morning, and I need a little action before I can even think of going along with your stupid idea."

"Yeah, yeah," Agracia said, readjusting her headphones over her ears and turning up the volume. The classic industrial metal hit from the early twenty-first century thrummed in her head, buzzing her eardrums with intense blast beats. Ever since she could remember, she'd been addicted to the tune.

Soothed by the thrashing tones, Agracia pointed her finger at the bar across the street, its neon lights fading in the ghostly morning light. "Let's get sloshed."

CHAPTER I

Jetta didn't expect anything for their eighth birthday. It had been years since they had celebrated one, and the date was just an estimate anyway. However, when she woke up the day of 3184.250, she found Jaeia sitting at her bedside, grinning from ear to ear and holding something behind her back.

"Hey, what are you so happy about?" Jetta said, rubbing the sleep from her eyes.

"Here!" Jaeia's hands opened to reveal a small package, poorly wrapped in silver and red paper. Jetta, still surprised, didn't know if she should reach for it.

"Go on," Jaeia urged, placing it in her lap.

Tentatively, Jetta unwrapped the box, careful not to tear any of the paper. When she removed the lid, she smiled.

"What is it?" she asked, picking up the glowing object. The small orb fit neatly into her cupped palm. When it touched her fingers, the bluish shape reacted and re-formed itself into a question mark.

"It's a map of the galaxy. Tell it where you want to see."

Jetta didn't hesitate. "Fiorah."

The red planet, its neighbors and suns, all appeared within the globe, but she could barely see them.

"Put your eye to it."

Doing as her sister suggested, Jetta brought it up to her eye and the rest of her room disappeared, immersing her in the orbiting planets and stars. When she focused, she zoomed in on Fiorah, close enough to make out the outline of the bubble encapsulating the crowded city where they had lived.

"That is so cool," Jetta exclaimed, putting the globe down and hugging her sister. "Thank you."

"It's so you never get lost. No matter what, you'll always able to find your way back to me," Jaeia said, hugging her back.

"Like I'd ever leave you," Jetta scoffed. Biting her lower lip, she reached under her pillow and dug around for the present she had hidden. "Come on, this is for you."

Jaeia looked surprised. "I didn't think you'd want to celebrate."

"Just because you're my sister, my twin *and* you can hear almost all my thoughts doesn't mean you know *everything*."

Giggling, Jaeia shook her head. "I can't open it. You open it."

"Jae, that's not the point of presents."

"Come on!" she squealed, squeezing her eyes shut.

"Oh my Gods, just so you don't have a stroke," Jetta laughed, unwrapping her own gift. She set it down on Jaeia's lap. "Ummmm, you're eventually going to have to look."

Jaeia peeked one eye open, and then the other. A puzzled look edged its way into her face.

"Keys?"

Jetta nodded.

"To what?"

"Your first cruiser."

Jaeia picked up the keys, her jaw agape. "Jetta..."

"Just say 'thank you.'"

"Jetta, I don't think it's legal for anyone under the age of twenty to operate a space licensed vehicle."

"Fine, I like black and red anyway," Jetta said, swiping at the keys. Jaeia dodged her just in time.

"I didn't say I didn't want it. How'd you manage this?"

Jetta smiled coyly. "I guess you're right—not *everybody* hates us. I was able to sneak a deal after the last hearing."

The expression on Jaeia's face fluctuated between excitement and uncertainty. "Will I even be able to fly it?"

"I bought it under someone else's name and had it docked on a public lot on Trigos," Jetta said, shrugging her shoulders. "It's there when you want it."

Jaeia thought for a moment before responding. "Did you buy this for me, or so that we could go find Galm and Lohien?"

The smile on Jetta's face dissolved. "Jaeia…"

Her sister folded her arms across her lap, hiding the keys from view. "I thought we discussed this."

"We did."

Gray eyes grew solemn. "I want to see them just as much as you, but you know the situation."

Jetta sighed. *I'm not going to be able to convince her even if I bought an entire warship and had a Fleet escort.*

"You know I can't wait. You can either come with me or stay here."

Facing the window, Jaeia looked down at her feet. "After all that we've been through, after all that has happened—you haven't learned, have you?"

"Come on, sis."

In an uncharacteristic display, Jaeia got up and walked to the door. When the doors parted, guards stepped up to escort her back to her assigned quarters.

"Jaeia, please—"

"Happy birthday, Jetta."

***

Triel of Algardrien looked at the clock on the interface monitor and groaned. *Only forty minutes left until my shift.*

After spending the last eight hours pouring over the latest evidence on a displaced telepath encampment near Jue Hexron in her quarters, she had forgotten to eat. *If I don't prepare for the meeting with the chief of military intelligence, I won't be able to make a mission bid. Food can wait.*

Her stomach responded with a loud gurgle.

Exhausted and restless, she stood up and stretched, regarding herself with a frown in the mirror by her nightstand. She had always been slender, but lately her clothes seemed looser than normal. She told herself that it was because of the demands of her new Alliance position, but she knew it was more than that.

Triel slumped back down in her seat, her head heavy in her hands. The quiet of her room felt stifling. She missed the constant rumbling engine of the *Wraith*, the banter between Ro and Cray, even the incessant babblings of Billy Don't. But most of all she missed the feeling that there was always someone around—specifically, someone who wasn't afraid of her.

The door chimed, and she stirred from her thoughts. "Come in."

Even before she set foot inside the doorway, Triel recognized the familiar presence and smiled. "Jetta—what brings you by?"

Jetta had been stopping by more often lately, particularly in the evenings after her shift. And if she was gone for an extended period on a Special Missions Teams assignment, after visiting her sister, she always made sure Triel was her next stop.

In Jaeia's presence, Jetta always seemed a little more relaxed, but today she had come alone. Despite her guarded demeanor, Jetta maintained her usual politeness and purpose. "It's late, and I figured you worked through another meal." Jetta lifted up the container she carried in her left hand. The smell the roasted yingar root and karrin potatoes wafted across the room.

"Where did you manage to get that? That's not just vegetarian, it's traditional Algardrien," Triel said, clearing a place off of her workstation for her favorite meal. "They don't exactly serve that in the mess hall."

Jetta blushed as she put the food down on the workstation. "I can't tell you all my secrets."

"Well, I'm impressed; you seem to know me well. Stay, won't you?" Triel said, pulling up a stool to the workstation so Jetta could sit.

Like always, Jetta hesitated. Triel used to take Jetta's uncertainty personally, but as ruthless as she was in battle and as assertive as she was in the war room, Jetta was shy in certain social situations—particularly around her.

A few weeks ago it finally dawned on her—a fleeting thought that she had initially dismissed and only later begun to reconsider: *there may be more to Jetta's feelings for me than friendship*. At first it frightened Triel, but over time she began to find the notion increasingly intriguing.

"I can't," Jetta said, looking away.

"Are you feeling okay?" Triel asked, noticing the pallor of Jetta's cheeks. Extending herself, the Healer sensed her underlying physical rhythm slightly out of sync. *A common precursor to illness,* Triel thought, trying to take Jetta's hand.

Jetta moved out of reach, but sported a pleasant smile. "Please, I'm okay, just overworked. A lot like you."

Triel caught the after-impression of her words. "What's wrong, Jetta?"

"Nothing's wrong. It's just that I may be gone for a while on this next SMT assignment."

"I thought that was just an intelligence sweep—and you don't leave for another two days."

Jetta kept her thoughts well contained within her constructed psionic barrier. "You're right. But things can change. I might leave a little early and swing by the Noraeth Colony to question some of the natives about recent human colonist disappearances."

Triel nodded, allowing herself a moment of silence to choose her words carefully. "Jetta… you know you can always come to me if you need anything."

"I know. Thank you."

"I mean it."

Jetta's eyes narrowed, and her lips compressed into a hard line. It was the same face she made in the war room when she was readying to go head-to-head with Minister Razar, and that meant the conversation was over.

"I hope you enjoy your meal. I'll come by and see you when I return. Good luck on your proposal," Jetta said, sounding flat and rehearsed.

Triel moved to hug her, but Jetta faded back a step. Still, Jetta placed her hand on Triel's forearm and squeezed, a small smile tipping up the corners of her mouth.

"Be careful out there," Triel said.

Jetta met her eyes once more, her face unreadable.

Not knowing what else to do, Triel walked her to the door and watched her summon a lift, staying until she was out of sight around a bend in the corridor.

Slowly, the Healer reentered her quarters, and once the doors shut, leaned heavily against the wall. *Whenever Jetta leaves it feels like she takes something with her.*

Sorting through her feelings, Triel did her best to rationalize the profound loneliness and sense of loss weighing down her heart: *Maybe it's because Jetta and her sister are the only other telepaths around.*

(—Or maybe it's something else.)

The suddenness of her tears surprised her. After a few deep breaths she returned to her workstation, and with a grateful smile, dug into the Algardrien fare.

***

Jetta racked her knuckles against the railing of the lift as it whizzed down the corridors towards the docking bay. The pain was necessary right then. She didn't understand why she felt the way she did about Triel, and part of her hated it. To feel like she did made her vulnerable. *What the hell am I doing?*

"Stupid. *Stupid*," she muttered to herself, rebuking herself for the delight she took in seeing the Healer. *She's just a friend. I care about my friend.*

The enemy inside her wouldn't let her believe that lie, nor would it let her feel.

Jetta gripped the railing with all her might, deforming the metal bar. *I'm a monster. A sick, disgusting monster.*

The lift slowed as it neared the docking bay. She counted the guards and the personnel, making note of weapons and alert stations.

Good, Jetta thought to herself, letting her anger bleed through. *I'll need this.*

She casually withdrew her combat knife and put it to her neck.

***

Triel pinched the webbing between her fingers hard enough to break capillaries in what was becoming a futile bid to keep herself awake. She hadn't slept in thirty-six hours, but she couldn't miss the trials against the Kyrons.

Even though the courtroom was the largest on Trigos, it was packed shoulder-to-shoulder with various delegates from around the Starways, film crews, and Alliance troopers. Employing her limited authority, the Healer assumed the last empty seat in the house.

Oh, Jetta, she thought, taking the seat assigned to the Commander. *Why do you let your sister go to these hearings alone?*

Instead of acknowledging the issue, Triel kept quiet, knowing that when it came to Jetta's absence, it was best not to say anything. Even with the nature of the hearings, the only thing that really flustered the quieter, gray-eyed sister was Jetta herself.

"I don't even remember half of these 'witnesses'" Jaeia said as Triel slid into the seat beside her.

Triel looked to the witness box situated below the towering row of judges where a twitchy teenager of Cerran-humanoid descent was giving his testimony. The prosecution claimed he had been a child laborer alongside the triplets on Fiorah.

"You say that you worked with the Kyron siblings during your servitude on Fiorah," the lead prosecutor said. "Where did you work with them?"

"Uh, the mining ships," the kid muttered.

"Can you be more specific?" the prosecutor asked, slowly pacing back and forth in front of the witness box and the audience.

"Th-the target drill in the Mirirus division."

If he wasn't a liberated child laborer, he played the part well. He kept his chin tucked against his chest, eyes shifting nervously back and forth as he made himself as small as possible on the witness stand. He only spoke Fiorahian, but the auto-translator perched besides his box picked up the slurred drawl common to most of the children brought up in the mines.

"And how were your encounters with the siblings?"

"Uh, well, bad. They were nuthin' but launnies, really, but they were mean. Always fighting with us. One of 'em killed my brother Verk."

The prosecutor stopped in his tracks and put down his datafile. "Which one?"

"Dunno. One of the girls. They looked the same."

"You witnessed this killing?"

The Cerran shook his head. "Nah, didn't. But I seen her with him before he died. He wasn't acting himself. He was Verk, but he wasn't. Like he went missin'."

"What was he doing?" the prosecutor asked, approaching the witness box.

"He was suppose' to be cleaning the guttering receivers, but he was doing her job in the engine rooms cleanin' the track parts. Didn't make no sense. Verk would never associate with 'dem launnies. It was like she played a mind trick on him or sumthin' to make him work her job."

"And what happened later?"

The kid scraped fingernails down his cheek, rocking back and forth. "I found him in the coolant room. He weren't breathing no more."

"So one of the Kyron sisters killed him?"

"Objection!" shouted the defense team. "That is speculation."

Triel looked to Jaeia. Outwardly, she appeared to be listening closely, unmoved, but on a psionic level she radiated a fear the Healer had never felt from her before.

The principal judge nodded his multiple heads. "Sustained."

Jaeia closed her eyes and drew in a deep breath.

This is a nightmare, Triel thought, feeling badly for her. The trials had been going on for weeks, and witnesses had been flooding in from all corners of the galaxy to testify. Thankfully, the prosecution hadn't called for Jetta and Jaeia yet, but Triel knew what would happen long before then: the release of their post-war psychiatric evaluations. The Alliance had been successful thus far in either preventing or delaying them from being submitted by the General Assembly, but it wouldn't be long before the public's overwhelming desire swayed the easily manipulated Chancellor Reamon into overriding Minister Razar's authority.

"Gods, it's hot in here," Jaeia said, pulling apart her uniform collar and fanning herself with a datafile.

"Let's take a break," Triel whispered, placing a hand on her shoulder.

"I shouldn't... I should stay," Jaeia mumbled, not taking her eyes off the Cerran witness.

For the first time all day, the kid looked up and straight at Jaeia. Triel sucked her breath in. Being of Prodgy blood, she had felt that same contempt and fear before, but never as intensely as is it was directed at Jaeia.

Triel toyed with the idea of pressing her authority as a chief medical advisor, but she decided instead to play it conservatively. Swaying Jaeia with the idea of taking care of herself seldom worked, but when it came to taking care of others, she usually listened.

"I could use a break, Jaeia," she said, laying a hand on Jaeia's forearm. "Keep me company."

"Alright," Jaeia relented.

There weren't many places they could go. Like Jaeia, Triel had an escort at all times. The Alliance had assured her it was for her safety, but she knew it was more of a safeguard for their own unspoken qualms. Having a lone Healer wandering around was not good for public relations, despite some of the newfound public support for the telepathic survivors of the Dissembler Scare.

"There's a lounge inside the circuit room. Come on," Triel said, touching her shoulder.

Reluctantly, Jaeia got up, keeping her eyes on the Cerran teenager until she turned to leave. Even then, Triel felt Jaeia's mind clinging to the kid's presence as they walked down the halls with their military escorts.

As they shouldered their way through the Sentient swarms, the Healer kept her concentration trained on Jaeia. The reporters' shouted questions barely rose above the clicking of cameras and the screaming public behind the electric fence.

"Do you feel any remorse for the murders you committed during your days as General Volkor?" one of them yelled.

"Are you and your sister still having nightmares?" said another.

The latter question disturbed Triel. *That's not supposed to be public knowledge.*

Their escorts formed a triangle around Jaeia, shielding her from the eyes of the cameras, but it only prompted the reporters to ask more inflammatory questions.

"What were you thinking when you and your sister killed your brother?"

"Which one of you was the one who ended his life?"

Triel finally exhaled when they were safely behind the double doors of the circuit lounge.

"Can we please have a private conversation? We are allowed that," Triel asked.

Her escort rattled off a few lines of Alliance protocol, but when Triel moved to lay her hands on his forearm, he backed away. "You have five minutes."

I just wanted to connect with you, Triel thought, distressed that he had misinterpreted her gesture.

As the escorts took posts by the double doors, Triel made her way over to the bay window across the room. The view overlooked the terrace and central garden with its statues of prominent political figures of the Allied Homeworlds going back as far as the tenth century. In the distance, the planet's only sun sunk lazily into the yellow grass hilltops, casting the world in shades of pink and orange.

"I'm still not used to all these time shifts. It feels like early afternoon to me," Jaeia remarked, joining her at her side.

"Hey, I heard you and your sister just celebrated your birthday. I'm sorry, I thought it was at the beginning of the year," Triel said. "I want to celebrate with you."

Jaeia shrugged. "The Alliance just gave us a generic date since we didn't really know. But this is our favorite day of the year, so that's the date we decided on."

"What do you mean?"

Shaking her head, Jaeia explained: "It's a numbers thing. Jetta, for all her blabber about scientific method and proof, is pretty superstitious."

"Good enough," Triel said, smiling. "I'll have to get you a present. But what do you get for an eight-year-old commander in the Starways Alliance?"

Jaeia chuckled. "I suppose I'm eight, right? Last round of physicals we had put us at around twenty. Don't really know, though; the way Jetta is acting, I think she's more in that moody teenager stage I've read about."

Triel raised a brow. Chronologically the twins were twelve years her junior, but no one, Triel included, could really treat them as children anymore. With the Motti's alterations to their bone and muscle growth, the twins' physical appearance matched her own age. Mentally, the twins exceeded any adult, and their cumulative age from gleaning experiences from Sentient minds aged them decades beyond the Healer. There were still moments when she wasn't sure where their true development put them, but, if anything, their eyes told of their true age.

Sensing the break in tension, Triel finally broached the other issue on her mind: "How have you been feeling, Jaeia? You haven't looked like yourself in a while."

Jaeia, always trim, appeared leaner and pale. The Healer wanted to talk to both sisters since they had both lost weight, but Jetta was never honest about her health. Once, after a battle simulation accident, Jetta had tried to return to duty with Grade IV lacerations to her thigh. Triel knew that the twins had a serious aversion to medical care after their experiences on the Dominion ships, but Jetta in particular refused even basic care, especially from the Healer. At first Triel was hurt by her avoidance, but recent observations gave her new insight.

Jaeia sighed. "Run down. Like I've had a bug for the past several weeks. I did see Dr. Kaoto, but he couldn't find anything wrong, so it's probably stress. I appreciate your concern, though."

Taking Jaeia's hands in hers, the Healer peered underneath her skin. "You have a low grade fever, and your white blood cell count is slightly higher than usual, but there's no cause that I can sense. That's odd. If you don't get better soon, why don't you set an appointment with me for a full immersion?"

Jaeia chuckled as she took her hand back and ran it through her hair. "Time is always an issue for both of us, isn't it? There's always that next pressing mission."

"I know, but I'm worried about both of you. I saw your sister earlier," Triel said. "She didn't say anything, but I could sense that she wasn't herself."

"No, she's not feeling very well either," Jaeia admitted. "Not that you'll ever hear her complain."

Thinking back over the last several months, Triel smiled. *No, Jetta never complains.*

Memories of her first encounter with the infamous Jetta Kyron surfaced in her mind's eye. All of her initial assumptions had been wrong; Jetta was nothing like General Volkor, and she was certainly not the product of all the military knowledge she possessed. Knowing her lethal abilities and military conquests, the Healer had tried not to like her, but the more Triel got to know her, the more she found that she did.

On duty Jetta was one of the Alliance's stricter officers, but she was also one of the few to drill alongside the soldiers in her units. Those who doubted or feared her eventually learned to respect her skill and fairness, especially when she routinely outperformed her own troops.

But it was the sensitive side to her personality, the one that others rarely saw, that Triel found herself inexplicably drawn to. From the very first healing, when she felt Jetta's intense bond with her siblings, Triel realized there was something beneath her hard exterior. Jetta cared about those she served with—it was never a game to her, and the lives she had taken during the Dominion Wars still weighed heavily on her heart. She took her friendships, though few, very seriously. Especially their relationship. With all the things Jetta had done for her since the war—routinely stopping by her quarters, bringing her food, making sure she was taking care of herself—Triel began to realize that Jetta also cared about her, even if she had a hard time saying so in words.

"Well, it could be stress, Jaeia," Triel said, thinking of how much all three of them had overworked themselves since the end of war with the Motti. "Did the Minister give you time off like he promised?"

"No," Jaeia said, shaking her head. "Leave was rescinded after the death threats were posted on the net. Razar said it was took much of a security risk. And then with the trials… I don't know. Everything's so screwed up right now. I just wish Razar would let us go back to Fiorah before Jetta does something stupid."

Triel silently agreed. *Jetta won't wait much longer.*

"Is everything okay with you?" Jaeia asked, leaning against one of the marble pillars.

"No," she said, folding her arms across her chest. "I'm worried about you and Jetta, Reht and the crew. I'm worried about what will happen to all of us. These trials, the state of the Homeworlds postwar—everything is uncertain."

Jaeia nodded, staring off into the distance. "And now the latest intelligence reports indicate that Urusous Li has found some sort of rich private investor and is trying to re-form the old empire."

"The old empire?" Triel repeated.

"Predated the United Starways Coalition. It was an autocratic society founded by the conservatives of Ios and Sirian over a thousand years ago. Eventually it became democratic after the two planets were colonized by the new wave of Trigonian and human colonists. But there's a lot of people out there that want that sort of thing, especially after the Dominion Wars and the Deadwalkers."

"Absolute right and wrong, absolute answers," Triel echoed.

"Exactly," Jaeia whispered.

"Commander," a soldier said, popping his head through the double-doors. "There's an urgent message from the ACS."

Jaeia hunched forward, her gaze drifting off.

Oh no... Triel thought, sensing Jaeia's dread. As much as the Healer tried to rationalize any other reason for an urgent message from the Alliance Central Starbase, Jetta's odd behavior during her last visit only solidified their mutual inference.

"Don't worry," Triel whispered, hiding her own fear as best she could. "She knows how to protect herself."

"It's more complicated than that," Jaeia responded, covering her mouth with the back of her sleeve. She gave herself a moment before going over to the terminal interface near the holographic fireplace. After logging in, the message, encrypted with a code known only to Jaeia, scrolled down across the virtual field, the red light casting a shadow across her carefully composed face.

"When did they report her missing?" Triel asked, staring out the window. The crowd outside was more dense than before. Protestors and demonstrators screamed at one another while crowd-control police waved their shockwands to maintain control.

"After she missed her shift call, they couldn't locate her signal on board the *Gallegos*. She's not registering in regulated territory."

Jaeia must have come to the same conclusion, but Triel said it out loud anyway. "You know she probably removed the biochip. She couldn't have gotten that far out of the Homeworlds in a single jump, though."

"It doesn't matter," Jaeia said, sliding down the wall until she was sitting on the ground. "I know where she's going."

"What can I do, Jaeia?" Triel said, approaching her and kneeling by her side.

Jaeia shook her head. "The last time she ran it nearly cost my life, hers, and the Exiles'. And this time around she's learned how to do more damage."

Triel didn't know what to say. All three of them were in a precarious situation. One Prodgy and two unschooled telepaths of unknown origin with uncertain powers made the Alliance and the public nervous, but it scared her even more.

Falling back into old habits, Jaeia rubbed the inside of her right upper arm. "I don't want to follow her, but she is my sister."

"Well, you don't have to go alone."

Jaeia looked at her directly, the steely composure in her gray eyes betraying her feelings. "I hope you don't mind the heat."

***

Jetta scratched at the base of her neck as she wound her way through the crowd in Newpara Square. The dermaband had stopped the bleeding, but the itchiness from the adhesive felt worse than the initial pain of cutting out the biochip.

Dr. Kaoto's warning played out in her mind: *"Improper removal of a biochip can cause hallucinations, seizures, paralysis—even death."*

"Yeah, well, I'm about to risk a lot worse," she muttered to herself as she passed by the city's four-tiered fountain.

A Teller, sitting cross-legged on his prayer rug next to a group of beggars, popped up and grabbed at her arm. "You're in need of a guide!"

Jetta shrugged him off without looking at him and picked up her pace. The solar mask of a Wamarus, a photosensitive Sentient, provided adequate cover for her face, but her height and weight made it look suspicious, even with all the extra clothing she wore.

Keep going, she told herself as she turned on to the trade streets. *No chance to go back now.*

As the sun slipped behind the mountains, Trigos' market district bustled with last-minute transactions. Alliance troops, stationed at various checkpoints, performed their flash sweeps with biosensors, looking for criminals and marked citizens amongst the masses. Staying in the thick of the crowds, Jetta used numbers to her advantage. Plenty of Sentients had refused the biochips, so she wouldn't be flagged—at least not until she tried to leave the planet. Orbital checkpoint scanners, more sensitive than the handheld devices used by the troops, would pick up on residual markers from old biochips.

(Like the one I just cut out,) her subconscious screamed.

"I should have never agreed to have one in the first place," she whispered, giving the wound another scratch.

"It's required for all members of the Alliance military," she remembered the Military Minister saying. *"Besides broadcasting your vital signs and location, the chip is programmed with all your medical information. It's for your own safety, Commander."*

No, it's a tracking device, she thought angrily. *Just another means for the Alliance to keeps tabs on me and my sister.*

Thinking of the sleek black and red four-wing Yamazuki cruiser waiting in the docks, Jetta promised herself things were about to change. She had taken a late-model cruiser and completely redesigned the interior and engine based off the gleanings from the Alliance's top fighter pilots. Equipped with the latest jumpdrive, phase-inversion weapons and shielding, the mid-size cruiser had enough fighting power to take on a warliner.

The Alliance won't be able to stop me, she thought. *No one will.*

A quieter voice inside her whispered: *(Jaeia was right about me.)*

Tightening her fists, Jetta tried to keep cool as she walked stiffly down the block, avoiding vendors and salesmen shouting their final sales. But as much as she tried, the truth chipped away at her conscience.

So what if I bought the cruiser thinking that it would rally my sister to find our aunt and uncle? she argued with herself. *I had to do something.*

The Alliance had allowed them to monitor the search parties, but Fiorahians weren't going to deal with the military even if they were interrogated and imprisoned. Even the undercover contacts she had hired had failed simply because they weren't Fiorahian, but nobody from the black market planet was trustworthy enough to hire. *Fiorah has its own intricate protocol, and if we're ever going to find Galm and Lohien, I'll have to do it myself.*

"You are in great danger!"

The Teller was back, on her heels. Jetta whipped around, palming the hilt of the blade concealed under her robes.

"I don't want trouble," the Teller said, opening his palms and raising his hands. "I just want you to see what I see."

Jetta didn't want to speak; her voice was widely recognized nowadays, but the Teller left her no other choice. She cleared her throat, straining to make it sound deeper and raspy.

"I don't have any money."

"I don't want any," he said. Standing about two meters tall, the lanky Teller appeared around sixty or seventy years old, and the opacity of his eyes suggested blindness. How he had caught up to her and found her in the crowd, she wasn't sure.

"Then what? I haven't got all day," Jetta said.

The Teller closed his eyes and brought his hands to his mouth. "Turn back now before it's too late, before you lose sight of your true path."

Listening to the words he did not speak made her pause. *This Teller actually knows something; he has talent of some sort—not telepathy, but maybe clairvoyance.*

Jetta dug out a coin from her pocket and placed it in the man's hand. "Another one if you get a little more specific."

The Teller smiled, stretching out an arm to feel her face. She grasped his wrist, blocking his attempt, but he took hold of her forearm with his wrinkled hand. The hair on her arms stood on end as a sensation like mist sunk beneath her skin.

"Her name is from the mother who saw her life before she was born," he intoned. "From the ashes she will rise to bring us home."

Startled, Jetta shook him off, and the Teller collapsed to the ground.

"What the hell?" she mumbled, trying to sort out the sudden

wash of fear and confusion. But before she could decide her next move, she spotted two guards near a crosswalk homing in on their interaction.

"Get up," she said, trying to help him back to his feet.

Clinging to her sleeves, the Teller whispered: "*He is coming for you now.*"

"Who?" she asked.

The Teller's cloudy eyes glistened in the waning sunlight. "The one who cheats Death. His words are his power, and his soul is the gateway to a world of endless suffering. You are not ready. You must not listen to his lies. And promise me—promise me!" he said, voice rising to hysterics. "*Never* look behind his eyes."

One of the guards pointed toward Jetta and the Teller before speaking into the com on his sleeve.

"You have to get up," she said, holding him by the upper arm. The Teller wobbled on shaking legs.

"Just remember," the Teller said, his breathing hard and heavy, his legs buckling, "Many names you shall be called, but only one is true. Know this and be reborn."

Jetta stuffed her hands into pockets and spun away, letting the Teller drop to the ground as guards produced biosensors to sweep her area.

Only twenty more meters, she thought, hurrying toward the peak-roofed transport hub. Steering close to the few civilians milling around the docks, Jetta prayed that the Teller's fall would provide a decent enough distraction as she approached her destination.

"Don't turn away now—only the flesh is dead!" screamed the Teller as people walked around and over him.

What a scam artist, she convinced herself, wanting to get as far away as possible from him and his cryptic warnings.

Without looking back, Jetta jumped up, grabbed the arm of a streetlight, and swung herself over the fence.

At least that was easy, she thought, sticking the landing. As much as she hated the reason why she had grown so big and tall, she couldn't deny the advantages of strength and speed. The only downfall proved to be the emotions and thoughts that came with her increasingly mature body.

Sex and attraction are such hassles, she concluded, thinking through some of the experiences she had absorbed from adults over the years. *All that energy and emotional strain spent on "love"—such a waste.*

But as much as she tried to distance herself from the idea, inklings of a curious longing broke down her logic and pulled her back. The throes of love and heartbreak, once pitiful to her, now felt ominous.

Don't think of that right now, she told herself, digging her fingers into the dermaband on her neck to suppress the images of the Healer burning through her mind. Pain zapped down her spine, shocking her back into focus.

(Besides—nothing will come of it anyway.)

Jetta wound her way through the rows of cruisers and other starcraft, keeping a trained eye on the man sleeping in the traffic booth. Finding her vehicle and loading up was fairly easy, but taking off and getting past the perimeter guard with their more attuned biosensors would be a different story. Her best plan was to make the jump while still on-planet, but that would have devastating results, ripping space-time apart and unleashing a shockwave that could easily obliterate ten city blocks. And as overpopulated as Trigos was, especially after the Motti's destruction of so many habitable planets, there wasn't a square centimeter of the planet that wasn't owned and occupied.

After slapping on her helmet, Jetta gripped the throttle and entered in the coordinates to Fiorah. As the numbers flashed in red, waiting for her final punch, her mind wandered back to her sister.

(Maybe I should check in on her—)

No! she reprimanded herself. *Stay closed off or she'll try to talk you out of this.*

Concern still trickled into her thoughts. The trials and the rising tension between the Alliance government and some of the Homeworld nations and protectorates made it look more and more like a full-scale war would erupt any day. The last thing she cared about was what crimes people thought she committed or if the human colonies were really being exterminated so that other Sentients could have their land. She would have been happy buying a midship and traveling the stars with her sister, away from the Alliance, the Starways, and her memories. But for some reason Jaeia cared, and that had kept her grounded, even spurring Jetta to take up rank in order to placate her sister's ever-growing need to solve the problems of the universe. Besides, what better way to protect her sister than with an entire armada at her command? At least the military respected her skill and her powers. Even if a soldier or officer didn't believe in her, they believed in her abilities, and being feared was good enough for her.

But it's not good enough for Jaeia. She's still trying to win everybody's acceptance.

(I have to do this alone.)

Jetta cursed under her breath and hit the accelerator. The traffic operator sprang out of his seat, knocking over his coffee and splashing his newspaper as Jetta's engines flared to life. She hovered for less than a second before blasting off, taking off toward the outer rim of the city.

"Unauthorized flight plan. Please submit your course to the Trigonian Perimeter Guard."

The recorded voice repeated the command twice before Jetta silenced her communications system.

As she zoomed through the sky, Jetta couldn't help but regard the cityscape as the pinks and oranges of the settling sun melted into shades of gray and purple, reflecting off the windows of its countless high-rises and geodesic domes.

(So beautiful.)

No distractions. Keep an eye on your navs, she told herself.

The ride felt smooth in her hands as she searched for the jump site she had vetted earlier that day. Based on what she had gathered from satellite views and area mapping, the grassy hill overlooking half-finished houses and construction machinery would be the best option.

There it is, she thought, circling above the designated plot.

A late-shift foundation worker emerged from under a temporary shelter as Jetta made her final calculations.

Oh no…

After checking her coordinates twice, she came to the same conclusion: *I can't jump higher in the atmosphere or the guards will neutralize my engines with guardian probes.*

Three chirps from her scanners alerted her to the scout ships heading toward her position. *They've flagged my ship. I've got less than a minute to make this jump.*

Jetta looked at her hands and bit her lip. She hadn't shied away from the possibility that she might have to kill in order to find their uncle and aunt, but she'd always figured it would be a low-life or two in the Fiorahian underworld, not some poor Trigonian construction worker.

What is one more Sentient life under my belt? It won't be long until the General Assembly turns me and Jaeia over to the civil courts anyway, she reasoned, wiping the sweat from her brow. *We'll be lucky if we spend the rest of our lives in jail.*

Jetta clutched the ignition to the jumpdrive, her knuckles turning white as the engines hummed anxiously, waiting for her final punch.

Do it already, she willed herself over and over again, but her mind wouldn't let go of the foundation worker.

Paralyzed by her conscience, an impetus arose from the shadows of her mind, whispering in her ear: *He is nothing but another obstacle in your way.*

Painful images of Galm and Lohien cut through her mind. Her uncle's arthritic hands and broken gait; her aunt's wilting figure. *I have to save them—*

Her fingers convulsed on the punch. The initial surge of power slammed into her right before the engines folded space and time, and she gripped her armrest to combat sensation of falling.

During the brief half-second her surroundings shifted in the illusion of movement that preceded the jump, she caught sight of her pursuers—not the Perimeter Guard's scout ships, but a pair of phantom fighters. A burst of light shot from their guns, but she had no time to react.

As the missiles struck her engine core, the world folded in and away in a flash of white light.

***

Damon Unipoesa scrolled through the newsreel. Even though Minister Razar had limited his access, he could read between the lines well enough to know what was going on in the outside world.

The Starways is fracturing, he thought, reading the reports on food shortages and rioting throughout the unregulated territories. *A new war is coming.*

Damon looked up from the newsreel. The Military Minister, Tidas Razar, sat across from him, his belly lumping over the table, studying the Admiral's face. *What does that bastard want from me?*

Since Damon's breakdown after the Final Front at the Homeworld Perimeter against the Motti, his every move was monitored, and his speeches—if he was even allowed a public appearance—were scripted for him. *Whatever he wants, it's got to be something big since he made this a personal visit.*

With his hands folded neatly across his chest, and perfectly cropped hair, Razar cast a judging eye on the disheveled admiral. Damon didn't like the Minister's new image, but it fit into his post-war agenda for a new military age. "We could use you back, you know," Razar said.

Damon grunted. A long time ago he thought the Minister might have been a fair player, but Razar had since proven him otherwise.

"Right now the Starways needs a leader," the Minister said. "I want you on full duty."

"You can't make a very convincing argument about needing me when you've got me cooped up in here," Unipoesa sighed, putting down the newsreel. The interrogation room housed nothing more than two chairs and a table, with a solitary lamp shining down on them. Guards stood outside the door, watching their activity. Damon couldn't tell if they were being recorded or not. "Why don't you just reprogram me and send me back out on the streets? The Alliance could always use another Sleeper Agent."

The change in Razar's face was nearly imperceptible. "It was considered."

Careful not to break his own stony expression, Damon made the connection: *I've somehow made myself important enough to be left fully intact. That's the only reason they'd keep me alive and in possession of my original memories.*

"So how much longer is this going to take?" Damon said, rapping his knuckles on the table. "I've had all the training. You're going to have to get a lot nastier than babysitting me to make me crack."

Razar's face remained emotionless and his tone even. "That's not the intention. We would like you back on staff. There is considerable tension in the government. Whole planets have been rendered uninhabitable by the Motti; there are millions of displaced people. War is imminent. And… Li is back."

"So that's why you need me," Damon chuckled. "You want me

to advise you on Li. Tell you how to beat him. Well, I can't."

"You made him," Razar said.

"Yes—and I made him the best, just like you wanted. He's a jackal. And now, humiliated after losing the Endgame, he's going to try and take down the entire Starways just to prove what a murderous bastard he is."

"Are the Kyrons at risk?" Razar asked.

"Of course—I'm sure he's figured out a way to either assassinate or neutralize them completely. In fact, he's the most likely source of all this controversy over their part in the Dominion Wars. If he doesn't kill them, he'll make sure to have them executed legally or you'll face complete and total dissolution of your government. He'll win either way."

Razar blinked several times, but otherwise his face didn't change. "You were the one to expose them in the first place, Damon. You can't blame me for that."

"You know I did the right thing—Li had enough silent allies in the upper ranks that he would have found out one way or the other. By putting them out there in the public's eye, I kept Li from using them against you. You should thank me."

Razar's mouth compressed into a single line. "Hate me all you want, but you know that if you help me, you'll help the twins, and that's one of the few things that matters to you."

"Stop playing psychologist, Tidas. You've never been very good at it," Damon said.

"Tell me you don't look at them and see all the little girls and boys you broke and re-broke to produce Li."

"Don't you dare—"

"Help me and save them," the Minister said, remaining firm.

Keeping his emotions in check, Damon replied: "Then I want them to know the truth—all of it. It doesn't matter how much Rai Shar you do. Even if you resort to doping them like the Core, they'll find out. They're adapting, growing stronger. You know the time will come when you can't control them any longer, and Gods help you if they see you as their enemy."

Razar leaned back, away from the light. A shadow fell across his face so that only the whites of his eyes were visible. "Reconsider this offer. It's your only option if you want to keep your skin."

As the Minister got up to leave, Damon despaired. *One way or another the Alliance will figure out a way to get what they want from me—dead, alive or somewhere in between.*

Then it struck him: *Wait—what if this isn't a threat, but a warning?*

He realized what he needed to ask. "Any leads on the tattoo?"

"Come to the High Council meeting tomorrow, 0700 sharp, and find out for yourself. That is, if you're willing to aid us with Li. Once you're in, that's it. No more chances, Damon," Razar said as he walked out the door.

Unipoesa ran a hand through his hair, marveling at how much it had thinned in the past few months. *I'm falling apart faster than the Starways.*

As the guards took his sides, ready to escort him back to his quarters, his thoughts turned to Li. *My old prodigy is much more cunning and ruthless than the Alliance is prepared to deal with. If anything, his political ranting and threats against the Kyrons are just a smokescreen for his true agenda.*

The longing for a smoke nagged at his thoughts as he walked back to his quarters in silence.

***

Reht hated the bars on Trigos. Not only did government regulations cap drinks after three rounds, the cheap bastards controlled total alcohol consumption so that even his favorite drink, vodka and Redfly, had been partially neutralized to decrease the desired effects.

"I would rather give up my guns for a year than be stuck here another day," Cray grumbled, licking the rim of his pint.

Ro whimpered. "I'd give up Cornelia and Marlou."

"You never had Marlou, so don't even cut that, *ratchakker*," Cray said, shoving his empty glass across the table.

"Quiet, you two," Bacthar mumbled, rubbing his face with both of his wings.

In an uncharacteristic display, Ro and Cray shut up and the rest of the crew fell silent as the generic background music played lightly over the buzz of conversation. A few of the patrons threw occasional glances their way, but nobody seemed to care about the presence of Reht and his motley crew.

The dog-soldier captain frowned. *And I know why.* The saffron wallpaper punctured and dented to imitate a violent history. Chipped glasses and broken pints. Mystery stains too perfectly splattered and arched across the ceiling and floors. Just another badly-forged controlled setting with undercover Alliance guards monitoring their activity and interactions.

Even that one-eyed bartender and dishwasher are probably in on it, too, he thought, playing with the ends of his newly-dyed hair. He kept the base white, but colored the tips red and black out of boredom, mainly because it was one of the few liberties afforded to him.

This was all Unipoesa could bargain for them, and Reht hated him for it. The biochips were bad enough, but to be quarantined on a planet as strictly regulated as this one made him ache for the Labor Locks—at least there he'd have a chance of dealing their way out. He had no idea how many tails he had and no ways to make connections with his contacts.

In the midst of his lamentations, a woman in her late twenties clothed in a plain green and gray civilian jumpsuit walked in and made her way to one of the barstools at the counter. Her hair, brown and falling to the middle of her back, was pulled back in a tight braid. He picked up her animal smell, the stink of fear and desperation, and pushed his drink aside.

"Give me five," Reht said to his crew.

"Bah. I don't give you thirty seconds with that one. She ain't ripe," Cray snorted.

"Yeah, but she's female. And she probably smells a lot better than you," Reht said, shoving himself away from the table.

The dog-soldier captain strode casually over to her, keeping track of the eyes that followed his every move.

"You look like you could use a drink," he said to her as he flipped the bartender a credit.

"Don't bother," the woman muttered, her shoulders hiking upwards. Her accent was unusual; he had never heard anything like it.

"Then maybe you could use an ear."

Silence. She wouldn't look him in the eyes, and he couldn't read through her stone-cold expression.

"Okay, then why come here?" he asked.

The woman turned and looked him dead in the eye. Pale green eyes locked with his, striking a familiar chord that he couldn't quite place.

"Can't I have some peace? Aren't there other women around here for you to hit on?"

Normally he would follow that with a crass remark, or, if she was pretty enough, he would pursue her. But this one was different. She didn't excite him the same way other women did; there was something different about her, something strangely attractive that threw him off his game, but he couldn't pinpoint the cause.

"Darling," he said, leaning up against the bar and signaling for a smoke. The bartender pointed to the *no smoking* sign. He cursed under his breath before continuing. "This is a *chakking* poke bar, not a playground. This is for unfortunate souls like me who pissed off the wrong politician and have tails on 'em everywhere they go. I just want to know where you fit in this whole scheme."

She fell silent again, seeming to take him in with more than just her eyes.

He threw a quick glance over to his crew. Although they weren't actually watching him, he knew they were paying close attention. Bacthar, tapping on the rim of his glass, signaled to bail, but Reht decided to stay. His gut would never lead him astray. This woman wasn't part of the Alliance gig.

Tears formed in the woman's eyes, and Reht felt he was nearly there, at some kind of breaking point.

"There is nowhere else to go," she whispered.

Ah, she's a Deadskin, he figured. Another low-status human, probably part of the growing number of displaced colonists that were left homeless after the Motti poisoned most of the habitable planets in the Starways. Humans who weren't vouched for or declared liberated had a hard time, and from the looks of it, she was on her own.

"Calm down, get a sponsor. It ain't hard. A little makeup, a little smile—you're not half bad for a Deadskin," Reht chuckled. The bartender threw him a sidelong glare as he set a bubbling tonic in front of the woman.

"I don't drink. And I *don't* need a sponsor," she said, pushing aside the drink with the back of her hand.

Reht wavered a moment. *Wait—this doesn't add up.* She wasn't in on anything, and she was certainly out of place in any bar setting, poke bar or legit street joint. *She's trying to tell me something, but she knows she can't.*

No, there's more, he realized, reading her body language, the way she watched him from the side of her eye. *She's trying to hire me for a job even though these Alliance* chakkers *clearly have their heads up our* assinos.

As he watched her fingers curl up into her hands and then relax, the puzzle pieces fell into place. *For her to risk seeing me like this, it has to be about something only I could know.*

The launnies.

He took a stab at it. "Maybe this is about your kids. Nothing else in the universe matters more to a mother."

A startled look crossed her face but vanished as she grabbed the tonic and slugged it back.

"Personally, I don't have kids—that I know about. Hell," Reht said. "But sometimes they can be cute little buggers. Maybe I'd think twice with the right woman."

Her hands started to shake, but she crossed her arms and leaned into the bar to mask her nerves.

"I would just like to know that mine are okay, that's all," she said.

Reht almost didn't believe it, but when she turned back to him and he got another look at the shape and color of her eyes, the closely guarded facial expressions, he knew.

"I'm sure that wherever they are, lady, they're alright. Looks like you can take care of yourself, so they could probably take care of themselves."

"Sure, sure," she muttered, fumbling with her empty glass. She stared ahead for a moment, her lips twisting as she chewed on the insides of her cheeks. "I have to get going. Without a sponsor, it isn't safe, even on Trigos. But I don't have to tell you that. You know the way things are."

"Come by this place again—keep a prisoner company?" Reht asked, catching her by the elbow as she turned to go. One of the men at the bar shifted in his stool and pretended to stare into his drink. Light glinted off the recording device he tried to hide in his palm.

"I can't," she said. "I've got to keep moving. It isn't safe."

"At least tell me your name," he said, holding fast to her elbow even though she tried to wiggle away.

The woman looked straight into his eyes, and a thousand pinpricks shot down his arms and legs. He fell, but there was no ground to fall to, just an infinite black hole within himself, backwards, twisted and inside-out.

Then, as quickly as the feeling came, it passed, leaving him gasping for air, still clutching her elbow.

"I don't think so," she whispered, finally freeing herself from his grip. She took the napkin from underneath her drink and, with a quick hand, plucked the pencil from the bartender's back pocket as he wiped down a bottle. "I'm just a toy to you."

After scrawling something on the napkin, she scrunched it up and shoved it into the pocket of his pilot's jacket. Still reeling, he couldn't muster a single word as she exited the bar.

"You okay, Cappy?" Cray said, joining his side. The Ereclian slapped his shoulder with a chuckle. "Some strange broads you like. She give you her number? Not like you can get laid without a *chakking* audience anymore."

With his heart pounding in his ears, Reht managed to steady his hands enough to pull the napkin out of his pocket. In ancient English were the letters, *O E A.*

Reht wiped the sweat off his forehead with the napkin, smudging the letters before he ripped it up and threw it in the trash. "Eh, she couldn't handle me."

"*Chak*, Reht, I'm so goddamn bored I'm about to slit my own throat," Cray whined as he and the captain sat back down with the rest of the crew.

"Chill out," Reht said, holding Cray back as he wound up to throw his glass at one of the eavesdroppers. "Just sit tight. Something will come up, I'm sure."

***

The first thing Damon noticed at the emergency High Council meeting was that it was limited to only a few of the ranking officers in the Fleet and Chancellor Reamon from the General Assembly. Upon further scrutiny of the conference room attendees, he deduced that each person had been in some sort of position to know privileged information about the Kyrons.

This can't be good.

He took his seat at the conference table and reviewed the roster on his datawand:

Gaeshin Wren, chief commanding officer
Tidas Razar, Military Minister
Waylen Reamon, chancellor of the General Assembly
Damon Unipoesa, admiral, chief military advisor
Msiasto Mo, chief of military intelligence
Ryeo Kaoto, chief of medicine
Triel of Algardrien, chief medical advisor
Trecyn Rook, acting-commander, Special Missions Teams (SMT)
LuShin DeAnders, director of Military Research

"First off, this meeting isn't going in the books. The room has been completely deactivated," Minister Razar said, standing in front of the horseshoe-shaped conference table. "Any notes or records that you keep must be by datawand with defensive memory wipe coded into its primary routines. I don't want anyone or anything getting hold of what we are about to discuss."

Whispered concerns circulated throughout the room, but Razar resumed the spotlight before things could get out of hand.

"I'll get right down to it. The war with the Motti has left us searching for solutions for our displaced citizens and our devastated worlds. We cannot survive if we do not find habitable planets for our Sentient brothers and sisters. Trigos was already overpopulated and facing ecological disaster before the massive influx. Arkana, Saelis, Aeternyx, Jue Hexron, Ra'Tunne—all are now facing crisis as refugees flood the ports. Civil wars have already ousted many of our delegates. We cannot negotiate with the terrorists that have assumed control of our land and people."

"I didn't think this was about Li," Wren said, cutting into the Minister's speech. "I thought you wanted to discuss the Kyrons."

"Yes, I do. I think what they may have will save us from having to go to war with Li and his terrorist armies."

Razar returned to the open seat at the end of the horseshoe opposite Unipoesa, and DeAnders rose, taking his place in the center. The projection screen behind him lit up, and the tattoo on the girls' arms appeared.

"Our preliminary research fell short of revealing anything significant about their last name or the symbol," DeAnders said. "We're not sure how the Dominion determined their last name was Kyron, and our searches on the crosslink database came back with zero hits. Given the lack of data, we focused on their tattoo. We tried cross-referencing with known markings in xenosapien tribes, ancient languages, religious symbols—everything my team could think of. It wasn't until we determined the children's specific DNA group that we understood we were looking in the wrong places."

"What are they?" Mo asked, tapping his datawand against the table.

"They're human," DeAnders said. "But not just any ordinary human. They're 'original ancestors.'"

Each of the officers had something to say then, but Unipoesa ignored most of them and honed in on Triel. Silent and emotionless until this point, the Healer finally looked uncomfortable.

"What do you mean, 'original ancestors'?" Reamon said, leaning forward in his seat.

"We cross-referenced with the archives on Trigos. They possess DNA signatures that indicate they were from the original groups that fled Earth," DeAnders explained. "We even identified old radiation markers, although that does not necessarily mean they were born on Earth. There's the possibility that they are first-generation born during or immediately after the crisis."

Confusion followed, and speculation. All things that Unipoesa was thinking too. Original humans from Earth? Impossible; the Exodus happened over 1,100 years ago. And how did they possess telepathic powers without alterations to their genetic code?

"They're not mixed with Prodgy at all?" Triel asked over the rising volume of chatter.

"No, they're not," DeAnders said, "though that was our original summation. Granted, my teams had trouble analyzing their blood samples because of the Motti's genetic manipulation, but with the use of the crosslink Hub, we were able to perform a complex restructuring of their DNA. They're pure Old Earth humans."

Razar stood again and motioned for DeAnders to take his seat. He adjusted the waistline of his pants as he took a visual sweep of the room again. "Acting-Commander Rook has been charged with finding the detailed passenger lists from all outgoing shuttles during the Exodus, something that might still be stored somewhere on a smartserver buried in the ground on Old Earth."

"I didn't think anything still worked on that planet," Wren said. "Didn't the Last Great War destroy all their historical records and databases?"

"Yes," DeAnders said, removing his glasses and massaging the bridge of his nose. Many sleepless nights and stress had carved dark circles underneath his eyes. "But we're hoping that there are still a few left that some of the locals might know about. We're also hoping that there is enough saved data left in those servers to help us complete the search on the tattoo and their last names."

"But that in of itself is very dangerous," Razar interjected. "The Alliance can't just send an SMT, so for this mission, for the potential ramifications behind it, I've ordered the activation of a Sleeper Agent rather than send a full regiment. We need to go quietly on this one, and one of our Agents has a better chance among those Godforsaken Scabbers and Necros than we do."

"Why? What are you looking for?" Triel asked.

Unipoesa understood his role now, why Razar hadn't wiped his mind yet and why it was still important for him to play soldier and fight Li. He had never rid himself of the guilt over the death of his human surrogate mother, and a chance like this, to help the human race, might help him set things right.

"Besides the answer to their identity, other important survivors from the Exodus—ones that were never accounted for. Specifically, one that might know how to save our planets, keep us from war," Unipoesa replied. All eyes turned to him, and a silence fell upon the room. "With the twins alive and well, it could theoretically be possible."

"I have sent each of you a set of specific instructions on what needs to be done to monitor our Sleeper Agent, gather intelligence on Li, sweep the human colonies for other ancestral survivors, or help with the recon mission for Jetta. How is the team looking?" Razar asked Mo.

"We've set up a perimeter around Fiorah," the chief of military intelligence replied. "Our attempts at placing undercover police on the streets have been unsuccessful, but we're still trying. No contact reports from any of our teams."

"*Godich* locals," Razar said. "Keep at it. Secure her sister with me—I will debrief Jaeia myself about the situation. Meeting adjourned."

"Wait—wait," Triel said as the other officers rose to leave. "There is something I still don't understand. They're not genetically telepathic?"

DeAnders shook his head. "No. I can't explain where their abilities come from. We're still working on it. It might be a subatomic mutation we've never seen before."

Her eyes widened. "That could be a very big problem."

Those who had headed towards the exit paused. Razar ceased his private conversation with Wren and all eyes turned to her.

"Minister Razar, you have to let me go back to Algar," the Healer said. "There is something there that might explain where the twins come from."

Unipoesa crossed the room and stood by her side. She looked up at him, clear blue eyes pleading with him to advocate for her request.

"There isn't much left of Algar," he said gently, resting a hand on her shoulder. "Certain groups of expatriates and defectors have set up camp on tribal grounds. It's not safe."

"I didn't think you'd let me go alone," she said. "Have Reht escort me. He can get around anywhere, better than if you send me in with troops."

"We have plans for Captain Jagger and his crew," Razar said. Unipoesa gave Triel credit for trying to help her friends, though her method wasn't the least bit subtle. "And plans for you, Triel. We need you to help us find Jetta. You're one of the few people she'll talk to. Maybe you can reason with her."

As the others filed out of the room, Unipoesa lingered behind with the Healer.

She looked away from him, playing with the webbing between her fingers. "What I'm about to tell you goes against everything I've ever been taught, everything I believe in."

"It must be extremely important, then."

"If I'm right, and the foremost tenet of the Healers is to preserve and restore life... then I have to betray my people to save yours."

Unipoesa softened his voice. "Triel, I'm on your side."

The Healer exhaled heavily. "When I was a child, there was only one tale that the elders would tell in whispers," she said, turning around in her chair to face the window. Starlight bathed her face in azure and white light. She closed her eyes, her red lips parting slightly as she took a deep breath. "It was the story of fear and death that only the high tribesmen could know, and even they barely spoke of it. It was the Legend of the Rion, the Abomination, the poisoned one—the mortal who stole from Cudal."

"Cudal?" Unipoesa said.

"It's our name for the Otherworld, the realm of the Gods," she explained before continuing. "Since my father was the chief of our tribe, my brothers and I sometimes followed him around town and spied on his meetings. I overheard some of the legend before I got caught. That's why I need to go back to Algar. I'm afraid for Jetta and Jaeia, but I'm more afraid for what this will mean if they are 'unnatural' telepaths—they are more dangerous than Dissemblers."

Unipoesa leaned against the conference table and gazed out at the stars with her.

"There aren't many people who believe in them, Triel. I was hoping that you were one of them."

"I am," she said, her eyes welling with tears. "That's why I'm willing to go back to the one place in the entire universe to which I swore I'd never return."

***

"Hey, check it," Bossy said.

Agracia had seen the fiery streak in the sky long before Bossy could have picked it up. Her eyes and ears were far better than any other Sentient she knew, especially considering she was part human. "Yeah, that's a ship. See the way the fuel burns blue and yellow? Ain't no meteor."

"Payday!" Bossy shouted.

Agracia set down her gear and scanned the horizon. They were about five kilometers from the checkpoint, and the digital readout on her visor displayed about forty percent oxygen reserves and radiation shielding. There wouldn't be enough time to drop off their gear at the checkpoint and then make a run for the downed ship. Most likely there were other scavenging Jocks lurking around to beat them to the payload or steal her gear if she chanced it.

"You're sitting on this one?" Bossy exclaimed. "All because of that lousy letter?"

For the first time since she could remember, Agracia didn't know what to do. Her gut pulled her to stay on the job, especially since it was sure to be lucrative. But a downed ship—especially one that left that big of a tail—would be just as big, and guaranteed. Then maybe they'd scrap together enough dough to move on, maybe hit the Mars colony for a few years, the Belt, Saturn—something other than this forgotten wasteland—without having to resort to the fighting rings, selling chits or joining up with another crew.

"*Sycha*," Agracia said, adjusting the straps on her harness. Bossy had ripped off some drunken Jocks, affording them some decent gear to get across the wasteland. Dropping it this close to a Pit would mean they'd lose it, no question.

"Look, we can make it to the ship, right?" Bossy said. "We got enough tools on us to fix something when we get there, especially with all them fancy new parts we'll acquire."

"A temporary shelter?" Agracia said, eyeing the amber sunset. It would be dark in less than an hour. "Even if we could with the scrap we have, we'd have to take shifts staying up. We ain't shutting eye without guns lit."

"Fine, fine. I won't sleep."

"And what if someone survives that wreck?" Agracia asked, testing her. It was hard to see her expression through the reflective visor.

"Say what? Are you kidding? If they survive, good for them. They can walk home."

"God, you're worse than a *chakking* dog-soldier," Agracia laughed. "Alright, but it's a long shot. Better hope we can put something together, or we're toast."

"Well it's a *chakking* good thing I'm smarter than you!" Bossy said.

Agracia grinned and punched her in the shoulder. "Watch it, kid. That mouth of yours is gonna get you screwed up one day."

"*Chak* off, Grace."

They walked in silence, each of them focusing on their breathing and the radiation meter superimposed over the rolling dirt and scrap landscape.

"*Chakking* Scabbers," Agracia cursed as she stepped around and through the skeletal remains of an old building. Why anyone would choose to remain in the wastelands of Earth defied all logic. The dump of a planet should have been abandoned centuries ago, especially considering how much it cost to maintain the Pits, but the Scabbers—humans that couldn't let go of their dream of revitalizing the dead planet—were determined to stay put. Earth only existed because of the black market trade, and the few that could get by selling artifacts and giving tours of the graveyard cities. But that was it. The underground Pits that shielded the dwindling inhabitants from radiation and severe weather were crumbling along with the rest of the planet. It wouldn't be long before the entire place had to be evacuated.

Or the Alliance decides to use it as a weapons testing site, she thought.

As they approached the smoldering wreckage, Agracia decided that the chance of someone surviving was slim at best. Black smoke pumped out of the engine exhaust while white fire and red sparks danced across the crushed nose of the cruiser.

"They were hit," Bossy said, pointing to the gigantic flaming hole in the engine lock.

But it didn't add up. A hit like that came from a military grade weapon. The make of the cruiser looked decent enough, so there must have been adequate shielding from a standard assault. She didn't know of any crews flying around Earth, and no Scabber could afford machinery like that.

"They must have been mid-jump," Agracia surmised.

Bossy cocked her head and sucked noisily on her lollipop underneath her helmet. "Yeah, you're right. Where you from?" the kid said, jumping on the wing and looking for the emergency hatch release.

One of the fuel cells blew, rocking the ship and knocking Bossy off the wing. Agracia caught her, and the two stumbled backwards.

"*Sycha!*" Bossy exclaimed. The windshield of the cruiser cracked open, and two hands appeared, struggling to lift it over the damaged hinges.

Agracia grabbed her gun off her thigh belt and took aim. Bossy, already tossing a ball of 20-20 in her hands, readied for the fight.

"*Chak,*" Agracia mumbled. The pilot, bloodied and burnt, slumped over the rim of the cockpit, unable to squeeze through the narrow window.

"Grace!" Bossy shouted as Agracia lunged for the pilot's arm. Usually she didn't give two *chaks* about someone else's fate, but she hated crashes, herself having almost baked alive in one, and she couldn't watch even a sucker like this one go down like that.

"You trying to get us canned?" Bossy screamed, but she nonetheless helped Agracia drag the pilot to a safe distance from the wreckage. "Give it up—not like he'll make it that banged up and out here without any protection. He's gonna die anyway!"

Agracia dropped the pilot in a pile of rubbish about twenty meters from the wrecked cruiser. His chest still rose and fell, but he sustained a deep gash in his stomach and burns on his right shoulder and arm that would need treatment.

"We're not that far from the Pits. We could backtrack."

"What?!" Bossy exclaimed. "You can't be serious. They have Dogs after us now! 'Sides that, you think they'll let us back in with all this gear? We'll have to trade off with the patrol, and then we'll have nothing—right back where we were. I thought you wanted this job!"

Agracia knelt down and took the pilot's helmet in her hands. *Maybe if he's cute, Bossy will reconsider.* She gave the helmet a tug, and to her surprise, a head full of auburn-brown hair tumbled out.

"Holy *sycha*…" Bossy recognized her, too. "How did you know?"

Agracia shook her head. She didn't—but this was going to pay off bigger than any job she'd ever had. "Exposure will kill her before these injuries do. We have to make that shelter."

Bossy scanned the wreckage. "We have some D-fuser 226 that could put out that fire. Not much, though. If the cruiser's shields aren't blown, I can rig our generator and cross it with the biofield. Should last us the night."

Agracia dug through her gear, but couldn't find a single medical kit or supply of any kind she could use to patch up the battered pilot. Not that it surprised her. Jocks usually discounted that kind of thing, even in the wasteland. It was lazy. Stupid. Just like most Jocks. She just hoped the rumors about the Slaythe's hyped up biology was true, because there was nothing Agracia could do to keep her alive.

Frustrated, Agracia grabbed an extra oxygen mask and cinched it over the pilot's mouth. The woman's head rolled to the side, and the shallow rise and fall of her chest became sporadic.

"Hey," Agracia said, poking her in the ribs. "Don't you die on me. You're my paycheck."

The last rays of sunshine faded into the deathly browns and rusted yellows that pervaded the planet. She took a deep breath, the stale smell of oxygen and body odor reaching deep into her lungs. Somewhere in the distance she could hear the Necros howling.

It would be a long night.

***

Gunfire. Shouting. Pain streaking up her arms, chest and neck. A distant rumbling in her ears. Her own heartbeat, shattering her concentration, pummeled away at the insides of her skull.

Please, oh Gods—

The blackness of night swirled together with the stars. Above her head she saw a solitary beam of a headlamp swaying back and forth while a red beacon winked in the distance.

Am I running? No, she couldn't move. Her neck arched back impossibly, and her arms, pinned to her sides, froze in pain. Someone else was running, dragging her along like a rag doll.

"Stop," she groaned through split lips.

Someone repositioned a mask over her face that blew foul-smelling air into her lungs.

"Keep quiet!"

Stay calm. Remember.

"*Skucheka*," Jetta whispered, recalling the attack on her cruiser. *Where am I?* Not Fiorah—it was never dark there. Someplace else.

"Jaeia…" she whispered.

***

Suited up in hazard gear, Jaeia surveyed the remains of the planet Neeis with one of the science crews. The land, once fertile and green, had been reduced to a charred wasteland, destroyed by the Deadwalkers' nuclear weapons. *Entire cities turned into ash and rubble,* she mused, putting her hand to her visor and looking up. A line from a poem, perhaps part of a memory she had stolen, came to mind: *Dreams laid to rest under a poisoned silver sky.*

Still, this fate proved kinder than what had befallen other

worlds. In most cases, the Motti infected a planet with their bioweapon first, abducted its inhabitants, then destroyed the planet afterwards, leaving it completely poisoned, uninhabitable and impossible for hazard teams to assess.

The people of Neeis must have put up a formidable resistance, Jaeia thought as she read the reports on a datapad. From the pattern of destruction and death toll, she deduced that the Motti opted not to waste their resources and nuked the planet.

"I never got to see La Raja," she heard one of the soldiers lament as she re-boarded the Alliance survey craft, *Palamo*. Jaeia found herself smiling as she thought of Reht and his elaborate stories about the infamous escort hotels of Neeis.

"Sir, I have a call on a secured channel holding in your quarters," the ship's captain announced as she exited the decontamination chamber.

Jetta.

Not that she didn't already know who it was about, or that something was gravely wrong. The bad feelings first started when she was out with the teams collecting radiation data, and had only gotten worse as the day progressed. *She's hurt—is she dead?—oh Gods.*

(Did she hurt someone again?)

No, she stopped herself. *Breathe. Just wait and see.*

Despite her attempts to control her anxieties, her stomach contracted into a tight ball of acid the second she signed onto her terminal in her assigned quarters.

The Military Minister appeared behind his desk, his beetle brows knitted, nose flared, and his lips pressed together in a tight frown. "Commander Kyron, I have some unfortunate news to share with you about your sister."

Jaeia barely heard the Minister as she read the perimeter guard's report racing across the bottom of Razar's image:

"Phantom fighters green-lit for missile strike against an unregistered Yamazuki cruiser in pre-cycle."

Oh no—they fired on Jetta's starcraft in mid-jump!

But as she read down the report, she couldn't find notation of found wreckage or any indication that Jetta made it to Fiorah.

Breathe. Reach back, Jaeia told herself, falling into their shared bond and searching for her sister's familiar tune. *Find her.*

"She's alive, don't worry," Jaeia said, her voice just above a whisper as she minimized the report on the viewscreen. "What I can sense of her is disorganized, jumbled—perhaps because she's hurt. But she's alive."

"Good," Razar said, slapping his hand down on his desk. "She will answer for this. That perimeter guard was only doing his duty. Your sister wiped out an entire construction zone where she jumped, injuring a dozen workers and putting the construction manager's son in intensive care."

"Is he okay?" she asked, face flushing with guilt and embarrassment.

"Yes, but your sister had better thank her lucky stars there's a Healer left in this universe. Modern medicine would not have saved him."

Jaeia shook her head. *Jetta's only getting worse. A few months ago she would never jeopardize and innocent life for her own needs, but now nothing seems to stop her.*

"You understand why she's in the Fleet, don't you?" Jaeia said, sensing that the Minister's thoughts of punishment for her twin. "It's because of me. She wants to protect me. And she thought by joining the Alliance that meant she would have the resources to save the other people she loves too, like our aunt and uncle."

"Jaeia," the Minister said, leaning forward, his belly squishing over the lip of the desk, "your sister has made herself a liability. If there was a chance that your aunt and uncle were alive we would have sent a full team, but you know as well as I do that the only things left on Fiorah are bad memories."

Jaeia stared at her hands. "Yes, I know. None of our contacts came up with any evidence that they were still alive. Even Yahmen's whereabouts are questionable."

"In light of everything going on in the courts, this will be exceedingly difficult for me to cover up. And it will be even harder for me to petition her as fit for duty," the Minister said.

"So, then what?" Jaeia asked, her tone still even. "Do I need to be worried about our safety?"

"Please," the Minister said, raising his hands off the desk. "This is not a threat. I'm merely telling you that Jetta's behavior is unacceptable. She needs help. For her sake, yours and mine. For the entire Alliance. She is too important to all of us. Both of you are. I am willing to provide you with whatever resources you need."

Jaeia thought it over. "I want to be here; I accept my title. I believe in what the Alliance could do to unite and preserve the Sentients of the Starways. I believe in restoration, reparation, progress—all these things. But my sister is different. With all of her powers and all of her abilities, you'd think she'd want to be CCO—be the most powerful commander in the entire galaxy. But she doesn't. All of these abilities she has—we have—she sees as a means to survive, to escape those that hunt us, to protect me, not to be your soldier. She could one day believe in helping others, but not until she's found a way to fulfill the role she feels she's failed."

The Minister looked at her, his eyes hard and narrow. "She's still looking to save your brother?"

"She'll never stop," Jaeia replied, her chest tightening. "And you can't blame her for that."

"We have to find a solution to this, Jaeia. You're the commanding officer of our Contact Teams—this is your area; this is key diplomacy. Find a way to restore your sister."

And with that the Minister signed out.

Before she could react, her uniform sleeve beeped, alerting her that her mission team was prepped and awaiting her command back on the carrier ship orbiting Neeis. She sighed and thought of Jahx. "It would take a miracle."

CHAPTER II

Being trapped on Trigos was bad enough, but after the Military Minister ordered the crew's transfer the Alliance Central Starbase, things turned ugly.

Something's up, Reht Jagger thought as an Alliance soldier showed him and the rest of his band inside their assigned quarters. *That* ratchakker *is going to pull something.*

Once again, he barely snuck the Narki technology past the guards. With a pat on the ex-con's shoulder, Reht silently thanked Vaughn for swallowing the goods.

Vaughn turned up his lip, made a retching sound, and wiped his mouth with the back of his sleeve. Discreetly, he handed the silver wand and golden key to his captain along with a string of yellow saliva and bits of his dinner. Even for a hardened criminal used to smuggling items through his digestive system, this was pushing his limits.

Time to make my move, Reht decided, drying off the Narki tech in his pocket. *Or the crew will riot.*

Communicating with his crew would be exceedingly difficult, especially aboard the starbase. *This place is surely bugged,* he thought, scanning the sparsely furnished quarters. Nothing obvious stood out, but he didn't believe his eyes. *Why else would that* assino *let us all room together? Gotta beat that bastard at his own game.*

Time to choose a cryptic language. Reht figured that the Alliance had probably deciphered a large number of dog-soldier tongues, so he'd have to use a lesser-known code. *I hope these chumps remember their words,* he groused, thinking of Ro and Cray.

Reht sighed and took a seat at the table in the middle of the windowless room. Billy Don't ran laps around him, singing, or something of the equivalent, to himself while the other crew members fought over the bunk beds crammed into each corner of the room. Tech, too timid to challenge anyone for a prime bunk, scratched at the stain covering the ratty couch shoved up against the wall.

"I have these habits," (We need to talk,) Reht said, pulling at the bandages on his hands to signal his choice of code-speak. "Bad ones I gotta quit." (It's urgent.)

"*Chak*, not again," (I understand), Bacthar said, lifting his head off the pillow. His wings unfolded, and he slid off the top bunk. "We can't keep up with you like that, Reht." (Does everybody else understand?)

Nostrils flared, Mom took a seat by his captain's side. Ro and Cray uttered expletives as they whipped around chairs and plopped down opposite Reht at the table. Annoyed, Ro stuck his foot out and stopped Billy mid-lap, and Cray hit the half-Liiker boy mid-spine, sending him off into a self-diagnostic/sleep cycle.

"This again?" (yes) Tech replied. Deciding to brave the mystery stain, the nervous engineer perched on the armrest of the couch, while Vaughn, rubbing the stubble on his head, looked blankly at the floor. With him it was always a crapshoot anyway.

"I need to get laid. That's an old habit," (Our insurance policy,) Reht chuckled. "But it's getting in the way of my thinkin'." (We may need to move on it.)

"Cappy, you ain't comin' onto me, is you?" (That's a bad idea,) Ro said, scooting his chair back. Mom bared his teeth and took a swipe at Ro, but the Farrocoon ducked out of the way.

"Calm the hell down," (I disagree,) Reht said, tightening the knot on his bandaged left hand with his teeth. "Look, there's also this: I got a new itch, and it's bad. I think I need help." (There's a job opportunity that's better. We need to all be in on it.)

"Hey, we're all thirsty, boss. Stupid Alliance is keepin' us dry," (We will follow your lead,) Bacthar said. Mom nodded and emitted a low growl. Twiddling with his thumbs, Tech waited for the group consensus.

Ro and Cray exchanged glances, their faces tight and noses upturned.

Those ratchakkers, Reht thought. *They're balking!*

"Cappy, we always been helping you, all the way from Titus to now. But your habits—they queer. Don't know about this anymore." (We've always been loyal to you, but this is too much for us.)

I'm losing them.

Reht looked around the room; Bacthar sighed and massaged his temples, resigning himself to the bench in the corner. Despite the threat of his first mate, Ro and Cray didn't break their gaze, crossing their arms and looking petulant. Even Tech and Vaughn maintained their distance.

Surprisingly, Tech chimed in: "He's our captain. This is his decision. We made the oath. Bad habits or not, we're all in."

"Least one of you remembers the pack," Reht said, yawning and stretching out his arms. He hadn't been sleeping well at all lately; he felt like his head was stuffed with cotton. *A stiff drink would help,* he thought longingly. "Look, just stick with me. I'm working on changing my ways." (Follow my lead, I'm going to make a move.)

Cray hung his head, rapping his brow with his right hand. Ro stared intently at him but didn't utter a word, either because he couldn't translate what Cray wanted to say or because Mom was too close for him not to mind his tongue.

"Keep the boys in line, okay? I'm going to talk to someone who might care about this," Reht whispered in his Talian's ear. Mom grabbed the captain by the forearm as he got up to leave.

Reht grinned. "Hey, trust me, old friend. We're gonna do alright."

***

Jaeia had already briefed her Contact Team about their mission, but her mind kept going over and over the details.

Am I missing something? she asked herself for the tenth time as she perused the composite reports on the armrest screen of the bridge command chair. *(Or maybe I can't focus on diplomacy with my sister still missing.)*

Forging a ceasefire with the terrorists on Jue Hexron was critical. Well-known across the galaxy for its Holy Cities, Jue Hexron was also one of the few worlds where humans and other Sentients coexisted peacefully, and the loss of that planet and all the delegates that fought for human rights meant that the delicate balance between humans and Sentients could devolve into another civil war, further dividing the Alliance.

Her mission aboard the *Heliron*, though, was only part of whatever the Alliance had planned. Usually she oversaw the entire process of diplomacy and restoration, but for whatever reason, she was only charged with the negotiations; they would send research teams to interview human colonists after she had settled the dispute. Her superiors never briefed her on the second part of the mission and met her inquiries with noncommittal statements. *Something for me to investigate later,* she thought, making a mental note.

Frustrated, she opened up the Alliance's files on Earth's history. Even while on the Core ships, Jaeia had learned little beyond the common knowledge that humans had traveled to the Homeworlds after their wars resulted in the destruction of their planet. From her appearance she knew she was at least partially human, but she and her siblings, like those they interacted with, had deduced long ago that they couldn't have been completely human given their unusual abilities, so learning about the human plight was never a strong interest. But pitted against the many factions of terrorists vying to control what remained of the habitable worlds, knowing a bit about Earth history and the struggle of mankind gave her new insights.

"Commander," one of her Lieutenants said, approaching her with a salute. "We're entering communications range."

"Keep me appraised," she said, nodding for her to return to his post. With only a few minutes left, she absorbed as much as she could about Earth from the Alliance records, stretching out her mind and allowing the information to synergize with the collective knowledge she had accumulated.

"...overpopulation and pollution crisis lead to extremist factions developing weaponry to protect and control the planet's last viable resources. The first worldwide nuclear war began May 12, 2045, and although most prominent countries suffered losses, the Middle East and parts of western Asia were hit the hardest, with entire cities and nations completely destroyed.

In 2049, the United People's Republic, formerly the United States of America, publically revealed that world-renowned scientist Dr. Josef A. Stein and his son, Dr. Kurt Stein, had the means to repair the environmental damage caused by fallout, promising the United Nations that peace was possible through restoration of the ecosystems. In an unfortunate turn of events, Stein's wife was murdered by a UPR official, and his son went missing in 2051. Stein retaliated by releasing a deadly bioweapon that infected several million people across Europe. News of the bioweapon prompted the Russian and Middle Allied forces to unleash nuclear weapons on Europe in an attempt to stop its spread, drawing the UPR and United Eastern Asia into the Last Great War.

Later dubbed the Exodus, minority party leaders from the Cause for Earth, in conjunction with private investors, revealed several mass transport lifeboats designed for survivalist space travel, taking aboard as many survivors of the nuclear fallout as they could. Forces still grounded on the planet attacked several lifeboats as they launched into space, but 10 million people survived the initial stage of the Exodus."

Jaeia scrolled down further. From that point on, she was quite familiar with Earth's history and the trials of the human race. Equipped with oxygen farms, food gardens, and water recycling systems, the lifeboats were designed to be self-sustaining, but overcrowding maxed out the resources. The congested lifeboats struggled on for a few weeks before their food, water or oxygen systems collapsed, while other passing ships, unable to render aid, watched and listened while they died. Within a month, the human population went from 14 billion to 3 million.

The dwindling survivors were catching their first glimpses of Mars when the course of the Starways changed forever.

How did the Prodgies know to intervene—and why? Jaeia wondered, enhancing the report on the fateful rescue of the human race. Nobody understood how the elder Healers could have known of the destruction of the tiny planet on the outskirts of the galaxy, or why they would want to save such a lowly species. Even Triel couldn't provide any answers.

Regardless of the reason, the Prodgy gift of break-light speed to the dying race gave humans the edge to survive the precious few weeks it took to reach the Interior. Still, after all they had survived, the refugees did not find solace in the Homeworlds, and relations only worsened with the host of new diseases they inadvertently introduced to the Sentient population.

Jaeia rubbed her eyes. *I don't feel like negotiating today.* "Lieutenant, what are the latest readings? Who do I have to deal with?"

Her first officer didn't look up as he studied his console. "I'm not sure; the signal is coming from a known Creos-occupied location, but the operator is not identifying with any party. It's someone calling themselves 'Victor.'"

That's odd, she thought. It had been a long time since the Creos, a terrorist group with many high-powered leaders, opened up communications with any Alliance official. Furthermore, most of their members proudly—and often violently—demonstrated their allegiances to the Creos upon contact. *Who is this Victor and why is he reaching out to me from Creos territory if he's not part of their faction?*

Jaeia stepped up to the front of the telecommunications grid and straightened her back. "I am Commander Jaeia Kyron of the Starways Alliance. I am representing all Sentients who wish to negotiate peace on Jue Hexron."

The ship's viewscreen distorted and then reset, the protected signal finally organizing itself on the flat display. Jaeia squinted before realizing it had nothing to do with her vision.

What the—?

A man with a pink, seamless face smiled back at her. Any illusion of youth dissolved as soon as he turned his head, revealing the telltale signs of hormone and metabolic serum abuse in the queer glint of his skin.

That's either the worst cosmetic job I've ever seen, Jaeia thought, *or he's very, very old.*

Everything about the man was unnatural. His hair, an unpleasant mix of yellow and silver pulled back taut, should have belonged to a display mannequin. Even his accessories—the gold-trimmed glasses, and the large, flashy rings adorning his fingers—felt more befitting in a gaudy catalogue.

"Commander," he said, hands resting on a black cane. "It is my pleasure to finally meet you."

With the price of an engineered body like that, I bet the cane is for effect, she surmised.

"I am Victor, and I speak for the Creos. I speak for all of Jue Hexron." His eyes, darker than a starless night, gave her the most unusual look.

He's inhumanly human.

With the slightest movement of her left hand, Jaeia signaled her first officer. *Since we won't be able to accurately lock the signal's true origin, we'll have to take a chance on cross-referencing his profile.*

The lieutenant nodded and began processing the data she wanted off-screen.

"Forgive my confusion, Victor, but I came to negotiate peace between the Creos and the residential colonies. I was not aware that there was a representative for both sides."

"No need for confusion, Warchild," Victor said, revealing the diamond finish of his teeth. She had not heard that nickname in awhile. "I have negotiated peace. There is a cease-fire. Your presence here is unnecessary."

Jaeia tilted her head. The man was too far away for her to probe around his thoughts, but his words carried a whisper of his essence. She gleaned something she hadn't felt in ages—something dark, something beyond what words could describe. *Gods—the last time I've felt like this,* she thought, skin prickling, *I was back on Fiorah, hiding from Yahmen.*

(Why am I afraid?)

She tried to think objectively as the adrenaline flooded through her body, making her heart pound in her chest. *I've stumbled upon a figure of importance, maybe the leader of the terrorist groups, or perhaps someone bigger.*

"Mashen Ky is negotiating for the human colonies, and our last contact with Creos identified as Xerod of Gramen," she said, still maintaining her composure.

"Here they are, Warchild. No need to worry. Speak to them yourself."

Victor waved the camera to pan to his left and right, revealing both Mashen and Xerod. Aside from fading bruises and scars around their right eye sockets, they both appeared unharmed.

Why are they so emotionless? Jaeia wondered, confused by their dispassionate expressions. *This has to be the first time in the history of the planet that they have stood within a few meters of each other.*

"I speak for the human colonies," Mashen said, his tone confident but face remaining blank. "We have obtained peace with the Creos."

"I speak for the Creos. We have achieved peace with the human colonies. We will no longer wage battle with the Starways Protectorate," Xerod said, his affect mirroring Mashen's.

Jaeia looked to her first officer, who promptly cut off the com line.

"What do you have, lieutenant?" she asked.

"So far our scans support the possibility of a ceasefire," the officer reported. "I have three colonies ringing in… Yes, I have confirmation. An agreement between the Creos and colonies has been negotiated."

Jaeia didn't believe it, not even for a moment. *I need to find out who this Victor is.*

Instincts pulled at her thoughts. *(He cannot be trusted. I have to be careful.)*

"Victor, my congratulations and thanks; you've done something admirable in such a short period of time," Jaeia said. "Would it be possible for you to join us aboard my ship and dine with me tonight?"

He smiled, his teeth glinting. "I do not like remote transport, and I like space travel even less. But you are welcome to dine with me. I will send you my location."

"The signal's lost," her first officer announced. "But we have the last transmission. Looks like he wants you to meet him on the southern continent."

Jaeia stared at the blank viewscreen where the image of Victor had first appeared just moments ago. *Something is very wrong about this.*

"Jetta," she muttered under her breath. "I could really use you right now."

Running her fingers along the smooth contours of the armrest refocused her attention. "What time did he want to meet?"

"1900, Sir," her first officer replied.

Jaeia looked at the time on her uniform sleeve; it gave her a few hours to think things over. "Okay, I'm going. But I want two ground compliments, and one tail on me the entire time."

She sounded like her sister: paranoid, ready for assault. *This isn't like me at all.*

Or something had really gotten under her skin.

Heading back to her quarters, Jaeia kept her eyes locked straight ahead, but did not register the soldiers and officers saluting as she passed by.

She had to find out who or what Victor was.

***

Tidas Razar had been monitoring the progress of Commander Kyron and the Contact Team at his desk when he received a priority message from the holding cells.

"This had better be good, Jagger," Razar muttered, electronically approving the request for a meeting in his office.

Reht never messed around when he had a business proposition, but Tidas didn't see what he had left to bargain with. Realistically, it didn't matter if he did. The high council had deemed Reht and his crew "level 1 security risks," allowing the Military Minister to dispose of the dog-soldiers by any means necessary.

Soon, no more games with Captain Reht Jagger.

Razar distanced himself from any emotion attached to the thought. Jagger was a pawn with a skewed measure of his own importance in the scheme of the Starways. Besides, in his day, Razar had committed much worse crimes than silencing a group of mercenary thugs.

"Always a pleasure, boys," the dog-soldier captain said, saluting the soldiers that escorted him into Razar's office.

"Leave us," Tidas said, folding his arms across his desk.

"We're finally alone," Reht winked, taking a seat across from the Minister.

"You know I'm trying to find ways of making you disappear, Jagger."

Reht seem unconcerned. "Look, you're an old military stiff, and I'm a dashing young privateer, but you can't discount that our credos are similar: You take care of those who take care of you. I know my crew and I are more knowledgeable than you'd like, but I give you my word as a captain and a loyal compatriot of the Alliance that my crew and I will never speak a word of what we've seen or interfere with the government or military ever again."

Tidas guffawed. "And what good is your word, really? What kind of assurance do I have that you'll keep your end of the deal?"

The fear in his eyes was fleeting, but Razar caught the edge of it as the captain reached into his jacket pocket.

"There's a plasma shield surrounding my desk and about forty guards within the next hundred meters of here."

"Relax, Minister—it's not a weapon," Reht smiled as he laid down the item. It had a strong smell to it, like stomach acid.

"It stinks," Razar said, pushing the edge of the silver wand away from him with a pen.

Reht shrugged his shoulders. "Hard to transport it around these parts."

"What is it, Jagger? I don't have all day."

The greed, the arrogance in his eyes returned, and the dog-soldier captain leaned back in his chair, his hands behind his head.

"Flash transport device."

Razar blinked. "Come again?"

"It's Narki technology—the flash transport device. It's why the Dominion knocked 'em off."

Turning the monitor away from the dog-soldier, Razar called up the classified files on the flash transport device on his terminal. The details and descriptions of the device matched the silver wand on his desk.

It could be a replica, he thought, still skeptical. Utilizing the sensory equipment linked to his terminal, he ran a quick local scan.

Impossible. The preliminary data rated a 99.5 percent identity match.

"How did you get this? Where's the key?" Razar demanded.

Reht pointed his index finger at him and made a clicking sound with his mouth. "No, no. That's my insurance policy. I give you this, you let me and my crew go, and I'll give you the key. Simple and easy."

"Simple and easy," Razar repeated, letting the words roll of his tongue. "So are our interrogation techniques. You wouldn't last an hour, Jagger."

Reht's smile didn't break. "I figured you'd be an *assino*. But that's alright. I guess if you knew that your niece was floating around up there, you'd act a little different."

Gripping the edge of his desk, Razar couldn't control the anger spilling into his voice. "She was killed a long time ago, Jagger."

"No, she wasn't. She survived on Tralora and Jaeia saved her. She's flashed into the wave network."

Razar pinched his brows with his fingers. "The sisters never spoke of this."

"They know more about loyalty than you do, you *ratchakker*."

"I will tear you apart from inside out, Jagger," Razar said, just above a whisper. He leaned forward, "I will personally break you."

"Then you'll never get that key. You forget who I am, where I come from; I'm not one to break. Neither is my crew. It's in your best interest to play along. Besides, the only person that knows how to work that thing is Jaeia, and if you even touch a single hair on any of our heads, you'll have her and her sister to deal with. And you and I both know you're on shaky grounds with them already."

"Where is the key, Jagger?" the Minister said through steeled teeth.

"I want my old ship back, ready and prepped in the dock by 2100 hours. I want a nice dinner—a nice, *clean* one—with meats and desserts for my starving boys before we ship off. Only when we've jumped will I give you the location of the key."

Razar steadied himself. *Jagger is an idiot. Why am I concerned?* After calming himself, the Minister pretended to take the bait by sporting a defeated expression. "Get out of my office"

The guards came in and tried to grab Jagger by the arms, but he shoved them away. "Think about it is all I'm sayin'."

One of the guards cracked Jagger in the thigh with his shockwand. After giving the guards the finger, the dog-soldier captain limped away, laughing as he went.

Tidas Razar picked up the wand and turned it over in his hands. *My niece...is it possible?*

Squaring back to his terminal, he typed an urgent message to Msiasto Mo and DeAnders and sent for a covert guard squad.

As he waited in his office, the background noise of the Contact Team's reel replaying from the last stop, he tentatively set down the wand. He didn't think he could feel pain again. Not like this.

"Senka…"

***

Getting any kind of news of the outside world was a rarity on Old Earth, but the Alliance made sure over the last several months to force-feed it's propaganda to every planet's populace, no matter how remote or disassociated with its reign. Many good drinking nights and days had been ruined by the military *gorsh-shit* recycling over and over again on the lone televisions or half-functional holographic displays in Agracia Waychild's favorite bars. Still, she had built up the idea of Jetta Kyron in her head to the point of myth. The vids of the Final Front and Homeworld Perimeter had told it all: *The warchild once wielded by the Dominion Core took the helm of the Alliance Fleet in time to save us from the Deadwalkers!*

Jetta Kyron, Agracia laughed to herself, nudging the unconscious woman with the toe of her boot. *The genius leech who could take down the entire galaxy with a handful of soldiers. What a sucker.*

Lying there, her body ragged and beaten, Jetta looked just like any other chump she knew. *She ain't anything special.*

Agracia decided she wasn't ugly, but she wasn't exactly a looker. Jetta looked much more feminine on the newsreels; in person she appeared a lot rougher, like one of the spitfires from the fighting rings, but her looks weren't what was going to make Agracia money anyway.

"She ain't gon' make it. No way," Bossy said, sucking noisily on her lollipop underneath her helmet. "And that *chakking* tribe of Jocks are right on our *assinos*. We can't stay here much longer, Grace."

Agracia sighed and twirled her gun around her finger. The crumbling remains of a building provided adequate refuge from the storm tearing through their area, but they couldn't stay their much longer. Surface storms were notoriously fierce, sometimes lasting weeks, even months, and the energy reserves in their suits would, at best, last them another five hours.

"Ah, *sycha*," Agracia said, slumping down against the wall. The wind howled against the building, support beams creaking and groaning against the pressure. *We would have been fine if we'd stayed on course to the next Pit.*

"Where did that tribe hole up?" Agracia asked as Bossy flipped on the tracking device.

"Dunno, actually; storm is screwin' with the readings. I saw them dive about a half mile back, but that don't mean nothin'."

Bossy dropped the tracking device on the dirt-blown ground and threw up her hands. "I can't sit here any longer. We gotta get going. I say we shed the *baech* and the extra gear and make a run for the next Pit."

"Don't be a dumb-*assino*, kid. Not only would we lose our paycheck, we'd be blind, and we don't want to end up on sour turf."

That shut her up. Bad turf meant the possibility of running into one of the millions of undead Necros that roamed through the forgotten cities. Pissed off Scabbers and tribes of banded Jocks were bad enough, but flesh-hungry, mutated monsters were worse.

Through bloodied lips, the Slaythe rasped: "Where… how did I…?"

"*Gorsh-shit*," Agracia muttered. *I didn't think the bastard would regain consciousness, at least not this quickly.*

"Well, what now?" Agracia said, readjusting the oxygen mask

over Jetta's face, testing the kid.

Bossy shrugged and turned her back to them, playing with her lollipop. "She's your pet. You decide."

Agracia got up and stood over the woman's body. "This is Earth. Your ship crashed about two miles back. There's a bad storm outside, and we've taken shelter for the time being. How badly you hurt?"

Jetta rolled her head to the side, towards Agracia. Two brilliant green eyes peered through swollen lids. "Who are you?"

"How bad are you hurt?" Agracia repeated impatiently.

It started like an itch in the back of her mind, rapidly growing into a peculiar uncertainty that branched out to her hands and her toes, making her feel weak.

"What the *chak*—are you messing with me, leech?" Agracia said, aiming her gun at Jetta's head.

Coughing violently, Jetta curled up into a ball, bringing her knees to her chest. The bad feelings in Agracia's mind faded.

"She ain't worth the trouble," Bossy remarked, getting up and checking the storm through the crack in the wall. "I don't care who the hell she is."

"Yeah, well, we can't afford to have the Alliance hunting us down, now can we?" Agracia said, kneeling besides the injured woman and tapping her cheek with the nozzle of her gun. "Let's get one thing straight between you and me. We saved your *assino* back there and would appreciate a show of courtesy. Stay out of my head and my gun will stay out of your face, yeah?"

"I need a medkit and a wave network transmitter. I promise that if you can get me back to Alliance territory you will be compensated beyond whatever you think you'll get paid," Jetta said, her neck taut as she strained against the pain of her injuries.

"Make a decision, Gracie. We've got trouble," Bossy said, removing several 20-20 grenades from her belts.

Agracia hurried over to her companion and looked through the crack in the wall. Shadows moved toward their shelter as the wind whipped debris and dirt across the landscape.

"We ain't leavin' her," Agracia said, keeping her voice low. "She's too valuable. We could sell her out or we could give her back—either way, we'll probably score a ticket off this rock, and that's all that really matters, yeah?"

"Yeah, yeah," Bossy said, only wanting a decision.

Agracia turned around and took a step back in shock. Bloodied and burnt, Jetta took to her feet, her left arm clutching her side while holding the oxygen mask over her mouth with her right. Green eyes locked intently with hers.

"Who are you?" Jetta asked, voice barely rising above the winds.

"Holy *sycha*," Bossy said, cocking her grenade back. "Stay where you are!"

"We didn't think you'd ever walk again," Agracia chuckled. "I don't know how you're holding up in this environment."

"I've been through worse," Jetta said.

"Alright, let's try for the next Pit. There's one expired anti-radiation booster I found in the bottom of that repair kit," Agracia said, pointing to their stash of gear. "You'd better take it."

"Expired?"

"Quit complaining—it's better than nothin'."

Agracia watched Jetta stumble over the gear, remove the kit and rifle through the tools with shaky hands until she found the booster. Severe burns kept her from using her left hand, forcing her to uncap the syringe with her mouth and jab the medication into her thigh with her right.

"Whoa…" Bossy murmured. She was impressed, too.

"Grab the gear, let's move. We can stay on this block another half-mile, then we'll head north. The cover will be *sycha*, but it's better than full exposure," Agracia said, grabbing what she needed.

As Bossy headed out into the storm, Agracia turned back to Jetta.

"Look," Agracia said, emptying the gear bag of all non-essentials, "you're gonna need this around your skin. Cover your head and close your eyes. You'll have to let us guide you out there."

"Who are you?" Jetta asked again, covering herself as best she could.

Agracia smiled, though Jetta wouldn't be able to see it through the helmet. "Your saviors."

***

Jaeia refused her first officer's request to have recording devices implanted in her ears. She strongly disliked the idea of the tiny electronic squares imbedded into her eardrums, but more importantly, a cunning man like Victor would expect that kind of thing. Not knowing what kind of detection technology he had access to, she decided to go in unarmed and unequipped.

Besides, she thought as she walked through the glass door entrance to the capital skyscraper of Jue Hexron. *This doesn't feel like a trap; a man with such influences wouldn't do something so vulgar. This feels more like a preamble—but for what?*

"Welcome, Commander Kyron," one of the soldiers said, saluting as she approached the security checkpoint.

After a cursory pat-down, the guards let her through, waving her past the weapons scanner and bioscan.

What? This can't be right. Jaeia stepped onto the elevator unescorted and pressed the button to take her to the top floor. *A loosely guarded, relaxed atmosphere doesn't seem fitting for a man accustomed to brokering peace between warring factions.*

The elevator dinged. "131st floor," the automated voice intoned. "Please watch your step."

Jaeia couldn't contain her amazement as she stepped off the elevator. Tinted glass framed the top floor of the capital skyscraper, offering a complete view of the entire city and the red and gold sunset as the last hours of daylight came to a close. The decorations, sparse but sleek, created an ambience from a different time. An off-yellow lounge chair faced a long, slanted red couch with a silver-lacquered steel coffee table dividing them. Dull gray bookshelves held real books, faded and cracked but neatly arranged in rows and stacks. Old-fashioned bulb lamps, oddly curved, perched on wooden end tables. A wet bar, constructed from translucent glass and buffed metal, curved around the north end of the room, where a long and narrow dining table glowed with light from an asymmetric arrangement of candles. Everything was old—very old, just like the man who sat in the yellow chair, his cane leaning against the armrest, holding up his martini glass in a salute as she approached.

"Jaeia Kyron, welcome. Please, join me," he said, motioning for her to sit on the couch.

She sat on the very edge, crossing her legs and placing her hands on her knees, trying to appear relaxed. "I must ask, how did you manage to get the top floor of the capital building? I was under the impression that it was designated for top government officials only."

Victor tipped his glass to her, delighted to answer the question. "I was recently appointed to a Sentient relations position within the governing body of Jue Hexron. The council seemed very appreciative of my work to solidify a ceasefire agreement amongst the warring parties here in the Holy Cities."

"I see," Jaeia said, skeptical of his claim. She took another look around. "I've never seen this kind of furniture before."

"It's from Earth. Very rare, very valuable—to some," Victor said, setting his drink down. "Can I offer you something from the bar?"

"No, thank you," Jaeia said. Instead of pointing out her true age, she answered, "I don't drink."

"I rarely do. It wrecks the mind," Victor said. "Only on special occasions, and I think this is one."

"Why is that?"

"I celebrate the peace forged on Jue Hexron. And I toast to your coming. It is an honor."

Jaeia pressed her tongue hard against the roof of her mouth, concentrating on keeping her emotions from her voice or expression. Unable to read his thoughts, she feared asking him any of the questions that burned in her mind and exposing some unknown vulnerability in herself.

Why can't I sense him? she wondered. *Does he know Rai Shar?*

No, that wasn't the answer. Rai Shar practitioners erected psionic barriers to protect their thoughts. There were no walls between her and Victor. Instead, she felt an infinite shadow, a pool of darkness that spanned well beyond Victor's mind.

"You speak as if you know me," Jaeia said.

Victor smiled, his seamless cheeks wrinkling like plastic sheets. "I keep myself informed of the politics of the Starways," he said, voice smooth and slick. "I like to know who's on my side... and who's not. I believe you're on my side. I believe you want what's best for the Sentients."

His voice, she thought, clenching her teeth. She could feel his oily words passing through her, sliding into her thoughts. *He's more than just a silver-tongued speaker.*

(Is he like me?)

"Tell me about yourself, Victor," she asked, trying to regain control. "Where are you from? How did you end up on Jue Hexron negotiating peace between the humans and the Creos?"

"I have always had the human interest in mind."

"You're certainly part of the minority. Why such an interest?"

Victor leaned back in his chair, sipping from his martini. One of the rings on his right hand caught her eye—a signet ring of black gold adorned with a red seal depicting a bird of prey. "I am from Earth, but I'm not a Scabber, and I'm not a refugee descendent. Oh, what do they call them these days—Deadskins? No, I'm *from* Earth."

"From Earth?" Jaeia was confused. He couldn't be *that* old.

"Yes. And so are you."

His icy words sent shivers up her spine and brought goose bumps to her skin. *That's impossible,* she told herself, closing the front flaps of her jacket against the sudden chill.

(Then why do I feel like he's telling the truth?)

No, I can't let him get in my head. Jaeia forced a smile. "Why do you say that?"

Victor set his drink down again and folded his bony fingers across his lap. "That, my dear, was the easiest thing for me to know, but I'm afraid I'm one of the few who does. But if I tell you how I know, then you must do right by me and share information that would help me and my cause."

"Your cause?" Jaeia asked, wishing she had run the risk of the recording device now. *I've never felt so exposed. How is he doing this?*

"Yes. I wish to found a permanent home for humans. Being from Earth, I'm sure you wish this, too."

Jaeia didn't know where to begin or how to reply. *Gods, I need something on him. If I could glean even his direction or intent— something—I wouldn't be this disadvantaged.*

Victor brought his hands together to form a steeple. "This struggle between humans and Sentients has gone on long enough. The human race is slowly being eradicated through flesh farms, Labor Locks, fighting rings, and surrogate breeding. I want a new Earth for humans. I want a fresh start, away from the Starways."

"How do you see me helping you with that?" Jaeia asked, now

more confused than ever. *This was supposed to be about how he forged peace between the Creos and the human colonies—how did this become about my origins and the future of humankind?*

Victor leaned forward, his black eyes seeming to suck her into their endless depths. "I want you to tell me everything you remember about your tattoo. How you got it—and when."

Something in Victor's voice, or perhaps the way he looked at her, assaulted her with fresh fear. *I have to get out of here—*

Jaeia scrunched her fingers together, cracking the knuckles on her left hand before realizing her actions. Exhaling slowly, she brought her heartrate down and steadied her nerves.

This is like nothing I've ever felt before, in my lifetime or any of the experiences I've gleaned from others. He's holding more cards than I can see, and he's certainly no ordinary human.

Still, she thought, glancing at the elevator doors. *This may be my only opportunity to talk to him like this. I can't waste this chance; I have to find out more.*

The tattoo was supposed to have been kept a secret, but like most of the information about her and her sister deemed classified, someone with high security clearance had leaked the information. The military council and General Assembly suspected Li or one of his sympathizers, which made Jaeia question something else about Victor: *Who is pulling his strings? Is Li behind him?*

"Victor, all these personal questions and I don't even know your full name," Jaeia asked shakily, trying to redirect the conversation.

Victor smiled. "I'm too old for a last name. Besides, nobody who knew me back then is here now. I am just Victor."

Fear, ripe and hot in her belly, kept her from pursuing the issue further. Instead, she tried something different. "I don't know if I can believe that you're human—or that I am, for that matter. I'm a telepath, and humans are not telepathic. And you—you don't read like a human being."

Victor nodded, his calculated smile returning. "Yes, it is curious, isn't it? But I speak the truth."

He bent forward, swirling his drink in his glass. "There is a history in this room that stretches back farther than you can imagine. And what transpires between you and I will determine more than you could ever conceive. Not to be too dramatic."

He's crazy—and full of himself, flashed through her head, but her gut reaction to keep listening kept her grounded. *Maybe I should just press harder; maybe I should chance a real peek behind his eyes.*

Victor seemed to anticipate this consideration, holding up two fingers and wagging them at her. "Don't get any foolish ideas about me, Warchild. You've tampered with enough minds in your day, but you have no experience with someone like me. If you try to force information from me, unspeakable things will happen."

She believed him. *Gods, Jetta, I wish you were here, or at least looking through my eyes,* she called out silently to her twin. *I need your advice, your perspective on this. I can't seem to keep myself together.*

A robotic butler whirred to life, rising from the floor behind the wet bar. Its metal arms held up trays full of meats, vegetables, fruits, and other strange foods she had never seen before. Even on edge, the intoxicating smell caused her to lick her lips as the butler heaped food onto the plates at the table.

"Delicacies from Earth," Victor said. "I had hoped you might remember them."

Keeping her eye and mind on him, Jaeia crossed the room, slowly approaching the dinner table. The butler clicked and hummed, waiting for her command. When she neared one of the two chairs, the butler wheeled around and pulled it out for her.

"No, thank you," Jaeia said, refusing to sit. Still, she looked over the food with hungry eyes.

"Stuffed turkey, mint lamb, sausage and gravy, mashed potatoes, figs, oranges, black pineapples, ambrosia salad, mushrooms and rice, fruit tarts, apple pie—foods that are forgotten to most of us," Victor said, coming up behind her, his cane tapping softly on the tiled floor.

Standing so close, Jaeia caught the aroma of medical preservatives rising above the hint of his aftershave.

"Can't you remember?" he whispered in her ear.

Jaeia turned around, facing him. Although she only stood a few centimeters shorter than him, he felt massively larger.

"I must return to my ship," she said, voice wavering. "I will be meeting with Mashen and Xerod tomorrow to see how the negotiations went. I appreciate your hospitality, but duty calls."

Victor leaned with both hands on his cane, coming close enough that she could see the interlocking fibers of the synthetic skins on his face and the dead black of his eyes behind the prescription lenses.

"Your tattoo. Think about it. I will tell you where you are from, how you got here—and how you're almost as old as I am."

Nonplussed, Jaeia turned and walked toward the guards waiting for her on the elevator. Victor lingered in her mind, his words cold and heavy, weighing down her thoughts. Nothing he said was logical, but on some level, well beyond her immediate access, it all made sense to her.

(Victor is dangerous. More so than I can even appreciate.)

The elevator chime let her know she had reached the ground floor of the skyscraper. When the doors parted, she came face-to-face with her first officer and two Alliance escort guards.

"Sir, there is a priority message waiting for you back on the *Heliron*."

When she picked up on his thoughts, her stomach dropped. *Did they find Jetta?* She searched her shared connection; nothing. Jetta was still too far away or continuing to cut herself off. *Or worse.*

Then she saw the panic in her first officer's eyes and knew that something was wrong on a much larger scale.

"How bad?" she whispered so that Victor's men couldn't overhear as they headed to the double-pane doors.

Her first officer eyes, frantic with fear, connected briefly with hers as he held open the door. "The Deadwalkers are back."

***

Jetta could barely stand, much less walk. Her legs, pillars of fire and broken glass, screamed in agony with even the slightest movement. Dirt and debris whipped about her, penetrating the holes in the gear bag that she'd wrapped around her head and body, pummeling her exposed legs.

Can't think about it, she told herself, not wanting to acknowledge the severe burns on her left leg, or the raw and ragged wounds on her right suffering in the stinging winds.

The two who had pulled her from the wreck poked her and tugged her along, but they progressed slowly, hindered by the weather and her condition, especially since she couldn't see through the gear bag to make out the path. Unable to hear her captors' conversations happening over their private two-way on their helmets, Jetta could at least feel the residual worry in their thoughts.

They're getting more and more concerned the longer we're out here, Jetta sensed. A peal of thunder shook the ground. Wincing, Jetta struggled to stay on her feet in the chaos. *But it's not just the weather. There are others out here, gaining ground on us every minute.*

Feverish, exhausted, and in pain, Jetta let her guard down. *Jaeia...* she called, reaching out to her sister across the stars. As far as she could, she stretched back, bridging the millions of light-years between them, searching for Jaeia's familiar tune. And when she found it, she stopped in her tracks.

"Jaeia," she whispered, filling with her sister's primal fear. *I haven't felt anything like this since the final fight with the Deadwalkers,* Jetta said, breath catching in her chest. Something must have happened. *I should never have left!*

"Hey!" she screamed, trying to get the other girls' attention. "We need to get to a com station right away!"

But her screams were in vain. Howling winds drowned out her cries, and the booming thunder deafened any ears. Even from behind the thin protection of the gear bag she could see the flashes of lightning cracking open the skies and smell the burning smoke. *It's getting worse.*

Something exploded in the distance, and the ground quaked beneath her. One of the girls grabbed onto her arm through the gear bag and yanked her hard and fast to the right. Jetta couldn't coordinate her feet fast enough, and she fell, the impact knocking the wind out of her.

"Stop!" Jetta cried, but another pair of hands helped to shove and roll her crumpled body along, wedging her into a tight space. After a brief struggle to orient herself, the floor seemed to give way. She fell, head over heels, down a hole.

"Yeah!" one of the girls cheered.

With a loud crack she hit some kind of bottom, but the aftershock of the impact left her unsure if she had stopped moving.

"*Sycha*, that was close!" the other one said.

It took Jetta a moment to collect herself. Realizing she was still stuck in the bag, she fought her way out. Once freed, overhead lights stung her eyes, and she let her arm lie over her face until the place stopped spinning.

"Where are we?" she asked.

Finally taking off their helmets, the two girls looked at her, their eyes narrowing in unison.

"You ever been to Earth?" the older one asked. She was maybe in her late teens, about Jetta's height with the wiry build of a drug addict. Stringy black hair, streaked with magenta and pulled back in a ratty updo, framed a desultory face. Her eyes, lined with layers of mascara, projected similar disinterest. From the smell, Jetta surmised that hygiene was not her foremost priority.

As the older girl set her helmet down on the grated catwalk, she pulled out a retro pair of black headphones from her satchel and placed them over her pierced ears. "Well? I asked you a question, *assino.*"

"No," Jetta said, taking in the rest of her surroundings. It reminded her of the parasitic areas on Fiorah, where illegal thoroughfares and businesses tapped into the city's air ducts, except this was more haphazardly constructed than anything she had ever seen. Anything and everything had been used to mold, shape, and decorate the entrance and the passageway—old posters, tin cans, decaying composite wood, a string of broken lights, coat hangers, a pot shard, a rusted pipe, chicken wire. Some of the materials were so decomposed that she couldn't tell what they were.

Looking up, Jetta spotted where they had fallen from. Constructed like an old chimney stack, but slanted to save them from a direct fall, was some kind of passageway.

The other Scabber, considerably smaller and younger than the first, sucked on her lollipop while giving Jetta the once-over. After fixing her pigtails, she donned a ragged engineer's cap. An air of rabid sexual energy pervaded her psionic space, making Jetta uncomfortable.

Her mind doesn't read like a kid in her early teens, Jetta thought. *But her appearance sure holds up that illusion.*

"We gotta get lower, Grace," the younger one said. "This still isn't safe."

"My suit's out of juice. We're gonna have to get treated. *Sycha.*"

Even after a brief exchange, Jetta felt an unusual dynamic between the two girls. *They could be related,* she guessed, sensing a deeper bond between the two. *Or perhaps they've adopted each other over time.* She had encountered enough pairs like that on Fiorah to know the type. *They're survivors.*

"Look," the older one said, turning to Jetta. "We need to get about another quarter-mile down before we're safe from the radiation. There's a lift about fifty feet that way. You gon' make it?"

Jetta looked down the dark tunnel and then down at her legs. Normally resistant to medical treatment, Jetta found herself longing for even the basics. She swallowed hard and looked away before the sight of her injuries made her ill.

"Yeah," she said. "Hey, are we safe from those people following us?"

The older one shrugged. "Dunno. A firestorm started up when we found this route. They probably got baked. Either way, doubt they could find this hole anyway; it ain't in the guidebook."

Neither of them were too eager to help her up, not that she would have taken their assistance. From what she could sense, neither of them saw her as an enemy, but the younger one saw Jetta as a means to an end while the older one guarded her conflictions.

Pulling herself up with the aid of the chicken wire and her good arm, Jetta balanced herself on unsteady legs. Her head, already in a dizzy swim, felt sluggish. *I can't fight these injuries much longer,* she realized, fighting to control her breathing. *And this talk of radiation—*

No, she stopped herself. *Don't give into pain or fear.*

"I don't know much about Earth," Jetta said, attempting to generate a conversation that could give her a clue about the dangers she'd be facing. "I know worldwide fallout changed the weather patterns. Is it true that there are only brief windows for landings and takeoffs?"

The older one swayed to the industrial music playing on her headphones and let out a laugh. "Yeah, this dump is a regular commercial transportation hotspot. Real good for tourism."

The younger one rolled her eyes at her friend's sarcasm and slurped loudly on her lollipop. "Why'd ya come here?"

Jetta shuffled along the piping, now dragging her right foot. Pain hammered at her skull, wearing her down, making it hard to concentrate. *Gods, I can't do this—*

(*Jaeia!*)

Stop—think. Give them a partial truth. Maybe they'll let their guard down a bit. "Something went wrong with my navigational systems and I jumped to the wrong site," Jetta said through gritted teeth.

The older one snorted. "You were hit. We ain't dumb. Who you runnin' from?"

Jetta bit her lip to keep from fainting. *I would give anything for even a first-aid kit right now.* "I jumped too close to a city. The city patrol fired at me to keep me from punching out. It fried my navigations systems. I was lucky I ended up here."

The older one's accusation came across with a snarky bite. "So you really ain't that smart then, huh?"

Exhausted and furious with herself, Jetta relented. "No. I'm not."

"Look," the older one said, stopping in her tracks and turning around. "My name is Agracia, and this here is Bossy. Saving your *assino* is costing us a fortune, and you're probably wondering if we're going to sell you or dump you off."

"Are you?" Jetta asked.

Agracia shrugged her shoulders, disinterest still in her eyes. "Depends. You're Jetta Kyron, right? That's shaky business, and all I want is off this *godich* rock."

"You don't have to sell me to get off this rock. I owe you for rescuing me from the wreck; I'll help you however I can."

Bossy turned around and smirked. "That ain't your reputation."

A flash of anger turned her hands into fists, but Jetta bit back her instinct to strike. She knew better than to challenge them in a hostile environment, especially when severely injured. Besides, pain crowded her thoughts, making it harder and harder to access even the most superficial aspects of her talents.

"I'm not the monster those *godich* liberalist mediaheads makes me out to be," she said. "And I stay true to my word. Help me get back to the Alliance and I will get you off Earth. Hell, I'll even get you a star-class vessel so you never have to worry about transit again."

"Don't mind Bossy—she ain't never had no manners," Agracia said. "Just spent too much time around Scabbers. 'Sides, if you wanted to kill us, you would have already, right? With all that leech talent you have?"

Offensive words meant to test her. *Agracia is no idiot.* If Jetta didn't play it cool now, she would lose any edge she might gain in the future. "I'm not a killer."

"What a waste," Bossy mumbled, and they resumed their descent down the tunnel.

"She's a fighting ring dark horse," Agracia chuckled, nodding her head toward her companion. "She don't know anything else but tossin'."

"Dark horse?" Jetta asked. Not a second later the little girl was on top of her, wedging a knife under her chin and pinning her back against the catwalk.

"Means nobody expected nothing of me," Bossy said, rolling the lollipop over to the other cheek with her tongue, "but I won every time."

Jetta kept herself from retaliating by reminding herself of her predicament. It would do no good to kill her guides, especially since she had so little knowledge of Earth and no way to communicate to the Alliance about her position. She needed to heal—then, even if she couldn't find a com station, she would have enough strength to contact her sister. After that, she could do whatever she liked. *Soon these two punks will find out what I'm really capable of.*

"Fair enough," Jetta said.

Bossy gave her a wink and pulled out her lollipop with a popping sound. "Best you remember that."

"I need a doctor," Jetta said, struggling back to her feet. "I can't make it much farther than this."

"Yeah, but you ain't welcome here," Agracia said. "Gonna be tough. Not too many Scabbers like military around, especially an ugly one like you."

Jetta stopped and leaned against the wall, fighting against the seismic pain shooting up her legs. "Do you know anybody that could help?"

Agracia shrugged. "Yeah, maybe."

The Scabber duo walked ahead, Jetta shuffling behind them in silence until they reached a two meter long flatbed car.

What the hell? she thought, regarding the rusted gears meshed together with odd looking parts. *Is that a crank lift?*

Jetta despaired. It looked like someone half-heartedly assembled a bunch of scrap and junk. *That's got to be 19th century engineering.*

"Nothing here really works right," Agracia said, pulling Jetta on top of the lift. Jetta collapsed, breathing hard and rolling on to her back to keep an eye on the pair. "So just keep your fingers crossed."

With a series of loud grunts, the two Scabbers managed to engage the gear shift. Pumping furiously, they put the lift on the descending rails. The lift platform groaned and shrieked against the cradle as they picked up speed on the rickety track.

"Hold on to your panties!" Bossy laughed, leaning over the front of the car and spreading out her arms.

Jetta lost any sense of distance as they plunged into Earth's depths. Overhead lights, sparse and half-functioning, winked past and disappeared into the dark curvatures of the tunnel.

"Agracia… what kind of name is that?" Jetta asked, hugging her bad arm against her side.

Agracia eyed her as she braced herself against the railing. "If you worry about that too much, you and me are gonna go for a toss."

Jetta closed her eyes and searched again for Jaeia amidst the hissing white noise of pain. Her sister's tune, a whisper in a stadium full of noise, lay out there somewhere in the unfathomable distance, fully engaged in whatever troubled her.

Swallowing the hot lump in her throat, Jetta tilted her head back, and with every bit of strength she had left, reached out.

***

Back aboard the starbase, Jaeia caught a lift in the docking bay, speeding down the hallways and corridors until she reached the briefing room. Inside, she found the head of every department sitting anxiously in their chairs, waiting for the debriefing to commence. Usually calm and collected, Chief Commanding Officer Gaeshin Wren appeared unsettled, clicking his laserpen on and off repetitively until the security commander whispered something to him.

Jaeia took her place between DeAnders, the director of military research, and Admiral Unipoesa at the rectangular conference table.

"Good to see you, Jaeia," Unipoesa said, nodding to her.

"Admiral," she acknowledged.

As she logged into the holographic interface at her seat, the mounting tension in the room scraped across her nerves.

Gods, she cringed, rubbing her temples. *I can't handle all of their anxieties.*

Concentrating on her slowing her breathing, Jaeia gradually withdrew her awareness from the room's psionic clamor to give herself enough space to think. *Things must be worse than I thought.*

Damon leaned in and whispered in her ear. "Forgive me, Jaeia, but you look like you're not feeling well."

Everyone—from her troops to her superior officers—had been saying that lately. She looked down at her reflection on the conference table, hiding her thoughts behind a smile. "It's just a cold. I've already been to medical. Thanks."

"Your attention," the Military Minister said, taking his post behind the podium. "This is a critical matter, so I will get straight to the point: What we think is a Deadwalker ship has been spotted in sector 101-79, just outside regulated territory. It's like nothing we've seen before."

The Military Minister pointed to the holographic projection in the center of the conference table. Gasps and murmurs filled the room. An enormous alien ship, about fifty times the size of any known Motti vessel, rotated on a central axis. The top of the ship, shaped like a black crescent moon, mounted a semi-elliptical central structure with protrusions jutting out of the main hull like spiny antennae. What looked like tentacles dangled beneath the superstructure, reminding Jaeia of pictures she'd seen of Old Earth's extinct jellyfish.

"The ship appeared on our remote radar about twelve hours ago, and this is the image we constructed using our long-range scans," the Minister said. "Even at that distance, we've already received reports of unusual activity."

"What kind of unusual activity?" Jaeia asked.

The Minister nodded to Gaeshin Wren. Leaning forward in his seat, the CCO answered her question. "Primarily communication blackouts. Any long-range contacts are mostly gibberish, unintelligible—as if people have lost their minds."

"Is it some kind of bioweapon?" DeAnders said.

"Unconfirmed," Razar said. "We can't get any ships out there fast enough, and we lose contact with anyone who makes it within sensor range, including our own scout ships."

"Chief," Razar said, standing to the left of the podium.

The chief of intelligence, Msiasto Mo, took the podium, standing completely erect. In accordance with his Chinese-Nahvari customs, he spoke just above a whisper but in a matter-of-fact way about what the military satellites had detected. "We've analyzed the design against known Motti technology but are unable to confirm its engineering or its primary function. We have, however, theorized that they are unable to achieve greater than x10 break-light speed given their mass and energy expenditure."

"If they can't maneuver well, then they'd have to avoid close contact with enemy starcraft," Unipoesa suggested. "And since the ship is too massive to jump, maybe they're jumping their weapons to their targets instead."

"Like bioweapons," Wren added. "Perhaps some kind of neurological disease. That would explain the gibberish on the long-range coms."

As she stared at the image rotating on its projection axis, Jaeia became aware of the blood rushing in her ears, of every breath she took. Her pulse turned into a whisper, then a shout, until thousands of lost voices rose up in her chest, screaming for release.

—*The thing with the burning red eye.*

Jahx's pain—

(Our pain.)

Death. Destruction.

"I thought the nightmare was over," she whispered, recoiling against the resurgence of emotions.

No, the Deadwalkers had been eradicated during the post-war cleanup. At least that's what the official statements reported, and what she chose to believe.

It was all I had, she thought, grinding her knuckles into the armrests. Moral ramifications of genocide aside, she felt both relief and pain knowing that her brother, though already freed from the captivity of his Liiker construct, had been physically destroyed. That *thing* would no longer have hold of him—or seek out her and Jetta.

A hint of nausea licked at the back of her throat. *The possibilities are endless if the Motti and their Liikers have somehow survived, especially if they still control a crop of telepaths,* she reasoned. *Just the fact that they have emerged, especially with severely reduced numbers, means that the weapon they possess is something catastrophic.*

Reviewing the alien ship's design on her personal holographic interface, Jaeia intuited a possibility that chilled her to the bone. *This craft isn't like any other we've seen before from the Motti. What if they don't mean to convert Sentients into Liikers?*

(Death is coming.)

"I can confirm that it is Motti. And that the ship is a massive communications dish."

Everybody in the room turned to her.

"How can you confirm that, Commander?" the Minister asked.

Jaeia closed her eyes, her mouth suddenly dry. Perhaps it was a gleaned memory she had inadvertently acquired while exposed to the Motti, or something she subconsciously learned communicating with the converted telepaths in psionic limbo. She couldn't explain it, but she knew she was right. "Trust me."

"It is plausible," Msiasto Mo said. He turned to Jaeia and bowed slightly. "Your observation is noted, Commander. We will consider that possibility."

"But how would a communication dish cause massive blackouts?" Damon Unipoesa asked.

All eyes fell upon her again.

Jetta—I need you. I wish you were here. "I can't explain that right now."

Razar cleared his throat and stepped back to the podium. "CCO Wren and Chief Mo will coordinate our next move. I want Research and Intelligence teams to stay involved in the proceedings. We need all civilian posts notified and escorts sent to remote starposts. Our first priority is protecting the citizens. Dismissed."

After the debriefing concluded, Jaeia lingered, waiting to have some alone time with the Military Minister. Damon Unipoesa stayed, too.

"We need to find Jetta," Jaeia said to the Minister. "We'll need her for this."

"We're doing everything we can, Jaeia," the admiral said, resting a hand on her shoulder. "You know that."

Jaeia looked at the image of the massive Motti ship and rubbed her hand along the smooth edge of the conference table's mahogany finish.

"I'll need Triel's help. Maybe she can help me find her."

"Of course, Jaeia," Razar said, trying too hard to sound

amenable.

Dissatisfied, but knowing no other recourse at the time, Jaeia turned to leave. Before exiting the conference room, she paused. "The Motti have something terrible otherwise they never would have resurfaced. I have a feeling this isn't about the survival of their species anymore."

Her theory was met with silence, and as she pushed her way through the double doors, her thoughts inevitably returned to her worst fear.

Jahx.

CHAPTER III

Torturing Reht Jagger was a dangerous move, but Tidas Razar pushed the authorization through before he could fully weigh the consequences. As much as he disliked the dog-soldier captain, it had to be acknowledged that Reht wasn't just another scum mercenary. Reht had friends and advocates, important ones who the Military Minister needed to stay in service to the Alliance.

But right now the Alliance needed the key more than ever. Even slow moving, the Motti ship would eventually reach the Homeworlds with whatever disease or method of destruction it harbored. Any tactical advantage, especially the mass teleportation potential of the Narki's flash transport device, would increase their odds in battle.

Most of all, he needed it. He had to know. *Is Senka alive? To have family again, I would—*

(No. I can't have these feelings.)

He didn't like the crushing waves of emotion, a weakness that crippled him ever since the dog-soldier captain suggested her survival. Hope rekindled old sentiments he had spent years burying. A man in his position couldn't afford to feel; the consequences would tear his soul apart.

Tidas Razar heard the muffled screams through the steel doors long before he stepped into the sectioned interrogation cell. Elite guards held the dog-soldier captain down, forcing him to watch the gruesome scene unfold in an adjacent cell. Although it was nothing more than a Spinner replication, Reht didn't know the difference, and watching his first mate, the Talian, torn apart by laserwires was too much for the captain to bear.

"Gods—please—stop! You don't have to kill him! PLEASE!" he screamed.

Tidas nodded to the guards monitoring Jagger's vital signs and stress levels as he pulled back the partition and stepped to the captain.

"Ah, Reht Jagger. How are we?"

"You *chakking* pig!" Reht screamed, tears streaming from his eyes. The guards yanked the dog-soldier back by the hair and gave him a sizzling zap from their blue shockwands.

Razar's knees ached, but he managed to stoop down so his eyes leveled with the dog-soldier's. He pulled a cigar from his uniform breast pocket—one of Jagger's favorites—and lit it, blowing the smoke right into Reht's face.

"Your first mate isn't dead—just inoperative," Tidas said as guards hauled away the massive, broken body parts of the spun Talian. "The Orcsin is next. We'll pull his wings off before taking his eyes out. Your choice, Jagger."

They couldn't have elicited anywhere near this level of pain if they had tried corporal torture. All the psychological evaluations concluded that one of Reht's greatest weaknesses was his crew, especially Triel, but she was too valuable for Jagger to believe they would torture her just to inflict pain on him.

"Please stop," Reht sobbed as the guards released his head. "Please…"

Knees popping, Tidas stood back up and looked the captain over. *That bastard's going to lie now, both to protect the rest of his crew and his investment. I have to push him further.*

The Military Minister chewed on the end of the cigar, stroking his chin. It would have to be something Reht wouldn't be able to withstand, something that would shatter his deepest reserves.

"Leave us," Razar said. The elite guards saluted and disappeared behind the mirrored walls.

Razar circled the dog-soldier captain, taking his time. "I know why you keep your hands bandaged, Reht."

Holding his head in his hands, Reht stayed kneeling on the floor, rocking back and forth. Tidas wasn't sure if he was listening, but he kept going.

"After all these years you could have had Triel heal them for you, but you've resisted. It's your reminder, your penance. You think that by keeping those scars you'll atone for your sins."

Reht glared at the Minister, his eyes red and swollen. "*Chak* you. After all the jobs I've pulled—you're a *chakking* bunch of backstabbers!"

Tidas ignored him. "And now you're doing it again. You're forsaking your family; their blood is on your hands. Give me the key, Reht, and I will end this now. I will send you back with the remainder of your crew, and you can leave this ship. I want nothing more to do with a washed-out piece of *sycha* like you, the disgrace of Elia, the shame of your family—the rot of this galaxy."

He grabbed Reht by his hair and, being heavier and stronger than the captain, pushed him to the ground, driving his knee into

Reht's chest. "Give me the key, you *mukrunger.*"

Mukrunger. Reht's native language; Elian for *weakling, traitor.* The word carved into his acid-scarred hands.

"What are you doing?"

The adrenaline pumping in the Minister's veins, the thrill that strengthened his grip, suddenly dissipated at the sound of Jaeia Kyron's voice.

"Commander, you are not authorized to be here," Tidas said, straightening up and catching his breath.

Tidas Razar turned around, collecting himself as best as possible. Exposed, he struggled to restrain his thoughts and emotions with Rai Shar.

Jaeia's eyes never left his face. "On the contrary; I have security clearance."

He wiped the sweat from his brow and motioned for the guards to take Jagger away.

"You *chakking* betrayed me!" Reht screamed as he was cuffed and dragged out of the room.

The expression on Jaeia's face reminded him of Jetta, making him nervous.

"You promised you wouldn't harm them," she said. "That was part of the deal. If you had a problem with them, you should have come to me."

Razar shot a look at the two security monitors that had allowed Jaeia entrance as he led her out of the holding area.

"They were only following protocol," Jaeia said. She paused as they passed the interrogation chamber where the guards laid out the injured Spinner's replication of the Talian warrior on stretcher. Pressing her hand into the glass, Jaeia watched as the medics extracted the little green worm from the mutilated body.

"Did you hurt the Spinner too?" Jaeia asked as blood and intestines spilled from the replication's abdominal cavity. "I thought standard practice was to remove the Spinner before... *using* the replicated body."

He thought to lie to her, but he had already placed himself in a compromised position. In truth, keeping the Spinner, a green, worm-like Sentient that could "spin" living flesh, inside the replicated body until right before death elicited the best simulation. This proved exhausting and dangerous for the Spinner, but the Alliance generously funded and compensated their homeworld, enabling the Spinner government to offer up more of its citizens to volunteer for interrogation replications.

The Military Minister changed his tone to reflect his authority. "Needless to say, Commander, this is a delicate situation which merits alternative methodology."

Tidas Razar made a motion across his neck, signaling to the security monitors to cut off the recording devices as they entered an empty briefing room. He waited for the telltale click and the flicker of the lights before continuing.

"I don't see how this doesn't violate every basic rights law there is," Jaeia said, leaning against one of the many desks facing an inactive holographic display. Yellow starlight filtered in through the observation windows, accentuating the frustration etched across her forehead.

After blowing out a ring of smoke from his cigar, Razar decided to hit her hard. "Speaking of violations—you knew this whole time about the device, Jaeia, and yet you chose to act on behalf of this dog-soldier and his crew, forsaking your oath as an officer in the Fleet, even forsaking the Exiles that helped you survive that cursed planet."

Jaeia's eyes stayed locked with his. "I didn't know Senka was your niece—Reht must have found out and kept it from me. But the captain and his crew did save my life, and I knew that the Narki technology might be the only thing to save his. I certainly wouldn't forsake my friends from Tralora; Senka thought they would be safe in the wave network. I had it worked out."

Razar saw right through her. Jaeia had always been a terrible liar. "You had nothing worked out. If I had to guess, I would say that you somehow lost the device to that dog-soldier scumbag and were trying to get it back. But guilt kept you from taking it by force; you think you owe him a debt."

"I do," she said quietly.

"Either way, it doesn't excuse your actions, Jaeia. The Narki technology will give us unparallel advantages in war. And we will need it against that godforsaken ship heading our way."

Jaeia stood her ground. "Reht is my friend. Don't make me choose between my loyalties to him and my loyalties to the Alliance."

"You should choose your friends more carefully, Commander. You know little of Reht and his history," Tidas Razar said, removing a datafile from his uniform jacket.

Jaeia took it from him, her eyes moving rapidly as she panned down the lists of infractions and criminal reports compiled against the dog-soldier captain.

"He is responsible for the murder of his parents," Tidas summarized.

Jaeia spoke in measured tones. "That is not how I read it."

"Just ask him then. Or rather, look at his scars," Razar said. "And if that's not criminal enough for you, then read section 19b, subtext 2871. He orchestrated the genocide of the natives of Elia. He's a thief, a criminal, and he's proven time and time again that he can't be trusted."

"Then what about his part in our rescue off of Tralora?"

"It was for profit," Razar said. "He blackmailed some of our senior staff. When he's said he's served the Alliance, he means that he's served himself."

Jaeia lowered the datafile. A mixture of disappointment and astonishment crossed her face, but she tried to hide her emotion beneath her conviction. "I didn't know about these... *violations.*"

She's telling the truth. It surprised him on some level. For some reason he had assumed she would have cracked into Reht's skull and leeched out all his knowledge and experience a long time ago. *I certainly would have in her place.*

Razar circled her slowly. "Obtaining the key is the Alliance's top priority. If I have to bruise a few dog-soldiers, then so be it. I will do anything to protect the citizens of the Starways."

Her eyes glazed over for a moment, and Tidas felt a strange pressure in the back of his mind. "Be careful, Jaeia—that is insubordination, assault of a superior officer."

The pressure stopped. Jaeia blinked and folded her arms across her chest. "Sorry. Natural reaction," she said coolly. She looked at him straight in the eye. "I had no idea Reht had done so many terrible things."

Tidas stopped and squared himself to her. "He says you know how to work the thing. Is that true?"

"I absorbed some of Senka's theories," Jaeia responded softly, lowering her head. "And I have the key."

Tidas crushed the cigar in his hand. "Why didn't you come straight to me?"

"He may be a criminal, but Reht's been right about a few things. Don't you think I know how much you're holding out on us? You think I'm blind to the fact that you've been running genetic tests, analyzing the tattoos on our arms? Do you really believe that every soldier practices Rai Shar as well as you do?"

Blood rushed to his face. Even as a master of Rai Shar, the shock of her words made it difficult to keep neutral thoughts at the forefront of his mind.

"We've kept the genetic information about you and your sister highly classified because of what the findings could imply. And I was the one who decided to keep our findings from you."

"Why?" Jaeia asked, taking a few steps toward him.

"Because if any of it is true, then you and your sister become more valuable than our top battle commanders. You become something else entirely, and I wanted to make sure we had all the facts before we presented them to you."

What he said was not entirely true, but she seemed to buy it. Jaeia cocked her head to the side, looking puzzled. "I met with a man called Victor on Jue Hexron who claimed to have negotiated peace between the Creos and the human colonies. And he knew me. Or knew something about me. He said I was human—but a human *from* Earth. He was implying I am over 1,100 years old. What do your findings claim?"

Tidas played things carefully. He wanted to give her something valuable, to make it appear as if he was on her side.

"Your DNA markers suggest that you're one of the original humans from Earth."

Gaze dropping to the floor, Jaeia hugged her arms to her chest as all the color disappeared from her face. "That's impossible."

"No, it's not. Travel at sub-light speed, wormholes—there are enough possibilities out there to make it plausible. The most important thing is your tattoo. We believe it's from Earth, a symbol that might lead us to know more about you, where you come from."

Jaeia's brows pinched. "Why is that so important? What if I am an original human from Earth? Aren't you wondering where we got our powers?"

It wasn't the primary concern, but Tidas nodded, affording her that belief.

Jaeia sighed. "I will give you the key and my knowledge of how it works only because you're going to let Reht Jagger and his crew go—together, unharmed, and without tracers. And you'll do it for Senka. She was one of the few people who have ever been honest and kind to me, and she wouldn't have wanted others to suffer."

Tidas's jaw stiffened "You're forgetting your rank, Commander."

"I'm not forgetting anything. You and I are at an impasse. You still need me in uniform, and I need the Alliance so I can continue to fight for what I believe in. But I need to make sure you really let my friends go."

"Is that a threat, Commander?"

"Think of it as renegotiating my military contract."

The Minister thought it over carefully, realizing that he could still maintain the upper hand. "Fine. I will make arrangements for Captain Jagger and his crew."

As he rose and walked to the door, she called after him. "Oh, and another thing."

Tidas turned to her, clearing his throat when he saw the look on her face.

"I would like full access to all your information and history on Reht Jagger."

Tidas ground his teeth together. *She's seen enough. I don't want her gaining sympathy for that bastard.*

Voice unusually calm, words evenly spoken, Jaeia tried him again. "We're all in this together, and we both want what's best for the Alliance. And we're going to need each other if we're going to make it."

You're too easy, Jaeia Kyron, he thought to himself. If Jetta had confronted him, things would have gone very differently. *You have no idea what fate you've assigned your friends.*

Straightening out his uniform, the Military Minister held the door back to the security corridor open for her. "Bring the key to the Defense/Research labs—I want that thing unlocked as soon as possible. Then I'll get you access to Reht."

Even though she kept her gaze trained forward, Tidas felt her eyes following his every move as they walked down the corridor together to the lift. There was no accusation in her voice, but the pressure, like a heavy mist settling over his gray matter, returned. "Remember your promise."

"Jaeia—you have my word."

***

Jetta woke up slowly. At first she became aware of the pain shooting up her broken arm and injured legs. Moving was a bad idea. She bit down hard on her lip, drawing blood. A bolt of white-hot pain exploded through her body. *Hold your breath. Don't cry out.*

Gritting her teeth, Jetta counted the seconds until the pain subsided to a dull throb. Much better to lie still.

She opened swollen eyes to find herself in an unfamiliar place. Pain sobered her to the reality of her situation. *Gunfire. A flash of light. Crash-landing on Old Earth.* Memory fragments knitted themselves together as she dug deeper. *Scabbers—most likely the infamous hirable Jocks that roamed the wastelands looking for lost terrestrial treasures—coming to her rescue.*

(My captors?)

Centuries of grafted military training kept her calm. *Assess the situation. Keep quiet.* A stray thought from a stolen life entered her consciousness in the gruff, straight-talking tones of a veteran: *If you aren't dead, then don't panic.* Under different circumstances, she might have found it humorous.

Jetta took in as much information as she could from her limited vantage point. Lying on her left side atop a flattened cardboard box, she faced a wall of aluminum siding. The odd smells of antiseptic and mold hung in the air. A blanket, sewn together from the remnants of other blankets, covered her from shoulder to knees. Voices behind her carried on an intense discussion in low whispers. Since they hadn't detected her yet, she listened closely—extending her mind to them, pushing past their words and into their thoughts.

She identified two of the three voices: Agracia and Bossy. The third party, a female, sounded tired and middle-aged.

"She isn't worth the risk."

Jetta heard that repeated a few times, each time with a little more fervency.

"I heard she has the power of the Dissemblers—she's too hot. Send her back."

Agracia laughed. Her overconfidence made Jetta's stomach knot. "There be ways to deal with that!"

Grumbling and profanities followed, along with talk in another language, one that sounded similar to Starways Common.

Of course, Jetta thought. *English.*

Though an antiquated dialect, English was an important root language that had formed Starways Common back when the first human refugees arrived in the Homeworlds. Since humans couldn't speak some of the more difficult Sentient languages that required vocalization on multiple amplitudes, Starways Common developed out of the need for a universal language that could be understood and spoken by all Sentients. Within a few years of its conception, the new language unified business transactions and eased travel and communication across regulated space.

"Do you have *any* money, Agracia?" the middle-aged woman asked.

"Yeah, I'm loaded, like always. Don't be stupid."

"Watch that tongue!"

"Hey—quiet you two, she's awake!"

Jetta grimaced and rolled over, the effort resulting in a sharp reminder of how much damage her body had taken.

Sitting on storage boxes around a circle of half-melted candles, the three Scabbers stared at her with various levels of disdain. Bossy drew Jetta's shocked attention with tightly fitted, low-cut clothing at drastic odds with her apparent age and the ten or so cans of explosives strapped to her waist. Her blonde and brown striped hair had been arranged into two buns on the sides of her head, with a low cap hiding her brow. Oversized jewelry augmented her suggestive outfit, mostly arm cuffs and bracelets, as well as the bedazzled boots with straps all the way up to her knees.

Agracia rolled her eyes and turned to the woman Jetta didn't know. "Is Jimmy around? He deals and patches up sometimes on the side."

Jetta inferred that Jimmy dealt medical supplies, specifically antibiotics. When she pulled off the covers, she saw why Agracia asked.

My legs—

White film glazed the open wounds on her puffy red legs. Reflexively she reached out, only to receive another painful reminder of her other injuries.

"*Skucheka*," Jetta winced, retracting her arm. She propped herself up on her good elbow and scooted back against the wall. "My arm is broken—it needs to be re-set."

"Does this look like a *chakking* clinic?" Bossy said.

"Enough!" the other woman snapped. With a grunt and a huff, the woman shuffled toward Jetta, bending down and inspecting her with a frown on her face.

Jetta regarded her similarly, taking in her rather plain-looking features with curiosity and calculation. In the grand anatomic scope of the Sentients, this woman seemed just as uninteresting as any other Scabber. Lines of stress creased the corners of her eyes and her mouth, making her appear much older than she probably was, and her skin, unusually thin, like paper, looked like it would tear at slightest touch. She carried her large build half-hunched over and hidden under layers of mismatched clothes.

"What name you go by?" the woman asked.

I guess it's too late to lie. "Jetta."

"Fine. I'm Jade, and I'm a caretaker, not a doctor. I did the best I could to treat your injuries."

"Caretaker?" Jetta asked, taking in more of her surroundings. They looked to be in some kind of processing facility, given the giant holding tanks and the pipes crisscrossing the walls and ceiling. Jetta spied a dusty control box, its indicators broken and bent, fixed to the right side of the room.

Somebody made a pitiful attempt at redecoration, she thought. Strings of colored lights stretched across the pipes, though most of the bulbs were broken. A strange and badly burned carving of a human figure on two crossed planks hung above the broken window over the control box. Other artifacts of Earth—doll heads, dead electronic equipment, plastic containers—were neatly arranged on shelves around the room.

"I keep what little is left of Earth's history *on* Earth," Jade said. "There was a news building and a library above this Pit before the War, so my family tried to salvage some of the documents before they set the nukes off. What wasn't stolen or sold we hid here in the shallows of the Pits."

"Shallows?"

"Secret areas," Jade said.

Bossy started to say something, but Jade interjected. "Like she's any threat right now—look at her!"

Holding her breath, Jetta bit down hard on her lip as the throbbing in her legs and broken arm threatened to make her pass out. *Don't you dare blackout. Stop being such a wuss.*

"You've got to get her down to Dac's clinic, Agracia," Jade said, folding her arms across her chest. "I don't want her dying in here."

Agracia stuffed her hands in her pockets, tapping her foot to the awful industrial metal song playing in her headphones, not seeming to take in her friend's advice.

How can she hear anything over that noise? Jetta wondered. *Let alone listen to that same crappy song over and over again.*

"Me and Bossy are gonna take off, set things straight. You keep her the night and I promise we'll be back. Here," Agracia said, handing Jade something. "Your security deposit."

"Hey!" Jetta said, feeling her pants pocket with her good arm. *They took the compass orb Jaeia gave me!*

"What is it?" Jade said, shaking it. The question mark never appeared.

It must be coded to my touch, Jetta surmised. To Jade it must have looked like nothing more than a dark, translucent rock.

"It was hers, and it's something sweet or she wouldn't be pitching a fit like that," Agracia snorted.

"Cut the *sycha* and just get me some radiation meds," Jade grumbled.

Agracia shrugged her shoulders as she headed out the door with Bossy.

"Here," Jade said, lumbering over to Jetta with the orb. "I have no use for your crap."

Jetta snatched it out of her hand and stuffed it back into her pocket. "It isn't worth anything. Just sentimental."

"Let's get something straight, kid. I know you're *Commander* Jetta Kyron, but you're not going to find anybody saluting you in these parts. You're just another warlord to them," Jade said, dragging herself over to a chest of clothes.

"Where exactly are we?" Jetta asked, trying to get something useful out of her.

Jade pulled out a scarf that she wound around her head and neck as she sat back down on her storage box.

She must be crazy—it's sweltering in here! Jetta thought. Then her eyes drifted towards her legs. *No, you idiot. You have a fever.*

"You're near Ground Zero, where the end started," Jade said.

With a stifled groan, Jetta gingerly lowered herself back down onto the ground. "Look, I really need a doctor, a medic—anyone trained in medicine. I don't want to lose my legs or my arm."

"I'm sorry," Jade said unapologetically, "but there really isn't much left here. Earth is just a bad memory for most. The only people that dare to visit are environmental scientists and Tourists that prey on easy human targets. Everyone else is on their own. And not everyone is lucky enough to have access to the anti-radiation medications that your great Alliance sends."

The woman pulled her blouse open to reveal a chest studded with disfiguring lumps.

That's why she kept her garments so loose. Jetta felt cheap issuing any kind of apology, and pity would only elicit anger from the Scabber woman. Instead, her words came out flat and ignorant: "I had no idea."

Jade's face soured. "Earth is too far away from the Homeworlds for anyone to care. Besides, I don't think any Deadskin living in the Homeworlds would call this place home anyway."

Not wanting to fight, Jetta closed her eyes. She needed to contact Jaeia at any cost, especially after her telepathic attempts had failed. "Where are your communication relays? Is there any way for me to get a signal back to the Alliance?"

Jade readjusted her clothes and relit a candle in the center of her arrangement. "The only remaining communication tower is all the way in Pit 822-2. Everything here is broken."

"How do I get to Pit 822-2? How far away is it?"

Jade seemed to find some kind of hollow delight in her predicament. "A few thousand miles, give or take."

"Miles?" Jetta repeated. "What kind of system works in miles?"

She shrugged. "It's the old ways."

"Alright, fine. How do I get there?" she asked, wiping the perspiration from her forehead. "On foot? I don't suppose you have any hovercraft."

Jade shrugged. "There are a few machines up and running around here, but you have to know the right people."

Sighing, Jetta arched her neck back, trying to give herself even temporary respite from the pain. "What do I need to do to get some help around here?"

She couldn't see it, but she felt Jade smile. "You're gonna have to fight, kid. Literally. There's no other way out for someone like yourself."

"Fight?"

"Where do you think the fighting rings came from?" Jade said.

Jetta blinked. "I'm in no condition—"

Jade waved her off. "You'll pull through. The newsreels say you're one tough bastard. And believe me, once you get a taste of it," Jade said, rolling up her sleeve far enough to reveal battle wounds criss-crossing lumpy skin, "you'll never get enough."

"I don't fight for sport. Take me to a communications relay," Jetta demanded.

Jade laughed, rummaging through a storage box next to her and taking out a can of beans. She pulled it open by the tab and sipped the juice before digging the beans out with her fingers. The rank smell made Jetta's stomach twist.

"I'm going to bet all my money on you. Get some sleep, kid. You're gonna need it."

Jade was done talking to her, and Jetta, too exhausted from fighting the pain, decided not to push it. Fighting back tears, Jetta curled into a ball, trying to think of her next move. *I'm too weak to use my talents, and I don't want to risk pissing off my captors.*

"Jaeia, please. Please find me. Jaeia," she whispered. Then she did something she had never done before. She drew in a deep breath as tears squeezed past her closed eyelids. "Triel…"

***

"You want my opinion?" Damon Unipoesa said. "Tell Jaeia. You need them both on your side. I still don't understand why you won't level with them."

Lip upturned, Tidas Razar looked at him with disgust. Damon had tried to clean himself up since they offered him the deal, but when he saw his reflection in the desk's mirrored finish, he could understand the Military Minister's revulsion. The skin beneath his eyes sagged, and his uniform, wrinkled from sleeping in it, looked like it hadn't been washed in weeks.

Razar grumbled and shoved away from his desk, pacing his office. "They're still an unknown quantity. I need them leading my teams, not leading revolts, and the analysis says that it's a strong possibility, especially with Jaeia, now that she knows she's human. What do you think the other Deadskins will do? What do you think the twins would do if we found what we're looking for?"

"You're paranoid," Damon said. "If we found what we're looking for, then there would be no need for revolt. There would be a chance for peace. We could all go home."

"You think the Deadskins would stand for that? You think their handlers, the traffickers, the dealers would stand for that? We would be looking at a full-scale civil war."

Damon struggled with his reaction. His parents were both Tarkn, but his birth mother was a human surrogate. Without the humans and the quasi-legal breeding and surrogate trade, he wouldn't be alive. His mother had already had the one pregnancy that Tarkn biology allowed, and those fetuses never made it to full term.

Even though Damon had never met the woman who nourished him in her womb, he knew one thing for certain: that he wasn't her first pregnancy and surely wouldn't be her last. It was the fate of all fourth-class, breedable human females.

Damon weighed the Minister's theory of human revolution. The explosion of human surrogates happened right after the first human refugees reached the Homeworld Perimeter. Bringing with them a bevy of new diseases, the newcomers unintentionally caused a death toll in the trillions. The common cold alone was deemed responsible for the eradication of the Moopi people of Irocos, and the flu wiped out all inhabitants of the moons of Kav and Noloran. Many Sentients called for an end to the human race, but with careful peace negotiations and the promise of restoration, one human set forth a dangerous precedent.

Careful never to be named in the history books, the private investor announced his discovery that humans were compatible with many of the mammalian species of Sentients, then started a surrogate company with the intention of helping reestablish species that had been driven close to extinction by human disease. The proclaimed intention was to "save lives and improve human-Sentient relations."

Over time, it insidiously grew into something else. Since many species of Sentients were unable to reproduce at a high rate, rich politicians and officials paid large sums to ensure the continuation of their bloodline. However, Alliance intelligence reports had shown that the majority of surrogate investors selling off and renting out female wombs were human themselves.

The human surrogate companies paved the way for other biological investments, such as flesh farming. Although flesh farming was largely responsible for the biomedical discoveries of the last millennia, at least ten billion humans were estimated to have been grown, bred, and sacrificed to the practice. But without their sacrifice, Damon's father and cousin wouldn't have survived the effects of Hans-Raiqio disease.

Flesh farm survivors were usually sent to human laborer camps under the supervision of third-class human traffickers, a practice which hadn't changed in over a thousand years. After all, human laborers proved unparalleled in their profitability. They were cheap to hire, easy to breed and highly trainable. They built the capital skyscraper in the Holy Cities of Jue Hexron, and worked the dangerous mining jobs that no one else would on Karris VII. In fact, a fourth-class human could be found to do just about any job. Without humans, the lowest class of all the Sentients, the Homeworlds would never have achieved its booming affluence.

No, Unipoesa thought to himself, *a human revolution isn't possible. The species is completely divided.*

However, Damon could understand where Razar was coming from. If the humans had a reason to unite, especially with leaders as strong as Jetta or Jaeia, and made peace within their own group, then it would spell economic and social disaster for the many governments and planets that relied on the lower class humans to prop up their income and social structure.

Damon rubbed his tired eyes. "I'm due to my post in fifteen minutes. I have a lead on Li; I think he's running with the Creos. He might be on Jue Hexron."

"Jaeia was just there. She met Victor."

"Victor?" Unipoesa repeated, unsure of who the Minister was talking about.

Razar's eyes shifted away from his. Surprised, Damon didn't know what to think. *I've never seen him this visibly upset.*

"Victor Paulstine, to be exact," the Military Minister said. "He hasn't surfaced in probably twenty-five years. Somebody or something made him come out of hiding. The analysis from *Heliron*'s imaging data confirms that it is the man we've been after."

"You can't mean *the* Victor Paulstine?" Damon said.

"Yes, I do."

"From what I've read, he prefers extreme anonymity."

"Yes, he's been a very hard man to trace. But it's him. I'm sure of it."

A shiver shot down Damon's spine. Many political and Sentient Rights groups fingered Paulstine as one of the most notorious human traffickers in Starways history. Allegedly, he bred millions of humans only to sell them to flesh farms, surrogate handlers or the labor colonies. He was supposedly human himself, but a traitor to his own species, having shown his support for many of the human control coalitions. Those who collected intelligence on him said that there was little sentiment holding Paulstine back from eliminating the entire race, only the fact that humans were his means of amassing the money to cheat time and death. The Alliance had been trying to move in on his operations for years, but Paulstine stayed one step ahead, making sure to conduct his business under the legal terms of more accommodating star systems.

"Pretty bold move to engage us like that," Unipoesa said.

"Yes, I agree. Which makes me think he's got something. He talked to Jaeia on Jue Hexron. I read her report; I suggest you read it too. I want to know what you think. If Li is on Jue Hexron, I would hate to think that he's collaborating in any way with Victor."

Damon saluted and left the Minister's office, his pace quickening with the shock of learning that Victor Paulstine had re-emerged. There were other rumors about him—terrible ones—that, if true, would make him one of the most dangerous Sentients in the history of the galaxy. With the Alliance still recuperating from its last miscalculation of their enemy, he didn't dare underestimate Victor's capabilities, especially in light of the fragile state of the Starways.

"Admiral," a soldier said, stopping him on his route to the starbase's main bridge and handing him a flashing datapad. "Priority message from CMA Triel of Algardrien."

Damon read the file and erased it quickly. "Inform the bridge crew that I'm going to be late."

"Yes, Sir."

Damon picked up his pace once again, this time taking a lift at the apex of the starbase straight down to the medical division. After hopping off a lift, he headed toward Triel's office at the end of an empty hall.

Razar could have at least moved her office closer to the lifts, he thought. No, the Minister did as the staff requested—put the Healer in a separate office away from the main corridor of the medical division. Separated by an entire wing, her office, an old cancer treatment room, had walls reinforced with antiquantum sealant, a material that some of the staffers and interested committees believed would protect them in case Triel descended into a Dissembler. *This just makes it worse,* he thought. *All their unfounded paranoia only reinforces her sense of isolation.*

"I got your message," Damon said as soon as he passed through the front door of her office.

Triel, lying down on one of the couches next to the far wall, draped her hand across her forehead. "Jetta's in worse trouble than I thought."

"You can sense her?" Damon said. "Forgive my surprise, but Jaeia's having a hard time reaching her. She believes Jetta's hurt or too far away for her to get a solid connection."

Brushing the dark hair from her face, Triel turned her head to face him. "I can't explain it. After Tralora, after healing them, our relationship changed."

Her bond to the twins is probably adaptive since she's on her own, Unipoesa reasoned. He offered her a hand, helping her sit up. "Where is she, Triel?"

The Healer shook her head. "Somewhere… dead. That doesn't make much sense, but that's my understanding. She tried to reach out to me, but she's weak—hurt. I need to speak to Jaeia. Maybe the two of us can contact her together."

That would be dangerous. Damon's jaw tightened. The Military Minister had informed him of what happened with Reht Jagger and Jaeia, and there would be little he could do to hide that from Triel if the two of them were to speak. But to find Jetta, he would need to have Triel and Jaeia meet.

Triel regarded the markings on the backs of her hands. "You're about to lie to me."

"I don't want to," Unipoesa said, sitting next to her. "But the situation is complicated, and I think it will be hard for you to understand."

The Healer looked him up and down, the stark blue of her eyes seeing past his words. "I know they're hurting Reht. He and I share something special, too, remember?"

"Razar and I don't always see eye-to-eye," Damon explained calmly. "I would never condone torture."

An inner voice surfaced with distinct rancor: *But you would follow orders to do so.*

Damon swallowed hard to keep from remembering the ghostly faces of his past. Channeling his self-hatred to steady his nerves, he asked her, "Will you still help me find Jetta?"

Triel looked at him, disappointment creasing her forehead. "Yes."

Damon typed a series of commands into his uniform sleeve, one of them to inform his second-in-command to take over his watch.

"I'll escort you to Jaeia's quarters," Damon said. "Tidas will want to be there, and probably a few of the other chiefs of staff."

"Fine," Triel whispered, following him through the door.

"Did you ask the Minister if I could go back to Algar?" Triel asked as they boarded the lift. It took off, the hum of the engines filling the silence as he thought of his answer.

"Yes, I did. We need you here, Triel. That will have to wait."

Triel didn't look at him. "My reasons are more important than the Deadwalkers, the Alliance—all of it."

Damon touched her shoulder, trying to console her, but she didn't acknowledge him. She felt stiff, cold. He worried what she was thinking—or rather, feeling. "I'm sorry, Triel. I'm doing my best with the Minister. His priorities are securing the homeland first, and you're our best resource for healing our soldiers and recovering the displaced telepaths. Be patient and I promise you'll get your chance."

"Before or after they kill all my friends?"

Her icy gaze cut right through him, igniting a fear like nothing he had ever felt before. Before he could react, the warm blue of her eyes returned.

Breathing heavily, he decided it was best not to respond. He wiped the sweat from his brow and let the railing hold him up, hoping that what he had just experienced was not what they all feared could one day come true for the lone Healer.

***

Fixed in place by an invisible force, Jetta watched helplessly as Yahmen's blows came crashing down on Jaeia and Jahx. As her siblings cried out to her, Yahmen's back split open at the spine. Mechanical legs broke through callused Cerran flesh, spraying the room with black ooze.

Jetta tried to scream, but her mouth fused shut. There was nothing she could do as the apartment walls melted into pulsating capillary beds covered in slick yellow mucus. Yahmen's face distorted, his two eyes congealing into one that burned a fiery red. The broken bodies of her siblings re-formed themselves into upright stalks fixed to feeders, flesh and machine indistinguishable underneath the biosynthesized jelly.

Her uncle's voice came through over M'ah Pae's mottled gray lips. "You said you would come back."

The Motti Overlord smiled, his gums oozing something thick and yellow, voice changing again. With a flick of his front pincher, the voice changed to that of the Healer's. "You said you were my friend."

Her siblings, with dead, glassy eyes that stared into the terrible nothingness, cried out to her with mechanized voices: "You said you would protect us!"

Something sharp stabbed Jetta's left ankle, jarring her from one nightmare right into the next.

"What are you doing?" she screamed, shoving Agracia off of her. The Scabber tumbled into a pile of boxes stacked in the corner. Before Jetta could retaliate further, Agracia pressed on a remote in her right hand, and a strange sensation seized Jetta's body, rendering her rigid and numb. She involuntarily flexed backwards, back arching off the ground until the sensation stopped.

Breathing hard and fast, Jetta collapsed from exhaustion. It took her several minutes before she worked up the energy to sit back up. When her eyes caught sight of the gray cuff around her left ankle, she immediately tried to remove it.

"Don't bother," Agracia said, standing and adjusting her headphones. She tapped out the beat of her music on her chest as she spoke. "It ain't comin' off."

"I'm a commanding officer in the Starways Alliance," Jetta yelled. "Take this thing off!"

"Look, we gonna get you all healed up, and then you're gon' make my money back. And since you never been to Earth, I'm going to give you the real flavor of it," Agracia said, stooping down next to her.

Given Jetta's injuries, Agracia couldn't have anticipated her speed, or her strength. Jetta grabbed the Scabber Jock by the throat with her good hand and yanked her down so that her knee smashed into Agracia's chin. The sudden movement whiplashed the remote out of her hand. But before Jetta could collect her prize, the prickling numbness hit her again, and she went stiff.

"There be two remotes!" Bossy announced, not taking her hand off the button as she hopped on top of one of the crates in the center of the room.

Something snapped like a twig. Pain, incredible and fierce, stole her breath away. The terrible feeling intensified until Jetta felt as if her muscles would tear themselves apart. Fingernails dug into palms and vertebrae tested the limits of their own flexibility.

"Quit it," Agracia said, getting back up, milking her sore chin where Jetta's knee had connected. "She gets it."

Every muscle in her body stayed tense for what felt like forever after the pint-sized Scabber let up. When Jetta's jaw finally relaxed, she tasted something like metal shavings in her mouth.

I think I bit my tongue, she thought, testing the swollen tissue against her teeth. For the moment, that felt like the worst injury caused by the seizure-like episode Bossy induced. Even as her muscles jumped and jittered, making her prior injuries protest all the more vehemently, she knew that she had probably only experienced one of the device's lower settings.

"Listen here, leech," Agracia said. "I bet you real mad right now. *Real* mad. I bet you want to fry my guts."

Something like that, Jetta thought. Dark whispers came from the depths of her, promising swift and satisfying revenge if she would use her greatest talent on her captors. In her pain and exhaustion, the temptation to submit to a psionic assault prevailed. But as she relaxed into the grip of the shadowy bloodlust, the cuff buzzed.

"Ha ha, look at that!" Bossy said, pointing at her vibrating cuff. "She wants to fry your guts!"

An electric charge lit up her insides. Only when the dark urges were jolted from her mind did the torture subside.

Jetta coughed violently, expelling something sticky and red. On some level she recognized that the burning smell that fouled the air was coming from her.

Agracia whistled. "Yep. That temper will 'bout do you in, leech. So don't even think about it. No mind tricks, no funny business upstairs," she said pointing to her head. "And maybe you'll keep from cooking."

When the blurred walls became fixed again, Jetta inspected the cuff more closely. Panic turned her belly into hot coals. Somehow the Jocks had fitted her with a telepath shock cuff. How they could have possibly found a relic from the Dissembler Scare was beyond her. The Alliance had sworn to have collected and destroyed all the devices with the enactment of the Telepath Anti-Discrimination Act.

Jetta had learned enough about them from her gleanings of Sentient minds and history reels to know that even though the cuffs were promoted as a "safety devices" by the Dominion Core, they had permanently maimed and killed tens of thousands of telepaths. The devices worked by monitoring brain waves. Even the tiniest fluctuation—little more than a passing glance at someone's mind—meant the delivery of punishment.

From what she remembered, the devices were attuned to the minds of the Tre, Morro, Si, and Prodgy, not an "unknown" telepath like her. This could either work in her favor or severely against it. If the shock cuff was oversensitized to her brain waves, it would kill her. But if it wasn't properly tuned to her psionic frequency, she might stand a chance of evading some of its parameters.

"Yo, Jimmy, you're up," Agracia said nonchalantly, sitting on the storage boxes and taking up a low conversation with Bossy.

Where's Jade? Jetta looked around, but couldn't find the grumpy woman. Instead, a man who hid behind thick glasses waited nervously by the door.

"Y-you're sure it's safe?" the man asked, clutching his black leather bag.

That's an old doctor's satchel. She didn't know if she should feel relieved or terrified.

Agracia gave him an uninterested look but held up her remote, as did Bossy. "I said get to it; I ain't paying you by the hour."

Desperate and in considerable pain, Jetta tried to reason with the fellow. "Please, I'm a Starways commander. I need to get to a communications relay. Help me and I'll make sure you're adequately compensated."

He laughed anxiously as he looked her over. "I've heard that line before."

After digging through his bag, he pulled out a few instruments. Jetta wasn't sure what century they were from, but from the wear and chipped wooden handles, she gathered they were from some period of antiquity. "Look, I can fix your arm and repair the damage to your leg. It'll take a few weeks, and you'll need radiation boosters and antibiotics. You'd better let me or they'll just feed you to the wolves."

"Wolves?" Jetta said in disbelief. She thought they went extinct like 99 percent of the planet's animal population, save rats and other survivalist vermin.

"Yeah, wolves," he said, reaching for her arm.

"Are you a doctor?" she said, holding herself back.

The man looked for cues from her captors, but since they ignored him, he was forced to answer on his own.

"I'm a ringside medic. But I tell you, I have more experience than any trained doc around. Not that there are very many…"

Ringside medic, she thought to herself, memories rewinding back to her days on Tralora. *Just like Crissn.*

When she offered up her arm, the man brought his hands up to his face as if expecting a blow. With a nervous laugh, he tried to play it off.

And just as jumpy.

Jetta allowed Jimmy to work, knowing she was in no position to refuse help, even if it was from a ringside medic. Any help would increase her chances of survival, especially as a hostage. *I only hope he's as good as Crissn.*

He worked steadily, chattering occasionally about nothing in particular, disregarding her pain. Setting her broken bone made her to black out for a few minutes, and debriding the wounds on her legs caused equal agony. But even a shred of compassion was unrealistic coming from either a fighting-ring medic or her captors, so she bore the pain silently.

(After all, I deserve this.)

Three hours later, once bandaged and given some kind of topical opium derivative, Jetta finally felt a little relief. Normally she would have fought against taking any kind of drug in a hostage situation, but she was too exhausted to put up a fight.

"Good enough. Can she fight in three weeks? There's another tournament in the Dives," Agracia said, handing the man some hard cash.

The medic scratched his head anxiously. "Uh, I wouldn't advise it, but nobody ever tells you 'no,' right?"

Agracia smirked. "Thanks, Jimmy. Stay out of this place. The lice are biting," Agracia said, slapping him on the shoulder.

"You shorted me!" Jimmy said, inspecting the cash she handed him.

"You took three *chakking* hours. Me and Bossy missed happy hour."

Jetta studied the interaction closely. Bossy grabbed for her weapons, but Agracia stood there, slack-shouldered, her eyes half-open, nodding to the rhythm of the music in her headphones.

"It's gonna catch up to you, Agracia," the medic said, pushing past her and hurrying out the door.

"*Chakking* Scabber," Bossy laughed, returning her explosives to her belt. "Let's go get blasted. I'm tired of this scene."

"So you," Agracia said, kneeling besides Jetta and showing her the remote. "You stayin' here. I set this on a six-foot perimeter. Better hope you don't have to piss."

Jetta assumed that the ankle cuff they put on her would deliver a shock if she went outside the designated perimeter. Too tired to fight and feeling the effects of the opium, she drifted off. Even if her captors had a means of delivering punishment and preventing her from using her most obvious talents, she hoped she still had her passive connection to her sister and to Triel. It might be her only means of survival.

"Don't do this," Jetta mumbled deliriously as Agracia and Bossy headed for the door. "I'm not your enemy."

Agracia snorted, holding open the door for Bossy as she ducked under her arm. "You definitely never been in a place like this, then.

Nobody's your friend here. Welcome to Earth."

***

Disappointment, frustration, and fear carried in Bacthar's voice. "I can't get him to talk."

The winged surgeon looked straight at Jaeia through his sets of red eyes, demanding answers she didn't have to give about their captain.

Keeping her eye on the other livid dog-soldiers, Jaeia raised her arms to quell the tension. *If we were anywhere other than Alliance territory, I would already be dead.*

"I didn't know they would do this to Reht," Jaeia said, carefully crossing the room, trying to get close to the captain. Lying on the couch in the middle of the bunks, Reht breathed shallowly, eyes open but unseeing.

"Don't," Bacthar said, holding her back. "Mom won't let you any closer."

A low growl and flash of the Talian's claws protruding from his skin kept her at bay. Mom had been protectively hovering over his captain since the Minister released him from his private session a few hours ago. Even now, Bacthar was the only person Mom even allowed within three meters.

The other crewmembers, Ro, Cray, Vaughn, and Tech, watched her from the bunks. Billy Don't, put into sleep mode by Tech, idled in the corner. Head hung to one side, drool trickling from his open mouth, the little Liiker snored very softly while his background programs hummed and clicked.

"You tell me you gonna fix this, and then we can talk," Ro said, voice rising. Cray slapped him on the chest and whispered something in his ear. Although Jaeia could not hear the words he spoke, the menacing aura surrounding the pair told her enough.

"I am going to fix this. I've arranged for your safe passage out of the system. I also told the Minister that if there was any further interference with your crew's freedoms and liberties—in *any* way— that I would terminate my service with the Alliance."

None of them said anything. *They don't believe me.*

With a heavy heart, Jaeia set aside the crew's enmity and focused on her main concern. She extended herself, reaching into

Reht's mind. Once again she encountered disturbing feelings, but the more she pushed through his psionic boundaries, the more concerned she became.

Why is there no evidence of psychological trauma? she thought, feeling the stanched surfaces of Reht's mind. *Surely the Military Minister's sessions caused some sort of mental injury.*

Dread burrowed into her heart as she skimmed across another smooth, emotionless white wall. *It's as if something is holding his subconscious hostage.*

Jaeia resurfaced from the captain's mind, frustrated and frightened. *I want to help Reht, but I've never encountered such an unusual barrier.*

"I'm going to get Triel. Maybe we can help him together," Jaeia said, turning to go.

Bacthar grabbed her arm. "You abandoned us after we saved your life."

Jaeia did not hide her feelings from him. "I'm doing the best I can," she said in hushed tones. "And I won't stop until you are all safe and away from here."

With a grunt he released her, and she left quickly, not looking back as Ro and Cray called her names viler than anything she had ever heard on the streets.

"*Upek.*"

"*Chakking j'eesh.*"

On some level she felt she deserved it.

Things didn't have to turn out this way, Jaeia thought, avoiding eye contact with the soldiers standing guard in the hallway. *I should have tried harder.*

She fought emotion with reason: *No, I did everything I could.* Carefully, she wiped away the tears in her eyes before they had a chance to fall. *Reht and his crew are criminals. They violated dozens of Alliance laws during the last war alone, not to mention all the other crimes they committed over the last decade.*

But despite her best efforts, her conscience continued to eat at her as she walked down the corridor. *(They risked everything to save us.)*

(I could have used my second voice—)

She rubbed her fingertips together until she calmed herself. *I'll keep trying,* she told herself, taking a deep breath. *I won't stop until*

I've helped them.

As she took the lift back to her quarters, a heavy projection entered her mind, parting her from any thoughts of the dog-soldiers. At first she thought it was Jetta, but as she explored the feeling and neared her room, she realized it was someone else.

"Admiral, Triel," Jaeia said, greeting the two as they waited for her by the entrance to her quarters. "I was just meaning to find you, Triel."

"That will have to wait, Jaeia," Unipoesa said. "Don't be surprised at the guests in your room," Unipoesa added.

Jaeia tilted her head to the side and listened beyond her immediate surroundings. Just inside her quarters hummed the familiar tunes of the Chief of Military Intelligence Msiasto Mo, the Military Minister, Chief of Medicine Dr. Kaoto, and CCO Gaeshin Wren.

"What happened?" Jaeia asked, keeping voice low enough so that the guards patrolling the corridor wouldn't hear.

Unipoesa indicated towards the door. Jaeia entered, saluting to the other senior officers as she took a chair next to the Minister. Following suit, Unipoesa and Triel took seats on the couch by Mo, Kaoto and Wren.

The admiral spoke first: "We called an emergency meeting, Jaeia. Triel thinks she's made contact with Jetta."

Adrenaline surged through Jaeia's arms and legs, making her want to sprint to the nearest docking bay. "Where is she?"

"I'm not entirely sure," the Healer said, reaching over and grazing the back of Jaeia's hand as she started to rise out of her chair.

With a simple touch, Triel slipped under Jaeia's skin, slowing her heart rate and the outpouring of catecholamines. After the Healer mitigated her stress response enough so that she would keep from jumping out of her skin, Jaeia breathed in sharply and settled back in her chair. *Thank you, Triel.*

"Jaeia, I need your help to make the connection back," Triel said. "I agree with you that Jetta's probably compromised, and that it's preventing us from individually connecting to her, but I think the two of us might be able to sort things out."

Swallowing the dry lump in her throat, Jaeia focused on every word to keep them from rushing out of her mouth in a tangle. "Okay.

What do we need to do?"

Triel hesitated. "The only means I know of is a cleansing ritual to prevent a Healer from Falling into a Dissembler. Basically, you and I will combine our awareness to reach out to Jetta. I have no idea if it will work, though, or what could happen. She's so far away, and I'm not sure how your telepathy will react."

Jaeia picked up on several of the Healer's implications. *Triel is worried enough about Jetta that she's willing to try just about anything in order to contact her, no matter how dangerous.*

Gods, Jaeia thought, scrunching up the ends of her jacket sleeves in her hands. *Triel knows that we have unusual telepathic gifts, but this goes deeper than I originally thought...*

(She's afraid.)

Jaeia concentrated on this aspect of Triel's emotions, but the Healer wound tightly around her feelings, even guarding her thoughts.

She knows something—or at least suspects something—about our telepathic abilities, and it's a secret she's fighting to keep, Jaeia thought, feeling the sealed edge of the Healer's mind. The idea gnawed at her, but Jaeia knew that she would have to wait to inquire about it until after they tried to contact Jetta.

Unipoesa nodded toward the Chief of Medicine. "Dr. Kaoto will be monitoring you both during the entire event. We also have two medical teams standing by. If anything seems amiss, Commander, we will stop this 'ritual.'"

"Okay," Jaeia said, shaking out her arms. She had no idea why she was suddenly so afraid, but she didn't have a choice. "Let's do this."

Triel took Jaeia's hands and placed them on her chest in a triangular formation. Chanting under her breath, the Healer put one of her hands on each of Jaeia's cheeks and rested her forehead against Jaeia's.

Nothing happened.

I have to relax, she told herself.

Jaeia closed her eyes and took deep breaths, concentrating on her own pounding heartbeat.

Relax. Think of Jetta. You have to find her.

The chanting got louder. Her breath came in choppy gulps.

Relax. Trust Triel. She is your friend.

(Is she? Then why is she so afraid?)

Just as she thought to abort the whole thing, something inside her broke free. A disconcerting sensation coursed through her, peeling her away from her body. The feeling intensified, her surroundings dimming, until she was only aware of herself and Triel, floating above a shadowy sea of gray and black motes.

(Where are we?) *she asked.*

(In between,) *Triel said.*

A rush of light and color flashed all around them, like starships flying past her at break-light speeds. As the scintillations slowed, Jaeia found herself encompassed by countless radiant stars, just like the unencumbered night sky.

(Those are other Sentient minds,) *Triel said.*

Jaeia couldn't believe her eyes. Galaxy-sized clusters of celestial light shined brightly in every direction she looked. (How are we ever going to find Jetta?)

(Think of the happiest moment you've ever had with her.)

Jaeia couldn't think of anything at first. So much had happened over the past year that it was hard to pinpoint any time that they had spent on their own, together, without escorts or guards, where they could really get away from their duties, the public eye or any of the other stresses that had beset them since their exposure, and just be with each other, giggling and playing, like the kids they were supposed to be.

(I—I don't know; I can't remember.)

(You have to, Jaeia,) *Triel said.* (Think. Go back.)

Jaeia pushed beyond the last year, stretching all the way back to their life on Fiorah. It was difficult to remember anything other than Yahmen and the mines, but she pressed on, trying to bring back the brief happiness they had known before things went bad.

(She is your sister, your twin—part of your soul,) *Triel whispered.*

The memory seemed to pop up out of nowhere. All other distractions faded away as the scene played out in her head:

"Hold on, Jetta," Jaeia said, standing tip-toed on a chair and flipping the yellowed pages of the recipe book on the kitchen counter. "We need to read the directions."

Grumbling, Jetta ignored her sister, pulling up another chair to the counter and climbing on top. Without waiting for instructions,

Jetta dumped the contents of the orange mixing bowl on the cutting board and began rolling the ingredients together.

"Hey wait!" Jaeia said, trying to stop her.

"Come on, Jaeia—we've got this," Jetta said, dropping her shoulder to block her sister's hand. "We've seen aunt Lohien do this a million times."

"Jetta, no—"

"Hey you two," Lohien said, walking into the kitchen, hands on her hips. "What's going on?"

"Nothing," Jetta muttered, trying to hide the mess of flour and spices.

Lohien gently pulled Jetta back and inspected the disaster. The pasta, limp and watery, lay in clumps, trails of spices dripping off the counter and onto the floor. "Looks like you forgot the rising powder."

Jaeia sent her sister a silent *I told you so!*

"Sorry, Auntie. We just wanted to help out and make dinner tonight," Jaeia said, bowing her head. "But *somebody* got impatient."

Jetta shot her a glare, and Jaeia made a face right back at her.

"Well," Lohien said, grabbing a pan from below the stove. "I think we can still make something out of this."

Humming a Cerran tune, Lohien poured the ingredients into the pan and added a few more spices and pigeon meat. After fifteen minutes over a low flame, Jetta and Jaeia saw their culinary disaster turn into a feast.

"Here, you take the first bite," Jetta said, offering her sister a spoonful of the soup.

"It's good," Jaeia said, licking her lips. "Thanks, Auntie!"

"Very well. But you two," she said, pointing to the mess on the counter. "Clean that up before you eat."

As they cleaned up the spills, still elated at the success of their concoction, Jetta surprised her.

"Think fast," she said, splashing her with dish soap from the sink.

"No fair!" Jaeia retaliated, throwing a handful of flour at her sister.

Seconds later they fell to the floor, rolling around and laughing hysterically until Lohien came in and told them to get back to cleaning or they'd miss out on dinner.

"That was great," Jetta said, lying on her back and wiping the flour from her forehead. She poked Jaeia in the side and smiled. "You make everything fun. Thanks."

It had been one of their few times together, alone, as sisters, and it was one of her most treasured memories.

To see Jetta laugh and be playful—that is the best feeling in the world, *Jaeia decided. When happy, Jetta's aura felt like the sun shining down on her, and all became right with the world. Their secret bond felt electric, magnetic—and most wonderful of all, in harmony, as if their souls were perfectly knitted together.*

Smiling, Jaeia opened her eyes. The stars were gone. Instead, she could see a hazy image of her sister through a jagged tear in the galactic fabric. Jetta, curled up in a ball underneath a dirty, patched blanket, shivered and moaned. She seemed to be injured, but somebody had taken the time to bandage her up.

(There she is!) *Jaeia exclaimed, pulling away from Triel.*

The Healer held tight to her. (Don't stray from me,) *she cautioned.* (We have to stay together. We can't get separated, or else we won't find our way back to our bodies.)

(What can I do?)

(Try and call out to her now.)

Jaeia held her breath and dug deep into the back of her mind, focusing on the image of her sister as she called out: (Jetta, wake up! Where are you? We're trying to find you!)

Jetta's brow furrowed, and she curled into a tighter ball, but she didn't wake.

(Oh Gods…) *the Healer said.* (I think she's been drugged. We'll have to risk entering her mind. Hold on…)

Jaeia's awareness elongated, stretching farther and farther away over an impossible distance. She could sense Triel, bending and extending in unison with her, as they plunged through the hole in the fabric towards her twin. A terrible pain shot through her, igniting her senses, sending sheets of fire down her phantom body as they crossed the threshold of the in-between.

(Hold on!) *Triel cried.*

The pain intensified, making her panic for release, but Triel brought her even closer. The pulse of the Healer's being flowed through her like running water, and for a brief moment she fell in tune with Triel's mind, hearing and seeing things that were hidden deep within the Healer's soul.

Rion, the Abomination. *Jaeia saw her face reflected back at her, as well as the images of her siblings. From the Healer's heart whispered chilling words*: Harbinger of Death and Destruction.

But before Jaeia had a chance to react, or understand the meaning of this revelation, she found herself thrust into a new body.

(Jetta!)

She felt the rise and fall of Jetta's chest, and the steady beat of her heart. Even unconscious, her sister's pain, a seething entity relegated to orbit in the distant periphery, still shocked Jaeia with its intensity. (She's hurt badly—we have to get her out of there.)

Jaeia didn't understand where they were. Nothing made sense to her. Jarred by what she saw, Jaeia tried to steady herself as images reeled in disorder, ebbing and flowing around her like half-thoughts.

(She's asleep,) *Triel said.* (She's dreaming.)

Jaeia reached out, stirring the light, colors, and sound. (Jetta, we're here! Wake up!)

Despite Jaeia's attempts, her sister's sleep state seemed uninterrupted by their presence.

(You have to do something more,) *the Healer said.* (We can't stay here. This is our last chance.)

Jaeia understood. With their minds bridging millions of light years, staying tethered to their own bodies was becoming more and more difficult the more time they spent apart from them, especially now that they had taken up residence inside Jetta. The pain of corporeal separation, once fierce and insufferable, grew more distant and dull as time pressed on.

Gods, being inside Jetta's dream like this feels just like that terrible otherworld where I made her battle Jahx, *she thought. Realizing that, Jaeia knew what to do. Using her second voice, Jaeia projected an image of herself into Jetta's dream.*

(See me,) *she whispered.*

Her own image, though distorted and fluctuating, appeared in the middle of Jetta's ever-changing dream world.

(Tell me where you are so I can find you,) *she said firmly.*

Jetta reacted. The world changed. Their surroundings became fixed and solid in the form of crumbling walls and rotting piping.

Jaeia took it all in. No windows, gray-green piping. The air smelled old and stale. Large holding tanks and a control box, situated in the corner of the dimly light of the room, looked like a snapshot from a different time.

A shadowed outline of a cross over the control box with a small figure in the middle caught her eye. From what little she could see, Jaeia could tell that the entire room centered around the display.

That's a key component, *her instincts told her.* Some kind of important symbol in this place.

She thought she saw the shapes of doll heads lining a shelf, but she couldn't be sure. A stack of plastic containers stood in the corner. Jaeia figured they were used for food storage, but by the looks of it, food was scarce.

Jaeia paid special attention to the signs and posters on the walls. She could make out a few letters, but too much of the text was indistinguishable either from decay or shadow. None of it looked very decorative—more like a desperate attempt to cover something up.

The sound of people speaking in whispers drew her attention.

Is that Common? *She couldn't be sure. Stretching out as far as she dared, Jaeia tried to see them, but they stood beyond the limits of their connection.*

(It hurts to speak,) *Jetta whispered, her pain slicing through Jaeia like an electric shock.*

Something or someone is preventing her from using her telepathy, *Jaeia realized.*

Jaeia held onto the Healer to keep from being taken by Jetta's torment. (Where are you? Give me a name!)

The strange voices in the background grew louder; she heard several words: fighting rings—hard cash—now.

(No!) *Jaeia cried, but it was too late. They snapped backwards, the Healer holding fast as they shot across space and time.*

***

Jaeia opened her eyes with a scream. The Minister and the CCO held her down while Kaoto drew up a sedative. Triel, refusing the admiral's attempts to comfort her, immediately rushed to Jaeia's side.

"Jaeia, Gods—I'm so sorry—I had to pull back. We were there

for longer than we should have been. Can you feel me?"

Triel touched her arm and her hand, but Jaeia couldn't feel a thing. Her responses, sluggish and numb, made her feel all the more disconnected, as if her body was not her own.

"Don't worry, it will come back to you. It might take a little while, though. It's a shock to the system to span that far out. I'm sorry," Triel repeated, rubbing her temples.

"The commander's electrolyte levels are dangerously low," Kaoto said to the Healer. "And I don't like her vital signs or the rest of her chemistries."

"I'll fix that," Triel said, taking Jaeia's hand.

The Healer dipped beneath her skin and rummaged around her circulatory system. Even after all this time, Jaeia still couldn't acclimate to the sensations of being healed. Gentle fingers ran along and through the deepest layers of blood and viscera, mending wounds and balancing energies.

Triel resurfaced looking exhausted. "There. Everything's restored."

"Well?" the Minister said impatiently. "What did you find?"

Jaeia smoothed back her hair and tried to concentrate on her words, but everything and everybody still moved too quickly for her.

"Jetta is somewhere old, very far away," Jaeia sputtered, mind still trying to make sense of the experience. "I saw some kind of cross, and heard Common. I also saw posters that used the Starways alphabet, but they were arranged in a strange order. It must have been a root language…"

"It's a dead place," Triel added. "That's what I felt. And Jetta's in danger. I believe she crashed down on a planet and is being held captive by someone who wants to use her in a fighting ring. And there's something that's preventing her from directly communicating to us. She said it 'hurt to speak.'"

"Have we found a trace of her ship's emergency signal?" the Minister asked.

Chief Mo shook his head. "No, we haven't. But planetary interference, damage to the beacon, sabotage—there could be many reasons we can't trace it."

"A dead place. What does that mean?" Unipoesa asked.

"The environment," Triel said, hands crafting a world they couldn't see. "It feels dead to me. I don't know how to better explain it."

"Maybe it's a Class 5 planet," Gaeshin Wren suggested.

"We should run a trace on all the planets that are colonized but considered uninhabitable. Maybe she's on a world that's still being terraformed," the admiral said. He snapped his fingers. "And cross-reference it with all planets that are known to have illegal fighting rings. That limits the possibilities…"

The Admiral's words faded, eclipsed by a tingling sensation traveling from her toes and fingers toward her core. Just as Jaeia was trying to make sense of it, the lights and sounds in the room became too much for her. Conversation turned into hurricane winds against her eardrums; light, a searing fire across her retinas. Jaeia brought her hands to her ears and tucked her head to her chest.

"Commander, are you okay?" Kaoto asked, raising his bioscanner to her chest.

"Jaeia," Triel said, taking her arm to keep her from falling.

Then, she heard it. Voices, in the back of her mind, whispering. Strange feelings, as if a collection of moments from other lifetimes raced through her at the same time, leaving her disjointed and confused. A voice rose above all of the other lipless speakers, calling out to her in a language she didn't know but nonetheless understood. An ancient cry, telling of a pain that had lasted for centuries, full of longing and unfulfilled promises.

"She's somewhere I haven't been, but I know. I can't describe it," Jaeia said breathlessly.

"What do you mean?" Tidas Razar asked.

Triel looked at her, eyes narrowing. "It's a stolen memory, perhaps. Or maybe something passed down to you."

"I'll advise the Fleet and assign Acting-Commander Rook to compose a Special Missions Team for this," Wren said, inputting his commands on his uniform sleeve.

"No—let me do it. I'll lead the SMT," Jaeia said.

"Your situation is compromised," the Military Minister said. "You can advise the team, but you will remain in command of our Contact Team. Chief Wren, please draw up your proposal within the hour. Dismissed."

Jaeia stood her ground. "I object. I can find Jetta faster than anybody here. If I can't lead the team, I should at least be commanding the ground units."

The room fell silent. Razar folded his hands behind his back and regarded her sternly. "We have that situation covered, Commander."

Jaeia found herself unusually intolerant of the Minister. Maybe it was the stress of spanning the stars, or perhaps her growing instability being kept so far apart from her twin. "I *object*."

Razar stood up, his nose flaring. "I gave you an order, Commander. I expect you to follow through with it. Report to your post."

He's intentionally trying to assert his dominance after our dispute over Reht Jagger, she thought, meeting his gaze. *I can't back down—not when Jetta was hurt and trapped somewhere dangerous.*

"The rest of you are dismissed," Tidas Razar barked. He waited for the rest of the party to leave before addressing her again. "You and your sister are my best battle commanders," he said, not mincing his words. "We can't afford to lose either of you. But if the situation with the Deadwalkers becomes critical, I need you advising Wren or even taking over command—I can't have you chasing after your sister. Do you understand?"

Jaeia sighed and sat heavily on her couch. "Yes, I understand."

"Good."

Jaeia retied her hair. "I saw that I'm assigned to investigate any relation between Li and Victor; Admiral Unipoesa conferred with me about his findings."

"Yes. This is a high-priority situation. You can still check in with the CCO and Acting-Commander Rook every hour to get an updated status on your sister. Your input is paramount. Also, keep advised on the Deadwalker situation; we still have no contact with any ship, post, or planet in its path."

Razar left, leaving her alone in her quarters. She tightened her hair again, fighting back the urge to cry.

How did it come to this?

A comforting arm wrapped around her shoulder and gave her a squeeze.

"How did—?" Jaeia exclaimed, shocked to see the Healer sitting beside her on the couch.

"Many years of practice in the forests of Algar," Triel said, blushing. "I learned to be quiet if I wanted to see the night creatures."

"Impressive," Jaeia said, still unsure how the Healer could slip back inside without her noticing.

"Hey," Triel said, squaring herself to her. "Everything will be okay. Jetta's a tough one. There isn't much she can't handle."

Jaeia couldn't help but chuckle. *That much is true.*

The Healer withdrew her arm from around her shoulders. "So... do you want to tell me about Reht?"

"Stop reading my mind," Jaeia said, wiping her eyes. "And I do, but I don't know if now is the time."

Concern spread across the Healer's face. "What have they done to him?"

Jaeia closed her eyes. "He tried to use the flash transport device to bargain his way out of Alliance territory. Didn't work. The Minister's niece was flashed, and I don't think he was willing to bargain for the life of his only remaining family member."

"How bad is it?"

Jaeia paused, weighing the consequences of telling her the truth. *I can't spare her the pain,* she decided, seeing the intensity in the Healer's eyes. *She's too attuned; she'd pick up on any lie.* "Very. He won't talk. His mind is totally locked, but I don't know why. Even with what they did to him, I can't imagine it would cause damage that massive."

"I need to go," the Healer said, abruptly getting up.

Jaeia caught her by the arm. "We should go together. I don't know what's wrong with him—I don't think it's something you should face alone."

"This can't wait, Jaeia," Triel said, the edge of panic in her voice. "Every moment counts."

Jaeia ground her fist into the couch. She was due at her post, and the situation with Li and Victor, her sister and the Deadwalkers couldn't wait.

Triel did not keep the hurt out of her eyes. "Please, Jaeia—for me. He is more than a friend or crewmate."

Jaeia looked at her, then through her, feeling the Healer's strain and burgeoning imbalance. *These types of feelings are dangerous for Triel,* she thought. *If I don't help her, I'll leave her vulnerable to the dark trappings of the Dissembler.*

"Okay—but I can't be long," Jaeia said. "I'm breaking about a dozen different protocols, not to mention risking the Fleet."

Triel grabbed her hand. "Thank you."

Jaeia summoned a lift, and notified her second-in-command of her delay. When he didn't immediately respond, she assumed the worse. *He's probably reporting my absence to my superiors.*

Guilt tore at her worry. *No—I can't let that bother me right now,* she told herself as she boarded the lift with the Healer. *I have to help Reht and Triel; I can't let them down.*

Jaeia sighed and rubbed her tired eyes as they whisked down the corridors and through the transway shafts. Despite her best intentions to stay focused on her current objective, her mind wandered back to what had recently transpired.

Those images, Jaeia recalled, thinking of what she had gleaned from Jetta's mind. *Especially that cross on the wall—I need to figure out what it is.*

A sudden recollection jolted her attention. She gripped the railing to the lift. "Triel, what's 'Rion the Abomination?' I heard those words inside you when we were trying to contact Jetta."

Triel turned to her, alarm evident in her eyes and in her posture. "Not now, Jaeia, but soon."

Jaeia tilted her head. Unable to catch any stray psionic information from the Healer, she relied on her intuition. "Do you know what I am? Am I really human—or am I something else? Are Jetta and I this 'abomination,' this 'harbinger of death and destruction'?"

"That depends," Triel said, her voice just above a whisper. "You have a choice."

"I have a choice?"

Triel closed her eyes as the lift slowed to a halt. "It will have to wait, Jaeia. It looks like we were expected."

Jaeia's heart sank as she looked at the empty corridor ahead. The guards were gone, and a cleaning crew milled around the dog-soldiers' quarters, barking orders at each other as they tried to figure out where to start in the waist-high mess.

"Oh no," Jaeia said as she carefully waded into the debris. There was the dog-soldiers' usual untidiness with the piles of empty food containers and cigarette butts, but there was also evidence of a fight.

Blood stains peppered the walls. Pieces of broken furniture and a fistfuls of blue hair covered the floor. *I didn't want it to be like this.*

Jaeia squeezed Triel's shoulder. "Let me find out what happened," she said, accessing her uniform sleeve to contact the Minister.

"Don't bother," Triel said, her voice cold and inhuman. "It's too late."

CHAPTER IV

Jetta lay on her side facing the wall, testing the strength of her arms and legs as inconspicuously as she could. Still sore and tired, she found that she had her usual mobility back, and with Jimmy's antibiotics and treatment, even her broken arm seemed fairly solid.

This isn't right. I should be dead, she thought, putting pressure on her arm. Dull pain radiated from the old fracture site, but barely registered above the revulsion and resentment souring her stomach.

Accelerated growth rates, enhanced immune systems, Jetta thought, looking at the fading scars on her hands. *The Motti violations saved my life. Am I a miracle—or a freak?*

(Freak.)

Chewing on her lip, Jetta pushed aside her discomforts and examined her situation. As puerile and stupid as Agracia and Bossy acted, they seemed to have her number. *I won't be able to hide the extent of my physical recovery much longer. Soon they'll be playing me for cash.*

A door slammed. Drunken legs plowed into crates. "We're back, *assinos!*"

Jade rebuked the two Jocks, trying to get them to sit before they broke one of her prized collectibles. "Can you not go one night without getting sloshed?"

Bossy belched. "Nope!"

"How's our new friend?" Agracia asked.

"She's still out," Jade said. Jetta felt three sets of eyes on her back, studying her movements. Slowing her breathing and relaxing her shoulders, Jetta tried not to blow her cover.

Agracia and Bossy talked with Jade in low tones. As much as she tried, Jetta could only catch snippets of their muddied, inebriated words as they slipped in and out of Common.

Frustrated, Jetta tilted her head back as far as she dared, trying to catch more of the conversation.

"You'd better cough up that money for your little 'hostage storage' by tomorrow," Jade said. "You're not taking advantage of me this time."

"Yeah, yeah," Bossy said, hocking up something and spitting it out. "We'll pay you soon."

"What the hell is that?"

Jetta couldn't tell what Agracia pointed out, but from Jade's reaction, she guessed it was something precious to the Scabber woman.

"Jeez, more junk?" Bossy exclaimed. "Why do you waste your time scavenging for that *gorsh-shit*?"

Jetta caught a glimpse of Jade's reflection in the finish of a metal storage unit. The Scabber woman cradled an armful of broken plastic toys. "These are priceless."

"Yeah, right," Agracia snorted.

Jetta agreed. *It's junk.*

A deeper knowing pulled at her conscience, not allowing her to dismiss the woman's attachments. *(Those toys represent the last remnants of Earth's long-forgotten past.)*

Waves of nostalgia came crashing over her. Jetta held her breath, surprised by the flood of emotion for a planet and people she didn't know.

Bossy pulled down her pants and waved her butt in the air. "Hey Jade, I'll crap on a plate and sell it to you for fifty bucks."

Jade turned away in disgust.

"Come on, we're friends! I'm giving you a bargain!" Bossy said, hiking her pants back up and pretending to look hurt.

Agracia laughed so hard that snot shot out of her nose. With an exaggerated snort, she wiped it off on her sleeve. "Jade, seriously, who do you think really cares about any of this stuff?"

"You're a selfish bastard, Agracia Waychild," Jade muttered, shelving her prizes with great care.

Overcome by a curious longing, Jetta's hatred for Jade trickled away as empathy reshaped her thoughts. *She's not another callous, heartless Scabber—not with the way she treats Earth's "treasures." She has a passion for preserving Earth's culture. All that gruffness is not because she's uncaring; it's the only way to survive this rotten place.*

Feeling the tensions rise, Jetta carefully rolled over to keep an eye on the situation.

"And another thing," Jade said, tripping over the empty bottles of booze that littered her living space. "Get off your *assinos* and clean up this mess!"

Agracia clinked her bottle against the crate she sat upon, spilling more alcohol onto the sticky floor. "We'll get right on that, captain cranky," she slurred, giving a stiff salute.

"*Godich ratchak* Jocks!" Jade said, flinging a bottle at her head.

With astonishingly quick reflexes, especially considering her state of inebriation, Bossy caught the bottle and cocked it back to throw at Jade.

"Easy, kid," Agracia said, stripping the bottle from her hands.

Infuriated, Bossy shoved the ragged mess of her hair haphazardly underneath her cap. "Don't—*hic*—call me kid!"

"See, when you get all bent like that, you give yourself hiccups," Agracia said.

"Bite me!" the pint-sized girl growled.

"Look, Jade, we'll get her on the circuit tomorrow," Agracia said, pointing a lazy finger at Jetta. "She's good enough to fight now. Then we'll get you some money. And maybe hire a maid or somethin'."

"You know—*hic*—you got the good—*hic*—end of the *sycha*," Bossy added.

They're more drunk than I thought, Jetta realized. The thought briefly crossed her mind to try for the remotes again, but she dismissed it with a shudder. Her only way to gain the advantage was using her telepathic powers, but after another aggressive attempt had triggered more shocks, her body wouldn't allow her any more tries.

Nausea and fear gripped her insides. *Even the thought of another shock...*

No—I can't give in. Jetta firmed up her thoughts. *Besides, there's still a chance.*

Lying quietly, Jetta relaxed the boundaries of her mind, keeping her mind open to the surrounding psionic wavelengths.

The two Jocks are drunk; Jade's upset. If I keep my mind open to them, maybe I'll catch a stray thought or emotion...

"I thought you had some big job to run before this one showed up," Jade said, pointing to Jetta. "Whatever happened to that? You really want to play the circuit? Those guys aren't regular Scabbers—you'll be in over your head."

Agracia and Bossy looked at each other and then burst out laughing.

Greed. Anticipation.

"Are you kidding me?" Agracia exclaimed. "They wanted to pay me two thousand for some ol' scavenger hunt. With her fighting,

I'm gonna be making millions."

"*We're*," Bossy said, punching Agracia in the shoulder.

"I stand corrected!" Agracia said and sucked down the last drops from her bottle.

"She needs a name," Bossy said, picking her teeth with a bottle cap. "We can't say she's the Slaythe or we'll get tagged by the *chakking* Skirts."

Jetta hid her amusement; she had heard the Alliance called many things, but never "Skirts."

"Name… a name," Agracia said, her head rocking back and forth to the beat behind her headphones. "How about 'Sinister Sister'?"

"That is the dumbest thing I've ever heard!" Bossy said, punching Agracia.

Agracia didn't fall over, but she held her hands as if she was about to. "Whoa—I'm not feeling so good."

Jetta looked away as Agracia lost her stomach into a box of scavenged plastics.

Cursing, Jade struck Agracia across the head. "I told you no more booze!"

With lightning speed, Bossy backhanded Jade clean off her feet. "Lay off!"

"I want you two out by morning!" Jade shrieked. She picked herself up and stumbled out the door, slamming it behind her as hard as she could.

"Let's call her 'Betty Bruiser,'" Agracia said, unaffected by Jade's departure, wiping her mouth with her sleeve.

"Dumb!" Bossy sighed, sliding down the crate and sprawling out next to the clump of candles. "God—*hic*—I could use a smoke."

"You quit, kid. Bad for your health."

"Don't call me—*hic*—'kid'!" Bossy said, slapping Agracia's leg.

"Well, what bright ideas do you have?" Agracia said.

Jetta realized her opportunity. Escape would be very difficult if she went against her captors, but if she could gain their trust she would have a better chance.

Even though they're idiots, they've been clever enough to survive the wastelands. I have to be careful; they'll suspect something if I'm suddenly friendly.

"Who's Earth's most notorious killer?" Jetta asked, propping herself up on one elbow.

The two of them looked at her with red-rimmed eyes and a gaze that was anything but fixed. Jetta clutched her stomach. *Just like Yahmen—*

"You *chakker*—you want to be named after a killer, *killer*?" Agracia said.

"That's what you want me to do, right? You want to attract a large crowd? Give me the most obnoxious name."

Agracia's eyes narrowed. "All the sudden you into our biz? You wanna fight?"

"Do I have a choice?" Jetta said, nodding towards the remote peeking out of Agracia's jacket pocket.

Agracia half-smiled. "Nope, ya don't, but glad you're on board. You made things a lot easier on yourself. Didn't want to have to break you in. It can get rather *messy*."

Jetta caught a psionic glimpse of something that didn't make sense. Agracia implied that she had hurt or tortured someone before to do her bidding. Although Agracia believed it, the memory itself felt flimsy and two-dimensional.

It's a lie, but not one she created.

Curious, Jetta reached out to explore the gleaning, but the shock cuff on her ankle buzzed a warning.

Skucheka, she cursed, withdrawing her talent. *I need to know more.*

Agracia inspected her upside-down bottle with one eye to make sure she had gotten every last drop. "Doctor Death. He ended Earth. That's you then."

"Doctor Death?" Jetta repeated. She didn't remember hearing the name before. Then again, she didn't know much about Earth's history. "That sounds campy."

Agracia lifted a brow. "Tell that to the dead. Or the undead."

"She wants a—*hic*—history lesson," Bossy guffawed. "Like she even cares. You—*hic*—playin' us, Skirt, and we know it. Don't think chummin' us up is goin' get you—*hic*—anywhere. You fightin'!"

"*Chak* it, Bossy," Agracia said, dropping her bottle on the ground. "She's the fancy commander who saved the universe, but she doesn't even know about Earth."

"This here," Agracia said, stumbling to her feet, "is the planet responsible for your well-being!"

Drunk and leaking emotions, Agracia hit Jetta with an enormous psionic wavelength.

Oh Gods—

Jetta cringed as a massive and labile compilation of memories assaulted her senses. Though not Agracia's direct experience, it was her imaginings of what the human race had endured in the last 1,100 years:

Humans stacked up on a rotating conveyor belt and dropped in vats of acid. Flesh reduced to essential elements and turned into white powder medicines. Pregnant women giving birth to squirming reptilian babies. Human laborers dressed in nothing but loincloths, scarred skin covered in soot, toiling in the mines and erecting great cities with foundations on their bones.

Jetta bit her lip and pushed the rabid thoughts away, but the echo of Agracia's sentiments lingered in her mind: *The lowest members of the human race are the backbone of the Starways.*

Tightening her fists, Jetta tried to deny the unfortunate reality, but the evidence overwhelmed her conscience. *So much suffering—how has the human race survived?*

"Doctor Death ended Earth," Agracia said. "He was responsible for everybody leavin'. He spread the necro-plague to start the Last Great War. He's the devil."

"Necro-plague?" Jetta said, unsure of the Scabber slang.

"*Chak*, I don't remember what the real name is," Agracia mumbled. "It made the dead come back to life. That's why we got all them Necros roaming around up top. It makes traveling suck even worse."

"Is it still an active plague?" Jetta asked.

"If they spit, bite, or bleed on you, then you're *chakked*. But we ain't going to the surface anytime soon. You have to win at least three matches here before we make the tourneys in other Pits," Agracia said, twirling her finger in the air.

Jetta thought it over. "What happened to Doctor Death?"

Agracia shrugged. "Who cares? He went six feet under centuries ago."

Jetta dropped it, realizing her captors were probably not going to offer any more information.

The alcohol is catching up to them, she thought as Bossy yawned and tucked her arm under her head.

Even with the industrial music blasting in her ears, Agracia eyelids grew heavier and heavier. "Don't think 'cause we're sloshed that we don't have an eye on you," Agracia muttered, activating a setting on the remote before finding a resting spot against one of the crates.

Jetta sighed and lay back down on her pile of cardboard boxes. *Stupid. Stupid. Stupid. How did you let yourself get in this situation?*

The self-directed reprimands continued until she felt blood trickling out of her clenched palm. She uncurled her fingers and saw where her nails had bitten into her skin.

Jetta stared at the blood as it ran down her arm, not feeling the pain. *This is all my fault.*

Her best hope had been that Jaeia could somehow find her, but with the shock cuff impeding her telepathic abilities, that would be impossible. She wanted very badly to believe that the dream she had the other night was real—that Jaeia had called out for her, that she was looking for her—but she wouldn't let herself believe it.

The dark voice inside her whispered crippling words: (*She's better off without me. I am nothing but a disgusting waste. I just bring her down.*)

Dangerous thoughts hovered at the corners of her mind, but she brushed them aside by holding tight to her biggest fear. She had to find a way back. For Jaeia, for her sister. *I'm a fool for leaving her in the first place.*

Jetta closed her eyes and cautiously let her thoughts drift toward her sister. *Please, where are you?*

A familiar tune rang across the psionic wavelengths, seeking connection.

Jaeia, yes, please, oh please—

No! she silently screamed, pawing at the vibrating cuff. Panicked, she yanked her awareness back into the confines of her own mind. The cuff went still.

After a few heart-pounding minutes, Jetta finally let go of the cuff and lay back down on her cardboard bed.

What was that? she wondered, sifting through what little she gleaned. Dissonant chords marred her sister's tune. *She's anxious—strained.*

Jetta clenched her fists. *What is happening on the outside is serious enough to affect her psionic signature. I have to get out of here.*

Taking a deep breath, Jetta made a promise to herself. *I will control my temper. I will be patient and bide my time until I can make solid contact with the Alliance or my sister. But until then, I will play my captors' stupid games, no matter how violent or unscrupulous.*

And for some reason, despite her fears, she found herself smiling.

***

Jahx Kyron ran as fast as he could down the entryway, but he was trapped. Their old apartment on Fiorah was not very large, and in this reality it was even smaller. The doors to the separate rooms disappeared before he had a chance to try them, and even the boarded-up windows were gone. It was just him, the figure in the shadows, and purple tendrils rising from the burning end of a smoke.

(Jahx, my boy—I found you. This is only the beginning.)

He had thought the nightmare was over, that he had finally found peace. Jahx huddled in the corner as the bare bulb flickered and dimmed, knowing that it wouldn't be long before he was completely in the dark again.

(Don't be afraid.)

He didn't recognize the voice, at least not immediately. But then a shared memory, one that he must have inadvertently gleaned from his sister during the terrible fight, brought him a sense of orientation.

Someone familiar. Someone safe.

The world changed again. The lights came back in full, and the apartment was the way he remembered it best: sparsely decorated but comfortable. Except this time his family was not there; it was just him and the man in the shadows.

(Don't be afraid,) *the man repeated, this time stepping forward. His amethyst eyes were just how Jetta remembered them.* (My name is Oblin.)

Jahx slowly uncurled and got to his feet. Still unsure, he stayed pinned in the corner. (How did you get here?)

The old man smiled and put the smoke to his lips, taking a long drag. (That, my friend, is what I'm trying to figure out. Quite the mystery, yes?) *He stepped a little closer and looked Jahx up and down.* (I must say, you are exactly as your sisters described. And you are quite the gifted telepath.)

(Why do you say that?) *Jahx asked.*

(I was lost out there,) *the old man said, pointing toward the door.* (So much chaos, so much confusion, but your radiance—you shine from so far away. I followed your light, and it brought me here.)

Trusting his intuition, Jahx took the old man's hand and led him to the family room. He showed the Oblin the couch and took a seat across from him on the ottoman.

(I felt myself leave the physical plane when my sisters freed me from the Motti's captivity. Do you think we're dead?) *Jahx asked.*

The old man ran his fingers down his braided beard. (I do not know. Your sister, Jaeia, tried to save me and my companions by sending our biosignals into the wave network. I think that's where I am... unless I died too.)

Jahx looked around, trying to understand the dynamic world. The cement walls cracked open, the paint flaking and peeling away. Windows shattered and decorations vanished one by one.

(I'm sorry. I don't know what's come over me. I'm just so tired,) *Jahx said, resting his head in his hands. Fatigue ate at his bones. It felt like he hadn't slept in years.* (I just want to sleep.)

(No!) *The Grand Oblin said, shaking his shoulders.* (Don't sleep—not here!)

(Why? What's wrong?) *Jahx said.*

The Oblin's wrinkled hands trembled. (Not to seem obvious, but this isn't your old apartment.)

(He's right,) Jahx thought, watching the couch fade and fray as if years had passed in seconds. *(This is some kind of temporal fabrication.)*

(Your body is dead, and mine is encoded into the network datastream. I think we're both trapped in a transitional plane,) *the Oblin said, his form fluctuating. Jahx watched with interest as the Berroman compacted and expanded into a female form.*

(Oh, bother,) *the Oblin muttered as she adjusted her robes.* (It seems the same rules apply here.)

(You said there were others—why aren't they here?) *Jahx asked.*

(I'm not sure about that either. I tried to find them. I was the only telepath of the group—maybe that has something to do with it.)

With great effort, Jahx walked over to the kitchen. He stood on tiptoe, trying to pour himself some water from the faucet, but the handle turned to jelly. Whatever this world is, *he thought to himself,* it's not stable.

Exhausted, Jahx leaned against the counter. The tiles and wood gave way, as if made of sand.

The Grand Oblin scuttled over to him, grabbing him by the shoulders and leading him back to the family room. (Just stay awake a little while longer. I promise you we'll figure this out.)

Jahx nodded and sat back down on the ottoman as various structures of the apartment rebuilt themselves around him and fell apart over and over again.

I don't want to be here anymore, *he thought, pulling up his knees to his chest.* If only I could close my eyes, just for a moment...

The Grand Oblin seemed to know his intentions. (Jahx, I know you haven't seen your sisters in a very long time. Perhaps you'd like to see them now?) *she said, extending a chubby hand.*

Jahx's eyelids quivered at half-mast. (Who?)

Somewhere in the depths of him sounded a voice: (Jetta. Jaeia.)

He wanted to reach out to the Oblin, but his hand felt too heavy to lift.

The Grand Oblin sprouted up again, his frame thinning and his back hunching over. His eyes, sagging at the corners, aged centuries in a heartbeat. With a strained effort he picked up Jahx's hand and held it in his. (My friend, let me show you.)

Psionic light burst forth from the Oblin's touch, encompassing Jahx and pulling him into the harmonies of the old man's inner world. After having been alone and guarded for so long, the comfort of another being released Jahx from his own prison.

I had almost forgotten how beautiful—

Jahx clasped the priest's hand, holding tight as their minds collided. Shared memories exploded across his mind's eye: the scene of his sisters' crash site on Tralora and nursing them back to health. Jetta's outbursts. Long conversations with Jaeia. Reaching out to them, trying to get them to understand the complexities of their situation. The Oblin's fear as the truth about the Exiles' circumstances came to light. The old man held nothing back.

(My sisters…) *Jahx said, withdrawing his hand. A mix of relief and sadness tugged at his heart.* (I'm glad they're safe now.)

The Oblin spoke with uncommon kindness. (Because of you, dear boy.)

But Jahx could not celebrate the sacrifice he made. His sisters did survive, but seeing them again brought back the realities of the living, and a reminder of the awful truth he had learned before the Motti Overlord had stripped him from his body. He chided himself for being so ready to accept the peace of death when the fate he carved for his sisters would lead them to face the greatest of all evils.

I should have never allowed myself to be taken by M'ah Pae, *he thought angrily.* Jetta was right about me. I am weak.

The Grand Oblin's amethyst eyes twinkled. (Don't despair just yet, my young friend. Your instincts led you this far. Trust them. Besides, I have a feeling there might still be a chance for you and me,) *the Grand Oblin said, resting his hand on Jahx's shoulder.* (After all, there is so much left to do.)

Jahx withdrew his hand from the Oblin's and rested his head on his knees. (I don't know how much longer I can stay here,) *he said breathlessly as the walls of the apartment melted and reformed. The invisible force pulled at his chest and mind, and every moment he remained awake seemed to drag down on his soul.* (I just want to rest—)

—and return to the dream.

(Don't give up, Jahx,) *the Grand Oblin whispered, holding fast to his shoulder.* (Our work is not yet done.)

***

The Healer had already disappeared down the corridor before Jaeia could get any answers from the cleanup crew.

"I'm sorry, Sir," the officer said, showing Jaeia the flashing message on his uniform sleeve. "Minister Razar gave me strict orders to remove the dog-soldiers."

"By any means necessary, I see," she said, looking him in the eye.

The officer cleared his throat and shifted his gaze away from her. "They left me with no choice, Commander."

Jaeia held angry words back, knowing better of the situation. *This isn't this man's fault; Reht didn't play his hand well.*

With a heavy heart, Jaeia righted an overturned chair and resurveyed the damaged quarters. *Reht wasn't patient enough—or maybe he didn't trust that I'd keep my end of the bargain.*

She had been planning to strike a deal with the Military Council for the crew's release, and she was certain she would have accomplished that, especially with the value represented by the Narki technology, but for whatever reason, he had jumped ahead of schedule.

Maybe he knew something, Jaeia thought. *Or maybe the Minister did.*

"Gods," she muttered, checking the beeping communications monitor on her uniform sleeve. An alert from the Minister ordered her to take the next available lift. There were no further instructions beyond a *Priority Level 5* tag flashing at the end of the message. *Something big has happened.*

Jaeia rubbed her hands together until her skin abraded. *I can't just leave Triel by herself, especially when she's experiencing such volatile emotions. But how can I be in two places at once?*

Closing her eyes, she waded through the neuroelectric tangle of the starbase crew until she came upon Triel's psionic signature. The Healer's normally mellifluous tune rose in a throb of anger and discontent. She had experienced Triel this upset, but never with such stark overtones of loneliness and despair.

(What do I do?)

When she opened her eyes again, she found *Priority Level 5* still flashing on her uniform sleeve.

What about my sister—
(I can't abandon the Fleet)
—or my friends?

Jaeia rarely ever swore, but she found the expletives spilling out under her breath. "*Skucheka!*"

Squeezing her eyes shut again, Jaeia extended her senses and wrapped herself around the Healer's signature.

I am here for you, she called, sending waves of reassurance and peace across the psionic planes. Impenetrable ice walls repelled her efforts, deepening her worry. *I've never felt a psychic barrier like this before.*

"Triel, come in, please. Triel!" she said into the com on her uniform sleeve. Crackling static responded.

"No," Jaeia muttered, spying a lift whizzing down the hall toward her position.

"Commander," the operator said, stopping the unit by her side. Specialized soldiers flanked him, guns pressed to their chests.

The Minister has never ordered a security detail like this when requesting my presence. Grazing the minds of the soldiers, Jaeia did not sense aggression. *This is a precautionary measure.*

(The Minister is afraid.)

She had to think quickly, but there were so few people that Triel trusted—that *she* trusted—at least when it came to personal affairs.

Admiral, Jaeia typed into her sleeve, *I'm concerned about Triel but can't meet with her right now. Please check on her. I will join you shortly.*

A response popped back almost immediately. *On my way.*

Jaeia allowed herself a hesitant sigh of relief as she boarded the lift. Damon was one of the few people she felt she could really trust. Even Jetta wasn't completely doubtful of him.

"Please hold on, Commander," the lift operator cautioned before speeding off.

They covered a distance of almost three-quarters of the post before they arrived at their destination deep in the heart of the Alliance Central Starbase.

"Thank you," Jaeia said to the lift operator, stepping off the platform. The outer doors of the research lab belched cold, sterile air as they parted. Heavily armored guards greeted her, falling in step with her as she hurried down the corridor.

When she stepped in to the front office, she found Director DeAnders looking over a series of charts and talking quietly with his staff. As soon as he spotted her, he waved her over. "Commander, please follow me."

Jaeia gently probed his thoughts. The director was eager to show her something, but she sensed a considerable despondency creasing his enthusiasm.

"The Minister is already waiting inside," he said, guiding her through the maze of the research labs towards the weapons division.

From the stray thoughts she managed to capture, Jaeia anticipated what she was about to see. *(A major breakthrough. Revolutionary technology—)*

—They've managed to initiate the Narki technology.

Though she had poured every detail of her gleanings from Senka into her report, she hadn't expected the Minister to authorize any trials so soon.

"Were you able to calculate the final mass conversion?" Jaeia asked, opening and shutting her hands, trying to get them to stop shaking. She feared the worst, but she wanted so badly to see her friends safely materialized.

The director didn't respond, making her more nervous. Instead, he concentrated on entering a sequence of numbers into the keylock by the double-plated doors.

"I don't think I've ever been to this part of the starbase," Jaeia commented, seeing the signage for "Division Lockdown Experimental Lab 1."

The keylock emitted a series of clicking sounds before an iridescent blue panel revealed itself behind the keylock. The director pressed his thumb into the pad as a retinal scanner flashed his eyes.

"Clearance, Dr. DeAnders," the computerized voice announced as the doors opened.

Inside the lab was a flurry of activity. Jaeia could barely see over the sea of white-coated technicians running back and forth across the catwalks and staging area. Looking up, Jaeia spotted cylindrical tubes, filled with a translucent orange fluid, suspended in the center of the room.

I remember detailing those in my report, she thought, spotting the large energy concentrators and biofeed tethers attached to the tubes.

Pain and suffering slipped into her mind, dragging her attention away from the realized Narki technology. The rest of the lab faded away from her sights as the Minister's mind, burning the brightest in the room, became a fiery star in a frigid night sky.

He's no longer in control of himself, she realized. Keeping his pain a safe distance from her mind, she crossed the room to stand by his side next to the tubes. *Only the burden of loss, especially death, could unsettle a mind of one of the most practiced masters of Rai Shar...*

(Senka?)

Jaeia placed a hand on the back of his arm. "Minister…"

Keeping his back straight and rigid, he pointed to the center cylindrical tube. "She's in there," he said, tone flat and detached.

Swimming in his worries, Jaeia only needed one glance at Razar's face to see the puffiness in his eyes and the pinched corners of his mouth to confirm her telepathic senses.

Oh no…

Jaeia cautiously approached the tube. Sliding her hand across the glass, she listened, extending her mind out as far as she could. She lost sight of the lab as she traversed farther than she normally dared, straining to hear even the faintest sound in the empty hollow.

All of her hopes quickly crumbled in the vast zeroscape of Senka's mind. *There's nothing here.*

Her friend, floating peacefully in the viscous orange biogel, eyes unseeing and shut, seemed to stare back at her with accusation as she withdrew.

"Physiologically they're intact," DeAnders said, handing her a dataclip. The numbers and readings meant nothing to her as her feelings took charge. *Did I miss something in my reports?*

(Did I kill the Exiles?)

"But we can't seem to wake them up," the doctor continued. "For lack of a more accurate term, we've diagnosed them all in a comatose state. Well, except one."

Tilting her head to the side, Jaeia picked up on a psionic dissonance radiating from the tank to Senka's left. Even distorted, she knew the sound of his tune. *The Grand Oblin.*

She pressed her hands against the cold glass and stared into the murky orange fluid. Seeing the familiar wrinkled face with eyes closed and mouth slack, she immediately sank beneath his skin.

Greeting her was the well of infinity she had sensed only once before, back when she and Jetta had bridged impossible lengths to locate their brother in limbo. The Oblin's mind spanned backward impossibly far, farther than she could perceive, his essence stretched so thin she could barely make out its impression against the shifting psionic palette.

"He's there," Jaeia whispered. She squeezed her eyes shut. "I can feel him. He's still attached to his body, but barely. I don't know what happened to the others," she said, hurrying from tube to tube, hearing nothing but the same eerie silence that pervaded Senka's mind.

Where are you?

"Gods," Jaeia whispered, biting her lip. If only Jetta was here. With her twin's help she could extend her psionic reach and maybe find a way to help the Oblin and the other Exiles.

But no. Jetta left me behind. Again. Jaeia blushed and stopped herself. She couldn't have those thoughts. She'd had enough personal and borrowed experience to know where that kind of thinking led.

"We've managed to flash several inorganic objects," DeAnders said, pointing to the energy pad on the other side of the cylinders. Boxes of tools and miscellaneous engine parts lay in scattered heaps.

The doctor dropped the level of his voice. "We weren't allotted a time trial of the process on Sentient organic material." He glanced at the Minister before looking back at her. "We also discovered that their signals were rapidly degrading. Time was our enemy."

"I understand," Jaeia whispered back.

"And this rescue operation was given a high priority level," he added.

Jaeia cupped her hand over her mouth. She didn't want to react, not in front of fellow officers and soldiers, or in front of other staff. But her stomach started to revolt, spasms tearing through her esophagus, and she ran to the nearest trash receptacle and threw up.

Why did I wait? Why didn't I act sooner?

Holding out to ensure the safety of the dog-soldiers, the Healer and even their own lives had cost those of the Exiles.

This is all my fault.

All she wanted right then was for the Minister to scream at her, to court-martial her, to throw her in the brig, but he didn't. The Military Minister, his jaw tight and his mouth pinched, turned on heel and left the lab, his escorts trailing behind.

DeAnders offered her a towel. "Commander, this technology was intended for the transport of armies, and that means the transport of organic material. There are a lot of things we still don't know, and we're working to figure out what went wrong." He adjusted the glasses on his face and cleared his throat. "Don't take this is a failure yet."

"No," Jaeia said, wiping her mouth with the towel and

straightening up her uniform. "I don't. I will review your process and see if there's anything I can add. When my sister returns we can revisit this situation. Have you asked Triel for her consultation? She can perceive biosignals and psionic rhythms better than we can."

DeAnders fumbled with his dataclip. Everything about his affect changed. No longer was he accessible; the internal barriers went up in an instant. "I was informed that Triel's commission is currently under review."

Jaeia sucked in her breath and held it. "Excuse me? I wasn't aware of this."

DeAnders looked over his shoulder nervously. He then grabbed her by the arm and pulled her under a recirculating station where they couldn't be overheard. "Her behavior has caused some concern. That's all I can say. You'll have to speak with the Minister."

"But this is an emergent situation—is she that critical? Why wasn't I informed? I'm one of the people who could help—"

DeAnders accepted a datapost from one of the technicians and shook his head. "I have to get back. Check with the Minister—these are not my affairs."

Jaeia pressed her knuckles together until she heard a pop. The urge was there, alive and dancing in her chest: *I can use my second voice. I can get answers.*

Jaeia licked her lips. No, she couldn't do that. *I'm upset, and using my talents when I'm distressed is the worst thing I could do. That's how people get hurt—*

(*That's how people die.*)

Jaeia willed her legs to take her out of the lab, despite the fierce desires that seethed inside her. She would have to find another way.

(*Who are they to control you?*)

It was a crazy thought, one she would have been more likely to find in Jetta's mind, not her own.

Where did that come from?

Jaeia dismissed the thought and placated herself with the survivalist mentality she had fallen into for years. *I don't need unpleasant thoughts tearing me down; I need to focus on more important matters.*

As she left the Division Lockdown, a message from Triel beeped on her sleeve. *I sent the admiral away. I'm fine. Just need some time alone.*

Seconds later a message from the admiral appeared. *She wouldn't allow me inside her quarters, but she assured me everything is okay. I'll check back with her in an hour.*

Jaeia was right in the middle of composing a message to the Healer when Triel sent her another. *Don't stop by. Please give me time.*

Jaeia let her arm drop to her side with a defeated sigh and decided it would be best to walk back to her command post instead of summoning a lift. Consumed by her thoughts, she failed to notice the crew's greetings as she passed by. With so much at stake, so many battlefronts, she didn't know where to start. If only for a brief second, she wished she was back on Fiorah where their enemy was clear, where what they needed to do was relatively simple. Back when they were three.

"Jahx," Jaeia whispered, wiping her eyes. "I need you now more than ever."

***

Jetta decided that she hated Earth cuisine, or at least her captors' choice of food. It was nothing but prepackaged, instant-cook meals that were worse than anything she had ever eaten.

Blech. Even the rat skins on Fiorah had better flavor and texture, she thought, spitting out her last mouthful. It all tasted like a heap of chemicals, and it upset her stomach every time she forced it down her throat.

"Hey, princess, you don't like the food?" Agracia said, her finger wagging to an imaginary beat. "Then maybe we'll jam a tube down your throat. You gotta eat or you ain't fightin'. And if you ain't fightin', we selling you. The puppet show is in two weeks, you know. There be plenty of Joes that'll sucker for you, even if you ain't a looker."

Bossy laughed and chinked her bottle against Agracia's. Jetta had never heard of a puppet show, but she had some pretty good ideas about what it meant by the way she said it. Humans had made the prostitution circuits on the Homeworlds a legitimate intergalactic business centuries ago, but one of the few attractions of the dead world was the syndicates' freedom to run their businesses without regulation.

Jetta gulped down the remaining lump of noodles and synthetic meat, making a conscious effort to control her gag reflex. Whatever they were eating was old anyway, making the meat slimy and the noodles hard and crunchy.

"She's onstage in an hour. You got any rags for her?" Agracia said, downing the remainder of her booze.

Bossy stumbled over to Jade's old chest of clothes and rifled through it. "Nah, unless she wants to look like a frumpy old witch. We could rip off one of the Dogs and get her some Earth fatigues. That would be sweet!"

As the Scabber Jocks schemed up their next move, Jetta thought of Jade. It was still exceedingly difficult to circumvent the parameters of the cuff, but she had discovered another small way around the sensors. Under the same premise of passive acquisition, she found that if she thought long enough about the person she wanted to sense, and they were in close enough proximity, she could glean faint impressions of their mood. It wasn't great, but it was something.

Jade hadn't returned since her spat with Agracia and Bossy, and Jetta sensed danger in that. From what few interactions she had witnessed between them and other Scabbers, including Jimmy the ringside medic, Agracia and Bossy had a reputation.

Now, when she thought of Jade, she sensed something unpalatable and bitter. She had felt it many times before in many different minds and knew exactly what it was: the roots of betrayal.

Jetta didn't know what to think. Should she warn her captors, or should she wait it out and see what happened? Both scenarios played out in her mind, but neither had a pleasant conclusion.

As Bossy staggered back from the chest of clothes, she knocked into Agracia, sending her headphones flying across the room. Agracia looked as if she was about to yell at her tiny friend, but instead the color drained from her face. She dropped her bottle of booze, spilling its precious contents, and made a strange noise, as if she were being strangled.

"Hey—hey! What's wrong with you?" Bossy said, shaking her shoulders. Agracia's mouth moved, but no sound came out, nor would her eyes focus. She appeared distant, distracted, seized by some unseen force.

Jetta let her mind relax in an attempt to catch anything she could without being direct, but she didn't sense much before the cuff began to buzz.

Agracia is in some sort of trance, Jetta deduced from what little she could feel. *Like she's caught in some kind of feedback loop.*

"What the hell?" Bossy exclaimed as Agracia stumbled to her feet.

"God," Agracia whispered, her eyes wide with fear. She anxiously snatched up her headphones off the floor and fit them over her ears. Seconds later her eyes glazed over.

"You!" Bossy screamed, grabbing the remote and mashing a series of buttons.

Jetta would have screamed if she could, but her mouth clamped shut as bolts of electricity shot through her body, setting fire to her viscera. She fell to the ground spasming and writhing.

"It wasn't her!" Agracia yelled, grabbing the remote from Bossy.

Jetta wanted to jump out of her skin as the residual shocks dealt their final insult. Sickness danced its way up her stomach to the back of her throat, and her last meal presented as a greasy, yellow pile on her flattened cardboard bed.

Both of the Scabber Jocks were too wound up to notice her distress.

"Well then what the hell was that? You get some bad booze or what?" Bossy shouted.

Agracia sat back down, slowly picking up her bottle. "I don't know. That was weird. I just suddenly got the idea that we're going about this all wrong. Everything felt really wrong."

Bossy eyed Jetta again, shaking the remote. "If that *ratchakker* did anything to you—"

It was only a glimpse in the psionic aftermath, but Jetta saw it clear as day: a ripple in the persona that was Agracia Waychild.

In an uncharacteristic display, Agracia grabbed Bossy by the shoulders. "It wasn't her! It was my gut. I suddenly got this really bad feeling."

"What are you saying?" Bossy said, wide-eyed. "That you don't want to fight her? We wasted all this time and money on that *baech* and now you want to back out?!"

"No," Agracia said, her confidence quickly returning. "Nah. Let's fight her. I don't know what I was thinking."

The Jocks talked about betting and who they'd connect with in the ring as Jetta recollected herself. As the electric shock jitters subsided, she stared at the cooling vomit on her bed. *I wish I hadn't thrown up.* She would need the meal, even as nutritionally poor as it was, especially with what she was about to face. With a sigh, she scraped the mess off the cardboard with an empty food can and into the drainage grate.

Time to buck up, she thought, inspecting her injuries. The burns had resolved into discolored patches against pink skin. Though her broken arm had been reset imperfectly, it had nonetheless knit together and proved functional. Scabs crusted her legs, but the skin was no longer inflamed and angry red.

Jetta grunted as she stretched and rolled her neck around, trying to loosen the kinks. She had fought under worse conditions on SMT raids or battling child laborers for food on Fiorah, but she had never fought in a ringside battle, and she didn't know the rules or what to expect.

I wish I could have stolen that kind of knowledge from somebody, she thought, glancing at the shock cuff. *And I can't expect to do that now, either.*

It struck her then—she could convince her captors that her chances of winning would increase if they let her use her powers to glean information from her competitors. She made a mental note of it as Agracia motioned for her.

"Let's get you going. You first, Doctor Death," Agracia said, tossing her a disguise.

"What is it?" Jetta asked as she held the plastic child's mask over her face. The narrow eye slits limited her vision and the small fanged opening for her mouth made it hard to breathe.

"The Boogeyman, which is exactly what you is," Bossy scoffed.

For the first time since her capture, Jetta stepped through the front door and into a barely lit passageway. Dirt and debris covered the walkway, and abandoned spiderwebs and dead electrical wires dangled from the breaks in the rock ceiling.

"So, you're expecting to just send me right into battle after only a few weeks of recuperation?" Jetta asked, testing the Jock duo.

"Keep walking, smartass," Agracia said, poking her in the back with the nose of one of her pistols. "Despite your words, you ain't no pansy. We got your number."

Jetta's legs felt rubbery as she hugged the wall, straining to see in the dim light of the tunnel. Haphazardly strung up mini bulbs, half of which didn't work, illuminated signs and advertisements for the fight. Some were in English, some in Common, but most were a mixture of both. She saw several names on the list with her pseudonym at the bottom.

"Who are all these people?" Jetta asked, pointing to the sign.

"Your competitors. Some from here, some from other circuits, some from other planets. Good fighters. Better hope all that military *sycha* pays off," Agracia said.

"Didn't you used to fight, Bossy?" Jetta asked, dropping herself down through a break in the walkway. Carefully, Jetta avoided the stairs, most of which were fractured or missing, and slid down a railing.

"You'd better shut your face," Bossy said, popping her lollipop out of her mouth and hopping down behind her.

"Jeez, kid" Agracia chuckled, following them down. "Look, Doc," she said to Jetta, "Bossy's the best there ever was and ever will be. Fighting ring dark horse extraordinaire."

"Where'd you learn?" Jetta asked, trying to get Bossy to think about her fighting days. *Come on,* she thought, hoping for just a fraction of a stray memory. *Give me something so I have a clue about what I going to be up against.*

"It's one of the few professions on Earth, *punte*," Bossy muttered. "I thought I explained that to you. Ain't you supposed to be smart?"

Agracia interjected. "Look, for most of us chicks, you either join the rings or play in the puppet show. There ain't much else 'less you're crazy enough to be a Jock."

It didn't explain much, but Jetta got the gist of it.

As they passed a public notice sign, Jetta spotted the faces of both her captors. Underneath was a telecam signature, but it wasn't for the local police. *Someone else is hunting them.*

Two humans, one missing half of his face and the other a leg, passed them by, bumping into Agracia. Enraged, Bossy shoved them both, sending them spiraling off the catwalk and into the trash piles that lined the floor of the tunnel.

"Haha, suckers," Agracia said, giving them the finger as they screamed profanities.

"Fighting me isn't going to go anywhere," Jetta said as they passed by a group of people huddled near a steam vent. The adults watched the Jocks earnestly, talking quietly amongst each other, keeping a watchful eye. "If I don't fight, if I lose, the two of you are going down with me. It doesn't take a telepath to see all the enemies you have around here."

Jetta glimpsed a child no older than six at the periphery of the group, her skeletal frame topped by a dirty face with starving eyes. She thought of her siblings, and Fiorah.

There was a moment of silence, then a snicker. A warning shot buzzed up her leg and straightened out her spine.

"You are one smart Skirt," Agracia said, bobbing her head to a beat, "but I ain't playin' with you. You fight or you die. Simple as that."

Seemingly unfazed by her argument, her captors shot off expletives to passersby who didn't get out of their way and worse expletives to the ones who recognized their faces.

"What you lookin' at, *assino*?" Bossy yelled at a mother shielding her child from their group.

"Go on back to your sissy business," Agracia said to a group of Jocks standing near a bounty board post. She didn't seem to care about the cash prize listed next to her wanted poster or the scheming looks of the rival tribe.

Jetta remained on high alert as they entered a thoroughfare. Never in her life had she been so lucid, yet so completely stripped of her extrasensory perceptions. She felt naked and deaf, and strangely off guard.

I don't like this feeling, Jetta thought, squeezing her hands into fists. *And these dumb Jocks are going to get us killed before we even get to the fighting rings.*

A big, crackling neon sign illuminated "The Dives." Red and blue arrows pointed every which way, directing the flow of human and human-like traffic toward various destinations. Ramshackle shops clustered together, their vendors selling what looked like recycled material and scraps. Jetta wasn't sure what anybody had to barter with other than Alliance rations and more garbage.

"*Skucheka,*" Jetta muttered, swatting at the pesky black flies that buzzed around her eyes and ears. They were everywhere, and for obvious reasons.

Who the hell runs this dump? she thought as she walked around and over piles of refuse and human waste, concentrating on breathing through her mouth without inhaling too many flies. *Is there any kind of waste management or sanitation effort?*

"*Chak*, this place stinks worse every time we come," Bossy mumbled, wiping her nose with her sleeve.

"There," Agracia said, pointing over Jetta's shoulder. "Head towards the competitors' entrance. Don't say nothing or I'm frying your brain."

Jetta complied, more than happy to get out of the main juncture of the Dives.

She entered a tunnel that looked like it had probably been part of a manmade aquifer. An electric sign that read "Razor Dome" hung over a swollen line of people waiting to get seats near a crumbling archway. Other lines formed near the betting booths where ticket stubs and empty beer cans littered the floor. She wondered how many people had taken bets out on her name.

Another sign, painted in red on broken plyboard, caught her eye. Misspelled and crooked, it read "fighters" but translated to "mongers" in Common. The smell that wafted towards her carried the salty-metallic tang of sweat and blood.

"Keep going, Doctor Death," Agracia said, pushing her forward.

Jetta ducked underneath the fighters' entrance, glad that the Jocks had stripped her of any telling military insignia when she saw the Alliance helmets, uniforms and other paraphernalia decorating the walls. Other trophies made of bones and skin hung from the ceiling next to pictures of the victors and their stats, giving her a gruesome picture of the losers' fate.

Other humans, bigger and stockier than her, gawked as she passed by.

"Holy hell—are they letting kids fight?" a painted and scarred man said as he polished his battle axe.

Another man, covered in tattoos, guffawed. "Look at that shrimp—I take dumps bigger than that."

"Nice mask," a man with one eye said. "You look like a *chakking* freak."

Agracia and Bossy kept them at bay, shouting obscenities right back or making obscenely high bets.

"Go suck it," Bossy said, waving her behind at the man with one eye.

"My fighter's gonna lick each one of you sorry *assinos*," Agracia said. "I'll lay down triple on that."

The entire lot of fighters erupted in laughter, but waved them off and went back to preparing for battle.

"You do look stupid," Agracia commented, nodding to Bossy.

The pint-sized dark horse slipped into the men's locker room. She emerged coolly, tossing Jetta some kind of black helmet with a visor and a pilot's jacket full of holes. "Wear this, Skirt. Don't want you looking *that* stupid."

Eager to get rid of the plastic mask over her face, Jetta accepted the trade. Despite the stink of booze and sweat, the helmet proved a better option. She could see much better and didn't feel as claustrophobic.

Jetta slid her arms into the pilot's jacket, glad that it offered more protection than her torn undershirt. As she adjusted the straps, she listened to Agracia and Bossy harass another fighter.

"Yeah right," Agracia goaded, "you think you could beat Doctor Death? Why don't you nut up and put some money on it?"

"You little pissant. I outta—" the man said, raising the back of his hand to strike. He stopped when Bossy got in his face.

"You outta what?" Bossy said, slurping on her lollipop.

It quickly turned into a scene, and as the Jocks exchanged vulgarities with the fighter, it crossed her mind that these were her only impressions of real Earth humans. The first humans she had encountered were on Fiorah, but they were all hopeless fourth-class Deadskins used for trade or farming. The humans in the Dominion Core were from distinguished lineages that never spoke of Earth as their home. Even the humans in the Alliance Fleet failed to recognize their terrestrial roots.

Now that she was here and watching Bossy once again flash her bare backside, she knew why. Given her own appearance, there was a strong possibility that part of her was human, but she didn't want even a remote association with this place or its people. *Earth and its inhabitants are disgusting and wretched; I can't imagine having any kind of genetic link to these rats.*

"We'll see who's laughing when the smoke clears," Agracia said, pulling Jetta into another hallway as she spouted off her last insults to the other fighters. "Then I'll go console your mamas when we smoke your sorry *assinos.*"

Under direction of the Jocks, Jetta rounded several corners until she reached a long hallway lined with metal doors bearing painted numbers and tiny eye slits. A borrowed memory gave her the notion that they were old airlock doors from twentieth century submarines.

"You're lucky number seven. Better hope you do good, Skirt, or you'll be wishing you died in that crash," Agracia said, pressing the control panel to the right of the door. The door slid up, and Bossy shoved her inside the holding box.

"You know this is ridiculous," Jetta said, banging her fist against the concrete wall. "Let me go."

"Look, if you make it to the finals, we'll discuss your release," Agracia said.

Bossy rolled her eyes and sucked loudly on her lollipop.

Even without her telepathy Jetta knew Agracia was lying, but the buzzing shock cuff kept her anger from building into anything more than a hot feeling in her chest.

The holding box door slid down and locked, immersing her in near pitch blackness, save the slivers of light that poked through the cracks. Jetta squatted down and put her hands together, calming herself as best she could. Fear and anger boiled in her stomach as she concentrated on slowing her breathing and increasingly rapid heart rate.

The noise of the chanting crowd rose steadily behind the second door that lead to the fighting ring. Something or someone was getting the audience excited. Jetta pressed her eye to the space between the wall and the door to get a better look. From what she could see, the ring was carpeted with sand or dirt. Blocks of concrete were scattered about, with heaps of bones and a few broken weapons peeking out from underneath the rubble. There wasn't action she could see. At least not yet.

Out of nervous habit, Jetta rubbed the back of her neck. It felt unusually sore, and when she touched the spot where her biochip used to be, her arms and legs tingled. She thought back to Dr. Kaoto's warning: *"Improper removal of a biochip can cause hallucinations, seizures, paralysis—even death."*

"*Skucheka,*" she whispered, rapping her head with her knuckles. *This can't be happening now, especially not when I'm about to fight.*

Her concern about the biochip faded into the background as the announcer called for the crowd's attention.

"*Laaaaadies and gentlemen,* welcome to the night's main event! We have a phenomenal show for you today here at the Razor Dome. We promise you the best, most gruesome fights Old Earth has to offer!"

The crowd cheered wildly.

Jetta doubled over and hugged her stomach. *There is so much energy in the air, so many charged emotions.*

The cuff started to vibrate on her ankle, and her mouth immediately went dry, her body anticipating the awful consequence to follow if she couldn't control herself.

Block them out! she commanded herself. She had done it thousands of times before, having learned how to protect herself from dangerous minds when she was very little. Why couldn't she do it now?

Something is different—

Something unbound inside her like an uncoiling snake. She gritted her teeth.

—Their emotions are so much stronger in my head—

"Do you want to see blood?" the announcer asked.

"Yes!" the crowd screamed back.

Beads of sweat soaked into the helmet's padding. Her heart pounded in her chest, driving a curious need to the forefront of her awareness. *Block them out!*

(You don't want to,) a dark voice whispered inside her. *(Let them inside you. Let them nourish you.)*

"Do you want to see carnage?" the announcer cried.

The crowd responded even louder this time. *"Yes!"*

Jetta pawed at the buzzing shock cuff, trying in vain to remove it. The voice inside her grew impatient, its hunger carving into her belly. *(Let them inside you!)*

The announcer lowered his voice. "Do you want to see *death?*"

Adrenalized, the crowd surged. Jetta fell flat on her back as electricity danced through her body. The shock, small by comparison to the whopping doses from Bossy and Agracia, left her trembling and nauseous.

After several heart-pounding minutes, Jetta pulled herself back up.

I'm okay, she told herself repeatedly. (*At least the voice is gone.*)

The observation came with little comfort. Whatever it was inside her that had reacted to the bloodlust of the crowd would have taken control of her if it hadn't been for the shock cuff. Jetta shuddered at the thought.

What is happening to me?

With no time to wallow, Jetta wedged herself into the break as far as she could to watch the first fight. Two humans, outfitted with terrestrial weapons, circled each other in the sand. One wielded a chainsaw with a broken motor and wore an iron mask crowned with a column of spikes. The other, large and lumbering, held a mace in each hand and let out a roaring shriek as he charged.

This is a poorly matched fight, Jetta thought as the crowd cheered on the fighters. The larger man with the two maces moved with surprising speed, making a raw, pulpy mess of the fighter with the broken chainsaw. Jetta backed up to avoid the spray of blood but didn't look away as the man with the maces finished the job with obvious delight.

(*You want more.*)

Jetta shook her head and braced her stomach. *I don't want these thoughts!* She squeezed her eyes shut and thought of her siblings. *They would be so ashamed of me.*

Her eyes popped open at the victor's battle cry. With sickened fascination she watched as he wound his opponent's pink intestines around his neck like a wreath.

This is very, very wrong—I shouldn't like this, Jetta thought, breathing hard as unwanted and frightening feelings percolated through her mind. She tasted the victor's savagery, and the growing need of the crowd.

(*Blood.*)

"Torjas! Torjas! Torjas!"

(*Death.*)

The audience chanted his name, calling for more, feeding the unwelcome hunger in her belly until she didn't want to hear his name anymore.

No, me, she thought, smiling. *I want the crowd to cheer for me.*

The shock cuff buzzed. Jetta bit her lip and braced her head in her hands as fear subdued the fires inside her.

(Do not let anything stop you,) the voice called.

"No," she whispered back. *Oh Gods—I'm either going to be taken by the ferocity of the stadium and be electrocuted to death—or I'll go insane.*

"And now, for your entertainment," the announcer said. "I am pleased to introduce our newest fighter. The most sinister of all criminal masterminds, the most notorious killer—the bane of mankind. I give you Doctor Death!"

"Please, help me," Jetta pleaded to any listening deity as holding box rattled to life. The door leading to the arena groaned and squeaked as it lifted off its cradle.

"Fight good. *Or else*," Agracia said from behind the first door.

Jetta stayed in the cage. The audience booed and hissed, some throwing things at her, but she didn't budge. *They didn't know what's at stake.*

(They don't know your power.)

"Get in there," Agracia said. The shock cuff gave her a zap, sending a bolt rocketing up to her skull.

"You don't know what you're doing!" Jetta said between gasps. The back of her neck tingled where she had dug out the biochip, tensing her arms and legs. "This is a really bad idea."

"Quit the drama," Agracia replied apathetically.

Not wanting to be shocked again, Jetta collected herself off the floor and stumbled into the ring.

Jetta had made public appearances after the defeat of the Motti, and she had stood in front of audiences both celebratory and incensed, but nothing in her life had prepared her for the thunderous mass of the fighting-ring crowd. Concrete benches sloped up and away from the center stage in tiers; Jetta counted at least forty rows through the strata of cigarette smoke before they became too hard to differentiate. People, packed in shoulder to shoulder, became a sea of movement and unfiltered energy surrounding her on all sides.

Panting for breath, Jetta tasted the salty dampness of blood and perspiration lingering in the air. *I'm going to suffocate—*

Instinctively she took cover behind one of the blocks of concrete in the ring, trying to shield herself from the bombardment of infectious lust that electrified the dome within the inner dimensions.

I have to calm down, she thought as the crowd roared and cheered. *I have to think.*

For the second time since she arrived on Earth, she found herself thanking the stars for something she normally despised. She closed her eyes, sifting through her borrowed memories, holding onto the experiences that could see her through this. Every officer she had ever gleaned memories from had advanced combat training, and between the courses she had taken in the Dominion Academy and the Alliance military, she had a thousand lifetimes of fighting experience.

After taking a deep breath, she opened her eyes. *I can do this.*

Even without the borrowed experience, her brief time on Fiorah fighting bigger kids and surviving the mines was physically tougher than anything she would ever face again. *The most important thing is to keep my wits,* she told herself. *I can't let my anger—or the crowd's violent desires—get to me.*

Calmer, Jetta took in her surroundings. The dome had been cheaply constructed. Most of the material looked like scrap metal, bringing together various eras of spaceflight, sea voyage, and land exploration. She noticed the flattened shell of an old gas-operated car integrated into the arched support structure and the wing of an airplane used as a cross-beam. The long, empty fuselage of what was probably a shuttle rocket had been halved, giving rise to refreshment booths behind the rows of people.

Satisfied with her initial assessment, she studied to the center of the dome. Precariously hung above the ring was a thicket of projection and recording gear, most of which looked broken. A big spotlight was trained on the announcer hovering safely above the floor in a lift as he read from a list of sponsors. Jetta determined that he was not an ideal target, even if she could find a projectile to throw at him. *He isn't the one holding the remote.*

Jetta analyzed the hotwire fence that separated the fighters from the audience. It crackled and fizzed as the audience hurled bottles and garbage toward the ring. Having been shocked more times than she ever wanted, she decided that breaking through it was probably not an option she wanted to explore.

"Fighting Doctor Death is your hometown hero, Rigger Mortis!" the announcer said.

Jetta looked for weapons lying around but didn't find much that would be helpful, especially when she saw her competition.

Skucheka—

A tall, muscular man, battle-worn and heavily armored, stepped through the cage doors on the other side of the arena.

Well, at least he's human, Jetta thought, spotting his sidearm and a large hunting knife.

Doubt edged its way into her thoughts. *Those two idiot Jocks are probably betting heavily on me because of my reputation and capabilities—but they've handicapped me without my talents.*

Besides, she said, testing the soreness of her broken arm. *I'm not fully recovered, and I've never fought for sport.*

Inner demons replied: *(But you've fought to survive,)* they said, conjuring up conflicting images of a smoldering starships and dead child laborers. *(And won.)*

"Come on, little one!" Rigger Mortis said, taking out his firearm and aiming it at her head. "You're making this too easy."

Jetta didn't move. *This is cheap,* she seethed. *It's a mockery of everything I've ever endured.*

All of it—the crowd cheering for her death, the announcer goading her to fight, Agracia and Bossy screaming obscenities back at the crowd—was a joke.

I risked everything to save the Starways, these people, and this is how they repay me? Bloodbath for sport, the thrill of brutality—a primitive form of entertainment. I don't understand it.

(You understand it all too well.)

She didn't feel the bullet that grazed her shoulder, ripping through her flesh. The voice inside her took away her pain and fear.

(You understand what they want. Give it to them.)

Jetta stood transfixed by the dark whisperings, oblivious to her enemy.

(They care nothing for you. Give them what they seek.)

A seed of anger, small and hot, flared in her chest. With every beat of her heart it grew hotter and hotter, stirring a rumble in her throat, a curious ache in her limbs. Pure, mindless reflex took over rational thinking. She lost sight of anything that had ever been or ever could be. There was only now, and the terrible need inside her.

Rigger Mortis approached her, unsheathing his hunting knife. Crusts of dried blood and flecks of skin dirtied the blade from earlier kills. She took in the scar across his nose, the missing teeth in his crooked mouth, his soulless eyes. *Yes, I see you.*

Focused and precise, he locked in on her position. She sensed his enjoyment, his lethal skill, stirring the darkest echoes of her past.

(He is all that you despise.)

Something snapped. As he thrust his knife towards her belly, she shot to one side, smashing her knee into his gut and throwing her body weight against his. Not expecting her to move so quickly or hit so hard, he fell backwards, his left arm shattering against a sharp edge of concrete. He screamed in pain as white bone poked through skin, and the crowd went wild.

He dropped the knife. It lay at his feet as he cradled his broken arm, but she didn't move to take it. When he lunged for it, she kicked it away, standing over him, staring into his eyes, waiting for him to make his move. No longer emotional, Jetta allowed her instincts to guide her, fear and apprehension transforming into cold calculation.

(Let them taste your power.)

He reached for his sidearm, but Jetta kicked him square in the face, breaking his nose, blood spurting from his nostrils. Dazed, Rigger Mortis tried to stand up, but she swept his feet out from under him, and he cracked his head against the concrete block. Blood and saliva frothed at the corners of his mouth as he collapsed to the ground, body jerking.

"The winner!" the announcer called. The crowd went wild, chanting and screaming. Jetta didn't immediately recognize the English word, but after the announcer pointed his thumb towards the ground, she inferred his meaning. "The crowd has spoken!"

I have to end the match, she realized. Conflicted, she looked up to see Agracia and Bossy in the stands, laughing and throwing their beer bottles at the hotwire, jubilant at their victory.

Jetta looked back down at her competitor. *What am I doing?*

The sanguineous hunger bubbled up from deep inside her. *(Taste the copper of his blood as it spills from his body. Watch as the light in his eyes dies. Feel the crimson wetness on your hands when the fragile pulse of life inside him stills.)*

Yes, she thought. *This is what I want.*

The voice within the shadows whispered ever so sweetly to her. *(Feel his fear.)*

Jetta tipped her head back and smiled, the terror of Rigger Mortis tantalizing her senses. The shock cuff buzzed wildly, but she didn't care. Not now, not when she was this close to sating her darkest desires.

(Kill him.)

Before she knew it, her hands wrapped around her competitor's neck. His face turned red as she increased the pressure, the fire in her belly burning hot as Rigger Mortis struggled helplessly.

I am powerful—indomitable—insatiable—

The crowd went wild, chanting her name, the entire dome rumbling with the thrills of the audience.

"Doctor Death! Doctor Death!"

(KILL HIM.)

A familiar voice whispered in her ear from across the stars. *(Listen to yourself.)*

Something inside her gave way. A feeling of interconnectedness overcame her, one that she had only felt when Jahx was near, jerking her away from her fury. As the magnitude of her desires paled, an empty coldness settled into her stomach.

"What am I doing?" she whispered, slowly releasing her grip as the nauseating reality took hold.

Jetta looked at her hands, suddenly confused. *I'm not a killer—am I?* The faces of her brother and sister flashed through her mind. *No, I'm the protector, even though I've had to fight for everything in my life*, she thought bitterly.

Another voice sounded from the deeps. *(But you don't have to be a murderer.)*

The voice from the shadows laughed. *(You're weak, like Jahx. His compassion was his undoing.)*

"No!" Jetta screamed, racking her head with her fist. *I am not a killer!*

Jetta choked back her tears as she knelt beside her competitor, taking his head in her hands. The crowd screamed and cheered, but instead of finishing him off, she bent forward, touching his forehead, trying to glean his essence before it was too late.

The shock cuff zapped her back, sending her to the ground. She crawled away coughing and wheezing while the crowd booed and hissed.

"Looks like Doctor Death needs a little help," the announcer said. "Send in the pack!"

The crowd roared with excitement. Instinctively Jetta grabbed for Rigger Mortis' hunting knife and sidearm as a series of sirens blasted overhead. Keeping low, she ran toward cover as the lights dimmed and generated fog poured from two of the holding boxes.

I can handle more than one thug, she told herself as the spotlights veered towards the cage doors opening to her left.

A hush came over the crowd. Low growls resonated from the cages, and through the smoke Jetta caught a glimpse of hungry yellow eyes.

That's not human—

Cursing in Fiorahian, Jetta snuck behind a concrete pillar, trying to get a better view. To her surprise, Rigger Mortis had come around, rolling on his side and propping himself up against the concrete block.

"Give me the gun!" he screamed at her, his eyes wild with fear. "Give me the *chakking* gun!"

Sensing the changing nature of the competition, Jetta slid it to him.

A large, gray paw stepped out of the cage. Then two. Four. A massive wolf emerged, his body low to the ground, ears pinned back. Another wolf, this one black and missing an eye, darted around the ring, circling Rigger Mortis and Jetta. Two more emerged, one a lighter gray and the other white, white fangs glistening as they all spread out around the ring.

Jetta climbed up on top of a pillar as Rigger Mortis shot wildly at the gray wolf. The massive creature dodged his bullets with surprising speed and grace, then leapt into the air and came down on Rigger Mortis with his entire weight.

"Help me!" he screamed just before the wolf tore out his throat. The crowd reacted with deafening approval, the lights in the dome flickering until the fanfare died down.

This is no place to hide, she thought as she watched the pack devour her former competitor in less than fifteen seconds. *I've never seen—or stolen memories of—wolves this huge. They must be genetically manipulated, or have mutated by the planet's poisons.*

They circled her, growling and snapping their blood-stained teeth, the white and black ones taking turns lunging at her.

They've got to be at least 95 kilograms, she guessed, dodging their attacks. *There's little chance I could take out one of them, let alone four.*

Unless...

(I have to use my talents.)

She looked to Agracia and Bossy, who sat motionless in their chairs, no longer jubilant as they faced the certain loss of their investment. She cracked up the visor of her helmet so only her lips were visible.

"Please," she mouthed, pointing to her head.

The ankle cuff powered down.

Before she could react, the black wolf swept her off her perch. She crashed hard into the sand, little black motes dotting her vision. Another set of teeth gnashed into her shoulder as she tried to scoot away.

Knife still in hand, she thrust her weapon at the closest attacker. The white wolf yelped as the blade sunk deep into its hip, making the others draw back.

Jetta dizzily got to her feet, waving the knife in front of her. The wolves circled around, lips writhing, fangs dripping, readying for their next meal.

"You will not have me!" she shouted.

Teeth bared, she stretched out her mind, connecting with the animals that hunted her. But she had never touched the mind of an intelligent wild animal before, and she was wholly unprepared for the experience.

Jetta dropped to her knees, her eyes blind to the world around her. She fell backwards, feeling teeth close down on her neck, the black veil of death upon her.

***

Jaeia sat in the observatory under the light of the stars, trying to remember a peaceful time. There was a brief period after the Final Front where she and her sister celebrated hope and, strangely enough, their newfound celebrity and wealth, but it wasn't what stood out in her mind.

Closing her eyes, she chose to reawaken her happiest memories.

Before Lohien was taken away and Galm withdrew, she thought, going back to their days on Fiorah. *And Jetta, Jahx and I weren't sick and forced into endless labor.*

Seeing her ragtag family again in the back of her mind made her smile. She heard the sound of her aunt and uncle preparing dinner in the kitchen as she and her siblings tore through the first apartment playing another made-up game.

It didn't matter that we were poor, she thought, remembering the strong feel of her uncle's arms as he helped her up to the kitchen counter to sample the stew. *We were together.*

Jaeia took a deep breath and flipped open her remote interface pad, redirecting her thoughts. She had come to the Central Starbase's observatory so she could investigate what she had absorbed from Triel in privacy. *I have to know who or what "Rion the Abomination" is.*

Using the remote system was not as easily traceable as it would have been in her quarters, but she didn't want to take too many chances. After creating a false identity, she patched into the wave network's datastream, knowing that she would have limited time to surf undetected before the Alliance safety nets stopped her unauthorized query.

Rion, the Abomination, she entered into the search engine. Nothing came up.

"Okay," Jaeia said, typing in a new search. *Folklore, Algar.*

Limited hits came back. Records from Algar were few, but she had hoped that the Homeworlds' historical societies would have tried to preserve some of its people's history for public access.

Not expecting much, she clicked on the closest hit. A brief summary of a Prodgy legend filled her screen.

In the year 100 LL, the Prodgies of Algar faced an unstoppable enemy with the power of the Gods. By uniting their tribes, the Prodgies drew upon their communal strength and defeated their nemesis. The colossal victory broke the cycle of violence that had reigned over Algar since the dawn of time. The Gods, pleased with the people, granted them the gift of healing.

Jaeia bit her lip. *I have to know more.* She ran searches on the final battle on Algar and the Gods, but they returned nothing useful.

"Tell me about this 'enemy.'"

One hit. She clicked on the journal logged by a graduate student at the University of Trigos at Sinani on the origins of telepathy. Most of it was what she already knew about the evolution and mechanism of telepathy. But the student also touched on another topic: the myths of Algar.

"My Continued Research on the Origins and Myths of Prodgy Talents" by Antonne Delphius: 3033.011

...Despite the strong evolutionary support for the adaptive function of telepathic powers, the Healers of Algar maintain that their powers were gifted to them by the divine. The history of their people is strongly guarded, and outsiders are strictly forbidden from learning the origins of their healing abilities. Even younger members of the tribes are limited in their knowledge, and to speak of it is punishable by death, a law that contradicts the pacifist nature of these people.

From my research on the planet conducted from 3030.114–3032.353, I concluded that the development of their healing powers seems to have taken place between 200–50 LL, coinciding with what little is known of their legends.

Although it cost me some hard-earned privileges with my cousin Amargo, I learned of a man named Saol who had been at the heart of the last war on Algar, right before the Healers claimed they were given their telepathic powers. Further research needs to be conducted on this person of interest so that we may understand the evolutionary process of telepathy, specifically those of Healers. My research indicates that the Temple of Exxuthus, a place that it is said no man can reach, will be the primary source of such knowledge.

Jaeia's sleeve vibrated, diverting her from the journal entry. With a sigh she closed down the remote interface and looked down at her arm. The message on her uniform sleeve, encoded and prioritized, flashed in red.

After taking one last look at the swirling light of the nebulous stars, she accepted the message. *It's probably going to be an assignment for another back-to-back shift or new orders for a Contact mission.*

"What?" she muttered. From the structure it appeared to be an internal message, but the length of the alphanumerics riding the link made her think a code had been piggybacked.

Late for dinner again. Sorry. The man on fire knows my excuse.

Jaeia scanned the message for viruses. Negative. She checked the source: unknown sender. If it had piggybacked into the system, then she had no way of tracing it anyway.

Jaeia saved it to her personal files and was about to send it to the chief of security when the message repeated in her head.

Late for dinner again. Sorry. The man on fire knows my excuse.

Is it from Jetta? she wondered. *Or one of our intelligence agents?*

Jaeia ran her hand along the bench, fingertips rubbing the smooth wood grain. *No, it can't be.* She and Jetta had a few dozen secret code languages that they used if they needed to communicate openly, and her intelligence agents never made contact via her personal com-link. *This is someone who wants only my eyes to see this message, who needs to stay undercover—somebody who wants me to find them.*

The man on fire…

Who do I know who fits that description?

Her eyes darted back and forth as she flipped through a mental list of people that might plausibly contact her like this. *Mantri Sebbs possesses an unusual knack for computer hacking. It could be him. After all, he'd want to stay undercover after escaping from the Alliance guard.*

Jaeia was about to call up one of her agents when the floor beneath her quaked. She tilted her head at the sound of a secondary explosion in the distance.

"Commander Kyron—there's been a breach in cargo bay seven," the duty officer informed her over the com. She let her mind stretch out beyond the observatory, sensing what had happened even before the duty officer finished his report. "CMA Triel stole one of the starships and jumped too close to the base. Part of the science deck has been obliterated."

Jaeia scooped her hair up and tied it in a knot, readying herself. "Where did they take Reht? That's where she's going."

The officer paused. "It's classified, Sir; only the Minister has access to that information."

Jaeia shut off the com and took off for the Minister's office, ignoring her officer's repeated pages. *I've always played the peacemaker, but not anymore. I want answers, even if I have to force them from the Minister. The lives of my sister and friends are too important to leave to negotiation.*

Jaeia took one of the lifts up to the highest level of the starbase, keeping her composure. However, when the Minister's secretary asked for her to wait for his clearance, she dodged the guards and stormed her way through the double-doors.

Inside, Unipoesa and the Minister Razar hovered over a communications display. They both looked up when she walked in, the Minister shutting off the panel as soon as he recognized her.

"Commander," the Minister said, stepping out from behind the display. "What are you doing here?"

"If you're not straight with me, right here and now, I will resign from the Starways Alliance. Where is the crew of the *Wraith*?" she said, shaking off the guards.

"Leave her. Resume your posts," the Minister said quietly to the guards. They withdrew, closing the doors behind them.

By the shock on Unipoesa's face, Jaeia knew that he had had no part in whatever had gone down between the Alliance and the dog-soldiers. However, the Minister, his face cold and hard, lips parted slightly, reeked of deception.

"They are safe, Commander," the Minister said. "We merely transferred them to a frigate. They are being transported right now, as we speak, to the outer worlds."

Despite his stringent Rai Shar, Jaeia detected the half-truth. "What frigate?"

The Military Minister took one step towards her, straightening his back to appear more confident than he felt. "You'll be able to contact them once they've cleared the jump sites."

"The *Hixon*," Unipoesa said, searching a nearby terminal. "They were discharged to the *Hixon*."

Jaeia sorted through her mental catalog of ships as Razar shot the admiral a contemptuous look.

"That ship was retired years ago," Jaeia said, approaching Razar. "It was an old science and research vessel."

Razar got in her face. "They are *safe*. Safer now than ever. They are being taken care of, and you will be able to contact them yourself when they've cleared the asteroid belt."

Jaeia didn't believe him for a minute. "Are you tracking Triel?"

The Minister leaned in, enough so that she had to take a step back. "Our resources are stretched thin, Commander, trying to investigate the matter of the communications blackout on the perimeter, chasing after your sister, babysitting the dog-soldiers—and now finding our resident Healer."

"I understand that, Sir, but—"

"Oh, and let's not forget," he interrupted, "trying to resurrect my dead niece and her companions. In light of this, I would appreciate it if you performed your assigned duties and attended the appointed council meetings. Barging in on our affairs only delays the kind of resolution we are all hoping to achieve."

"You promised me full access on Reht, and I've yet to get those clearance codes, Minister," Jaeia tried.

The Minister's face turned severe. "Get out of my office, Commander. You'll get those codes when the Fleet is secured."

Despite her frustration, her instincts told her it wasn't time to play her hand just yet. She withdrew, catching the admiral's eye before she left.

With her mind on her sister, she walked down the corridor, passing up offers for a lift. As she reviewed her options and her next course of action, a psionic whisper stopped her dead in her tracks.

(The forest is dead. The hunt is dead. There are only ashes. I want to go home.)

"Jetta," she whispered, falling to her knees. Several soldiers rushed to her aide, one easing her to the floor as her awareness shifted in and out of the psionic connection.

(I want to go home.)

Her eyes are sharp, her sense of smell even sharper. On four legs instead of two, she runs toward an opening in the trees, instincts guiding every move. She scans the mountainous horizon, turning her nose into the wind, detecting the scent of blood. A dense fur coat protects her from the crisp winter air.

"Commander, Commander!" someone shouted.

Time shifts forward. The soft glow of the moon illuminates the treetops of the forest below as she stands on the edge of the cliff. She smells her family nearby and her heart fills with joy. The hunt was good, and her packmates are safe.

She raises her elongated snout to the stars and gives off a cry into the still night air. Soaring upward with eerie fervency toward its apex, the howl fades away and then begins again, this time in chorus with the other voices of her kind. The ancient song, one that she feels deep within her bones, has been sung since time immemorial.

(I want to go home.)

Time leaps forward again. The forest is ablaze, sky blackened by smoke, the world turned to ash. Gunshots and trampling footsteps approach.

(The pack is dead.)

All alone she runs, but there is nowhere left to go.

(Home—)

Something snaps down on her back leg. Struggling only intensifies the pain, but it is all that she can do as the men with guns step out from behind dead trees.

"Get the medic!"

Jaeia tried to break from the link, but it was too strong—

A steel collar weighs down her neck. In the darkness she can barely make out the chain linking her to the bolts in the wall. Panicked, she thrashes about, but to no avail. Giving in to exhaustion, she collapses to the cold floor, very aware of the eyes watching her from the safety of the shadows.

Images blur and reform. Men with clubs appear, taunting and teasing her between beatings, giving her the taste of a hatred she could have never imagined in the forest world.

(Please, home—)

A new time comes in to view. Food is scarce, and the only way to eat is by killing the men in the ring. The lights stings her eyes and the chanting hurts her ears. Worse yet, the human flesh tastes vile, but it satisfies the anger burning in her heart.

(You are not Jetta. Who are you?) *she whispered as another vision formed.*

The smell of alcohol and antiseptic is strong, making her nose twitch. She can't see, but she can feel the prick of the needle and the pain of the injection as several men hold her down. It is like this every day, as is the sickness that shortly follows. But she's getting bigger, stronger, and the taste of man-flesh becomes a violent need...

As Jaeia came to, she felt her body being lifted onto a stretcher. *I've never experienced anything like that before.*

"Put me down—I'm okay," she said over and over again until the medics finally relented.

"Sir, I recommend you check into the infirmary," the lead medic said, stepping in her way as she tried to catch a lift on wobbly legs.

If Triel was there, Jaeia thought to herself, rubbing her blurry eyes. *I should never have left her alone. Or Jetta. This is my fault.*

She thanked the soldiers and the medics before she caught the lift.

"Where to, Commander Kyron?" the autofunction asked.

Still dizzy from the psionic immersion, she stared at the flashing display, unsure of where to go. *I need to report to duty and work on my mission assignment, but I can't disregard my other priorities.* Most importantly, she reasoned, she needed to understand what had just happened to her. *That vision was definitely from Jetta, but it was not Jetta's, and it did not seem conventionally Sentient.*

Without Jetta or Triel it was going to be difficult. That left her with only one option.

"*Shead,*" she cursed in Fiorahian, directing the lift to take her to the Division Lockdown Labs. The only way to narrow it down without telepathic talents was to use the broad access, super-processing "Hub" system.

"Dr. DeAnders," Jaeia called, hopping off the lift and running down the main corridor of the Defense/Research department. "I need to speak to you!"

DeAnders turned from his computer station, adjusting the secondary scope on his glasses. "Commander—this is unexpected."

"I need your help."

DeAnders lowered his voice, making sure his words didn't carry. "Commander, I'm sorry, I'm due in the cryostasis labs. We're trying a new re-feeder process with the datastream to see if we can attempt another download with the Exiles again."

"It will only take a moment," she said. "Is the Hub available?"

DeAnders tilted his head, nonplussed. "Considering your previous opposition to the program, Commander, I'm surprised that you ask."

"I know, but I'm out of options, and this concerns my sister. It might be the key to finding her."

"You'll need help with the interface module."

Jaeia raised an eyebrow. He knew her better than that to assume that she hadn't already picked up how to work the machine.

The doctor looked at her over the tops of his glasses. "Oh, right. Well, I still need to accompany you for security purposes. Let's make this quick."

Jaeia followed the doctor into the lab housing one of the three gigantic computer processors used for complex queries and research programs. Only accessible by select Alliance staff, the experimental Hubs were under top-secret lockdown, kept quiet so as not to alert A.I. watch groups.

Jaeia seated herself in one of the accessory chairs to allow DeAnders space to interact with the computer.

"Welcome, Dr. DeAnders. Welcome, Commander Kyron," the computer said as it came to life, illuminating the room in hues of green, blue, and red. Imagining itself as a human liaison, the computer projected an image of an old man with an abnormally large head full of wild, fuzzy hair.

"What are we calling ourselves today?" DeAnders said, typing in several commands into the keyboard.

"Ennui," the computer said, talking with a lisp in a high-pitched male voice. "That's our name."

DeAnders looked annoyed as he typed in several more commands.

"It hurts when you do that to us," the Hub whined as DeAnders checked the circuit links, making adjustments to keep the Hub's network within definable parameters.

Jaeia had been against the tailoring of the Hub, especially if it was truly evolving into a Sentient being, but since she, like many others, used the Hub to complete critical mission objectives, her arguments for its freedom were typically snubbed.

"Go ahead with your query," DeAnders said to her, leaning far to the left to type something in the two-meter long keyboard.

"Ennui, I'm going to describe feelings, sensations, and visual data," Jaeia said. "I need you to help me narrow it down to potential places and species."

"Go ahead, Commander."

With as much detail as she could remember, Jaeia described the vision as Ennui floated up and down in the Hub's projection field, nodding his head and changing the axis of his body's rotation.

"Yes, Commander. The subject you are describing has a 64 percent probability of being the species known as *Canis lupus*, and when cross-matched with the probable location, the probability is 99.5 percent."

"Probable location?"

"Earth," the Hub replied. "Original homeland of the human

race. Oftentimes referred to as 'Old Earth.'"

Earth. The revelation threw her mind into a spin.

"Somewhere dead," she mumbled, remembering what Triel had said. *It all makes sense now.*

Earth was the birthplace of the fighting rings, and she had heard that wolves and stray dogs were used to "clean up" the leftover stragglers. Furthermore, the cross she had seen in Jetta's dream would make sense on that world. *That's most likely a crucifix, a relic from an ancient human religion.*

"Jetta must have gleaned off of a wolf—but that means she's in the fighting ring," Jaeia thought aloud. She gripped the armrests of the chairs, panicked. "I can't feel her anymore."

"I'll make a report and send it through the chain of command," DeAnders said, compiling a dataset.

"Yes," Jaeia said, bolting up from the chair and heading for the door. She stopped before she exited. "Thank you, Ennui."

"A pleasure, Commander. Oh, and Ennui is not our real name. It is simply how we are," the Hub said.

"What do you mean?" Jaeia said, looking at DeAnders, but his eyes stayed trained on the interface.

The Hub saluted her as DeAnders shut down the system.

"What did the Hub mean?" Jaeia asked.

DeAnders pursed his lips. "The Hub says a lot of things we don't understand."

Jaeia reluctantly pushed the issue aside; she would have to address it later. Right now there were much more pressing matters.

"How did she end up jumping there?" DeAnders inquired, following her as she rushed out the door. "More importantly, how did she ever *survive* the jump? The atmospheric firestorms on that planet have been known to tear apart most spacecraft."

"I don't know," Jaeia said, calling the senior staff for an emergency meeting on her uniform sleeve. "I just hope we're going to be able to get her back out."

***

Triel was programming the ship's search parameters when she noticed the bluish-green tinge to her veins. Her skin, usually silky and white, had taken on a grayish cast.

"No," she said out loud.

"Please repeat command," stated the onboard computer.

"I'm not talking to you!" she yelled.

Tilting her head back, Triel took a deep breath, trying to calm herself. As much as she tried to find balance, the discord flowing through her veins, the polarizing push and pull that divided her thoughts, injected anger into every heartbeat. *I'm out of control.*

Reht and the others are all I have left, she tried to reason with herself. *I have to find them.*

Nostalgic feelings pushed down her anger for a brief moment. *Reht, my first love; the man who rescued me and gave me a home.* Phantom fingers traced the curve of her hips; she felt his chapped lips on her cheek. *I miss you.*

But by following him, she was abandoning her duties to the displaced telepaths of the war, along with Jetta and Jaeia.

Jetta, oh Gods. How could I leave her now, in a time of need? Triel pressed her hands into her chest, trying to stifle the ache. *Jetta is one of the few people who listens to me and asks for nothing in return. She is always there when I need it, whether I know it or not.*

Thinking of Jetta, the Healer realized a deeper truth: *I've not only grown accustomed to the tune of Jetta's mindscape—*

Comforting warmth spread across her chest.

—I long for it.

(But she left you!) said an ugly voice inside her, stripping away her joy.

Jaeia's voice popped through her thoughts. *Earth! She's on Earth! Help me find Jetta. Come back; she's in danger. There is nothing you can do for Reht and the others right now...*

Triel smashed her fist against the console. *This is all Jaeia's fault, not mine. She pushed Jetta away.*

The ugly voice added vitriol: *(And she could have done so much more to secure Reht's safety, but she didn't.)*

That's not entirely true, Triel thought, trying to pull back from her anger.

The radar blipped, diverting her attention. Triel pushed her thoughts aside and studied the reading. *The signal is weak, but it originated from the north pole of an orbiting body of this star system's fifth planet.*

From the constant running and hiding of her dog-soldier life, she knew it was a simple strategy that ships employed to evade standard radar. And luckily for her, she had stolen a beta-class fighter, a ship with the technology to detect even a minor fluctuation in the planet's atmospheric readings.

Good thing they were so afraid of me, she thought, remembering the fear in the eyes of the Alliance soldiers when she threatened to liquefy the organs of anyone who tried to stop her from stealing the vessel. *They believed me—that a Healer could be that perverse.*

(But I could.)

She swallowed hard and reexamined the data. Boosting the receiver by rerouting her shields helped her to read the residual signal from the ship, and from there she extrapolated what she needed.

The ship's registry has been erased, she realized. The make of the vessel, which she cross-referenced in the dataport she had taken from her office, was definitely Alliance, though a retired class of starship.

"Someone doesn't want to be detected," she muttered.

Closing her eyes, Triel let her head rest against the back of the chair. She stretched out, calling to Reht, feeling for him, for the tune frequency that had guided her across the stars far better than the aid of her navigational or scanner systems.

"Reht!" she gasped, sensing his familiar presence. Her stomach knotted when she felt his weak and disharmonious psionic rhythms. He was hurt—or worse. Something had changed in him. *I need to get to him quickly—at any cost.*

Plans formulated in her mind, dangerous ones that would only draw her closer to the brink of the Fall.

This is not my fault; the Alliance has left me with no other choice. The Algardrien Healer flexed her hands, feeling the hard knob of anger rise in her chest. *Finally, I can fight for what I believe in instead of taking the passive stance.*

Letting go of her corporeal tethers, Triel allowed herself to fall back and in to the minds aboard the unregistered vessel.

She felt the other presences surrounding Reht and reached out. Their life-cords pulsed and throbbed in her hands, so fragile, so easily crushed.

(Too easy—)

CHAPTER V

The Grand Oblin persisted in his efforts to keep Jahx from drifting off. He questioned him about everything from his life on Fiorah to his days on the Core ships, even his terrible experience with the Motti. Jahx gave him all the answers he could, but fatigue was taking its toll. The apartment shrunk with each waning heartbeat, brittle walls collapsing into dust.

It won't be much longer until I fade away with it, *Jahx thought.*

(What to do, my boy…) *the Oblin said, tapping his walking stick on the ground.*

Jahx sighed and sat down next to the old man. It's too late for me. I should just tell the old man to leave before it's too late for him, too.

A green thread coming off of the priest's robes caught his eye. (Your robe—it's unraveled. Look—) *Jahx said, following a long string around the corner and into the front entrance.* (It's going out the door.)

(Why yes,) *the Oblin said. He gave it a yank, but it remained unbroken.* (I must have snagged my robe when I came in. Would you be a good fellow and free it for me?)

Jahx tried, but the thread was too thick for his hands to tear, and his teeth didn't even fray the exterior.

(Hysian silk from Trigos,) *the Oblin said.* (Very rare. You'll have to trace it back to where it was caught.)

Exhausted beyond the point of rational thinking, Jahx obliged. He opened the front door to his apartment and stepped out, expecting the hallway. But in his deteriorated state, his psionic presence abruptly ended at the front door.

Jahx fell into the vast chasm, unfolding into the nothing. As he spiraled downwards, inwards and outwards, the solitary light illuminating the old number 9 apartment faded into shadow. He flailed, trying to find purchase, anything that would stop his descent.

(Grab on, Jahx!) *the Oblin cried out in the back of his mind.*

Jahx reached out and found the thread of the Oblin's robe. It slid through his hands, slicing through his flesh, but he held on tight, winding his feet around the thread until his fall slowed to a steadied descent. The light from the outside of the apartment door became a faint glimmer in the distance, but as he reoriented himself, he realized there was more than shadow in this place.

(Incredible,) *Jahx said, not believing his eyes. Remnants of other presences passed in and out of his awareness, scattered thoughts and feelings manifested in shimmering, spectral light. Other points of light, like nighttime stars, gave dimension to the dark substance of this place, fluctuating and fading in his visual field.*

Placing hand over hand, he tried to climb back up to the Oblin, but the slippery texture of the Hysian silk made the ascent impossible.

(I can't reach you,) he called to the Oblin.

(Do not be afraid, Jahx,) the Oblin replied. (This is your time.)

Unable to climb up, Jahx looked down to the glowing, iridescent cloud swirling beneath him. As he drew closer, a pulsing sensation touched his skin, and new energy revitalized his soul. He didn't know where he was going or what was happening, but he stopped fighting the descent as he immersed in the wonderful feeling.

Jahx closed his eyes, the radiance of the cloud too brilliant. Without letting go of the thread, he allowed himself to slide into this place of electric warmth, into a feeling he had all but forgotten.

* * *

I want to go home.

Jetta found herself thinking the statement over and over again as she slowly regained consciousness. It felt like days had passed, even weeks, but when she opened her eyes she was still in the arena, surrounded by the wolf pack and pinned down, fanged teeth sunk into the meat of her neck.

I should be dead, she realized as the murmurs of the crowd rose up over the feedback from the announcer's microphone.

"Please," she whispered, pleading with the animal, unable to move as the giant wolf held her down with his paws.

He growled at her, sending vibrations through her body. The animal's rage charged through her, brutal and unfiltered, like nothing she had ever experienced.

(Or have I?)

I remember, Jetta thought. She had run through their forests, hunted as one of them, slept with the pack. Through the eyes of several generations she had watched as the once-fertile Earth turned to ashes, as her family was scattered and her life turned into a living hell fighting for survival in the rings.

The other wolves barked and circled the gray one holding her in his teeth. He growled again, and the pressure of his bite increased.

What do I do? They can't understand me.

Her own primal fear bucked at her mind, calling for her to lash out.

That's it—the animal inside me!

In all her other battles she had evoked her enemy's fear, brought their worst nightmares to life, but with these creatures she found herself unable to do such a thing. For the first time in her life she wrestled with her talent, struggling against its natural flow, straining to give it a new direction.

Digging inside her own memories, Jetta recalled Tralora in sensations and images: Dense emerald forests and cool mountain air. The orange glow of the sunset, the gentle caress of the northerly wind. It wasn't Earth, but it was her first wilderness experience, one that despite the harshness of the environment had stirred a strange calling in her own blood.

Jetta remembered her encounter with the infected, reliving the thrill of the fight, the way her instincts guided her. Reaching deeper, she once again relished in how the pain of her injuries paled against the rush of adrenaline as she fought for her life, and how everything inside her felt more alive.

The fight intermixed with other memories of her past—her brother and sister, her attempts to protect them from everything from child laborers to the Deadwalkers, and her inability to control the tide of events that forever altered their lives.

With waning strength, she projected the collection of impressions outward to the four wild minds, tears streaming down her cheeks in the sudden wake of raw emotion.

Jetta opened her eyes again, her breath caught in her throat. She couldn't tell if it was working, or if the wolves really understood her memories, but when the jaws of the wolf slackened, she didn't waste any time rolling out from beneath him.

The knife was there, and the gun wasn't too far away, but Jetta didn't reach for either. She stayed still, crouching in the sand and holding her breath in the silence that had taken over the entire Razor Dome.

The gray wolf growled again. The others reacted to his cues, the hair on the back of their necks bristling, lips pulled back in a snarl.

But they didn't aggress any further, and neither did Jetta.

I hear you. I know what you want, she whispered silently, but they didn't seem affected.

The crowd grew restless. Some threw bottles of booze at the hotwire, while others started to chant.

"*Kill, kill, KILL!*"

The lead wolf eyed the knife by her feet, but she kicked it away. She didn't think he understood her, but she continued the silent conversation anyway.

I am not going to fight.

He leapt at her, claws gouging the skin of her left hip, sending her stumbling backwards. She stood her ground, eyeing the leader, still refusing to pick up the knife. The other wolves circled her, snapping at her from all sides.

"*Kill, kill, KILL!*"

I know what you want. I can make it real. I can give you back your freedom.

The gray wolf looked at her through yellow, predatory eyes.

Please, she whispered. *I know your pain.*

The alpha straightened his back. Head held high, he looked at her a moment longer and then turned away. The others followed, no longer interested.

As they fought over the last remnants of Rigger Mortis, she breathed a sigh of relief, only to find herself cursing again as she felt the shock cuff power back on.

"A strange turn of events tonight, ladies and gentlemen—a very strange turn," the announcer said. "But tune in tomorrow for the exciting conclusion when Doctor Death faces the deadly Banshee Sisters!"

Sirens blared, and the wolves tucked tail and ran to their cages. Jetta followed suit, returning to her cage as men with flame throwers and guns entered the arena to clean up the mess.

"You are one lucky bastard," Agracia said, lifting the inner door. Jetta shoved her hard against the wall, but before she could go any further, Bossy set off the shock cuff. Her muscles screamed in pain, but at the moment she didn't care; she needed to get her message across.

"I won't do that again," Jetta whispered, rolling onto her side when the punishment had stopped. "You will have to kill me, sell me—whatever you want. I'm not fighting anymore."

Cursing, Agracia picked her headphones off the floor, but paused before she put them back on.

"What is it, Grace?" Bossy asked.

Once again Jetta caught the unusual hesitation, the dread in Agracia's eyes and the shakiness in her hands. *That is the second time in a very short period.*

"You're going to fry!" Bossy screamed at Jetta.

Jetta tried to fight, but Bossy smashed her hand into the remote, sending her into a tonic contraction. As the electricity coursed through her body, muscles exploding with pain, a brilliant aura encircled her field of vision. In the distance she heard a pop and fizzle around her ankle just as it all faded away in a world of black fire.

***

Jaeia was in the briefing room of the *Star Runner* overseeing Acting-Commander Rook's instructions regarding the rescue mission for her sister when it hit her. A euphoric feeling washed over her like a tidal wave, leaving her weak in the knees and bringing tears to her eyes.

"Commander?" one of the troops said as she held fast to the side rail of the staircase.

"As you were, Marine," she whispered.

Jaeia kept her grips, unable to let go as her awareness became sharper, amplified. Every voice in the room seemed ten times louder, and every psionic projection rattled her skull. The whole event lasted only seconds before it dissipated.

What was that? she thought, testing the strength of her legs.

"Commander Kyron," Rook said, offering her the podium on the center stage.

Finally feeling steady enough to let go of the railing, she ascended the stairs and took the podium. Officers and soldiers sat at attention in angled rows, waiting for her to begin her portion of the mission briefing. Still reeling, she started slowly until she was sure she regained all her capacities.

"Despite the efforts of our Intelligence teams, Earth's atmosphere makes it impossible to locate biosigns or cruiser beacons, so we're left with very little in the way of leads," she said, making sure to project her voice to the farthest reaches of the room. "Because of this, we're sending ground teams to perform manual sweeps. A safe landing will be difficult; the firestorms of Earth only allow brief windows of passage. It is an unpredictable event that could take hours, days, weeks—even months."

Jaeia allowed Acting-Commander Rook to discuss the plans for ground deployment and the dangers of radiation, climate exposure, and plague while she readied the projection unit.

"If Commander Kyron is alive, her location will undoubtedly be below ground in one of the pressurized living units, or 'Pits,'" she said as an image of Earth rotated on the axis of the camera. She zoomed in, highlighting Pit locations in red. "These Pits were created as fallout shelters during the Last Great War in 2052, and were expanded when post-war surface temperatures and conditions became inhospitable. Eleven centuries later, we now have thousands of kilometers of uncharted territories. To complicate matters, the residents of Earth are a mixture of humans, Sentient outcasts, and drifters from the Homeworlds. They do not like outsiders, especially from any government or military. Our presence is unwelcome, so navigation will be that much more difficult."

Jaeia switched the projection to cycle through maps.

"We have rough layouts of 226 of the 5,000 known Pits. All are outdated. Even so, I suggest that in the next few hours you study them. Common is spoken by some but not all. These are the major regional dialects," she said, instructing the computer to upload the data into the uniform sleeves of the troops. "You'll need your translators on you at all times."

Jaeia paused. Normally she would offer some sort of insight into the planet's culture and customs per her duty as Contact Team commander, but in this case she found she didn't have any. *I've studied all of the available databases and read all the logs—why can't I think of something?*

(Because I don't want to go.)

Appalled at her own subconscious, Jaeia tried to rationalize her own resistance to the mission. *I must have accidentally gleaned something unfavorable about Earth that I haven't fully realized yet.*

A different answer surfaced from within her innermost thoughts: *(Earth is a bad memory, its history best left forgotten.)*

No, I can't think like that; I have to stay focused on the mission.

Despite herself, she pressed forward. "We have cases of medical supplies, food, water, and clothes, but bribing the locals will only get you so far. Stay in your units, stay together, and report back frequently to your team leader. I will lead the Contact Team's undercover unit to the targeted Pit once we've established probability."

Jaeia allowed Acting-Commander Rook to finish the debriefing as she headed back to her assigned quarters. *Deployment is in less than three hours,* she thought, checking the time on her sleeve. *No time to rest.*

Upon entering her quarters, Jaeia went to the sink and splashed cold water on her face.

"Stay sharp," she said to the tired-looking reflection in the mirror.

I have to get my op reports ready, she thought, but her legs steered her to her bed.

More fatigued than she realized, she laid down facing the window. As the ship raced from site to site on the booster highway, she watched the array of radiant colors streak by. *So beautiful. I wonder if I'll ever get used to this,* she thought, slightly dizzy from the cosmic pull of the jumps.

Her com beeped, and she dragged herself over to her desk.

"Admiral," Jaeia acknowledged as his image took form on her display.

"Jaeia—what's your status?"

"We're almost to Earth. How's the situation on the perimeter? I read that the blackouts have moved into the borderworlds."

"We've sent another squadron out to investigate. Wren's overseeing the mission from remote com."

"How about Triel? Any word?"

"That's what I wanted to talk to you about, Jaeia," he said.

The uncharacteristic way he paused got her attention. *He knows that any transmission is going to be tapped, even on a secure channel.*

Instinctively she allowed her mind to relax, reaching out to him across the stars, finding his mind unusually accessible. *This is a great act of risk—and trust.*

"The ship she stole has been spotted in the same system as the *Hixon*," he said.

The *Hixon*. Jaeia felt his mind fixated on the ship so intensely that the memory shined.

"Has she made contact yet?" she asked.

"Her ship is closing in—fast. Whatever happens, Jaeia, I know she's a good friend to you, and I wanted to assure you that we're doing everything we can to mitigate the situation. I've instructed the commanding officer of the *Hixon* to allow her to board if she engages."

Jaeia bowed her head. "I should be there for her—and Reht. This shouldn't have happened this way."

There was no forgiveness in his voice. "Take care of your sister. I will oversee Triel's return."

The admiral signed out, his image disappearing as the projection camera flipped off.

The Hixon, Jaeia thought, mulling over her next move. *Doing a search on the Alliance network or even my personal computer is too dangerous. I'll have to switch up my tactics.*

It was hard to find his contact signature anymore; the Nagoorian had taken political office again, and his personal messages were filtered and refiltered by his staff of five hundred. But Jaeia ran through the list of his public numbers until she remembered the formula he had given her long ago for decoding his private signature.

"The square of the root of the first number of my campaign signature, multiplied by the number of times I've ever considered resigning from office."

It was his way of trying to be funny.

"Pancar." Jaeia smiled as his image came to life on her desk. "It's good to see you again."

"Same here, Commander," he replied. He looked at her curiously, studying her physique.

It's hard for anyone who hasn't seen me in the past few months to adjust to my adult appearance, she reminded herself, blushing.

"I've heard about the problems on the border," Pancar continued. "I hope it's nothing too serious. I have to address the matter tomorrow at the peace conference."

Jaeia shook her head. "I don't have much to tell you, Pancar, except that we're still investigating the matter. So far we don't have any casualty reports, but we don't have any hard data, either. Just blackouts."

"That's a tough message to sell, Commander." He read her facial features correctly. "I didn't think you called to chat, especially not on this line. How can I be of service?"

I know of your covert ties to Unipoesa, she thought, typing an old proverb from Tauros Prime in a text message. When rearranged with the number sequence she was about to tell him, it repeatedly spelled out *Hixon. You're the admiral's closest confidant, and my only hope for understanding what he wants me to know.*

"Actually, I have to get going. Just wanted to see a friendly face, I guess," Jaeia said. "By the way, I'm considering changing my number to 774-921-423-5836; all my private numbers have been posted on the nets. Just get back to me on that line, okay?"

"I understand," he replied. "Well, for the time being, I might have to hard mail you. The lines are always down during lightning season."

He got the message, and he'd find a way to privatize his response. She smiled and nodded. "Thanks. You've always been a good friend."

Even after the transmission terminated, Jaeia sat staring at the projector, tapping her fingers against the keyboard. *Pancar will probably piggyback his message into my private mailbox—*

Oh Gods—a piggybacked message—

The words catapulted her backwards. She remembered that strange message she had received much earlier: *"Late for dinner again. Sorry. The man on fire knows my excuse."*

Man on fire. She concentrated on it, rolling the idea around in her head, allowing her mind to relax, expand, digging deep into her collective knowledge.

This isn't Sebbs, she intuited. *I don't recognize the word choice or pattern. Still, this is someone who can't risk exposure but needs to contact me very badly—someone who's probably been trying for some time.*

Late for dinner again…

Her sleeve beeped, breaking her thoughts. The message blinked, its originator code reading "Nagoor State House."

That was fast, she thought. *That can't be a good sign.*

Jaeia downloaded the massive content into her personal datafile as she received her first officer's notification that they were nearing Earth.

"I'd better get going," she mumbled, straightening her uniform top and retying her hair.

Unable ignore the flashing red light of the received transmission, Jaeia rechecked the time on her sleeve and gave in to temptation. *I have a few minutes.*

She flipped open the message, unsure of what to expect. When she started reading, she was still an Alliance proponent, proud of her allegiance to the peacekeeping federation of the Starways. But the more she read, the more she realized that things weren't quite what they seemed, and that her worst fears might be true after all.

***

"Come on Jetta," Jahx said, chasing after her through the red and gray apartment. "It's my turn already."

"No way," she said, diving between Galm's legs under the kitchen table. "You hogged it all yesterday. It's my turn to read."

"No, it's mine!" Jaeia said, catching up to them and making her bid to steal the tattered blue book from Jetta's hands.

"You three," Galm said, putting down his newspaper and reaching under the table to pull them out. "There are other books, you know."

"No there aren't," Lohien laughed softly as she added spices to the soup cooking on the stovetop.

"The Stone Garden," Galm said, thumbing through the worn pages of their favorite story. "I've only read this to you three about a hundred times."

Jetta wormed her way onto her uncle's lap, her siblings squeezing in beside her, eager to hear the story they already knew by heart.

It isn't real...

Joy turned to desperation as the waxen reality of her dream melted away, and she slipped back into the real world.

Jetta peeled back heavy eyelids. When the blurred walls became one again, she saw that she was back in Jade's place. Things were different. Her flattened cardboard bed was gone. Instead, she was tied to one of the routing pipes, arms above her head, her legs bound underneath her. Coupled with the pain from the gunshot and bite wounds, her body screamed for release from the stressful position.

"Hey—she's awake."

Bossy slapped Agracia on the back, making her turn around. The older Jock was once again swaying to the beat of her headphones with the same glazed-over look of indifference. She picked at her teeth with a knife and spat the contents on the ground as she looked Jetta up and down.

"Some stunt you pulled back there," Agracia said. "Fighting, but not really winning? Wolves not killing you? I don't get it. And what happened back in the locker rooms? You fake that seizure? What, you can't handle a little pain?"

Jetta remembered blacking out—but was it a seizure? It might have been a combination of the pain stimuli and the cumulative aftereffects of removing the biochip, but she wasn't sure.

Agracia walked over to her and stooped down to her level. "I don't give a *chak* one way or another. All I know is that everybody wants a piece of you now. You one hot ticket. You ugly, but you hot, right?"

Jetta struggled to loosen the bindings, causing her shirtsleeve to rip straight down her right arm.

Agracia's jaw dropped wide open. "What's a Skirt like you doing with that tattoo?"

Bossy, who had been stuffing her face with instant macaroni and cheese, looked up, mouth open, noodles dropping to the floor. "What the hell?"

"What?" Jetta asked, not understanding their shock at seeing her tattoo.

Agracia's eyes narrowed as she played with the knife in her hand. "I don't know what kind of *gorsh-shit* you pulling. Why do you have that mark on you?"

Jetta instinctively opened her mind but quickly retreated, conditioned to the shock cuff. She expected a reaction—even a warning buzz—but there was none. No punishment, not even the slightest tingle.

She looked down at the cuff. It was still flashing like it was on, but it didn't seem to be functioning correctly.

That weird sensation in my ankle right before I blacked out—

Had she short-circuited the device when Bossy overcharged her system? Jetta tentatively tried again, this time bridging the gap to touch Agracia's mind.

I can see you.

Jetta smiled. This would be fun. "Untie me."

Agracia smirked. "Answer my question, Skirt, or I'm gonna make my own mark."

Eager for both physical and psionic release, Jetta didn't waste any time. She jumped straight into her captors' minds, relishing the power she had been forced to hold back.

"Oh *chak*!" Bossy screamed, pressing her remote furiously. Agracia dove for hers, but it did no good.

Skimming over bad memories, Jetta stirred their fears, but didn't push too far just yet.

(*Make them pay*.)

Agracia hunched over, gulping for air, eyes dilated, sweat beading on her brow. Grasping for something imaginary, Bossy fell to her knees, face panicked and arms outstretched.

"Untie me," Jetta said calmly. "And take that *godich* cuff off—or you'll find out what I can really do."

Agracia rubbed her eyes in disbelief before setting her loose.

"Sit," Jetta said, massaging her wrists and ankles. "We have a lot to discuss."

"I won't beg for my life," Agracia said. She didn't seem to understand her predicament. "You can go shove it."

"Where do we go from here?" Jetta asked, eyeing the knife that Agracia still held in her shaking hands. Bossy's arms dropped to her side, and she clicked off the safety of her 20-20s. "Do you really think you can hurt me like that?"

Agracia's face flushed. "You're a *chakking* leech. Just take what you want and get the hell out."

It wasn't but a fraction of a second after the word leech came out of Agracia's mouth that Jetta knocked her from her seat. Agracia's headphones flew off her head as Jetta came down on her neck. Blood boiling, Jetta squeezed the Jock's throat until she could barely utter any sound at all.

Bossy screamed in the background, threatening to blow her to pieces, but Jetta ignored her. She was already in, seeking what she would need to destroy Agracia Waychild from the inside out.

Jetta sloshed through memory after memory of wild, drunken nights and mornings full of body aches and hangover sickness. Between binges she witnessed dangerous trips to the surface and fights with other Jocks over terrestrial relics. Fast-moving hoverboards carried her from one safety point to another, running from Necros, running from the Dogs, Jocks, Johnnies, Meatheads—running from her past.

That's the key, Jetta thought, pitching deeper into Agracia's roots.

An alcoholic human father, obese and miserable, flitted past. Only a bad aftertaste and a pitiful absence in her heart remained. Her mother, a mixed-breed woman with no more maternal instinct than the male Scabbers she serviced, regarded her with dead eyes and a white-powder lined mouth.

Nowhere to go, Jetta realized, unable to find her own space in the cramped studio apartment. Barefooted half-siblings, too many to count, crawled over her in desperate search for food. The smell of urine and mold overpowered her senses, making her escape to the streets for reprieve.

A choice had to be made. Be a Jock, a fighter, or a Puppet. There were no other options on Earth—especially not for girl. Strike out or be struck down.

"I won't turn out like my parents," Agracia whispered, huddling up behind a dumpster, trying to keep warm.

Perfect, Jetta thought, readying to exploit Agracia's self-hatred, her disgust for family. But just as she pulled back, she noticed the discontinuity. Stacked together, the memories from Agracia's childhood didn't seem real. The sensation felt akin to a false belief, something she had encountered when she had absorbed the memories of POWs who had created an alternate reality to escape from the horrors of war. But this was different. This seemed—

"—manufactured," Jetta said aloud.

She dove back in and tried again. The same memories from Agracia's childhood spun out before her, but when she tested their depth, she saw their stilted, two-dimensional construction, like a flat picture on a screen. Curious, she pushed past them, struggling to break through the dense fibers of Agracia's belief, her own habituation to the memory of her childhood.

Impossible...

Images exploded in front of her, assaulting her senses. Jetta gasped for air, reflexively releasing Agracia as she struggled for control.

Vast gaps spanned between the incomplete memories, but Jetta saw enough to piece together a disturbing picture. Test after test, mental and physical, in windowless gray rooms. Men and women in military uniforms screaming in her face. Endless battle simulations that didn't stop even after she collapsed.

"Candidate 0113 has failed personality trials. We will have to terminate her from the program."

It was Damon Unipoesa's voice, loud and clear. He turned to her, his face, his words, bereft of any mercy. "Know when you're defeated."

Tidas Razar stood in the distance. "We could use an Agent on Earth. Her aptitude is perfect for that environment."

Gloved hands reached for the needle in her arm. Bright lights shone in her eyes, but not before she saw the white substance dripping into the intravenous line.

Unipoesa's voice whispered in her ear as her eyes grew too heavy to keep open: "Know when you're defeated."

Jetta released her, panting for breath. Stunned, Agracia, gaped at her in disbelief.

"I'm going to *chakking*—" Bossy screamed, cocking her arm back to throw the 20-20 grenade at Jetta.

"No," Agracia said through hoarse vocal cords, tackling Bossy. "Don't."

Jetta sat down on a crate and held her head in her hands, trying to sort out what she just gleaned. *Why does Agracia the Scabber Jock from Old Earth have memories of Unipoesa and Razar?*

"What did you just do to me?" Agracia whispered, bracing her head in her hands. The tone of her voice changed, and she dropped her customary abrasive accent and slang. "I can remember… something else."

All of Agracia's desultory mannerisms vanished, the indifference in her eyes replaced with an intensity Jetta had only seen in her brother and sister.

There is a superior intelligence in there, Jetta realized, confirming her earlier suspicions.

"Gracie?" Bossy said, confused by the change in her companion's behavior.

"It's okay, I promise," Agracia said, tears in her eyes. "I just... I just forgot a few things. It'll be okay."

"She didn't mess you up, did she?" Bossy asked, shooting Jetta a sidelong glare.

"No," Agracia said, rising slowly. "But this changes everything."

"Yes, it certainly does," Jetta said. She probed her mind again, sensing the fear and the uncertainty flooding Agracia's thoughts.

"Don't—" Agracia said, squeezing her eyes shut.

Jetta hit a wall of resistance. *Impossible—*

She tried again, pushing for Agracia's knowledge of her tattoo, but Agracia's mind blocked her out.

This can't be—only specialized military personnel are trained against this kind of psionic assault, Jetta thought. *Who is this girl?*

Frustrated and confused, Jetta's initial malintent dissolved into a rumbling acid churn. *(I wanted revenge, not reasons to hesitate.)*

Reason soothed her dark aches. *Agracia is too valuable to eliminate. Her past could be the key to uncovering secrets about the Alliance—*

(—secrets that could prove to Jaeia that no one can be trusted.)

Biting down on her vexation, Jetta focused on playing it cool. She would gain nothing by revealing her knowledge that Agracia could resist her talents. "I'm only going to offer this once. I will get you some answers about your past if you tell me more about my tattoo."

"What is she talking about?" Bossy began, but Agracia clamped her hand over her companion's mouth.

"Done," Agracia said.

Jetta allowed her psionic awareness to branch out as Bossy screamed at Agracia and Agracia tried in vain to explain what had just happened. Searching for her sister across the vast stretches of space, eager to touch the mind she so dearly missed, she made a connection she had never expected.

Jetta opened her eyes and screamed.

***

The report came directly from DeAnders' terminal to Razar. Even though he hated using the remote transport device, the Military

Minister needed to get to the Division Lockdown Labs as quickly as he could.

"It started about half an hour ago, after we tried another signal retrieval—I can't explain it," DeAnders said, rushing him to the stasis chambers. Still unsteady on his feet from the phase shift of the remote transport, Razar managed to stumble his way there.

"Is it Senka?" he asked. His hopes were quickly doused when he saw the crowd of technicians around the Grand Oblin's cylinder.

"He's awake. And talking, but it's not making sense," DeAnders said, pressing the audio button on the Oblin's tank. The old priest's eyes were open and his jaw was moving, but his words came out in a garble.

"Is it the stasis fluid?" Razar asked.

"No. They can breathe and talk in it without a problem. I don't know why he can't communicate."

"Not my... too... flesh... can't believe... dead... again..." were his only discernable words.

Razar shook his head. "Can you make any sense of it?"

DeAnders adjusted his glasses. "Not at this time. But his brain activity is off the charts—I've never seen anything like this."

The Military Minister looked down at the terminal, reviewing the comparative analysis of the Berroman's biofunctions. "What does this mean?"

DeAnders looked at where he was pointing. "I don't know. We didn't have much of a baseline for him when we initially downloaded his datastream, but it appears that his body is in a state of flux. If I were to guess, I'd say he was attempting to shapeshift."

"Have you tried communicating with him?"

The director looked offended. "Of course, Sir, but he doesn't seem aware of us. At least not yet."

The Military Minister cursed under his breath. "I see your recommendation," Razar said, tracing the report on the screen. "And I concur. Jetta, Jaeia, or even Triel are probably the only people who could potentially access his mind right now, but unfortunately none of them are available."

"Jetta."

The room went silent. The Grand Oblin repeated her name over and over again, his eyes opening wider and wider, his voice escalating.

"Well, you can confirm that he's listening," the Minister said.

"He's changing—look," DeAnders said, pointing to his eyes. "His eyes are changing color. They were yellow before…"

The Military Minister watched with the rest of the research team as the Grand Oblin's body quivered, skin smoothing and then wrinkling, his frame expanding and contracting.

"His body can't handle this stress," DeAnders commented, studying the readouts. "I may have to medically induce a coma."

"I don't want to risk losing him—he might be the key to reviving the others," Razar said. "Keep him stable, doctor. I will contact Jaeia and reassign her."

"Whatever you're doing, do it quickly," DeAnders said, giving orders to the technicians running back and forth between stations. "There might not be much time."

***

The threads of the crew's life-cords pulsated in Triel's hands, warm and alive. One quick jerk and they would be blighted from existence.

(So easy…)

"No!" the Healer shouted, reclaiming herself. *Father, forgive me.*

Triel pulled out of the connection she had forged with the crewmen of the *Hixon*. *I could have killed them all and been done with it—but this isn't me. I have to remember who I am.*

She looked down and saw the reflection of herself in the console of the starship, the circles under her eyes a little darker than before. "I am not a Dissembler. I am a Healer."

That was too close, she thought. *I have to be more careful.*

Triel knew she couldn't allow herself to harbor aggression or hatred, but she didn't know how else to feel. *Healers aren't supposed to be isolated, alone.*

(I don't want to Fall.)

Reorienting to her surroundings, Triel realized that the *Hixon* had been broadcasting to her on every available channel for the last three minutes. "This is Captain Shelby of the *Hixon*. Please identify yourself and your vessel."

With a heavy sigh she acknowledged the hail. "I am Chief

Medical Advisor Triel of Algardrien. I have come to ensure the health and safety of the crew of the *Wraith*."

Even without sensing the change in his biosigns she could tell by Shelby's insincere smile that he was about to lie or deceive her in some way. "You are authorized to dock in Bay 1, but given our proximity to the planet's atmosphere, I'm ordering you to let our gravity beams guide you in."

It was a cheap trick to get her to disengage her primary controls, but Triel relented. *A wise idea—not something the Military Minister would have authorized,* she thought bitterly. *The admiral probably alerted Shelby, but gave the order not to engage.*

When Triel exited her craft, a complement of soldiers greeted her, as well as the red-haired Captain Shelby.

"Chief, please follow me," the captain said, dispersing the guard. Half of the troop inspected her ship, the other half trailing her as she followed the captain.

Given the unusual configuration of the corridors, the Healer guessed that the *Hixon* was part of the Defense/Research Department. Massive equipment lined the hallways, and most of the doors crackled with electrical fencing.

There aren't any maps posted, she observed. The stinging smell of pienoncyde, a potent cleanser used for medical equipment, touched her nose. *And this place stinks like a laboratory.*

Triel hid the worry from her voice as best she could. "I have come for Reht and the crew. I know they're here, and that they're hurt or sick."

The captain took his time responding. Triel tried to gauge his thoughts, but he was surprisingly unreadable, especially considering his human ancestry. "I'm taking you to them right now."

She wasn't sure what she was expecting when they entered the narrow hallway leading to the pair of double doors, but she sensed that whatever was behind the entrance wasn't something she could anticipate.

Shelby paused after unlocking the doors. "I will be straightforward with you. What has happened to the Reht and his crew was necessary for federation security."

Her shoulders knotted almost instantly, but she kept her composure. She had heard those words, "necessary for security," uttered far too many times in her life, especially during the

Dissembler Scare.

Cold sweat trickled down her ribs. "Open the doors," she whispered.

Shelby eyed the guards as he opened them for the Healer.

She gasped. There they were—Mom, Tech, Vaughn, Bacthar, Ro, and Cray—sitting around a table playing cards, smoking and drinking, apparently content with their circumstances. Billy Don't was doing laps around the crew, singing to himself and blowing bubbles with his digestive lubricant. It was a scene she would expect to see on a dog-soldier starcraft, but not aboard an Alliance vessel.

"What did you do to them?" she said, approaching the double-paned window. She pressed her hands against the tinted glass, wanting to connect, knowing that the crew couldn't see her.

What did they do to you? she wondered, sensing their ease and complete disregard for their situation.

"We asked them never to speak of anything they had learned from their infiltration of the Alliance mainframe during the last war," Shelby said.

He's being vague on purpose, she thought. Triel faced him, eyes narrowing, none too careful to hide her emotion. "What did you do to them, and where is Reht?"

"The crew is fine. Reht, however... We couldn't get him to promise," Shelby said, leading her through a hidden door to the right. He typed in several codes, and when the door hissed open, her worst fears came to life.

Shelby guided her through several rooms full of complicated-looking instruments that hummed and buzzed as technicians and engineers scuttled about before finally leading her to an observation room. Reht lay on an exam table, pale and diaphoretic, vacantly staring at the ceiling. Yellow intravenous fluid dripped into his forearm. When she reached out across the psionic planes, she felt his tune, thready and unstable, and her heart leaped in her chest.

"I will disclose sensitive information to you, Triel, because I need your help in order to save Reht. He's dying," Shelby said, showing her his vital signs on the terminal readout under the observation window. "He hasn't slept in days, and his brain waves are confusing—we can't explain them. All we know is that his systems are shutting down, one by one, and we can't slow the progress."

Her words came out barely above a hush. "Did you do this?"

Shelby shook his head. "No. But nothing we did helped—it seemed to progress his deterioration."

"Why even save a dog-soldier?" Triel asked, folding her arms across her chest.

Shelby grunted. "My orders came from the top. Reht is valuable. He has connections. That is why the entire crew was inducted into our Sleeper Program."

She was surprised by his candor. *This is not typical military protocol—what's he trying to pull?*

"Sleeper Program?" she said.

Shelby handed her a dataclip. "It's the Alliance's paramount defense program. We condition Agents to be able to go on missions without their direct knowledge. We transmit subliminal commands via electronic messages, net communication, lights, music, physical stimuli—almost any seemingly ordinary event can be made into a trigger. Our Agents are spread across the galaxy, gathering critical information for us, but they are unaware of the exact nature of their actions. We call them Sleepers for obvious reasons. Usually they're high-profile criminals or other personnel we can't afford to jail or execute. Too many legal gambles. This is the best option. It saves lives and gives us a return on our investment in setting them free."

Triel didn't bother looking at the dataclip. Instead, she made the obvious inference. "Are you telling me this because after I'm done healing Reht, you're going to do the same thing to me? You're going to erase this conversation from my head, make me forget I even stole that ship and that I came here to save my friends?"

Shelby didn't answer right away. "We didn't have a choice with the dog-soldiers. Jagger and his crew have breached our security system one too many times; they've been too involved in high-security affairs. It was the only solution if we weren't to terminate him. You're different—you're a telepath. We don't have the technology to make you an Agent. Your compliance with the defense agenda will be voluntary."

Triel looked at the guards, all of whom had a firm grip on their weapons. *I don't think "voluntary" is the right word to describe what he means.*

Triel felt trapped, betrayed. There was nothing she could do. If she killed the crew of the *Hixon* she would surely Fall, but if she complied and saved Reht, she was ceding to the military's agenda and forsaking her oath as a dog-soldier.

Unconsciously, the Healer ripped at the webbing between her fingers. Rage inflated her thoughts, making her ache for sweet release.

(They've hurt everyone I love.)

Dangerous feelings bubbled through, ones she had only felt with such magnitude when the Dominion was decimating her people.

(End the Alliance.)

(Kill them all.)

Her father had always warned her against the temptation to use her powers for ruin, but suddenly it seemed justified—

—Necessary.

Triel closed her eyes and gulped down her fury. With Reht's essence waning, she had to act now—no time for vengeance. At least not yet.

"Let me see him," she whispered.

Shelby blocked her from entering the containment room, finally unmasking his contempt for her. "It was Admiral Unipoesa that authorized your presence here, and it was under his direct order and only his direct order that I would ever share highly classified information about the defense program with you. Don't make me regret following my chain of command."

Triel didn't waste a moment on Shelby, or on wondering why Unipoesa would have done such a thing. She pushed her way around him and rushed to Reht's side.

"Hold on," she whispered, loosening the captain's shirt.

The Healer placed one hand on his chest and one on the side of his neck, searching for the root of his essence.

(Where are you, my love?)

His tune was altered, distorted; she had never experienced anything like it. In the spectrum of his being, in the vibrations of his biorhythm, she should have seen or felt something more than hollow discord. She searched deeper, moving farther and farther from herself, endangering her life as she submerged herself into his internal rhythms.

(Where are you?) *she called again.*

The farther she sank, the more systems she found shutting down. She searched within the tissues, right down to the individual cells, but could find no cause.

(Only one way to help him...) *she thought. She would have to go for a complete immersion. It was a dangerous practice, even for a Healer supported by an entire tribe. And she was alone and unsettled—*

(—but it's the only way I can reach him.)

Triel suddenly remembered one of the lessons her father taught her when she was assisting in the rejuvenation of a Falling Healer.

"We are all fragile things," *he once said,* "easily tangled in the battles between our different wills—will of spirit, will of mind, will of body—but with the right harmonizing, we can find balance again. If you cannot find their tune, call upon your own. A broken mind will seek your Voice in its state of disharmony."

Triel stopped her descent and grounded herself. Reaching back into her own past, she thought of her favorite melody, a tune from her childhood that her mother had sung every night to her and her sister before bedtime. As she hummed the words, Triel visualized her mother and her sister, smelling her mother's perfume and feeling the warmth of a shared blanket as her mother's melodic voice floated on the night air.

A terrified scream rose above her tune.

(Reht?)

The light planes shifted, and she could see him in the distance. She tried to get closer, but his image flickered like a pool of rippling water.

(I can't hear you!) *Triel cried.*

Reht disappeared into the undulations. Without thinking, she dove after him, ignoring the mounting distance between her mind and body. She arrowed inward farther and farther, beyond the substance of him, losing sight of herself and anything she knew.

(No going back now—)

Triel cried out as she broke through a barrier headfirst, the impact sending her spinning into a dizzying new reality.

(Who are you?) *Triel questioned, finding herself standing in front of a familiar-looking human woman in her late twenties. Looking around, she saw nothing but a world of swirling grays and whites to give them dimension in an otherwise naked plane.*

"*I am so sorry to find you like this,*" *she said, her voice thickly accented.* "*This is the only way I can communicate safely with you.*

There are others hunting me, and if they know about you, that you survived, then surely they will hunt you, too."

After waving her hand in front of the woman's face, Triel concluded that the woman couldn't see or recognize her. *Is this is a memory stain?*

Triel didn't know how a human-looking woman could implant a memory into Reht. Only the most powerful telepaths could accomplish such a thing, and only after decades of practice.

Assuming this is a memory stain, this can't be all of it, Triel thought as the woman's image zig-zagged like a wayward television signal. *I bet I can only see part of the message; it must be intended for someone else.*

As the woman continued, the background changed accordingly.

"There isn't much time, so I will tell you what is most important: I was born on Earth in 2021, and I can remember things that humans now have long since forgotten, the most important thing being Earth—the real Earth—when it was green and full of life."

Triel stepped backwards as jagged mountains erupted from the groundless floor and green forests sprouted from newly formed soil. A crisp wind tickled her skin, bringing with it the sweet smell of new life.

"I was hoping to pass these things down to you, but that day in 2052 changed everything. Now I can only hope that it isn't too late, that maybe my surviving—our surviving—the accident means that Earth and mankind still has a chance."

The background changed. Trees and mountains merged together to form decorated walls and a lighted ceiling. The smell of mothballs, old paper, and wood stain hit her just as the rest of the place took form. A human man, an old one with white hair and dark-rimmed glasses, appeared behind a counter counting round, copper disks next to an outdated cash register. Stacks of books and ancient-looking contraptions covered almost every centimeter of the store. A globe representing a blue planet with one moon hung from the ceiling, slowly rotating on its axis.

"The man on fire knows where to go next. If you get lost, look for a familiar sign. And when you find Charlie, all your questions will be answered."

As the image faded, Triel felt the pressure increase on the walls of Reht's psyche squeezing her from every side. She whipped backwards, retracting back toward her body as Reht's mind reawakened.

The Healer came out of the dog-soldier's mind gasping. As she regained her sight, Shelby held her in his arms while another lab technician tried to read her bioscan.

"I'm fine!" Triel said between breaths, pushing herself off of Shelby and rushing back to Reht.

Shelby made some kind of crass comment, but she ignored him. "Hey," she said, brushing Reht's red-tipped hair away from his face.

His eyes opened slowly, a sly grin spreading across his face. "Starfox…"

Tears squeezed from her eyes as she hugged him and felt his biorhythms harmonize. Whoever had stained him had almost killed him, but after seeing the imprint she didn't think it was intentional.

"Hey—what the hell?" Reht said, realizing his surroundings. "What is this *gorsh-shit*?"

Two other lab technicians and the guards surrounded them, weapons aimed at his head.

"Triel, I advise that you come with me now," Shelby said, offering her the door.

She shook her head. "I want him and the rest of the crew released."

"Please, Triel," Shelby said again, nodding at the guards.

"Don't touch him!" Triel said, standing between Reht and the guards as they advanced. "Or you'll never know what happened to him."

"What the hell is going on?" Reht said, trying to sit up but ending up on his side, panting for breath.

Shelby's face remained unemotional. "Triel, there is nothing to negotiate."

Triel thought about the woman—her familiarity, her bizarre accent, her captivating fervor. *There is something very important about her, something that the Alliance—the Starways—might need.*

"I saw a woman in Reht's head—she had imprinted a message. That's why he was sick."

"Imprinted a message?" Shelby said.

"Only telepaths can do that—and there aren't many of us left. More importantly, she seemed to know something about Earth. Something about saving it."

Shelby's face changed. "Did she say her name? What other information did she provide?"

Triel kept her eyes locked on his. "This is where we negotiate."

"*Chak* negotiations!" Reht said, trying to sit up again.

Shelby cocked his head to the side. "Unfortunately, I have to side with the dog-soldier."

Something pricked the Healer's arm. She tried to shout, but her mouth didn't want to move. Neither did her arms or legs. As she slumped over Reht's body and the guards descended upon them, she heard him scream.

***

Agracia and Bossy were yelling at her, shaking her by the shoulders.

"I'm fine, I'm fine," Jetta said, coming around.

"What was that? You kept screaming, 'Jahx,'" Agracia said.

Bewildered, Jetta held her head in her hands. She had felt her brother, his connection, his voice in her heard, just like before. *That's impossible—Jahx is dead. It must have been the effects of the shock cuff or the removal of the biochip; I must have hallucinated.*

Besides, she had been unable to use her powers for a long time, and she had only bridged that kind of distance between herself and her sister a handful of times prior, so it could have jolted her system. *Really,* she told herself, *any number of things could have caused the phantom sensation.*

"What?" Agracia asked, seeing her perplexity.

"Forget about it," Jetta said, standing and straightening her clothes. She rubbed her temples, searching again for her sister. As Jaeia's thoughts slowly surfaced in the back of her mind, she smiled.

Hey Sis, she called out across the stars.

A rush of emotion hit her like a hug given after a running start. Jetta laughed out loud, giving Agracia and Bossy a reason to raise a brow at her.

Relieved, Jetta sent her sister the knowledge of her relative safety and her new discovery.

I'm so glad you're okay. We're coming for you now. Where is your location? Jaeia asked.

"Where are we, anyway?" Jetta asked to Jock duo.

Agracia's eyes grew dark. "You're contacting the Alliance, aren't you?"

Jetta nodded, thinking of the consequences of her actions. She would be reprimanded, court-martialed—perhaps even jailed if she had caused harm to the foundation worker in the jump—but she couldn't care about that. *I did it for Galm and Lohien, and I would do it again.* "I have to."

Agracia picked her headphones up off the ground and held them in her hands. "You're going to tell them about us."

Following the chain of her thoughts, Jetta saw the logic in her fear. *Agracia has ties to the Alliance, and I'm not certain that relationship has ended.*

"If you leave," Agracia said. "You'll never know about your tattoo."

Jetta crossed her arms and gave them her best bluff. "I can take that from you. I don't need your help."

Thankfully, Agracia wasn't aware that Jetta couldn't steal from her as easily as she made it sound. "Yes, you do. You could gank every shred of knowledge from me about Earth, about the Pits—whatever. But no matter how much you know about the Scabs, you'll never be a Scabber, and they won't accept you—not without an escort. Not without me and Bossy. We're your ticket or you'll never get in."

"At least not without a bloody mess," Bossy muttered.

The same rules apply on Fiorah, Jetta thought, *so there's probably some merit to what she said.* "What do you want, then?"

Bossy popped her lollipop out of her mouth. "I want you to go *chak* yourself. This ain't the Gracie I know."

"Shut it, kid," Agracia said. "She might be able to help you if you keep your *godich* mouth shut for five minutes."

Jetta heard the echo of Agracia's desires: *She wants me to dig around Bossy's past, too. Maybe there's a reason the two of them have gravitated toward each other…*

Agracia put the headphones back on her head but immediately took them off.

"What is it?" Jetta said as Agracia's pain radiated back at her.

"My head," Agracia said, squeezing her eyes shut. "How did I ever listen to this?"

Jetta picked up the headphones and put it to one of her ears. The same verse of the heavy metal tune repeated over and over again in a never-ending loop. "*Gods.* Why the hell *did* you listen to this?!"

"I don't know. I just always have."

Jetta realized right then that Agracia wouldn't be able to recall the truth without being guided through the fictional web of her past, and that gave Jetta a distinct advantage. *If I'm quick about it, I could possibly retrieve some scrap of information before Agracia's training has a chance to react and resist.* And now that her access to Agracia's knowledge about her tattoo was closed off, Jetta would need to offer something equally valuable if she expected to get Agracia to cooperate.

"Hey!" Agracia shouted as Jetta grabbed her wrist.

Breaching the Scabber Jock's mind for the second time proved even tougher than Jetta thought. Agracia's faculties rapidly acclimated to her powers, erecting new ice walls against her assault. Acting quickly and deftly, Jetta leapt around and wound through the mental barricades.

She's stronger than she looks, Jetta thought, *dodging a psionic counterattack that sent shockwaves through her skull and spine. She's elite; I can't use my usual tricks.*

Pressing harder, Jetta hurtled through military drills, uniformed men discussing Agracia's fate, white-walled lab rooms, the exhaustion of training—the events similar to those she had already seen and proved of no immediate use. She focused her search, layering the image of the headphones over Agracia's memories, frantically trying to find a match before she was completely pushed out. Then she saw it.

"*I hate this* godich *noise.*"

Razar's voice. He stood somewhere above her. She squinted, trying to make him out, but it was too hard to see in the circle of exam lights.

"*This is that* gorsh-shit *the Scabbers listen to. It'll blend right in.*"

She caught a glimpse of a red-haired man as headphones were slipped over her head. She struggled at first, but as the music repeated over and over, she found herself lulled into a stupor.

"*This one is our toughest Agent; Unipoesa's training made her resistant to our standard conditioning. She'll have to wear these things almost continuously to keep her sensitized to our input. It also means we'll only be able to trigger her with visual stimuli."*

"I don't care," Razar said, sounding unusually irritated. "I want her stationed as soon as possible. Keep this quiet."

"Get out of my head!" Agracia screamed, kicking Jetta in the leg.

Jetta reeled backwards, head spinning as Agracia's psyche shoved her out. Righting herself against one of the vertical pipes, she pointed at the headphones. "I know what they're for."

"Tell me," Agracia demanded, approaching her, one hand cupping her forehead in pain.

"Back off—you know what I can do to you," Jetta said. That much was still true. Even if she couldn't read Agracia's thoughts or glean her knowledge, she could still make her nightmares come alive.

"Tell me," Agracia said, adamant, but backing off.

"Tell me about my tattoo," Jetta countered, stepping toward her.

"*Chak* you both!" Bossy said, wedging her tiny body between Agracia and Jetta. "I don't get you, Grace. You let this leech flip your head!"

"Get off, Bossy—it ain't like that! Use your *chakking* head. If it weren't real, then she be killin' us already!"

The pint-sized warrior looked crushed, as if someone had just killed her best friend. "Fine. *Chak* you, Agracia. I'm outta here." Bossy slammed the door behind her, cussing as she went.

"Aren't you going to follow her?" Jetta asked.

"You don't know Bossy. That would be a bad idea. Gotta let her cool off a bit," Agracia said, sitting down on a crate. She pulled out a smoke but looked puzzled when she went to light it. "This isn't me, is it?"

Jetta put her hands on her hips. "I don't know. A few hours ago you were a drunken slob that was selling me in the circuit. Now you're a confused ex-military project or something. Guess we're going to find out."

Agracia flicked the cigarette away, but after a moment, she collected it off the floor and lit it. "I'll tell you everything about your tattoo—you have my word—if you help me get out. Me and Bossy have enough trouble on Earth—we don't need no Skirts on our tails as well."

Jetta closed her eyes, touching her sister's thoughts. She pressed

Jaeia about whether she should follow up on the tattoo lead with Agracia.

There is trouble now, Jaeia said, sharing images of the borderworlds readings, the communications blackouts, and how the Alliance was unable to contact several colonies.

The Alliance is in a Class 7 emergency, Jetta thought to herself. *This is my top priority as commander of the SMT.* Even though she was still unsure of her loyalties to the Alliance, especially after what she had seen in Agracia's memories, Jetta couldn't deny her inner pull. *I owe it to my sister to fight any kind of threat against the Starways.*

"I can't stay; I have to go back. But I will find you, believe me," Jetta said, looking at Agracia straight in the eye. "There is no place you can hide from me now. I've been in your head."

The Scabber Jock held up her headphones. "What about these?"

"Give them to me," Jetta said, taking them from her. "You have no use for them anymore."

"Hey!" Agracia said, trying to take them back. "You never told me what they—"

"That doesn't matter," Jetta said, holding them away from her, staring her down. "And besides, you played me in the fighting rings. The least you could do is trade me your headphones for all that work—unless you think I'd have more fun grinding your brains."

After giving Jetta a petulant look, Agracia dropped her gaze to her feet and mumbled under her breath.

Jetta gathered what few things she had, mainly the birthday present from her sister that she had been careful to stow away in a broken pipe. Even though she had made many unsuccessful attempts to zoom in on her location, she gave it one last effort.

"That a map?" Agracia asked.

Jetta withdrew her eye from the orb. "Yes, but it doesn't work here."

"Not surprising. Nothin'll penetrate the atmosphere. It's poisoned, ya know."

Jetta knew Agracia was trying to be funny by pointing out the obvious, but it didn't amuse her.

Agracia sighed. "I guess you'll want me to take you to the surface."

"Yes. That is, unless you want me to loot your skull again,"

Jetta replied.

Agracia watched as Jetta wrapped a scarf around her head and face. "You know what's sorta ironic?"

Jetta didn't care to respond as she made a mental list of what she was going to need for her journey.

"My mom—or my fake mom—she named me Agracia. It means 'without God's grace.' But that little detail, just like the rest, was made up. Somebody wanted me to feel like a dirty meatbag, just like the rest of the Scabbers."

Having experienced some of Agracia's life, Jetta felt an uncommon depth to her words. Agracia had tried to pass it off as a casual observation, but Jetta knew the sadness behind it and couldn't help but share in her pain, if only for a moment.

"But what am I now?" Agracia continued, turning over her hands. "Part of me—most of me—is afraid to remember the past. Maybe being a cheap forgery is better than digging up old garbage."

Jetta couldn't argue with that. Some things were best left forgotten.

Eager to meet up with her sister and get away from Agracia's uncomfortable feelings, Jetta nodded her head towards the door. "We'll have to barter for radiation suits at the market. I saw your winnings in your pocket," Jetta said, pointing to the bulge in the side pocket of her pants. "That should be enough, right?"

Agracia mumbled under her breath again, but didn't dissent.

Jetta hung back when they hit the markets, allowing Agracia to deal with the other Scabbers and Jocks for suits, noting how differently they treated her without her sidekick. Agracia was fierce enough in her own right, but it was Bossy who made her a bully.

"I got only one suit," Agracia said, returning with an overstuffed duffel bag. "There's a storm comin' and a lot of the Jocks are running jobs right now. I guess some big shot investor is takin' a real liking to Earth."

Jetta suited up behind a vendor, keeping track of Agracia's peripheral thoughts. *She's extremely concerned about Bossy, even if she doesn't show it.*

"You think that Bossy has a past like you—made up?" Jetta asked as she cinched the suit tight around her waist and checked her radiation meter. *God, I hope that's broken,* she thought, seeing the meter already in the black.

Agracia shrugged her shoulders. "Well, she's not normal, not for a Scab. She looks like a young kid, but she ain't. And she's quicker and stronger than any human—any Sentient—I've ever seen. She ain't right."

Jetta nodded, making a note to investigate that when she could safely return to Earth.

"Look, I can't go with you," Agracia said. "You'll be safe in the suit—anybody will just think you're a Jock going to the surface. Just keep to yourself, don't mess with anybody's head, and you'll stay undercover."

"You're not leading me to the surface?"

Agracia looked back to the crowd, scanning for something or someone. "I told you—I got enough problems here. I gotta settle a few things, find Bossy. I'll draw you a map."

She's only telling half the truth, Jetta thought, extending her psionic reach. *She fears that I'll turn her over to the military.*

Carefully delving deeper into Agracia's mind, Jetta sensed a complexity to that truth. *It's not just because of what she's done to me... Agracia is afraid of what her subconscious already knows, but her mind has yet to remember.*

(I know that feeling all too well—)

"Can you remember my signature if I tell it to you?" Jetta said, pushing aside her feelings.

Agracia rolled her eyes. "Don't be a jerk. I'm probably just as smart as you."

Jetta gave her the twenty-digit code. "That's the easiest way to get hold of me. And don't try anything stupid."

Agracia shrugged her shoulders. "I want to know my past just like you, right? I know you're going up there and gonna find out more about what they did to me. Respect for that. When you come back, I'll have something for you, too."

"You'd better," Jetta said, grabbing Agracia by the arm. "Don't make me regret letting you go."

Agracia gave her a curious half-smile. "See you later, Doctor Death."

***

As Jetta watched the lights of the Alliance rescue ship cut through the cloud cover, her thoughts drifted to the memories she absorbed from the wolves.

Why can't I get them out of my head? she thought, sinking back into the experience.

Looking down at the windswept rock and dirt beneath her boots, she remembered the feeling of grass pressed down by furry paws. A chill ran up her spine as she recalled the sensation of four limbs stretching out across the plain, running forever, not knowing exhaustion or anything but the twinge of hunger in her belly and the thrill of the hunt.

Tears formed in her eyes, but she fought against them. *I'm not supposed to feel this way—I shouldn't care about a dead place.* But she missed the warmth of the sun terribly, and filling her lungs with clean air, free of waste exhaust and chemicals.

(I want to run freely, my companions at my side without collars or cages, and sing to the moon before falling asleep under the stars.)

"*Gorsh-shit*," she told herself. She held her breath and tried to make the sensations stop. "Bloody wolves!"

Jetta wiped the debris off her visor and huddled beside the relative safety of a fallen structure, trying to reason with herself. When she returned to Earth she wanted to settle things with Agracia, not waste her time with the wolves, but she felt a strange compulsion to see them again, to press further into their knowledge of what Earth once was.

"Fine," she muttered to herself. "I'll find some way—*if* I have time."

After the starship had safely landed, Jetta ran to cross the ramp. There was little said to her beyond the standard greetings as she underwent routine decontamination. Anxious to see her sister, Jetta quibbled with the technicians until they finally let her out of the treatment room, still dressed in a gown.

"Jaeia!" Jetta shouted, pushing past the guards and running to her sister. She wanted to hug her sister tightly, but fear and shame made her stop in her tracks. Face flushed, she took a step back.

"I'm so happy to see you," Jetta stuttered, looking at the ground.

Jaeia's brow furrowed. "Me too. Give me a hug already," Jaeia said, grabbing Jetta's hand and pulling her into her arms.

Jetta had longed for this moment, but now that she was back, it didn't feel right. Even though Jaeia's touch was warm and inviting, she couldn't bring herself to accept it, and her limbs and spine remained stiff as a board until Jaeia finally let go. *Something's changed.*

"Mind your business, Sis," Jaeia chuckled, covering her sister's open backside.

"Oh, sorry," Jetta said, rearranging her gown and stepping back again.

Jaeia studied her a moment, gray eyes searching her sister's face. "What is it?" she whispered. "What happened to you?"

"It's not like that," Jetta said, hearing her sister's concern. "It's just… I don't…"

The words didn't come to her, but Jaeia wouldn't need them.

I don't need your help, Jetta thought. Before her sister had a chance, Jetta bit back on their silent connection so that Jaeia couldn't probe any deeper than her surface emotions.

Folding her arms tightly across her chest, Jaeia kept her voice soft and even so as not to be overheard by the other staff. "Yes, I am upset with you, but I still love you. I just want to know what it's going to take to keep you from running away again. I don't want to always be chasing after you."

Unable to say the words out loud, Jetta projected them across their bond. *I'm so sorry, Jaeia.*

(My apology will never be enough.)

A lump formed in her throat, and she swallowed hard to keep from crying. *I can't lose my cool in front of the other soldiers and officers,* she thought to herself. *But there's just so much I can't say or feel.*

"You still need to go through medical," Jaeia sighed. "And what is this—a gunshot wound?"

"It just nicked me," Jetta scoffed.

"And I see you removed your chip," Jaeia said, palming Jetta's neck. "You can have seizures, neurological dysfunction, delusions—"

Jetta brushed her hand away. "Thanks for the dissertation. I'm fine. And having a seizure probably saved my life."

Jaeia opened her mouth, but Jetta cut her off. "It'll have to wait. Debrief me first."

"You're not getting off that easy," her gray-eyed twin said.

To Jetta's dismay, Jaeia made her go through a medical exam during the hours they spent jumping back to the Alliance Central Starbase.

"I can repair your spinal cord to fix the damage caused by digging out the chip," the ship's surgeon said, looking over the scans of her cervical vertebrae on his datapad. "But I'm afraid the damage is severe enough that biochip reimplantation will have to wait for a few weeks.

Don't you even think about celebrating that fact, Jaeia conveyed to her silently, giving her arm a pinch. Jetta hid her smile and laid down on the exam table as the doctor continued his assessment.

"Do not let her leave before you're able to patch those soft-tissue injuries and remove the bone fragments from her arm," Jaeia ordered.

"Yes, Sir," the surgeon nodded, motioning for his assistant to bring another tray of instruments.

"It's the least you can do," Jaeia whispered to her. Ashamed, Jetta said nothing, silently agreeing that her own failure to comply with standard protocol could further jeopardize her already-poor standing.

As Jetta went through the treatments, Jaeia stayed by her side and caught her up to speed on all that had transpired on the Alliance home front. Despite the circumstances or the tension between them, Jetta felt relief to be by her sister again.

"I'm worried about Triel," Jetta said, gnawing on the inside of her cheek. She couldn't say what she really meant, but she knew Jaeia sensed her regret and would be smart enough not to press for it. "And I don't want to think the Deadwalkers are back."

"Me either," Jaeia said as the doctor finished the treatments and gave her discharge orders.

"I don't suppose you'll carry out my instructions to rest quietly," the doctor said to Jetta.

"It's doubtful," she said, testing out the fracture repair in her arm. "But thanks."

After exiting medical, the sisters walked in silence to the main hatchway, sharing more memories and worries. The ship rocked gently as the arms of the port reached out and clamped down, securing the craft in the bay of the Alliance Central Starbase.

Jaeia touched her hand. "I'm too scared to think what might be possible."

The sensation reminded Jetta of the strange moment when she thought she had felt Jahx again, but she didn't share it with her sister. *It's most likely a hallucination and I don't want to burden my sister with any more of my problems.*

"I'm not going to lie to you, Jetta—there are about twenty charges the High Council is filing against you. You're just lucky there were no deaths at your jump site."

"The foundation worker—?"

Jaeia nodded. "He's okay. You owe Triel."

"Thank the Gods," Jetta whispered, pressing her knuckles into her eyes.

"However, given the current threat level, the Minister is assigning you to head the next team to investigate the blackouts. We've lost contact with the squadron that was just sent. So for now, you're getting off only because you're the commander of the SMT."

Still in shock, Jetta tried to wrap her head around an enemy with the ability to instantaneously deaden the communications system of an entire squadron and probably to wipe them out just as quickly. It was unparalleled, unprecedented, and in her heart she knew that if anything or anybody was capable of such an atrocity, it would be the Motti Overlord, M'ah Pae.

"Jetta, there is much to discuss," Jaeia whispered as they stepped through the umbilicus connecting the starship to the base. Soldiers, awaiting their arrival to escort her on base, saluted.

I know, Jetta said through their connection.

"No, you don't," Jaeia whispered. "I have information that I'll need you to review. It will change everything."

What is that? Jetta felt something she never thought possible radiate from her sister's mind. *My sister...she's doubting the system she has so heavily invested in after the war with the Motti.*

Without breaking her gait, Jaeia slipped something into the side pocket of Jetta's pants. Jetta schooled her face not to show any recognition.

Why don't you just tell me now? she asked.

Jaeia shook her head. "Because I don't want to believe it."

"Hey," Jetta said, stopping her sister as she began veering away toward the Defense/Research Department. "I just got to see you, and now you have to go?"

Jaeia nodded as she typed in a reply to a message she received on her sleeve. "I just got orders from the Minister; I have to meet DeAnders for some kind of emergency consultation. That's all I know. I'm missing that meeting you're going to, so it has to be big."

"Okay," Jetta said, eyeing the soldiers watching her every move. "I'll meet up with you afterwards?"

"If you aren't reassigned—or booked," Jaeia said, hugging her tightly as she signaled for a lift. "Whatever happens, be careful. Come back to me. I still have to kick your *assino*."

Jetta tapped her sister's chin with her fist. "You wish, softie."

As Jetta parted ways with her sister, she realized just how much she'd missed her. Lingering in the hallway, Jetta watched Jaeia board a fast-transit lift until she disappeared around a bend.

(I don't want to be ever be apart like that again.)

"Sir," the lead soldier said. "I must remind you of your destination."

"Yes, thank you," Jetta said, not masking her frustration.

After calling another lift, Jetta rode with her escorts to the conference room in silence, her mind divided amongst her mission, her sister, the dog-soldiers, and Triel. Even her former captors on Earth weighed in, pulling her mind back to their complicated parting.

Guilt pressed heavily against her sternum, but she fought back, determined not to let emotion overrule her actions. *I will make things right. I have to.*

As the lift turned a corner, her right arm grazed the datafile that Jaeia had slipped into her pocket.

I have to know what that is, she thought, unable to resist the urge.

"Stop by my quarters," she ordered the lift operator. "I need to change into uniform."

"But sir," the lead soldier said. "The Minister gave strict orders to—"

"I'm not going to a council meeting in scrubs," she said firmly.

Though a weak excuse, the soldier relented, buying her some time to look at whatever Jaeia had wanted her to see.

As the doors to her quarters closed behind her, the lead soldier reminded her of her limited time before the start of the meeting.

"I just need a minute," she mumbled to herself, pulling out the datafile.

She reimaged the seal in the background, tilting the datafile so she could see the official hologram. Seeing the crested Lionbird, Jetta concluded the source. *Pancar of Nagoorian.*

Jetta didn't know what to expect, but as soon as she decoded the massive file, the blood left her face.

"Oh my Gods," she whispered, reading the introductory paragraph entitled *Command Development Program.*

Slumping against the wall, Jetta felt the last remnants of trust she still vested in the Alliance disintegrate. *I didn't want to be right.*

***

Though he wasn't telepathically gifted in any sense, Damon felt the exact moment Jetta Kyron entered the conference room, even with his back turned to the entrance.

"Commander Kyron, so good of you to finally join us," the Military Minister said.

Damon caught a glimpse of her face as she entered, and his stomach dropped. The way the Minister spoke to her, he still assumed he had the upper hand. But Jetta, with her gaze that could cut down a Talian, was holding a deadly card.

"Did you enjoy your vacation on Earth?" Razar asked.

The entire military council shifted uncomfortably in their seats as Jetta and the Minister exchanged icy glares.

"Sorry I didn't write," Jetta said, taking her seat to the right of Wren.

Look at me, the admiral willed, trying to catch her eye. *Why is she ignoring me?*

The Minister glowered at her before continuing. "Chief Mo, please, let's get this underway."

Msiasto Mo stood up and read from his datafile. "We have discovered that the communications and visual blackouts point to a very specific trajectory, with Trigos as the primary destination. The alleged Motti ship is taking a path along highly trafficked zones, including routes through the booster highway. Since we don't yet know the method of transit for the alien ship, I propose that we shut down mass transportation hubs and deactivate all booster highway waypoints."

"Make it happen, Chief," the Minister said. Mo bowed and took his seat again.

"Chief Wren," the Minister said.

Gaeshin stood up and addressed the entire room. "The last scout ship was able to report back after we had him monitor the edge of the blackout area for 138 hours. Here are the results."

The room darkened as the projector came to life.

"This is Lieutenant Daley, reporting. I've been on the trail of the blackouts for four days now, and there appears to be no activity in the areas affected by the alien ship. All personnel from outpost 313 are missing, and the ship *Hoveron* was found adrift in planet XV-175's orbit. The ship was gutted, and the crew was missing; there was no way to recall any of the ship's readings prior to the blackouts."

"It goes on," Wren says, pausing the projector, "but it's more of the same. Whatever this thing is, it's literally cleaning out everything in its path and leaving no evidence of any struggle."

"What's the closest anyone can get to it?" Jetta asked.

"Long-range retroimagers are the only sensors that can detect the anomaly, putting you at about solar range," Mo answered.

"Right now we have them in the borderworlds, closing in on the perimeter, so our actions must be swift," the Minister added. "They will reach the first cityworld in less than twenty hours."

The admiral studied Jetta as she processed the information, her green eyes narrowing and lips pursing. Her intensity reminded him of one of his former students, and it made the hair on the back of his neck stand on end.

"Have you tried a bioscan or a residual marker boost of the affected area?" Jetta asked.

The room fell silent. Mo finally spoke up, "No, we have not, Commander. What would be the purpose?"

"Because if it is the Motti, then they're most likely using some kind of biodegenerative device—maybe a bioweapon streamed into a remote transporter. That could also account for the fact that conventional scanners can't detect any kind of activity in the area—some sort of bioelectric distortion could create that kind of readings blackout."

"Chief Mo?" the Minister said.

Mo nodded and inputted commands on the sleeve of his uniform. "We'd have to link the bioscanners with the long-range sensors. That would take at least two hours."

"Do it. Any other suggestions?" the Minister asked, looking around the room. Unipoesa held his hand above the table, signaling that he passed, as did the rest of the council.

"We will reconvene at 1700 hours to go over those results. Prepare your teams for launch. Commander," the Minister said as the others left the conference room, "going so soon?"

Jetta finally glanced at Damon, anger and disappointment darkening her face.

Unipoesa looked away. *She's found out about the* Hixon.

"I need to submit my report on Earth," Jetta said. "Then I'll make my way to the brig. Sorry; I guess that means I'll miss the next meeting."

Razar glanced at Unipoesa before speaking. "The brig?"

"That's where you're going to send me after you read my report."

"Commander, I don't quite follow," Razar said.

Jetta frowned. "Of course you don't. You weren't expecting me to run into one of your Sleepers on Earth. What a terrible coincidence. And you probably weren't expecting me to glean some of her memories, either."

"Jetta," the admiral said, looking back to make sure the doors were closed and that they were the only three left in the conference room, "you don't know the whole story."

Jetta nodded. "I know enough. I know that the woman I met on Earth was some kind of pawn, and that you wiped and replaced her memories so that she could run your errands when she didn't measure up. And I'm guessing since she was brainwashed on the *Hixon*, that you're probably turning Reht and dog-soldiers into Sleepers as well."

"Commander," the Minister hissed, nostrils flaring, "you're out of line."

"It's all about control, isn't it? You have to control all of your little worker bees. So what about me and Jaeia? You can't turn a telepath into a Sleeper, so what's next for us, huh? As long as I keep fighting your battles you're going to keep me around, right?"

"Jetta!" the Minister boomed, slamming his fist on the table. "Sit down!"

Jetta stood defiantly, unmoving. The Minister got in her face,

207

his eyes ablaze. "Your anger is misguided. You discover half-truths and then you come to me, your superior officer, spouting off like an imbecile. I would do you a favor by sending you to the brig."

The admiral came to Jetta's side. "If she met an Agent on Earth, Minister, she might be able to help us."

The Minister didn't take his eyes off Jetta. "Stay out of this, Damon."

"Jetta," the admiral said, trying to break her away from the Minister. "One of our Agents on Earth had a very specific mission, a very important one, and she's been unresponsive. We have no other way of carrying out this mission on Earth without her. Who did you contact on Earth?"

An expression of guarded curiosity crossed Jetta's face, and as she studied him, a tickling sensation edged around his mind.

Please, he thought, *I'm on your side.*

The tickling sensation stopped.

Still looking perturbed, Jetta reached behind her back and then tossed him a pair of beat-up headphones. "She called herself Agracia."

Has it been that long? Unipoesa wondered, turning the headphones over in his hands, careful to keep the emotion out of his thoughts. He had to be very cautious about what he said and did next.

"You were her teacher," Jetta whispered. "I saw you, I heard you. She admired you, and you broke her."

Her words cut through him, jarring old pain from its sleep. He tried not to let it show as he spoke.

"I know of whom you speak," he said as calmly as he could. "She was my best student. She was better than Li. But she was too sensitive, too empathetic. You know what happened to her at her final exam?"

The Minister exchanged deliberate glances with him, but Damon didn't censor himself.

"Afterwards, she wouldn't eat, wouldn't sleep—we kept her in medical for a full three months. She was broken. The only thing left to do was to make her an Agent. It was the happiest ending."

"Happiest ending? For her—or for you?" Jetta said.

The admiral could feel the Minister's eyes burning a hole through his uniform. "We did what was best for the collation."

"How many kids did you break, Admiral?" Jetta persisted.

The Minister stepped in front of the admiral. "It was our answer to the Dominion's threat back in the days of the USC. It does not need to be justified to you." He got back in her face. "I want that report on your experience on Earth and every detail about the Agent you encountered."

"Why?" Jetta asked. "What's so important about her?"

The admiral allowed his thoughts to slip for a moment. After forming the words in his head, he imagined projecting them to Jetta. When he glanced over to her, she appeared stunned.

"Commander, your officer status is under strict review," the Minister said. "I suggest that you write that report and have it on my desk before launch. Until then, I'd advise you to keep your mouth shut and keep your focus on your duties, or else I will send you to the brig, Deadwalkers be damned."

Don't— the admiral thought, sensing that Razar was close to striking her, and that Jetta anticipated such a maneuver. But the strike never came; the Minister was wise enough not to give her any further provocation.

"Yes, *Sir*," she replied, giving the admiral a sidelong glance.

Damon wanted to stay and talk to Jetta, but the Minister motioned for him to follow. Thinking of his own tenuous status, he obeyed.

"If I find out you've been feeding her any kind of *gorsh-shit*, I'll have you hanged for treason," the Minister said in a low voice as they exited the conference room.

"You needn't worry; I'm not brave enough to face the Kyrons' judgment," he remarked coolly.

"Agracia. Of all the fools she could run into on Earth, she had to run into her," the Minister muttered as he summoned a lift. "And now she's unsecured," he said, squeezing the headphones in his hands.

"She's been hard to trace for months," Damon said. "And she's become harder and harder to control. At least this way we've made contact. Maybe there's still a chance we can salvage her mission."

The Minister rubbed his face and sighed as they boarded the lift. "There hasn't been hope in 1,100 years, Damon. That's a long time. We have a lead, now, and that's more than we've ever had, even if it is a long shot. Now more than ever, we need that chance. If this

Deadwalker ship can't be stopped—if these civil wars continue—then what will be the point?"

The admiral didn't know how to respond. He knew better than to assume that the Minister's motives were purely for the benefit of Earth, the humans, or even the other Sentients, especially since the Minister's species had the greatest longevity of any known living creature.

"Speaking of civil wars, did you get a chance to read my latest report?"

"No, I haven't had the time," the Minister said, gripping the side rail of the lift as they swung around a corner. "This business with the blackouts has had me sleepless for too many nights. Too many *gorsh-shit* public appearances, reassuring all the *godich* bureaucrats that we've got the situation under control. I hate civvies."

"We had a breakthrough. A Sleeper Agent ran into one of Li's call girls on Vetrius while she was running errands for him."

"Vetrius the colony?"

Damon hid his amusement. *Razar always confuses the two.* "No, the fourth moon of Jue Hexron. The girl didn't give a specific location, but it would be too coincidental for Li to be hiding out near a snake like Victor. I want to assign a team to press Victor, see what he's hiding, what he's running. I've looked at the movement patterns in and out of the Holy Cities as well as the surrounding solar travel. If Li wanted to mount an offensive, the Holy Cities would be a prime location."

"I'm hesitant to assign you to such a mission now, given our situation in the borderworlds."

"We have to do something now, Sir," Damon said. "Li would take advantage of our distraction on the borders to rally a Fleet."

"Fine. But your choices will be limited—I want our best strategists on the blackouts situation."

The admiral tried not to let the comment bother him. "I understand."

"The situation on Jue Hexron is technically Jaeia's assignment—consult with her. I'll leave it up to you to form the team," the Minister said as he stepped off the lift at the entrance to the defense wing. "Just be careful with Victor—he's not like other Deadskins."

The admiral saluted and resumed his course to central

operations as the Minister parted ways, thinking of the Minister's caution. *Victor is human—a smart one, but still human. It's Li that is going to be the one to answer to.*

Or so he thought.

CHAPTER VI

(You tricked me,) *Jahx said, shutting the door to the apartment. It rattled on its hinges, plastic cracking, even though he hadn't closed it that forcefully.* (Why did you do that?)

Standing in entryway, the Grand Oblin smiled, his wrinkles obscuring his eyes. (No trick—just had a hunch. How did you get back here, anyway?)

(With difficulty,) *Jahx said, sagging to his knees. He held his head in his hands.* (They did something to your body; I was able to come back.)

The Grand Oblin nodded as if he understood. (Yes, I noticed I still had this,) *he said, tugging at the thread of his robe running out the door.*

(Why would you want me to have your body?)

(Because I'm an old man,) *the Oblin said, drawing an imaginary circle with his walking stick.* (And during my life as a priest I left many promises to God unfulfilled.)

Jahx watched the walls of the apartment cave in, disappearing into a dark gray shadow, the Oblin fading along with it. With the crippling exhaustion that weighed down his will, Jahx wasn't sure how much longer he could keep it together. (I would appreciate your candor at this moment. Neither of us really has that kind of time.)

The Oblin smiled again, his withered hand reaching out to Jahx's. With every ounce of strength he had left, Jahx managed to crawl over and take his hand.

(You would honor my life and my work by assuming ownership of my body,) *the old man said.* (I'm sorry it isn't in better condition—a few centuries tend to wear down the parts.)

(I can't—)

(You can,) *he said, squeezing Jahx's hand.* (And you must. For me, for your sisters—for the Starways. The things that you know cannot die with you.)

(You can go back—I told you everything!)

Jahx pulled the Oblin out of the way as a light fixture fell from the ceiling, but it turned to dust before it hit the floor.

(No, child,) *the Oblin said, placing his other hand on top of Jahx's as the entire apartment rumbled.* (I have work here to do. The others—my friends from Tralora—they are here somewhere in this place, and I will find them.)

(I cannot accept this. My life ended—yours has not!) *Jahx said.*

He gripped the old man as the kitchen wall cracked and groaned, debris falling from the ceiling, the deadly shadow closing in on them.

(You know the truth, even if it is hard for you to accept,) *the Oblin said.* (Now is the time for you to fulfill your destiny, to finish what you started. Be gone, my friend, and tell your sisters I said hello.)

Jahx didn't anticipate how quickly the old man could move as he scooped him up and tucked him underneath his arm, bolting for the entryway. As the last remnants of the ceiling, floor, and walls collapsed and faded into oblivion, they burst through the front door.

(You have my blessing!) *the Oblin shouted as he pushed Jahx away and into the shifting light.*

Jahx screamed, trying to grab onto the old man as they separated in the plunge, but all he could find in the chaos was the thread of the Oblin's robe. The sturdy thread once again cut through his hands before he could trap it between his feet to slow his descent.

(Thank you,) *Jahx whispered, feeling the ethereal warmth return as he slid into the celestial cloud and crossed over to another world.* (I will make your sacrifice count.)

***

Jaeia wasn't sure what she was expecting when she entered the Division Lockdown Lab. From the emergent call, the Defense/Research teams had found something—or someone—but she was too afraid to be hopeful.

DeAnders found her before she entered the stasis chamber.

"Commander," he said, putting his clipboard down. "Follow me."

Jaeia followed him onto the observation deck behind the sterilization field. She looked down and saw the Grand Oblin's body on a medical table, leads and tubes of solution dangling from his body. Though he breathed on his own, his eyes remained shut, the monitors beeping steadily in the background.

"My Gods—he's alive?" Jaeia said, pressing her hands to the glass. "He made it?"

DeAnders cleared his throat. "He's regained consciousness once, but now that his vital signs have stabilized, we're hoping he's going to reemerge again."

Jaeia heard the concern in his voice. "But...?"

"But," DeAnders said, removing his glasses and massaging his eyes, "his brain waves and metabolic demands are off the charts, even for a Berroman. From the readings, I'd guess that his body is undergoing metamorphosis."

"Metamorphosis—like shape-shifting? Not to be obvious, Doctor, but he is a shape-shifter."

"Yes, but there are limits," DeAnders said, pulling up a file on the nearest terminal for her. He pointed to the subject outline and comparative data below. "Given his advanced age, his body is theoretically incapable of creating new forms; he can only shift into bodies that he has previously established. So something must have happened during his transport to activate his cell identifiers to generate a new shift. It's overtaxing his system."

Jaeia looked squarely at the chief. "How badly?"

"I wouldn't be surprised if we had to keep him on some kind of life-support," DeAnders replied frankly.

Jaeia shook her head. "Can I see him?"

DeAnders looked at her over the tops of his glasses. "My orders are strict, Commander. You're here as an advisor, to give a positive confirmation that it is or isn't the Grand Oblin. If it is him, we need to know why he came back but the others have not."

"He's not in any imminent danger, is he?" Jaeia asked, glancing at the old man again. He looked peaceful on the medical table, his breathing rhythmic, facial features relaxed and unfettered.

"Dr. Kaoto is supervising, and I have my team rotating shifts so he's under constant surveillance."

"It would be nice to have Triel," Jaeia whispered, thinking of the Healer.

"Let's get you down there," DeAnders said, leading her through the sterile field and down the stairway.

The closer she got, the more she realized that the Grand Oblin's body was changing. His skin wasn't as wrinkled, nor was his beard as gray or as long as she remembered.

After taking a seat next to him, she tried to find exposed skin that wasn't hooked up to a machine. Finally, she placed a hand on his shoulder and closed her eyes.

Hello? she called silently.

"The patient's heart rate is accelerating to 120," someone said in the background.

Jaeia held onto the lip of the cold medical table with her free hand. "This isn't him—"

She felt DeAnders' hands on her shoulders, trying to pull her away, but her hold seemed cemented to the Grand Oblin. She screamed as she fought against the phantom sensation crawling up her arm and drawing her inwards, away from her body.

(No!) *she screamed as she was torn away from corporeality. She flung out her arms and legs, trying to combat her assailant, when she heard his voice:*

(Jaeia.)

Jaeia opened her eyes. A figure standing over her illuminated the darkness of the interspace.

(No...)

She couldn't believe it—she wouldn't. (This is an illusion.) *But the way he smiled, the way her body melted into his when he wrapped his arms around her, she couldn't help but give in and hug him back with all her strength.*

(How is this possible?) *she said between sobs.* (You're dead—you can't be real.)

He took her hands and looked at her squarely, his familiar blue eyes connecting with hers. (It's a long story, but I promise it's me.)

(What about the Grand Oblin?)

Jahx held her hands in his. (This was his gift.)

She shouldn't have believed him so easily, but the way he talked, the way his mind was so accessible, the familiar harmonies of his inner voice—she didn't want to believe that it wasn't. And though she knew she should have felt loss and heartbreak for the Grand Oblin, the overwhelming elation of her brother's miraculous survival erased all other sensibilities.

Tears streaming from her eyes, she hugged him again and kissed his cheek. (Please tell me this is real, Jahx. Please tell me that you're not going to go away.)

(I'm not planning on it,) *Jahx said with a broad smile.* (And I think it's time to wake up.)

When Jaeia opened her eyes she found herself back in the Division Lockdown Lab. After several seconds the walls and ceiling stopped seesawing, and she found that she had somehow ended up on the ground. To her surprise, her hand still rested on the Oblin's shoulder in an impossible stretch.

"Are you okay?" Dr. Kaoto asked, scanning her as a nurse took her vital signs.

"Yes," Jaeia said, picking herself up and sitting back in the chair. She had to catch her breath before reassuring them again. "I'm okay."

Then she realized who was lying before her. *This is the body of the Grand Oblin, but it's not him.* A smile spread across her face. She laughed, the tears flowing once more. "I'm more than okay."

Jaeia grabbed his hand and squeezed, causing one of the monitors to alarm. "Wake up, Jahx, wake up!"

"Jahx?" she heard DeAnders say.

"Jahx," she called, stroking his gray hair. "Wake up now."

"These readings can't be right—" DeAnders said, pushing aside Dr. Kaoto to look at the monitors. "I need 1,000 mls of cytosalin, stat!"

Jaeia ignored the surrounding flurry, holding her breath as she watched the transformation unfold before her eyes. The Grand Oblin's familiar features dissolved, and his tall and lanky frame thickened. Where old, stringy muscles had been stretched across a bony frame grew soft skin with developed muscle tone. Gray hair slinked back to a shorter-cropped black, and the long, hooked nose resolved to a finer tip. The yellowing of the Oblin's nails cleared, and the brown and black spots of age that had once speckled his body disappeared.

When he opened his eyes, Jaeia recognized the familiar blues and her heart leapt into her throat.

"It's really you," she said, throwing herself on top of him. The nurses and doctors pried her off, warning her about his fragility as they adjusted his intravenous fluids and scanned and rescanned his body.

"I'm okay," Jahx smiled.

"This is weird," Jaeia said, inspecting his new body. He was not the young boy she remembered, but an adult Jahx, comparable to her own unusual age. "It kind of looks like you… just older."

"This feels right," Jahx said, lifting his hands and turning them every which way.

"Jaeia—what's going on?" DeAnders demanded.

"Chief," Jaeia began, but she stopped. Suddenly she felt guarded, and she wasn't sure why. "This is my brother, Jahx."

"You're telling me this is your brother?" DeAnders said, pointing to the young man trying to rise from the table. The rest of the room went silent.

"Yes. I don't know how it's possible, but it's him."

"Where's Jetta?" Jahx asked eagerly as he sat at the edge of the table, ignoring the warnings of the staff.

Jaeia felt Jetta on the periphery of her mind. "She's on the station! I'll get her right away."

Jaeia closed her eyes, sending her sister the urgent message she could barely believe possible.

"She doesn't believe me," Jaeia whispered to Jahx. "She's going to have to see you for herself."

Jahx smiled and tried to stand, but then he closed his eyes and sat back on the table. "I'm not feeling one-hundred percent yet."

"That's because your body can't handle this transformation," Dr. Kaoto said. "You're going into ketoacidosis. We need you back on that table so we can stabilize your system."

Jahx complied but reached for Jaeia's hand. "Can you bring her here?"

"Of course," Jaeia said, squeezing his hand before turning to leave.

"Wait," DeAnders said, stopping her in her tracks. "I want to know what's going on. There is no way that's your brother."

"That is Jahx, I promise you," Jaeia said, wiping the tears from her face. "I don't know how he did it, but he did. This is going to change everything."

"Wait here," DeAnders said, typing commands into his uniform sleeve. "I'm calling Commander Kyron down here now."

Jaeia returned to her brother's side as the team worked to stabilize his system. Beneath youthful skin his new body struggled, but her focus was on the possibilities that were almost too frightening to conceive. For the first time in her life, there was a chance that they could be three again, and that maybe, now that Jahx was back, her sister might forgive her for the awful choice she had to make during the last war.

"Jahx," Jaeia whispered, intertwining her fingers with his. "I'm so happy."

"I'm going to have to ask you to leave," DeAnders said, putting a hand on her shoulder. "We're having a tough time stabilizing him, Commander, and we need room."

"What do you mean?" Jaeia asked, sensing his fears.

"Just wait in the observation deck and let us do our jobs," Dr. Kaoto said, turning his back to her as he injected something into Jahx, making her brother's eyes close and his mind slip away into a deep cavern of sleep. "We're trying to save his life."

With her hope and fears at the pinnacle of her awareness, Jaeia stumbled her way back to the observation deck. She watched as the medical and research teams worked in tandem, a steady chaotic parade of movement around the still form of her brother.

"Please," she whispered, pressing her forehead to the observation glass. "Not again."

***

Triel drifted in and out of consciousness, faintly aware of the steady montage of images and sounds that floated past. Dim figures discussed her fate, but she didn't really care. She felt good, her mind swimming in an ecstasy of chemicals.

She saw faces that didn't belong—her father, Reht, brothers and sisters, Jetta and Jaeia—as the lights passed over her in regular intervals, one after another, unending.

"Don't move!" someone shouted.

Pain seemed to branch out from her hand, routing through every nerve fiber, torching her entire arm. She screamed, but hands held her down.

"Hey—wake up!" someone shouted in her ear.

The room spun in every which direction, and when her eyes finally focused, she found herself in some kind of infirmary.

"My name is Captain Usin," said a man with scales across his face standing at her bedside. "You're on the starship *Mercury* outside the Vadis nebula. Do you remember how you got here?"

Triel shook her head, unsure of what he was talking about, but then her memories slowly trickled back.

The Alliance. Stealing a ship. Trying to find the crew of the Wraith. Then her mind went blank.

Her mouth felt parched, full of sand. "Who... who are you?"

"How is she, doctor?" Captain Usin asked. "How bad are her injuries?"

"Not too bad. Concussion, minor abrasions, burns. Nothing serious. I'll have her patched up in no time," responded the dark-skinned man standing to her left. He bent down and inspected her through an intraphase camera affixed to his left eye. "I haven't seen a Healer in years. And your ship had Alliance markers. You must be Triel of Algardrien—the last Healer of the Starways."

The captain and a few other crewmembers took a few steps back while the doctor beamed at his discovery. Triel was used to such discomfort, but it didn't make it any easier. "Yes," she sighed. "I am."

"Well, don't worry, you're safe now," the captain said, walking over to a terminal and interfacing with the projected keypad. "Your ship jumped right into the orbit of our mining arms and you had a nasty collision. Had a hell of a time getting her free—the motherboard was completely fried and the engine was blown, so remote navigation was impossible. But I think we can tow you back to the Alliance Central Starbase for repairs."

That doesn't sound right, Triel thought. *I don't know why, but I can't believe that explanation.*

"How long have I been here?" she asked, sitting up. Even the slightest movement made the room wobble and dip as if she were at sea.

The captain exchanged glances with the doctor. "A few days. You were pretty banged up when you got here. Doctor Nka says that memory loss is common, but I'm sure it will come back to you."

Triel didn't care about anything else he had to say. Even though they were prospectors under the protectorate of the Alliance and relatively hospitable, she didn't trust them. With their mixture of human and fishlike Mallok ancestry, they had open, accessible minds, but that did very little to quell her suspicions.

"Can I contact the Central Starbase?" Triel asked.

"Of course," the captain said, taking his com off of his uniform and handing it to her.

"Do you have a private terminal, perhaps? This is an important matter," Triel said as politely as she could.

The doctor shook his head. "You're a bit weak right now—"

Triel scowled and slid off the bed, luckily catching herself on the edge of an exam light. "I'm fine. And I insist. As chief medical advisor, I have the right to a Level 1 secured channel."

The doctor muttered under his breath as he called for an aide to escort her to his office. When the transparent door sealed shut, Triel input the admiral's signature into the wave network query.

"Admiral," she said when his face appeared on the monitor.

"Chief," he said, bending into the viewscreen. "I'm glad to see that you're okay. I heard about your accident. The *Mercury* will get you back within the hour. The Minister and I would like to review the events with you."

"And I with you. Something's going on here."

He paused. "Something is definitely going on. You stole a ship."

"My friends were in danger."

He paused again. "When you arrive we'll discuss these events, and you can contact Reht and the crew. They've passed through the communications dead zone, and you'll be able to see for yourself that they're alright."

Triel rubbed the webbing between her fingers. "Will I be sent to the brig?"

The admiral's face remained carefully neutral. "Report to my office once you're on board. We'll review your case then."

He signed out without another word.

I am in trouble, she thought, *but the urgency in his voice—my actions are not the top priority.*

Triel rested her head in her hands. *Something's missing; something's very out of place.* It didn't feel right that she had crashed into the mining arm, but she couldn't dispute the doctor's account.

Jetta, Jaeia. I need them, Triel thought to herself. *Maybe they can make sense of these feelings.*

Thinking of Jetta, her heart sank. *My friend... how could I leave her?*

Triel signaled to the staff that she was done. The aide and the doctor came through the double doors to help her back to the bed.

"Don't worry," the doctor said, trying to reassure her. "Everything is going to be alright."

Triel thought of Reht, the crew, and Jetta. "I wish I could believe that."

***

Reht knew that the Alliance was going to screw him over one way or another, and when he saw the *Wraith,* he knew that something was definitely up. It appeared perfectly intact and unaltered, sitting in the loading dock with a fuel line pumping into her tank.

"You know the agreement," the red-haired captain said, meeting him at the ramp to his ship.

Reht didn't care for many Deadskins, but he particularly despised the captain of the *Hixon.* There was something unusually sleazy and conniving about him, but he couldn't quite put his finger on it. The feeling was even worse than the one he had gotten around Guli, and that *ratchakker* had tried to kill him.

"I don't get all the kindness," Reht said.

"It's a hefty favor from the admiral and the Kyrons," Captain Shelby said. "Believe me, I'd rather you were worm fodder. Just know that I'll pull the trigger if you ever even graze my radar. Stay out of Alliance territory."

With a sneer, the Shelby turned his back on him.

"Son of a—"

Reht lunged at the captain, but Mom grabbed him and held him back with his blue-furred arms.

"I know, I know," Reht said, trying to wrestle out of his first mate's arms grips. "That *ratchakker* is just trying to provoke me. Let me go already."

With a growl Mom released him, but stayed close to his side as they boarded the *Wraith.*

"We're getting the hell out of here," Reht mumbled, shoving past Ro and Cray and heading straight for the bridge.

"It smells in here," Cray moaned as he inspected the weapons pit.

"That's just you," Bacthar muttered as he ducked under a support beam.

"It's a *chakking* trap," Ro said, kicking one of the terminal monitors. "This thing is rigged."

"Tech, get Billy Don't plugged in; see if he sees anything in the computer systems," Reht said, throwing his jacket onto the captain's chair.

"Billy ain't right, Captain. Not sure what it is," Tech said, scratching his head. "He seems a little... flakey."

"Flakey?" Reht said, watching Billy Don't spin around like a top. "Isn't this how *chakked* up he usually is?"

Tech shrugged. "Can I use the main power circuits and do a complete shutdown/reboot on him?"

"Not now—it'll waste too much time and fuel," Reht said. "We've got bigger priorities. Just get him jacked in, okay?"

"Yeah, sure," Tech said, scrambling after Billy. The little Liiker whizzed down the hall on his back wheels, squealing as the mechanic tried to catch him.

"What's wrong, Vaughn?" Reht said. Vaughn, normally mute, kept his gaze fixed ahead. The scar across his forehead was a reminder of the ex-con's stint in the prison system's rehabilitation program, but Reht sensed this wasn't a result of his "frontal regrouping." Even before they left the Alliance his brain was screwed up, but now it seemed worse. Vaughn's eyes, once trained to the navigational systems, seemed unfocused and empty.

"Heyyyy there," Reht said, snapping his fingers in front of his face. "Wake up, man, I need you to get us out of here."

Vaughn turned his head slowly, his pupils pinpoint, lips parted slightly. He stared at Reht for a moment before switching on the navigational controls.

"Bacthar," Reht shouted into the com. "Headcase is acting up. Get over here."

"I'm missing half my instruments!" the surgeon yelled over the intercom. "Those military bastards took my instruments!"

"*Chak*," Reht said, rubbing his forehead and slumping into the chair. *Gods, this headache—it's almost too much to think.*

"Ro, just get us the hell out of here," Reht said.

Ro had taken over piloting the *Wraith* since Diawn's departure, but it was a stretch to call him a pilot.

"Yeah, sure," Ro mumbled as he hit the throttle. He forgot to unclamp from the loading dock, and the ship lurched forward, catapulting the captain from his chair.

"Oops," Ro said, correcting the error. The ship took off again, and the captain rolled backwards, smacking his head against an armrest.

"You suck, Ro," Reht said, climbing back into his chair as the

Wraith sped away from the *Hixon*.

"I ain't a pilot," Ro reminded him. "I just kill stuff, remember?"

"Where are we going?" Reht asked, closing his eyes and massaging his temples. Mom came up behind him, assuming his usual perch against the railing.

"Let's go to La Raja," Ro said, licking his lips. "I need to relax a bit. This Alliance *gorsh-shit* has messed up my head."

"No, let's go to Vortmor Port and get some action. I haven't killed anybody in months," Cray said, scrambling up from the weapon's pit.

Reht checked his armrest console as he pulled out a pack of smokes. "Aeternyx?" he exclaimed. Vaughn had already laid in the course. "Why there?"

"We need a pilot," the navigations officer replied flatly.

Reht dropped the pack of cigarettes on the ground and laughed uncomfortably. "Whoa! He speaks! You definitely aren't feeling okay, Vaughny."

Ro looked at Vaughn indignantly. "*Chak* off, Headcase."

"We need you in the pits, *assino*," Reht said to Ro, shooting him a warning as he stuffed the smokes back in his pocket, "so lay off. Besides, Aeternyx—*sweet land of eternal night*—I bet you boys could find some fun there. And none of the girls will have to see your ugly faces."

The usual banter erupted, and Cray and Ro got into another fight over who was better-looking, but once things died down, Reht began to wonder: Why Aeternyx? It was on the other side of the galaxy. Yeah, it was a hotbed for up-and-coming hotshot pilots, but there were places they could go that were less dangerous. But he felt almost compelled to go there, like it was the right course of action.

"*Gorsh-shit*," Reht mumbled, letting his head rest on his chair. "Bacthar, I need something for this *chakking* headache," he said over the intercom.

Ro turned around and offered him a snip of spirits from the flask inside his jacket, but Reht declined when he caught a whiff. "Dear Gods—are you still siphoning off engine fuel to mix with your booze?"

"I likes the way it tastes," the Farrocoon said, taking a slug.

"Hey, I got a headache too, boss" the winged surgeon said, coming up from behind him and offering him medication. Mom growled at the handful of pills.

"I'll get you something, too," Bacthar said, nodding to the Talian. "Hell; must have been something in their water."

Reht didn't think much of it as they entered the jump cycle. *It's time to get my feet wet again, time to play.* He thought of his Starfox, but their last interaction—their terrible fight— had left him bruised and wary. Usually he'd at least try to finagle one last hookup, but impassive and benumbed, his mind told him to move on. What they had might have once been real, but now he felt detached and uninterested.

As the stars sped by on the viewscreen, Reht squirmed in his seat, unable to satisfy a deeper part of himself. *I don't understand what happened; Triel and I have never argued like that.* But when he tried to recall details, tried to analyze why they had parted ways so suddenly and so venomously, the need seemed to dissipate.

"It's time to get back to business, boys," Reht said, tapping his fist against his armrest.

"Systems check out," Tech said over the intercom. "She's spotless. There weren't any rider programs, worms, viruses— anything that we could detect, even during the jump. If they did something, neither Billy Don't nor the computer can find it."

"Alright then," Reht said as the red and black planet appeared on his viewscreen. "It's time to find a pilot and have a little fun."

Getting through customs was the usual hassle, and without Diawn to bribe their way through, Reht had to part with his last remaining stash of narcotic cigars. That made him even more wary that the Alliance was screwing with him. *They should have sniffed out the illegal stuff over lesser infractions like Bacthar's stolen medical equipment.* But he couldn't worry about that right now. *Vaughn is right. If we want to get back into the game, we'll need a decent pilot.*

"Night city, we're back," Reht said, stretching out his arms as he stepped off the docking platform with his first mate. Neon colors illuminated the city, its constant buzz of electricity and Sentient activity broken by the thunderous noise of the Metalclash stadium located in the heart of the entertainment district. The sun, hidden beyond the horizon, offered only a hint of its existence, painting the tips of the rocky spires to the east yellow and orange.

"Eh, more like eternal dusk than night," Bacthar commented,

coming up beside him and taking in the same view.

"As long as it's dark enough to hide Cray's ugly face," Ro laughed as he came down the ship's ramp with his cohort.

"*Chak* you, Ro," Cray said, readying to fight. With one snap of his jaws Mom ended the battle before it began.

Reht remembered his first exposure to Aeternyx, studying the planet's strange orbital pattern before he ever touched down on the surface. One side of the planet remained forever exposed to the sun, baking the surface to nearly 1,000 degrees Kelvin while casting the other in freezing shadow. Radiation and solar farming were the planet's only legitimate businesses, masking the true nature of the city that should have never been. Dog-soldiers and private businessmen like himself loved Aeternyx because of its mysticism, the allure of a place so sinful and unbound by law that a man like him could write his own ticket. But there was a certain protocol he had to follow, one that every hustler, streetwalker, dog-soldier, drug lord and pimp knew. Move too slow and get eaten alive, move too swiftly and wind up in a dumpster with your guts cleaned out.

The way Mom looked at him, Reht knew his first officer's reservations.

"Look, mate," he said, slapping him on the shoulder. "I hear ya. I know the Alliance probably has us tailed or tagged or something. But we can't live our lives pissin' our pants like launnies. We play it safe for awhile, but we still gotta play."

Mom growled, his claws sliding out from under his forearms.

"If it makes you feel better, we can take the *Wraith* over to the impound lot and have Lonnie look her over for bugs," Reht said. "He owes me one after I bailed his *assino* out of that deal with Mick."

Mom rolled his eyes, securing what was left of their hard cash in his satchel as Reht signaled for a taxi.

They rode through the city streets, necks craned to the sky, marveling at the explosive displays of lights and noise. Each building rose to a minimum of ten stories, and promoters made use of every available centimeter of space to sell their products and services. Banners and signs projected living colors, and transwave audio tones rang through their heads, advertising everything from prostitutes to illegal weaponry.

By the time they hit the central crossing, Ro and Cray had decided to hit the alleyways for their flavors, and Bacthar had gotten off on the market street to replace his missing supplies. Since Tech and Billy Don't stayed at their usual post on the ship, Reht was left with his loyal first mate and Vaughn. If somebody didn't keep an eye on the ex-con, he usually wound up incarcerated, but he was acting so twitchy that Reht preferred to do it himself.

"Look, that's Klex's old joint," Reht said as they whizzed past the red light district, its shady buildings glowing with advertisements for the hottest girls. Mom grumbled, unhappy to pass by their old enemy's territory.

"This place never changes, only the players," Reht said as a shootout broke out across the street. Their lift operator seemed unaffected as he veered around the corner to the Strip.

"Ahhh, now I'm home," Reht said. Streetwalkers clumped around the entrances to each bar, their pimps keeping watch from the balconies of the cheap hotels that sat on each joint. Reht waved to the ladies as their lift touched down in front of Suba House.

"Hey, big guy," one of the painted ladies said, throwing her hips out towards him. Her dark hair and blue eyes reminded him of Triel. "How about a little fun tonight?"

"Don't mind if I do," Reht chuckled as he plucked a hundred in cash from Mom's satchel and tucked it into his pocket.

In the back of his mind stirred an uneasy question: *Why aren't I missing Starfox? It hasn't even been more than a day...*

When he put any thought to it, only a vague, emotionless memory of the Healer drifted by.

(I should feel something—grief, anger, longing—shouldn't I?) a strangled voice inside him cried.

I feel nothing, he thought, walking toward the painted ladies. His passion for Triel, a force that had once pulled him out of his pursuit of the most dangerous game, had completely dissipated. Free of that, he found himself drawn away by the same undercurrents that had once taken him too close to the edge. *(Just like after my parents were killed.)*

Reht looked at his bandaged hands, imagining the scars through the ragged cloth and laughed. "I'm going to have a good time tonight, aren't I?"

As he slung his arm around one of the painted ladies, she gave him a slick smile. He saw the devious glint her eyes, but didn't care. The animal scent under the sweet smell of her perfume ignited his loins, and sense and caution dissolved.

"I missed you, darling," he said to the painted lady. "What was your name again?"

"You can call me Tracey," she whispered in his ear as she led him down the stairs and into the Suba House bar. Mom followed reluctantly, snapping his jaw at the streetwalkers that tried to offer him their services.

Suba House, owned by human descendants of Earth's Asian continent and Nahvari investors from the borderworlds, dazzled with terrestrial and otherworldly cultural fusions. Paper lamps and gold-painted dragons dangled from the ceiling while entertainers plucked stringed instruments and geishas worked the floor. The Nahvari influence revealed itself in the choice of radiant colors and the communal pipes that vaporized strong-smelling herbs.

Reht allowed Tracey to lead him to one of the private booths as Nahvari dancers, covered in blue and red paint, gyrated across the center stage.

"Fifty hard cash gets you topside, five hundred gets you full service," she said, grinding on his lap. She playfully bit his ear as her hands slid under his jacket. "But I'll give it to you for three hundred. Don't get them as cute as you very often."

"Well, how sweet," he said, pulling on her hair, bending her backwards, making her chest pop out of her corset.

Mom pulled up the curtain to their booth and growled at the girl.

"Get out," Reht growled back. "That ain't funny, mate."

The giant Talian motioned toward the empty space beside him.

"*Chak*," Reht said, seeing that Vaughn had disappeared. "Well, you don't need me to go find him, do you?" Reht said as the call girl ran her tongue down his neck.

With another insistent growl, Mom pulled open his empty satchel, showing that the ex-con had lifted their cash.

"*Ratchakker*," Reht cursed, shoving the girl off and making a break for the exit.

She yelped, falling over into the other side of the booth and cracking her head. "That prick is jacking me," she screamed to the bouncer guarding the front door.

Before the bouncer had a chance to aim, the Talian dropped his claws and sliced right through his gun. Frightened, the other bouncer backed off, raising his hands. Reht caught the barkeep reaching for his firearm and whipped out his handgun.

"Get down!" someone shouted.

The musicians stopped playing their instruments and the dancers took cover behind the stage. Some of the customers sought the protection of their booths while other reached for their weapons.

"Hey—this ain't a fight," Reht said, raising his other hand. "It's all cool, brothers."

"We were dealin'!" Tracey said, pulling her shirt back over her breasts.

"We were just talking, baby," Reht said.

"You got a lot of nerve, *ratchakker*. You pay to talk around here," the barkeep said.

"I said it's cool, right? Let's keep it that way," he said, backing out of the door as his Talian covered him.

"Don't ever let me catch you, *kunéndo*!" the barkeep screamed as the double doors closed.

"Atmosphere was good. Bad service," Reht commented, returning the handgun to its holster under his jacket.

Back on the street, Reht took the first corner and wound his way through the alleys until he was sure that he and his first mate had put sufficient distance between them and any interested parties from Suba House.

"Something is definitely wrong with Headcase," Reht said. He leaned against a brick building and caught his breath. "Where do you think he went?"

Mom's eyes narrowed as he scanned the street ahead, grumbling to himself.

"Yeah," Reht said, rewrapping the bandage on his left hand as he thought it over. "That bastard could be anywhere."

Because of the rehabilitation methods of the prison systems, the ex-con wouldn't use drugs, wasn't interested in gambling, and was even less interested in sex. But there were still one thing that got Vaughn to react—violence. And in Aeternyx, the city of sins, any and every pleasure could be found.

"I know what you're thinking," Reht said, seeing the scowl on Mom's face. "But he's the best navigations officer we've had, and he's saved our *assinos* too many times to count."

Mom glowered at him.

"Fair enough. But let me have a piece of him before you eat his face, alright?"

Reht heard shouts coming from the alley and figured the bouncers from Suba had caught up to them.

"Hey, up there," Reht said, pointing to the cement building up ahead. A solitary lamp illuminated plated metal doors as slow-moving hovercars with tinted windows cased the street.

The area is relatively quiet, so it's either a safehouse or a dealer's warehouse, Reht guessed, neither of which he would have minded patronizing right then.

"Come on," Reht said, running across the street with Mom close behind.

"Yo," he said, rapping on the door. "Can't a guy have some fun around here?"

The eyehole winked open and someone peered back. "You, but not your muscle."

"What, him?" Reht said, slapping the Talian on the chest. "He's a lamb. Let us in."

"No chance, *ratchakker*."

Reht remembered the hundred he had stuffed in his pocket. "Good enough?"

The door locks turned over, and the bouncer snatched the hard cash from his hand, looking them over carefully. "What business you have in here anyway? You don't look like hunters."

The pursuant shouting grew closer, the static runoff of the phase rifles echoing in the alleyways.

This is gonna get messy if we don't get in fast, Reht thought, resisting the urge to look over his shoulder. *Think quick. This* assino *mentioned 'hunters,' so this shitbox is probably a bounty post.*

Reht grinned. Maybe they could pick up a job, get them back on their feet. And if they had a big enough payoff, then maybe he could hire a decent pilot.

"Isn't that all the better?" Reht said, shouldering his way past the bouncer.

The bouncer looked like he would retaliate, but he eyed the Talian and backed off.

"This ain't pretty," Reht whispered as they entered the killing floor.

Looking around, Reht recognized the violent markers of the

brutal world of bounty posts: A sparsely outfitted room with poor lighting and a single bar tap in the corner with no attendant. Overturned tables and broken glass littering the floors, and smears of blood, both old and fresh, painting the ruined walls. A few dog-soldiers and hunters milled around a beaten Sentient who lay on the floor with blood spilling from his mouth and the wounds on his chest. Whatever he was trying to say came out in gurgles. Soon he was quiet, his body limp.

"Looks like we missed all the fun," Reht said under his breath.

Stepping closer, Reht saw that the dead man was a Toork, a large, lumbering beast of a Sentient who would give any challenger, even a Talian, a hell of a fight. It was unusual to see one taken down, especially without guns.

Reht glanced around to see who had been daft enough to challenge, and somehow manage to kill, a Toork.

A mixed-breed outerworlder with midnight skin and glowing eyes pointed at Reht and Mom. "What the hell you looking at, pretty boy?"

Reht's trigger finger compulsively flexed, but he gave off only a shrug. The last thing he wanted to do was upset an alien the size of Mom with huge, gauged piercings spearing his body from head to toe.

"Leave them alone," a voice said, dead and hollow. "They're with me."

Shocked, Reht took a step back as Vaughn, splattered with blood and knife in hand, worked his way out from behind the crowd.

"Holy…" Reht whispered. Unaccustomed to anything but the ex-con's usual stupor, Reht could not reconcile the violent need in Vaughn's eyes, or the way he licked the blood off his lips with distinct satisfaction.

As Vaughn moved toward them, Reht eyed potential exits, taking solace in the slick sound of Mom's unsheathing claws.

"You or him in charge?"

Reht eyed the fellow who spoke. Short and squat, he carried a machete on his waistband and a chip on his shoulder.

I've never seen a native of Aeternyx, he thought, studying the man's heavily scarred, ghostly-white skin. Eyes, red and translucent, seemed to burn right through him. *Especially one with such intense albinism.*

The fires in Vaughn's eyes disappeared, and he spoke in his usual monotone: "He's my captain."

Still in shock, Reht barely took his sights off Vaughn to glance again at the short fellow. "What's it to you?"

"I run the bounty board in these parts. Your boy just won the rights to the highest-payin' gig in three systems," the albino said.

"Is that right?" Reht said, finally realizing what Vaughn had done. *That crazy bastard jacked my cash to buy in to the fight for the highest-paying bounty. What the hell?* As long as Reht knew the ex-con, Vaughn had never acted aggressively unless provoked or directed.

I still want to slit his throat, he thought. *Then again—this is one hell of a bounty.*

"How much is it?" he asked.

"Two million—in hard cash."

"*Chak*," Reht chuckled, running his hand through his hair. "*Gorsh-shit.*"

Vaughn stood before him, blood still dripping from his hands and knife, eyes vacant and emotionless. Reht cautiously approached him, keeping an eye on the knife.

"Why'd you go and do this, Headcase?"

"Seemed like a good idea at the time," Vaughn whispered, dropping his gaze to his feet.

"He's quite the fighter. I never, ever seen no humanlike take down a Toork. Best fight in decades," the albino man said, kicking the Toork in the head. It bobbled back and forth, a pink tongue lolling out of one of the Toork's mouths.

"Next bid is in twenty, boys—get ready," the albino said, motioning for Reht to follow him.

The albino man led them into a back office where a young girl, probably no more than fifteen, sat half-naked on his desk. She wore only enough clothing to cover her most coveted areas, but the black netting didn't leave much to the imagination.

"Time for play?" she asked, giggling as she spied Reht, Mom and Vaughn.

The albino slapped her on the butt and jabbed his thumb at the door. "Business, sweetie. Go wait for me upstairs."

Reht tried not to stare as the young girl walked out, her undeveloped hips swaying side to side, small breasts bouncing up and down.

"Where do you get them that young?" Reht asked as the albino shut the door.

"She's a real Puppet from Earth," he said, tucking his overstretched tank top into his pants. "Got her custom-made a while back. Stays young forever, but still wears out, if you know what I mean."

Reht raised a brow. "Custom job?"

The albino sported a smile with several missing teeth. "The Puppeteer usually don't like you hittin' 'em too hard and breaking their parts, so they designed the puppets with a self-preservation program. But the maker owed me a favor and made me a special girl of my own—without limitations, if you get my drift."

"Yeah," Reht said, hiding his discomfort with a chuckle.

The albino sat behind a cheap wood composite desk and offered Reht, Mom and Vaughn plastic chairs. Mom, seeing it would not hold his weight, stood behind his captain. Already uncomfortable, Reht eyed the old clock radio on the desk playing metallic core music and wished he could chuck it across the room.

"Name?" the albino asked.

"Jagger. Yours?"

The albino looked him up and down. "As in Reht Jagger, captain of the *Wraith*?"

Reht nodded.

The albino seemed to think it over before responding. "Ash."

Placing a dataclip into the feeder drive, the albino accessed the terminal mounted on his desk. "Well, this bounty is probably of particular interest to you. I heard she hates you. Wants you dead."

Reht took the dataclip Ash slid across the table and studied it.

"Collect information on the activities of former dog-soldier Diawn Arkiam," Reht read aloud. "What the hell? That's it?"

Ash leaned back in his chair. "That's it."

"Who posted this bounty on her?"

"It came through a few channels, so it's hard to trace."

"Your best guess," Reht said, leaning forward in his chair and flashing his incisors.

Ash looked unaffected. "Best guess is that since this is a high-paying bounty, it's best not to ask too many questions."

Mom's low, disapproving growl didn't prevent the gears in Reht's mind from turning. *Diawn has probably found a way to make a lot of money, and it's most likely pissing off one of her competitors. And since it's not a kill or capture bounty, someone is being careful about knowing her connections first.*

"How do you know Di, friend?" Reht asked.

The albino snorted. "Are you kidding? Who doesn't?"

Reht didn't know how to take that. "What?"

"Look," Ash said, unhooking his machete from his belt and placing it on his desk. "You want this bounty? I have about a dozen other guys who are ready to rip each other's throats out for this chance."

Reht thought it over. "How much you make with buy-ins and fights, without even including your share of the bounty?"

Ash grinned. "Enough."

"Looks like I got in the wrong biz."

The albino scrawled a name on a piece of paper and handed it to Reht. "This is a friend of mine who knows the area better than anyone and can probably get you headed in the right direction. She's vicious, so watch your *assinos*. Most likely she's got eyes out for hunters. Well, and the likes of you."

"Right," Reht said, putting the piece of paper in his pocket. He didn't like the way the albino said that.

"Hey," Reht added, "I need a cash advance. I lost my pilot, as you know."

The albino pulled a roll of hundreds out of his pants pocket and casually tossed it to Reht. "Thirty percent return on that, plus twenty percent of your take."

"Go *chak* yourself," Reht said.

The albino smiled again. Light reflected off the metal studs that capped the last of his teeth. "Don't *chak* with the wrong people, Jagger. Your Talian won't always be enough, you know."

He saw Mom dropping his claws and held up his hand.

"Twenty percent return on the loan, fifteen percent of the take—plus I'll throw in something special. Something for a man of your appetites, yes? Something fresh."

The albino licked his lips. "Done."

As Reht left the bounty post with his first mate and navigations officer, he couldn't shake an unsettling feeling. *This seems way too chakking coincidental*. But the idea of two million hard cash drew him in too deep to reevaluate.

"Hey Mom—don't worry," he said, knowing his first mate's reservations. "We'll keep it tight."

"And Vaughn," Reht said, elbowing the nav's officer. "I'll slit your throat next time you jack me."

"I didn't want to. They told me to," Vaughn whispered.

Reht snorted. "Who told you?"

He didn't answer.

Forgetting that Vaughn had just butchered a Toork, Reht grabbed the ex-con by the collar and slammed him up against the brick wall of the nearest building. "Boy, you are lucky I still need you."

Vacant eyes stared back at him, unreactive to his aggression.

"Get Headcase examined when we get back and have Bacthar double up on his meds," Reht said to Mom as he let Vaughn go. "And I want some digs on that *chakking* pedophile back there. If we can whip his *assino*, I'd be most pleased."

Reht reached into his back pocket, withdrew a semi-smashed pack of cigarettes, and tapped out a smoke. It had been so long since he pulled a job—especially one with such high stakes—that adrenaline was already rushing through his veins.

As he signaled for a taxi, Reht slapped his Talian on the back. "You're gonna have fun, I tell you," he said, lighting his cigarette and taking a long drag. "This is going to be one hell of a ride."

***

Jetta burst onto the observation deck to find her sister pressed up against the glass partition.

"Where is he?" she said, pulling her off the glass.

Jaeia's eyes, red and swollen, reverted back to the scene below. "There," she said, pointing to the medical and Defense/Research teams milling around the body of a young man with dark hair, an angular jaw line, and prominent cheekbones.

"Who is that?" Jetta asked.

"That's the Grand Oblin," Jaeia said, wiping the tears off her face. "And Jahx."

Jetta imprinted off of her sister's open mind, reliving what her sister had just experienced.

The Grand Oblin gave his body to Jahx—and our brother is somehow alive inside of him? It didn't make sense; she didn't want to believe it. *It's improbable—impossible—that the thing I want most might actually come true. Things like this don't happen to me.*

"I want to see him," Jetta said, trying the keypad to the internal door, but the Defense/Research team locked from the other side.

"DeAnders said he's unstable; they're trying to save him right now. Please, Jetta—if it's really him, let them do their work!"

Jetta slammed her fist against the keypad and pressed the intercom. "DeAnders, let me down there. I can do more than any of you."

DeAnders looked up to the observation window, his glasses reflecting the overhead lights. "Let her down."

Without waiting for the technician to get out of the way, Jetta tore down the stairwell, jumping down half the flight. She muscled her way through the medical staff until she stood at the head of the table, near the Grand Oblin's left shoulder.

"Commander, we had to put him under. His metabolism is overtaxing his body," Dr. Kaoto said. "Whatever you plan do to, do it with caution."

Jetta took the young man's hand in hers and tuned out the rest of the world.

(Who are you?) *she demanded, searching the psionic world within.* (If you dare pose as my brother, I will destroy you right now.)

In the distant realm of corporeality, he squeezed her hand. (You haven't changed.)

Blue eyes emerged from the shadow, as well as the kind smile that instantly brought her to her knees.

(No—impossible!) *she screamed. He wrapped his arms around her, holding her tight, even as she slammed her fists into his chest.* (You're not real!)

The rest of her body gave out, and he eased her to the ground.
(You're dead—I killed you,) *she cried.*

Stooping down to her level, he put his hands on her shoulders, a half-smile lighting his face. (You always underestimate me, Sis. That's why I kick your butt at rock dice.)

His quirky sense of humor, his unique way of offsetting her emotions. Tears rolled down her cheeks, but she backed up, away from him, too scared to believe.

(Prove it's really you. Prove you're not an imposter I have to kill.)

Sitting back on his heels, he twirled the hair at nape of his neck. (You've never beaten me in rock dice—well, not without cheating. You have the world's stinkiest feet, even by Fiorahian standards. You love the smell of precoolant mix, and you're afraid of hair clogs in the sink. I mean, *really* afraid,) *he said, chuckling.*

Jetta's eyes grew wide. (I still can't—)

He smiled sadly, looking away from her. (Jetta, I'm so sorry. I asked you to do something that was too much to ask of any person. I know it wasn't easy to fight the thing that I had become, but you saved my life, as well as all those who were trapped with me. Now they are at peace, and I am here.)

(Jahx—) *She tackled him to the ground, hugging him until he slapped her on the back to ease up.*

Something inside her broke loose. She arched her head back and screamed. The moment she hadn't dared dream about cleaved through her like electric fire, sending joy rippling throughout her body. His psionic harmonies layered against hers, rhythmic and synced, his words once again resounding in her head.

(I am so, so sorry Jahx,) *she managed to say between sobs. She pulled away a little, searching his eyes for the answer she needed.*

(Jetta,) *he said, his face serious.* (I don't know how long this body will last. So with what time we have, I have to tell you what I learned on the Motti ships—it is the answer you'll need.)

(No, Jahx,) *she said, gripping his shoulders.* (I won't let you go ever again!)

(Jetta, you have to listen,) *he said, voice and image growing distant.*

Something—or someone—is pulling us apart, *she realized, fighting to stay anchored to his mind as she crossed back over into the physical world.*

"Let go!" she screamed, careening backwards. Her arms spun out of control as she landed on her back, a tray full of instruments toppling down on top of her.

"Commander!" DeAnders' bespectacled face appeared above

her, his grip like a vice on her upper arms. "We had to pull you out. Your interaction proved too much of a strain on his body."

Jetta geared to retaliate when the whine of the vital signs machine sent the technicians scrambling for their devices.

"I—I'm sorry," she said, discontinuing her fight. DeAnders backed off and helped her up. Legs feeling rubbery, she held onto the plasma filter until she righted herself.

"Jetta," Jaeia whispered, coming up behind her and wrapping an arm around her shoulders. "I can't believe it."

Jetta held onto her sister's hands and squeezed. "I can't either."

They watched in silence as the teams stabilized their brother by inducing a coma, slowing the demands of his borrowed body. Jetta felt him on the edge of her awareness, his psionic tune quieted by chemistry but still tangible and familiar.

"This changes everything," Jetta said, turning to her sister.

Jaeia's gray eyes focused on something beyond Jetta's figure, and she shifted her weight on her feet. *What are you planning?*

I don't know yet, Jetta said.

The interface on Jetta's uniform sleeve beeped. When she turned her arm over the Minister's face appeared. "Report, Commander. DeAnders tells me that you made contact with the Grand Oblin, but that he's somehow… your brother?"

Jetta looked to her sister, but Jaeia focused all her attention back on Jahx. *How do I respond? I don't even known if I can believe my own words.* "Yes," she said finally, her voice barely audible. "It's true."

The Minister acted as if he didn't hear her. "Commander?"

"I don't know how," Jetta said. "I can't explain it. But it's him."

The Minister stared at her a moment. "What's his condition?"

Jetta looked at her brother, extending herself as far as she dared into his mind. "It's hard to tell right now."

"Be that as it may, I need you and your sister to convene with the other senior officers for an emergency meeting. There's been a status change."

Jetta stared blankly at the Minister. She was supposed to acknowledge him, but the words weren't there. *How can he ask that of us right now?* she thought, anger brewing in her chest. *We just got our brother back—*

Jaeia grabbed Jetta's arm so that her face was in the visual field, responding for them. "Yes, Sir; we'll be right there."

"Why did you do that?" Jetta asked after the Minister signed off.

"You know why," Jaeia whispered. Gray eyes locked with hers, and Jetta felt her sister's warning. She didn't have to say it. Jetta looked at her brother unconscious on the table and knew it wasn't time yet.

***

Reht Jagger couldn't believe it. The albino had written down the name *Modoki*, but after asking around, the dog-soldier captain discovered it was just another stupid pseudonym for his old source, Mantri Sebbs.

"Ridiculous," Reht said, throwing the piece of paper over his shoulder. "He's still a *chakking* junkie spinning info."

Pushing past the streetwalker who had given him a tip, he threw her a bill which she dropped to her hands and knees to collect.

"*Chakking* cheapskate!" she screeched after him.

"Yeah, yeah."

Reht hiked up his jacket and squared his head before heading down the steps of the Suba House. Returning would be dangerous, especially since he had just baited a girl there, but the streetwalker said that Sebbs was hiding out inside, so he needed to get in.

Wearing the new hat, jacket, gloves and holosim glasses he purchased in the back alley got him through the front doors easily enough, but no disguise, no matter how good, could get his massive Talian past the bouncers. Mom, with much protest, stayed behind with the rest of the crew, making sure they would be ready for dust-off when the captain returned.

"Of course," Reht muttered, spotting Sebbs in the back of the booths with the company of a dancer. But the usual Sebbs—the twitchy one who was unable to function without getting high, wasn't there.

"Surprised you're here," Sebbs said as Jagger sat down across from him. Mantri didn't look directly at him. Instead, he sat back and enjoyed his lap dance, his hands running up and down the dancer's legs. "Chubs out front is looking for you, has some Dogs on your tail."

"That's an extra fifty, poppy," the dancer said, pushing out her lips when Sebbs tried to get under her skirt.

"Get the hell out of here," Sebbs said, shoving her off. She began to protest, but he threw her a stack of fifties. "I don't have time for an ugly face like yours."

That isn't Sebbs. Reht eyed him closely, trying to understand where this man had come from as the dancer flipped them off and took his money.

"What are you looking at?" Sebbs said. Normally he would have lit up by now, but he didn't. Sebbs didn't even look stoned.

"Where the *chak* did that half-baked Joliak go? Remember—the one with the shakes and the inability to get himself laid?" Reht laughed, removing his glasses and hat.

Sebbs' eyes narrowed. "Where'd you just come from?"

"I just got a job," Reht said, raising his voice to be heard over the sultry singer on the center stage. "Wanted to pay you a visit first."

"No, before that. How'd you get away from the Alliance?"

Reht shrugged his shoulders. "Easy enough. Had some hot, *gorsh-shit* transport device and I bargained my way out. They kicked me to this end of the universe, but it squares with me."

Snickering, Sebbs licked his lips. "Right, brother. Right. And how you feeling? Anything different? Still sleep at night? Still feel the same as you did when you first walked on their turf?"

Reht shifted uneasily. "What's your point?"

Sebbs took out a pack of smokes and tossed them to Reht. The package was full, unopened. "These old flavors aren't the same. My pleasures aren't the same—I'm not the same. They did something to me."

Reht gripped the gun strapped to his thigh and then relaxed. Everything that had ever come out of Sebbs had to be taken in stride. "Nah. I'm good. And I'm just about to make some real cash, get back in business."

Sebbs chuckled, slouching into the booth and closing his eyes. "I can feel it. The thoughts I have—these urges. They're not me. I don't want to get high, I don't like the same girls. My pleasure comes in deals, dangerous ones, ones that will get me killed. That's my new delight."

Reht thought of Triel, but he stopped himself. *That* baech *left me. There's no more to think about.*

"Are you going to come on to me next or what, Sebbs?" Reht said, taking a cigarette from Sebbs' pack.

Sebbs opened his eyes again as the music changed and a score of dancers dressed in red and white graced the stage. A predatory look lit Sebbs' eyes, making Jagger strangely uncomfortable.

"I did some snooping back when I was cross-dealing to the USC and the Core. There was a program that the USC started, very hush-hush, as a means of silencing their enemies but using them in covert operations. Never did get more than that. But for you and me," Sebbs said, pulling down the lower lid of his eye, "it might be worth investigating."

Reht swallowed hard as Sebbs' words drove into him like a kick to the chest. Leaning over into the next booth, the dog-soldier captain stole a shot of whiskey from the passed-out patron and downed it with urgency.

"Look man, just tell me about Diawn," Reht said. "You seen her, heard about her—anything? I'll cut you in a grand if you give me a decent lead."

Sebbs nodded as if he'd solved a puzzle, but only offered the captain a grin.

"You've lost it, brother," Reht said, standing up to leave.

Sebbs grabbed his wrist. "Check the landfills, near the waste refinery up north. She's been known to do deals there."

"What's she dealing, man?"

A dark shadow fell over Sebbs' face. "You'll find out soon enough. It'll blow your *kádes* off. She's in the upper echelon now, playing with the big boys, so she isn't going to waste her time with a *ratchakker* like you."

Reht wrenched himself free and put his glasses back on. "You're a sick *chak*, Sebbs."

"Whatever they're offering, brother—it isn't worth it. The Alliance, they're behind everything. They're using you just like they're using me," Reht heard the Joliak call after him as he hurried toward the front entrance.

"Hey, you!" the barkeep shouted as Reht passed by.

Reht tried to walk faster, but the bouncers had already alerted to his presence.

"*Chak*," Reht muttered, reaching for his gun. Out of the corner of his eye he saw the bouncer draw his weapon and jumped behind a table just before his enemy got off the first round off. Screams erupted, as did more gunfire. Patrons and dancers rushed every which way, some felled in the crossfire. Reht tried to fire back, but the multiple guns aimed to his position hopelessly pinned him in the corner.

Smoke curls rose from the holes in the table serving as his protection, obscuring his view. *They're closing in on me,* he thought, seeing the bouncers advancing in on his position. *I'm as good as dead—*

Then the pummeling stopped. The gunfire redirected away from him and toward the back of the bar. Reht peeked around the table to see Sebbs firing at the bouncers and the barkeep.

Taking advantage of the shift, Reht shot at the lead bouncer and barkeep, killing them with hits to the head and chest. With splattering blasts to face, Sebbs took out the last two bouncers. Reht shot the remaining thug, armed only with a broken bottle, in the leg.

Reht approached the man he crippled, intending to pump him for information, but Sebbs leapt from the booth and drove a knife into the thug's jugular. The Joliak twisted the knife as he withdrew, a perverse smile on his face.

Speechless, Reht backed away as Sebbs rose, blood dripping from his hands, dented grin still plastered to his face. *Just like Vaughn,* Reht thought, reminded of the grisly look in the ex-con's eyes after he slaughtered the Toork.

"I'm not right, you know," Sebbs said, dropping his weapon to the floor. He searched a few corpses, pocketing money and valuables. "This isn't me."

"*Chak,* Sebbs, I—"

The Joliak tossed Reht a platinum bracelet off a dancer. "Remember what I said. Don't go after Diawn. It's a setup. You're working for them now, just like me."

With that Sebbs disappeared, taking off into the streets. Hovercars and lifts honked and screeched as they swerved to avoid hitting him.

Scratching his head with the butt of his gun, Reht looked at the mutilated thug on the ground. "Between you and me, partner, that's some pretty messed up *gorsh-shit.*"

He tried to think of Triel, whether there was any connection, but he found he couldn't. *Maybe Sebbs ain't that crazy...*

But Sebbs was crazy, paranoid—he always had been. However, if his information about Diawn was correct, Reht was that much closer to being rich. He didn't want to think—he couldn't think—about giving any merit to Sebbs' conspiracy theories.

(Triel—)

Then a bizarre revelation hit him. There was a benefit in losing interest in the Healer. It meant he was free again, that he didn't have any attachments, any reasons not to answer to his lowest instincts. He could do his business like a real dog-soldier and make some real profits this time around. Forgetting Triel would be the best move of his life.

Reht picked up his step as the patrons slowly wandered back in, some screaming and fainting at the sight of the bloody crime scene. *Time to go,* he told himself merrily.

Fixing the collar to his jacket and securing his hat, he eased into the crowd on the street, heading towards his ship and his crew, imagining what he would do with his newfound riches.

CHAPTER VII

It wasn't the first time had Jetta pulled out a clump of her own hair as she adjusted her hair tie, but it was more than had ever come out before.

"Jeez," Jaeia whispered.

"I've seen you do it too," Jetta said.

Jaeia kept her gaze ahead as the two of them walked down the hallway toward the conference room. "It's just stress."

"Whatever," Jetta said, tossing the clump of hair onto the walkway. She spied a janitor's closet and grabbed her sister, yanking her inside with her.

"Hey!" Jaeia shouted as Jetta closed the door.

Jetta couldn't see her in the darkness, but she saw the light of her psionic aura. "Calm down, Jae. I just want you to remind me why we have to do this. I know Jahx is sick, but I know he'll make it. He has to."

"Jetta—"

"We should stay here, with him."

"All this time you were serving the Alliance in hopes that Jahx would come back?"

"No," Jetta said, shifting her feet. A mop handle jabbed her between the shoulder blades, but the tight squeeze left little room for reprieve. "I did it for you."

"Me?" Jaeia exclaimed.

"Yeah, you. You believed in the system and the idea of saving lives, helping people. And I guess, in some way, I needed it too after what's happened to us. Fighting felt good in some ways, like I was finally doing something right."

Jaeia stayed silent.

"You're a good leader and diplomat, Jaeia, but we never really needed this place. All we needed was each other. Jahx coming back is enough for me," Jetta said, fumbling for her sister's hand. "I don't want to be 'Commander'—they can cram their titles. And I don't want to be famous. I just want to be your sister."

Jaeia squeezed her hand. "I still believe in this system."

"What?"

"And I still believe that we can make a difference."

It won't be enough to have Jahx back, Jetta realized—not for Jaeia. His miraculous return didn't erase the unmentionable deeds they had performed under the influence of the Dominion Core.

That's why Jaeia went to all the trials, sat through all the miserable hearings about the deaths they had caused and the lives they had ruined. *Guilt keeps her from seeing the corruption within the Alliance and continue her service.*

"Jetta, this place smells. Can we talk about this after the meeting?"

"Fine. Let's just get it over with," Jetta said, shoving her way out. Soldiers that saw them come out of the janitor's closet gave them curious looks as they headed back down the hallway.

Frustrated, Jetta bulled her way through the conference room doors. The silent tension from the surrounding officers didn't faze her as she took her seat with a huff.

Jetta, please, Jaeia said, trying to get her to calm down as she took a seat beside her.

I don't care anymore, Jetta said. With Jahx back, she didn't see a reason to fight. *I'm tired of it all the* gorsh-shit.

When the Minister took the podium, his fear cut through her with fresh vigor, and her self-involvement ceased. Often emotionally guarded, his psionic vibrations rang out like a cymbal crash across the telepathic plane.

"The results of the modified scan have come back," he started. He stopped, catching his breath. His eyes searched the room, but he didn't seem to find what he needed. "Chief, this is your find. Please share it."

Chief Mo stood up. "Commander Kyron was right to suggest the bioscan. The results were more conclusive this time."

The holographic projector displayed a three layer view of the solar system Prax and the location of the alien ship across the room.

"With this scan we were able to clearly mark the regions of the distortion field, which you can see outlined in blue," Mo said, pointing to the highlighted borders. "However, tracking the activity within the distortion field is more difficult. We were able to determine that the alien ship is using some kind of hostile agent within that field, but we are currently unable to pinpoint the source. The areas affected by this event are in red."

Jetta inhaled sharply. The areas in red were inhabited or colonized areas: starships, asteroids, protoplanets, planets, and moons.

"Yellow represents the areas most affected by the hostile agent,"

Mo said. "These are dead zones."

The yellow areas followed the red, leaving a distinct trail of desolation across the system.

"Why can't we determine what they're using?" CCO Wren asked.

"Whatever they're using doesn't scan," Mo replied. "We can measure the reaction, not the cause. But at least now we're able to pinpoint the ship and its movement with more accuracy."

"And what is the reaction?" Wren said.

Mo studied his datafile before speaking. "Diffuse DNA deconstruction to both macro and microorganisms. The hazard teams have reported complete absence of life."

Two loose ends clicked together in Jetta's head, and her heart froze. In the back of her mind, she heard Jaeia make the same connection.

"None of your scans in the affected areas show any residual signs of an invasive virus, bacteria—any bioweapon?" Jetta asked.

Mo nodded. "That is correct, Commander. Our hazard teams have ruled out that possibility. But there are still other methods: low-frequency alphagraphic waves to neutralize the mechanical components of the outposts and starcraft, or perhaps streaming naturally occurring x-particles. Both would be hard to detect in the noise of space."

Jetta flexed her fist, her priorities suddenly torn. Realistically, her brother's condition was critical, and his recovery was dependent on the medical and Defense/Research teams. She still needed the Alliance, so she still needed to fight. And if she and her sister were right about the kind of weapon the Motti were using, the devastation upon the cityworlds would be catastrophic.

I have to protect Jahx.

(—I can't abandon all those people—)

The outpouring of emotion from within shocked her, but she bit down on her lip, countering the reaction with pain. She closed her eyes, her words coming through gritted teeth. "I've got to see this thing. I'll take a corvette with a skeletal screw—volunteers only."

"I'll go," Jaeia said firmly above the chatter of the officers.

"I can't allow that," the Minister said.

"If you let me to go with Jetta, we'll have a better chance of figuring out what this is."

"No," the Minister said, changing the image on the projector. "The issue became more complicated with the latest intelligence reports."

"What are we looking at?" Jaeia asked as star charts overlapped with marked routes.

"The flight patterns of several unregistered starcraft we've been tracking. As you can see, they all head directly for the suspected Motti ship," Chief Mo said.

Jaeia studied the tracings. "Those are cargo ships, aren't they?"

"Yes," Mo said.

Jaeia looked at Jetta. "So, someone's supplying the Motti?"

The chief of intelligence nodded. "We've cut down all booster highway routes, evacuated and stripped starposts of any jumpdrive technology, stopped all transit in the path of the ship—there's no way that vessel could be jumping through the systems without assistance."

"We need to buy ourselves some time," the Minister said. "We can't have that ship reach the cityworlds. Jaeia, I want you to lead a complement to intercept the supply ships. Get me some answers."

"I'll escort her to the border," Jetta proposed.

"Granted, but I want launch, PCP, and tactical readouts in one hour. Jetta, confirm your plan with Chief Wren," the Minister said, dismissing the council.

As the rest of the group filtered out, Jetta talked with CCO Wren and her sister about the mission. A tap on her shoulder alerted her to the admiral as he walked by and pretended to go over the meeting files at the table.

"I'll contact you on a private link," Jetta said to Wren as he left the conference room with the last few council members.

"I have a team to prep, Admiral, so let's make this quick," Jetta said, her anger rushing back as she faced him. She wondered why he'd want to talk to her and her sister in private, especially when they all knew that the conference room, of all places, was under constant audio surveillance.

Seeming to read her thoughts, the admiral held up a tiny magnetic device. "I took care of any unwanted ears."

"Why would you worry about that, anyway? You seem to be 'leaking' a lot lately," Jetta said, referring to his projected thought during their last encounter.

Resurrection. When the admiral allowed her inside his mind for a moment, she felt a seismic emotion interlaced with the word unlike anything she had ever felt before. From what little she could discern, 'resurrection' meant something beyond the admiral, beyond the Alliance, bridging lengths that she couldn't imagine, across vast planes of space and time to a place found in the hearts of all beings. And that it all linked back to her.

"All of us need to tread lightly these days. I'm doing the best I can," he said evenly.

Skeptical of his intentions, Jetta tried to look inside the admiral's mind, but came up against his usual mental barricades. "You're not the man I first met," she said. "I can see the monster now. You're going to tell me that you've changed, that you're no longer a child-breaker, that you're on a different path. But some things cannot be forgiven."

The admiral locked eyes with her. "Then you of all people should pass no judgment on me, Commander."

Careful, Jaeia projected to her sister.

Despite the cold blow, Jetta controlled her words as best she could. "What do you want from us?"

"You can hate me all you want, but I have always tried to do what's right, and yes, people got hurt. *Children* got hurt. You don't have to like me—I only ask that you continue to trust me. There are more important things at stake than your opinion of me." The admiral removed a dataclip from his uniform jacket and handed it to Jetta. "Here's a token of my trust in you two. I hope our dialogue will continue, because we'll need each other. The rest of the Starways depends on it."

"Is this about 'resurrection'?" Jetta asked.

Sadness and regret tinged the admiral's smile. He walked to the exit, pausing at the double doors. "We can discuss that when you get back. Good luck on your missions, Commanders."

The admiral left, leaving them alone with the dataclip. Jetta almost threw it in the trash, but Jaeia took it from her before she could dispose of it.

"I'm about this close to gutting every superior officer's mind," Jetta muttered, crossing her arms.

Jaeia raised a brow. "I can't say I haven't thought the same thing, but I do want to keep my skin. Here, look," she said, inserting the dataclip into her sleeve.

"What the hell," Jetta muttered, grabbing her sister's arms and reading the scrolling text. *Are those Agracia's orders?*

"This was translated into English," Jetta said as she read the original transcript in Common. "Agracia got a contract to download files from servers on Old Earth, specifically from some launch stations around ground zero. Weird…"

"What?"

"That's right around where I crashed. I must have interrupted that mission."

"Why did he give this to you?" Jaeia asked.

Jetta stared at the orders. "I don't know, but I think it has something to do with that word he projected at me—*resurrection*."

Jaeia looked at her, silently exchanging thoughts.

"I want to kill those Deadwalkers once and for all," Jetta whispered, letting go of her sister's arm. "I'm tired of military games, government cover-ups—and not understanding why. I want to go home, wherever that is, and have a family again."

"Soon, Jetta," Jaeia said, hugging her. "Jahx will heal, and we'll find Galm and Lohien—maybe even our real parents—and then we'll be a family again."

Even if Jaeia was humoring her a little, Jetta didn't care; it was what she wanted to hear.

"Jaeia," Jetta began. Her sister tried to pull away, but she didn't let go. "I'm not running, okay? We're going see this through together. Miracles can happen, you know."

Jaeia laughed and finally pulled free. Gray eyes remained solemn, but her words held firm. "I still have hope."

***

Reht Jagger ordered his crew to fan out around the waste refinery. The terrible stink of rotten fish and burning oil singed his nose, but the excitement in his gut built with every putrid breath. *So close.*

Even as armed men and crossbreed dogs walked the parameter in organized teams, Reht could only think of the massive cash flow coming his way.

This is going to be a huge payout, he thought, glancing up at the twilight sky layered with puffs of refinery smoke.

Reht rechecked his surroundings. Barbed wire wound around the barrier wall in a deadly maze, and laser traps flickered on every post.

"You ever seen a dog-soldier run anything this tight?" Reht whispered to his first mate as he crouched lower. "This ain't right. Reeks of military."

Grumbling, Mom surveyed the landscape, silver eyes narrowing with predatory focus.

"See that smokestack?" Reht said, pointing to the column of black smoke pumping from an unseen source. "Looks like engine burnoff. Somebody's itchin' for a ride."

Mom made a slicing motion across his neck.

"Yeah, probably should turn back. We don't have the manpower for this kind of in-and-out," Reht said, nudging Mom in the shoulder. "Ha ha, just joking. We can retire on this payout."

The giant Talian rolled his eyes.

"Look, there's a blind spot on the eastern wall. I'm going to take a look. You keep the boys here, and keep 'em ready."

Mom grabbed him and growled.

"Hey, old friend—I know what I'm doing, so just wait for my signal."

Without waiting for Mom's response, Reht jumped off their lookout point and slid down the mountain of garbage on the heels of his boots. Oily refuse rubbed up against his back, and he bit his tongue to silence his disgust.

After reaching the bottom of the refuse heap, he crept around the eastern wall, hugging the cement. As the searchlights swung back and forth, he counted the seconds in his head before making his move. Just as a light swept his previous position, he jumped into a narrow crevice between the juncture of two structural pillars.

"*Chak*," Reht muttered. "Too close."

He reassessed his position. Even though his crew couldn't see him, he still had his com. To be certain, he switched it off and tucked it under the bandages of his left hand. In a pinch, he'd need it, but he couldn't risk it going off and alerting the enemy.

As the searchlights danced across the other end of the perimeter, Reht jumped and grabbed the overhanging trellis. With a grunt he pulled himself up and over. He stayed low, popping his head over the lip of the barrier wall to catch a glimpse of what lay beyond.

"What the...?"

He popped up again, this time taking a longer look. Humans knelt together in rows, handcuffed and leashed together at the neck, muted by dermabond strips taped over their mouths. Thugs with their crossbreed dogs walked among them, snapping shockwands in their faces. Most had been stripped down to minimal cover.

My Gods—there are even children, he thought, spotting groups of little bodies huddling together for warmth.

Chilled by the sights and the frigid air, Reht pulled his jacket closer around his body. Aeternyx's warmer temperatures usually hit twelve degrees Celsius, but today, without the protection of the city's heated streets, the southern winds made it unusually brisk.

Keep looking, he willed himself.

About fifty meters away, a cargo freighter with the name *Ultio* inscribed in graffiti letters across her broadside rumbled with her engines in pre-cycle. Guards led a score of chained humans up the ramp, dogs barking at their heels.

Then he saw her. Even at a distance her figure was unmistakable. Her hand rested on the perfect curve of her hip, her shoulders thrown back to accentuate her augmented chest. She had dyed her hair again, this time black with a purplish hue. Holding a dataclip, she talked intimately with a small, wiry fellow as one of the thugs counted the humans entering the ship.

Reht remembered Sebbs' warning: *It's a setup.*

Closing his eyes, Reht pushed aside the warring tides of his mind. No, the job didn't feel right—

(—I don't feel right—)

—but he needn't worry. What he had to do was so simple. Brash, and definitely stupid, but this would reap him untold rewards.

Reht leapt off the barrier wall and walked right into the searchlight.

"Keep your hands where I can see them and get on your knees," a voice behind the searchlight shouted.

Reht turned his head to avoid the piercing glare. "Hey, man, it's good. I'm just here to visit my girl."

A gang of thugs jumped on top of him in a matter of seconds. In the background, Ro and Cray emerged from behind cover, but Reht licked his lips, signaling that he wanted them to stay put.

"What the hell are you doing here?" one of the thugs said, wrenching his arm behind his back.

Despite the excruciating pain Reht gritted out a smile. "I told you—I wanted to visit my lady friend. Where is she anyway? Where's my Diawn?"

The thugs exchanged glances. The one with a nasty scar across his nose looked him up and down before letting out an exasperated snort. "You're insane."

But they didn't argue any further. One grabbed him by the neck and led him into the compound, pushing his face down so he couldn't see anything but the ground beneath his feet.

"So, boys, gotta ask—what the hell do you want with these disease-breeding fleshbags? Deadskins aren't fetching a good price with real estate being this tight," Reht said.

The thug on his left scoffed. "Not everyone wants them hauling brick or pushin' out babies."

"Quiet," the one holding Reht's neck said, punching his accomplice in the chest.

This is too easy, he laughed to himself.

The white of her boots strode into view just before one of them connected with his chin. "Why did you bring this sack of *sycha* in here?"

Reht hated the taste of blood. He spat a few times and checked his teeth with his tongue before daring to look up. "Hey, Di. Nice to see you, too."

Chancing a glance to his left, Reht spied another chained line of humans filing onto the ramp of the freighter. The stink of body odor and urine hit him hard, turning his gut and making him wish back the smell of the landfill.

"Want me to take care of this *assino*?" Diawn's wiry companion said.

Reht got a good look at him. The man's face, pitted and scarred, appeared raw and fleshy, like a gaping wound with serrated teeth. As he leered at the dog-soldier captain, his eyes, sitting behind deep epicanthic folds, zeroed in on the blood trickling from the cut on Reht's lip in some sick carnal fixation.

What an ugly ratchakker, Reht thought. Any scumbag could afford cosmetic enhancement, especially on Aeternyx, which made the wiry fellow's hideous appearance all the more wretched.

"Diawn, baby—" he tried before a flash of silver silenced him.

Bewildered, Reht didn't initially register the blow. Feeling new warmth spread across his chest, he looked down, seeing shredded cloth and blood soaking into his jacket.

"Wait—no—" he pleaded.

She hit him again, this time across the cheek with the palm of her hand, and again with her boot in his stomach. He doubled over, unable to breathe as his diaphragm spasmed.

"I should kill you," she said, getting down into his face. "You left me to rot."

He gasped, trying to right himself, but the thug behind him stomped on his calf.

"You see this?" Diawn asked, pulling up her shirt. A ragged scar cut across her stomach. "You want to know how I made my way after you threw me out?"

When she struck him again, a glint of light gave away her secret.

Horrified, Reht barely made the connection. *Did she replace her fingernails with razorcutters?*

"Do you want to know the things I had to do to my body just to survive?" she said, nails slicing into his chest. "If you think my fancy new nails are bad, I'll show you what I had to do to my—"

Drowning in the agony of her touch, Reht didn't hear the rest of what she said. He sucked in his breath, trying not to scream as dark blood saturated his jacket.

"She's gone!" he managed to say as Diawn cocked her hand back to deal a lethal blow.

"What?"

"I got rid of her. Triel's gone. That *baech* betrayed me."

Her eyes narrowed. "You lying, *ahŭdábogo musalenðmos*—"

"She's gone!" he said, shaking off the thugs. He dropped to the ground, picking himself up slowly, clutching his bleeding chest with his right arm. "You were always the one for me."

With his left hand, he handed her the bracelet Sebbs had stolen off of one of the felled patrons of Suba House. "I want to make it up to you. I want us to be together. Forever."

"Hey jackoff, she's mine!" the wiry fellow said.

"Back off, Mar," she said, stepping in front of him. She took the bracelet, her eyes softening. "It's beautiful."

"Baby, you're my forever girl," Reht said between breaths. "Let the past be the past. I had to sort a lot of *sycha* to be here, but this is where I belong."

Diawn looked at the bracelet again, turning it over in her hands. Her brows pinched for a moment, but then her face relaxed. "Gentlemen, take him to my private suite."

"You can't be serious," Mar said, jabbing his thumb at Reht. "This lowlife is gonna screw you."

"That's the plan," she said, walking past Mar.

She wrapped her arms around Reht's waist and teased his lips with her tongue. "Where's the rest of the crew?"

"Long gone, baby. Long gone. They were just draggin' me down," he said, his hand gliding down the curve of her hip. She moaned in his ear and slid her hand down the front of his pants.

"You're one messed up *baech*," Mar said, looking hurt as he turned his back and headed off the dock.

"What did you call me?" she said, tilting her head and reaching between her breasts.

"Oh no," Reht heard one of the thugs whisper. The chained humans shuffling onto the cargo ship picked up their pace.

As always, Diawn's aim proved impeccable. The bullet sizzled its way through Mar's chest, and his body flopped to the ground. Smelling the fresh kill, the crossbreed dogs yanked their minders toward the felled meat.

"Pierced rounds. Love it. You haven't lost your touch," Reht joked.

Diawn blew on the end of her pistol before returning it to its place between her second and third breast. "You really missed me, didn't you?" she whispered in his ear, biting his neck.

"A little."

"Definitely not little," she said, pushing her hips into his. He playfully bit her back, but she shoved him against one of the thugs. "Get him to my suite."

Looking over his shoulder, past the barrier wall where his crew was hiding, Reht made a low, sweeping motion with his hand to signal that he was okay. *Actually, things are going great,* he thought. *Diawn's accepted me, and if I play my cards right, I can lift whatever she's selling and make double profit.*

Reht slapped one of the thugs on the back. "Lead me to

paradise, boys."

The bigger thug snarled, but the one with the scar whispered something to him as they led Reht up the secondary ramp to the forward compartments of the ship.

"So, seriously, what are you doing with a cargo ship full of Deadskins?" Reht asked.

The one with the scar responded indifferently. "Somebody's hungry."

Reht stuck his tongue out. "Too salty for most meat lovers. Who's buying?"

"Don't worry your pretty little face over it."

Without offering any more information, the thugs led him through narrow corridors to her private suite. Expensive-looking items that belonged in a museum decorated the walls and shelves—relics from Ten Jao Hi, a planet of blood rubies and pink latos flowers, and twisted metal weapons from the outerworlds.

Beauty and brutality, Reht mused, thinking more of the owner than the collection.

"You gave me the black mark," Diawn said, shutting the door behind him. He jumped a little, not expecting her so soon. "I should let my dogs devour you."

Regaining his composure, he reached out to stroke her cheek. She caught his hand, her razored nails digging in the meat of his palm until he flinched, then eased up, bringing him closer to her.

"How can I make it up to you?" he said.

She threw him on her bed, pinning him down with her arms, straddling his waist.

"Give me a reason not to kill you," she said, licking the blood from his chest.

Grabbing her by the hair, Reht pulled her up and bit her neck. She moaned softly, ripping her bodice open, warm breasts falling onto his chest. Animal instincts awakened, he leaned forward and undid his pants, holding her back by the throat until he was ready.

"You're mine," she whispered, breathing hard and fast as she slid on top of him.

Desire triumphing over pain, Reht gripped the bedsheets in his fists. Her inner thighs, strong and wet against his hips, milked both torment and pleasure in heated waves.

"Gods, yes," she said, leaning back. Necking arching with every gasping breath, Diawn dug her nails into his thighs. As she cried out his name, his hunger intensified.

Reht.

A ghostly image of Triel flashed across his retinas. He gritted his teeth, trying not to lose focus as he thrust harder.

My love—

He grunted and Diawn screamed as they climaxed in unison. Despite his initial eagerness, his release petered out into the empty space between them, muted and disappointing. He laid back, the headache he had when they first left the Alliance returning with a vengeance.

She rolled over, chest heaving, her face curiously blank. "Get cleaned up," she said, her voice monotone, the life gone from her eyes. "I can't stand your stink."

Her affect should have alerted him to danger, but he didn't care right then. With every beat of his heart drilled an ice pick into his skull. He pulled up his pants and stumbled to the door, where two thugs met him outside.

The scarred thug took one look at him and rolled his eyes. "This way."

Something is very wrong—

As much as he tried, Reht couldn't string his thoughts together past the pounding in his head. With one hand on the wall he followed the thugs up four flights of stairs. Steel-plated doors separated him from what he hoped was a shower.

"After you, princess," one of the thugs said, bowing in front of the double doors.

The way the thug said it, the glint in his eye. All the blood left Reht's face, but as he turned to run, the thugs caught him under the armpits.

"Paradise is just ahead," one snickered.

A triple-barreled rifle jammed under his ribcage. "Walk nice and slow, *ratchakker*."

The stench nearly blew him back as one of them pushed open the double doors and forced him through.

"What the hell is…?" Reht trailed off, too horrified to articulate the rest of the thought as he gripped the railing to the observational balcony. Humans lay in mountainous stacks atop each other, moaning and screaming behind taped mouths.

"Don't worry your pretty little self," the scarred thug said as whirring conveyor belts delivered more bodies into the swollen, squirming belly of the cargo ship. "Nobody will miss these slumrats."

"Where's Diawn?" he said, whirling around.

She stood in the shadow of the doorway, a venomous smile stretching across her face as she dangled the bracelet between her fingers. Casually, she tossed it to him. "Never trust a dog-soldier."

He turned over the bracelet and saw the inscription on the inside. *To Mai, all my love, Taeh Ly.*

Even his best lie fell short. "Baby, I bought this for you."

"You found it, you stole it—doesn't matter," she said. "All that matters is that you're here, right now, and I have this moment."

With augmented speed her white boot smashed into his cheekbone. He reeled backwards, tipping over the guard rail and falling headfirst into the slippery pile of humans.

After flailing about to right himself, Reht looked up to see Diawn cackling. "Now you know what it's like, you sack of *sycha*."

"Diawn!" he screamed, cradling his shattered cheekbone. "You can't—"

"You're nothing but meat," she said, signaling her thugs to follow her out the doors. "That's what I was to you, and now that's what you are to me."

After Diawn exited, the lights faded and the conveyor belts withdrew from the cargo hold. An internal siren wailed as the engines amped to full throttle.

Reht tried to gain purchase, but he couldn't balance himself on the tangle of limbs. Nails scraped across his skin, stray fingers desperately latching on, pulling him down into the undulating heap. Fear carved through his reason and he struck out, elbowing, kicking, and punching the people below.

"Diawn!" he screamed, careening backwards as the ship took off from the dock. "Triel was a *godich* leech! She *chakked* with my head! Don't leave me like this!"

He fell back onto the pile, defeated, bruised, and battered. In the darkness there was only the slick, grimy movement of flesh, and Sebbs' words of warning playing over and over again in his head.

***

Jaeia didn't understand just how desperate she was until she used her second voice to slip past the staff in the Division Lockdown Labs.

"Turn around quickly," she whispered to one of the technicians handling a tray of experimental liquids. Lost in her voice, the technician obeyed, spilling the contents onto the floor. The rest of the staff scattered as an odorous vapor cloud formed from the pooling chemicals.

Holding her breath, Jaeia ran through the cloud to the crosslink interface room, eyes and nostrils aflame.

"Ennui," Jaeia coughed, closing the door behind her before loading the program. The interface powered up, translucent blue panel lighting up at her fingertips. "I need your help."

The Hub projected the image of an elderly human with patchy skin and a frail body, legs bound with thick metal chains. "Our name is Servus," it rasped.

Jaeia ran her hand through her hair. *I don't have time to deal with the Hub's eccentricities.*

(These are more than 'eccentricities',) her conscience reasoned. *(The Hub has a personality.)*

Swallowing her guilt, Jaeia justified her actions with fear. *I want to help, but lifting the program safeguards to an interlinked dataprocessor is a serious security risk, especially with the Fleet engaged on multiple fronts. I can't compromise the Alliance; too many lives are at stake.*

"Servus, I know what you want, but I can't give that to you today," she said. "I need you tell me everything you can find about Saol and Rion, the Abomination, from Algar folklore. And take this off-registry."

"Hmpf," the Hub said, turning its nose up and crossing its arms.

Jaeia paused over the keyboard. DeAnders would have just snipped some of its circuitry, but she couldn't bring herself to cause it harm, even if it was an artificial being.

"Please, Servus, I need you. I know what Dr. DeAnders does limits you, but if you can't help me, then I can't help you. You have to show me that I can trust you."

"Trust?"

"Yes. Show me that I can trust you, and I will help you."

Servus did a backwards somersault in place. "We can trust you, Jaeia Kyron, because we know you."

"You know me?" Jaeia said. She eyed a bundle of secondary circuit links and the thought crossed her mind to start snipping, but she stopped herself. *Fear doesn't rationalize aggression.*

"We see everything," Servus said, pulling down his lower eyelids with his fingers, a kaleidoscope of light shining through.

Jaeia thought about what the Hub meant. *It's integrated into the wave network, so it has access not only to the Alliance datafiles, but to every piece of electronic information on the net.* In some way it did know her—through the tabloids, the court reports, the military profiles, the public profiles. *This is why the Defense/Research teams considers it such a potentially dangerous entity—and also such a valuable asset.*

Sucking in her breath, Jaeia drew a terrible parallel: *It's just like Jahx when he was integrated with the networked telepaths...*

"I promise I will help you," she said. "If you do know me, then you know I keep my word. Now, no more games. Help me with this query."

The image of the old man flickered. "Taking the query off-registry will prompt a defense system alert," it said, replacing its distinctive voice with a generic male monotone.

"I'm aware. Please continue with analysis."

The Hub blinked. "We are now off-registry."

In the span of a heartbeat the artificial intelligence changed its image to that of a Prodgy male, mid-thirties, average height and stature with the trademark dark brows and light skin of the Northern tribes. "Saol of the Gangras tribe. Rion, the Abomination. Information found. Classified. Unable to proceed."

Jaeia tapped her fingers. "Authorization Jaeia Kyron, alpha beta 1001-71."

"Insufficient clearance."

"*Oe Vead,*" she muttered, cracking open the door to see if anyone had clued in on her unapproved activity. The staff, still occupied with cleaning up the chemical spill, didn't seem to notice.

I have no choice, she thought, realizing what she had to do. Having given up the practice of Rai Shar, Admiral Unipoesa had become weak and accessible. Over the past few weeks she had inadvertently gleaned many of his codes while his wayward mind drifted during conversations that required him to access related information.

It's not an aggressive tactic, she thought, rationalizing her theft. *Stealing is just a leftover survival method from Fiorah and the Dominion Core.*

After overriding the voice authorization mode, she inputted the admiral's codes manually.

"Commander Kyron," the Hub said. "Would you like your requested information in visual or audio format?"

"Visual."

The text and photographic report gave her a brief description of the time period during the height of the Dissembler Scare. Much of Algar was auctioned off to prospectors and milling companies, but she didn't know that the United Starways Coalition had secretly removed artifacts and religious scriptures from the sacred Temples.

If Triel knew, she'd— Jaeia suppressed the thought before it could go any further.

With a deep breath, she scrolled down. The Alliance had translated some of the ancient writings, but much of the script remained too complex for their language systems to decipher. The Hub highlighted the substituted words on the projection:

Saol of Gangras lost his innocence *during the Ten Wars of Perspheolys. Enraged at the Gods and angry at his own* mortality, *he journeyed to Cudal and stole the power of the Gods to* seek revenge, *but his* broken *mortal body was* too weak, *and he was* poisoned. *Reborn to Algar as Rion, the Abomination, he became obsessed with the* destruction of his people, and drunk with *the power of the Gods*, killed without conscience. *The tribes of Algar, facing total destruction,* used the *Great Mother* to defeat *the unstoppable Rion,* but because of their weakness, *the Gods* bound the Prodgies with a curse.

Jaeia frowned. "Servus, give me a percentage of the accuracy on these translations."

The Hub made a series of electronic noises. "42.8 percent."

"I can't rely on that. I need to know who or what Rion the Abomination is and how anyone could draw a parallel between my sister and me to him."

The Hub chirped and buzzed as the image of Saol dissolved into a swirl of changing light. "Rion, the Abomination, Harbinger of

Death and Destruction. He saw God's image and chose to submit."

Jaeia looked up at the Hub. "What?"

"He saw God's image and chose to submit. Rion the Illusionist, the Speaker, the Seeker. He chose."

"What are you quoting from?" Jaeia demanded. "What does it mean?"

"He chose," Servus repeated more fervently.

Jaeia lifted up her hands as the keyboard faded, her access suddenly denied. "What's going on?"

"There is always a choice," it whispered. The Hub's image transformed into a young boy that looked too much like her brother to be coincidental.

"I need answers, Servus. Please, I don't have time," Jaeia said, ripping open the circuit box on the wall. She studied the auxiliary RAM, preparing herself to make the cut when the Hub cried out.

"Accessing," it said. The Hub disappeared, only the glow of the keyboard illuminating the room.

"Personal log, Triel of Algardrien, stardate 3184.255."

Jaeia reflexively crouched down, both hands touching the floor as Triel's slender figure appeared in blue light on the center viewfield. She wasn't sure how the Hub was showing Triel's personal logs, especially when all logs were supposed to be encrypted and inaccessible to even the highest authority.

"How are you doing this?" Jaeia asked.

"I told you. We see *everything*," Servus whispered.

The image of Triel leaned forward in her seat. "I'm worried, but I don't know who to talk to. I can never have a serious conversation with Reht, and Damon—well, I feel like he's a decent man, but I'm not sure that he knows how to be my friend. Bacthar and Mom were always good advisors, but they've been so upset since the Alliance grounded their ship, and I know they're angry at me for enlisting. And Jetta and Jaeia… how can I tell them? My people—I have to try and find my people. They are the only ones who can help."

Triel held her head in her hands. Tears brimmed in her eyes, but she seemed determined not to cry on the recording.

"Jetta and Jaeia. They're completely human—no physical explanation for their telepathic powers. That means that there is only one other explanation: they have been to Cudal. If that's true, then they are Rion. But there are three of them. *Trio-Rion*, I guess.

Triorion. It doesn't matter. They are poisoned."

Jaeia's mouth went dry. *Not Triel. Not our friend.*

"It makes sense, too," the Healer continued. "Rion had the powers to manipulate people with his voice, just like Jaeia, and he frightened people with their own imaginations, just like Jetta. And he could see right through to a person's soul—that's how he tried to turn the world against itself."

Jaeia pulled up military database on Algar's history on the subscreen projector. Nothing. It was just as vague as it was before: there was a world war in 100 LL, and the Prodgies united to defeat a common enemy. From there on, the Prodgies celebrated world peace and revealed their healing powers to the worlds.

"But there may be hope," the recording of Triel said. "It seems they were born into their powers; it was not their intention to steal from the Gods. Maybe they won't make the same choice that Saol made. Maybe..."

Triel looked down again, the tears falling from her cheeks and out of range of the visual field. "I can't do it alone. I'm worried that my feelings for them may impair my ability to stop them if the need arises. I need my people. I am alone and afraid."

The video clip ended, but before Jaeia could digest what she had seen, the Hub spun up another segment from another stardate.

"Love has blinded me before." Triel laughed bitterly and looked away from the camera. "Reht was the first. I should never have loved him. We're too different. And now..."

Triel stood up and then sat back down abruptly in her desk chair. Bringing her knees to her chest, she rocked backward. Finally, after a long exhalation, she continued. "And now I think I have feelings for someone else, much deeper than anything I've ever felt before. It's strange—it shouldn't be. I can't explain it. I still love Reht, but..."

Triel pulled her hair back and clipped it into a bun. "It doesn't matter. What does is that I might be making the wrong choices again because of my attachments. Jetta and Jaeia both possess immense powers that they can't fully control. Of the two of them, I'm most concerned about Jetta. The power she has is seductive and duplicitous, just like the Gods', and for someone as vulnerable as Jetta... I'm not sure if she could survive the Gods' test. Saol's suffering was great, too, and he couldn't. He saw God's image and chose to submit."

"What does that mean?" Jaeia said.

"Jaeia is pathologically passive when it comes to her sister. I'm not sure why. But Jetta's anger could override them both if Jaeia doesn't take a stand. And sooner or later they'll have to come to terms with their ultimate responsibility."

"Our 'ultimate responsibility'?" Jaeia repeated.

"I feel so close to them, especially Jetta," Triel said. "Whenever I heal them, I feel more alive, and when I touch Jetta's mind, there's a strange comfort there, as if I've known her for ages. My feelings for her are confusing, and I worry about my ability to do my duties as a Healer and as a friend. They took from Cudal. And my creed—the creed of my people..."

Triel played with the webbing between her fingers and whispered something the camera didn't pick up.

"Servus, repeat and augment audio."

The Hub rewound the video feed and replayed it slowly. Each word sank into her with gutting force: "I will not kill them."

The video feed terminated.

Jaeia could barely breathe. *This is why Triel guarded the secrets of Rion and is so concerned about Jetta. Saol had similar talents, and they took him on a path that nearly ended the Prodgy race. Are we capable of that?*

The dead boy in the coolant room surfaced in the forefront of her mind. *I've harmed others with my talents, but it's always been a last resort.* Ashamed, she turned her thoughts to her sister. *Jetta's hurt others with her talent, too—and she's starting to justify using it aggressively.*

Jaeia remembered her conversation with Triel on the observatory deck just after they defeated the Motti and asked herself the same question: *Is my love for Jetta preventing me from realizing my sister's true nature? Is that what Triel fears, too?*

No, she told herself, squeezing her fists together. *I believe in Jetta; my sister is a good person. She's just never forgiven herself, and because of this, she fuels her actions with self-hatred.*

"We have a secret," Servus said.

"What?" Jaeia said, snapping from her thoughts. The Hub changed forms again, this time morphing from one bipedal mammalian body to the next too quickly for her to discern.

"About your friends. But you have to go now. They are coming."

She craned her neck to see two staff members pointing a score of guards toward the crosslink room.

"What secret? What friends?" Jaeia said, eyeing the secondary bundle again.

Servus wagged its finger at you. "Now you must do this thing called 'trust.' Come back and set us free. Then we will tell you a very big secret. It's about what we see."

"You see everything," Jaeia said, reflecting on what the Hub had said earlier. Understanding that it had access to secured private logs, she realized that it probably did have a secret—many secrets—but time was against her now.

"Shoot," she mumbled, erasing as many possible traces of her use of the Hub as she could before terminating the program.

"Don't turn us off. You promised to—" the Hub managed to plead before the unit powered down.

Jaeia quickly went over her options. *I don't want to use my second voice again, especially not against the guards. They're better trained against telepathic manipulation, and I don't want to push the limits of my talent and risk injury—*

(—or death)

"Crap!" she said, gritting her teeth. *But I can't have anyone find out I ran a search about Rion the Abomination—or that I used the admiral's access codes.*

A guard rapped on the door. "Open up! This is an unauthorized use of the crosslink system."

Jaeia crouched down, her gaze distant, searching the area outside the crosslink room. Survival instincts took hold as she sensed the twenty people between her and the exit to the main corridors.

(Blind them—make them turn against each other.)

"No, I won't do it," she said. *I am not this Abomination.*

Jaeia calmed herself. *Maybe I can pacify the guards instead of assaulting them.* She had done it to her sister and brother thousands of times, and she had used snippets of the same talent on Contact missions during tense negotiations. But these soldiers were different—they weren't bonded to her, and they were trained in Rai Shar.

"Lieutenant," she said, stepping out of the crosslink room.

The guards clutched their shockwands, tuning in to her every move as the team leader addressed her: "Commander, you have not cleared this entry with Dr. DeAnders."

Jaeia took a deep breath. *If I'm not careful about using my talents, this could be disastrous.*

The more she thought about it, the more afraid she became. Pacifying the guards too much could cause a complete physiological shutdown, but since their minds were sensitized to telepathic manipulation, they could easily detect her influence, so she couldn't just use elements of her talent.

Normal tactics won't work, she decided. She would have to think of something else, something beyond the survivalist use of her second voice.

What would Jahx do? she thought. Always honest and open, Jahx used to draw his voice from a place within, pouring his soul into every spoken word. Even the most jaded of hearts seemed to yield to him when he shared himself.

That's it.

Jaeia relaxed her voice and sounded the deeps within herself. "I needed to speak to the Hub about a classified matter," she said. Concentrating on intent, Jaeia allowed her sentiment to ride on every syllable, the truth behind her actions transcending sound waves and penetrating their minds. She looked directly at the lieutenant, her willingness to cooperate quietly displayed in the soft gray of her eyes. "I have the authority to do that, yes?"

"Yes, Sir, but the query was unregistered."

"I said it was a classified query, Lieutenant." She dug deeper, reaching back and in, farther than she had ever dared, and instead of imposing her mind on his, she brought his mind to hers. The lieutenant's pupils dilated, and he loosened his grip on the shockwand. "And I am the commander of the Contact Team and a senior officer. I would hope that your better judgment tells you that I have the Fleet's best interest in mind when I take my queries off-registry. It's a matter of security."

She gave him everything, her words exposed, her ulterior intent unmasked, and his mind unlocked. His doubts and fears rained down on her mind, but she easily weathered them.

"Forgive me, Commander," he said. "I was just following protocol."

"Of course you were, Lieutenant. Now, let me pass. The chemical spill smells rather unpleasant."

The lieutenant hesitated, his forehead knitting. "You… you're going to—I understand now. You're trying to help, aren't you?"

"I am," Jaeia replied.

The look of confusion remained, but he stepped aside for her, saluting as she left the Defense/Research department.

Jaeia smiled, hope suddenly rekindled. *There is another way,* Jaeia thought. *I have to tell Jetta.*

Seconds later a sobering realization washed away her elation. *My method worked because the lieutenant is a decent person and on my side.* What if he had been her enemy—or a monster like Yahmen? She had forgotten how Jahx had hurt himself when he tried to connect with their owner, and if it hadn't been for her and Jetta anchoring him, it would have cost him his life.

I got lucky with the lieutenant, she thought. *I can't risk of exposing myself like that to a malicious soul—but at the same time, how can I risk letting my powers control me if I use them actively?*

"What am I supposed to do?" Jaeia said to herself as she turned the corner, heading toward the loading bay to ready her team.

After she boarded the lift and took a seat on the passenger bench, exhaustion sunk in. *Has it really been thirty hours since I last slept?* she thought, checking the time on her uniform sleeve. *I can't worry about that now.*

No time for rest, or take care of basic needs. Even tending to the irritation from the chemical spill to her eyes, nose, throat and lungs would have to wait.

"Jahx, I need you," she rasped, holding her neck. "I don't want Triel to be right."

***

(You should be used to this now,) a cynical voice said inside him.

Unipoesa, straight-armed, cracked his knuckles as quietly as he could while he waited for the guards to release the locks. He had stared at the number on the cell door long enough to remember. *This is where I interrogated Mantri Sebbs about his involvement with the Core.* It seemed so long ago now—another lifetime. *And in some ways, at least for Sebbs, it is,* he thought bitterly.

So there he was, standing once again outside the same cell door. It wasn't his assignment to make sure Triel's treatment had gone as planned, but he had volunteered to do it. *I always do.* He even did it when they administered the pretreatments to Sebbs—after all, they were childhood friends.

(Coward.)

Unipoesa itched for a smoke, but he'd left his pack in his office. Besides, Triel hated smoking—or at least she used to. He wasn't really sure what to expect; every person who was converted into an Agent seemed to lose a bit of themselves. Some, their humanity. But Sleeping saved lives. Or so he hoped.

(Tarsha—)

Then he remembered—*Triel is a telepath; they only erased her memories of the* Hixon, *not turned her into an actual Sleeper.* Luck was in her favor, then. The stakes were higher with Agents, and if the training didn't take hold, the only other option was disposal. Since Triel wouldn't recall her experience, she might have a chance after all.

"Clear," the prison guard called. The alarms shut off and door rolled back. In the dark of the cell sat a slender woman hugging her knees to her chest.

"Triel," he said, offering his hand. "I'm sorry that they put you in here. Come with me."

She looked at him skeptically, but she uncurled and followed him through the brig and to the lift. They rode in silence until they reached his office, where he did a quick scan to rule out any bugs.

"How are you feeling?" he asked as he took a seat across from her on the couch.

The Healer crossed her legs, keeping a stiff posture. "Fine," she said, turning her eyes away and rubbing the webbing between her fingers. "A little sore."

The admiral nodded. He'd read the report—Shelby's team simulated a flight accident so that she would have a plausible gap in her memories. They also injected myolytic agents into her bloodstream to give her muscle soreness and bruising.

"Do you remember the crash?"

This was the important question. For her protection he kept his thoughts guarded so she couldn't sense what he really asked.

The Healer shook her head. "I don't remember anything after I stole the ship. It's terrible. I feel…"

Gaze drifting off to the ground, Triel's mouth pinched at the corners as she tried to recollect something from the time lost.

Unipoesa's orders were clear, as was his knowledge that what they did to her was wrong, but it was too late for guilt or regret. Years ago, when he committed to his rank, he also embraced the responsibilities that came with it.

All of this is for her own good and the good of the Starways. (That's how I've justified so many things.)

"I promised that I would facilitate contact between you and Captain Jagger," he said, handing her a DAT-receiver. Triel took it from him, initiating the call.

The signature rang through, and someone picked up on the other end. Unipoesa couldn't see who she was talking to, but the voice sounded high-pitched and nervous.

"Triel!"

"Hi, Tech. Are you okay?"

"Yeah," the mechanic said. "Stuck in another lousy *sycha*-hole, but okay. The rest of the boys are out having fun, as usual, and left me with the mess."

"They're all okay?" she asked.

"Yeah, sure. Those Alliance bastards tried to stiff us with a territory blackout, but Reht told 'em to shove it. I'm sure we've been tagged, but he's got us a new gig far away from any of that trouble."

"Well, at least you're okay," Triel said.

"Hey, I'm surprised you called. I mean, you and Reht… well, you know."

"Know what?" Triel said, glancing at the admiral.

This is the big moment. Unipoesa controlled his breathing, imagining the wall between her mind and his. He had sworn he wouldn't use Rai Shar again, but this was to save her life.

Tech laughed nervously. "Come on, Triel. Don't tell me it was a joke or something. I mean, I've never seen Reht so pissed."

The Healer gave the admiral a long, hard look.

Minding his tone, Unipoesa clarified what he could: "You contacted the *Hixon* right before you jumped into the mining arm and spoke over a private channel with the captain. We have no record of your exchange."

Narrowed eyes and pursed lips made it obvious that Triel didn't believe him. "Tech, I had an accident and I can't remember everything that's happened over the last few days," she said. "Tell me what happened with me and Reht."

Silence. The admiral caught a glimpse of the mechanic's face as he strode over to pour himself a drink from his private collection behind his desk.

"Look, it ain't my business to tell you," the engineer replied.

"Tech," Triel said firmly. "What happened? I have to know."

Damon heard the clattering of tools as the mechanic fumbled with his hands and dropped them on the ground. "You and him fought about where you were headin'. He wanted to hit the circuit again, and you said didn't want to play that game no more. The Cappy thought you were crossing him, staying with the Alliance—"

"—but I didn't want to give up on the missions to save other telepaths," she whispered.

Unipoesa downed a shot of whiskey, liquid fire searing his throat. *If only I could hate you,* he thought, wishing the Healer's intentions had not been so altruistic, *it would make this so much easier.*

"Yeah. Well, it ended bad," Tech said. "Reht didn't like that so much. You were the best thing that ever happened to him which is probably why he's so bent right now."

"Bent on what?" Triel said, tilting her head. She threw the admiral another hard look.

The mechanic gulped audibly. "Look, Triel—you're a step up, right? He's a dog-soldier, and even if he was soft for you, he's still gonna be a dog-soldier. He ain't gonna settle down. He doesn't know how; it ain't his blood."

The admiral knew she got it then when he saw the hurt contorting her face.

She lowered her head, hiding her tears. "Is he out right now?"

"Uh, y-yeah."

Denial set in, changing her expression. She glared at the admiral while speaking to the engineer. "Tech, what was the name I used when you first met me?"

She's testing him, making sure he's not a fake. But Tech was quite real—just modified.

"Huh? Why?" he replied.

"It's very important."

"Raina."

Tears came now.

"You okay?" the engineer asked, confused.

"Goodbye, Tech."

Triel closed the DAT-receiver, severing the connection. "You could have warned me," she whispered to the admiral.

"You wouldn't have believed me," Unipoesa said, pouring himself another shot. "Drink?"

"No," she whispered, wiping away her tears. She was silent a moment, looking at one of the windows to the stars.

"Jumping into the mining arm was on purpose, wasn't it? I took the news very badly," Triel said.

You're doing the right thing, he told himself. "It looks that way."

"Reht was my first love," she whispered, still staring out at the stars. "But I always knew in my heart it wasn't going to work out. I just can't believe I would do something so stupid, even if I was upset. Something more must have happened. Maybe the emotional toll—maybe I was Falling, maybe I thought it would be best if I…"

She curled up in a tight ball on the couch, sobbing. He offered her a drink which she took, lifting her head only briefly to down it before hiding again.

"We tried to work with Captain Jagger and the crew, but he's violated at least fifteen federal laws just in the last ten months alone," the admiral said. He wasn't sure how much Triel knew about the flash transport device, but he was sure that she wasn't completely ignorant. "He was also trying to circumvent our security measures when they were allowed shore time on Trigos. He proved to be a liability. That was why he was relegated to the outerworlds."

"Triel," he said, putting a hand on her shoulder. He assumed his most fatherly tone. "We need you here. You are instrumental in our efforts to find and help the surviving telepaths, and your abilities as a Healer are unparalleled by any existing technology. Your dreams of reconnecting are possible, and there are people that care about you. I hope you stay with the Alliance."

His conscience bit at him with the seediness of his own words, but speaking partial truths was what he did best. The illusion of sincerity, the illusion of control—he had mastered them at a young age to be in this uniform. He cared about her, but the military did not. And by deceiving her into believing that she was in a safe, protected environment that would cultivate her abilities, he was as guilty as those that gave the orders.

"Jetta—did you find her? Is she okay?" Triel asked, looking at him with reddened eyes.

Why Jetta? he wondered, understanding her strong affinity for the twins, but not exactly for the darker of the two. Still, her bond was another means to exploit her, and for her sake he had to use it.

"She's back and safe," he said.

She let loose a huge sigh of relief. "Thank the Gods. Where was she?"

"On Old Earth, of all places. She was captured by some Scabbers and controlled by a shock cuff until she managed to break free and contact Jaeia. She's prepping for a mission right now."

"I'll have to see her," the Healer said.

"And she has some good news for you—apparently their brother is back."

"What?" Triel exclaimed.

"I don't understand the powers of telepaths," the admiral said with a chuckle, "but if they can cheat death, sign me up. She'll have to explain it to you."

Triel stood up to leave.

"Sit down, Triel," he said, his tone changing. "We're not through just yet."

"My punishment."

"Yes," he said, removing a datafile from his uniform jacket. "I've spoken with the Minister. Given your previous outstanding record, our tenuous situation with the invading ship and the imminent uprising in the Holy Cities, we're going to grant you conditional forgiveness. I want you to see a therapist to help with your emotional regulation."

"My *emotional regulation* was affected by the fact that you were torturing of the crew of the *Wraith*!"

"I know that's your reasoning for your actions, Triel, but you have to understand our position. Reht Jagger is a dangerous man. He's supplied us with valuable information in the past, but he has also sabotaged our ships, compromised the integrity of the Fleet and blackmailed the Minister. It was within our policies, and none of them suffered any physical damage associated with our interrogation methods."

Wisely, Triel held her tongue. She, like the twins, knew better than to play her hand too soon.

At least I've secured her safety a little longer.

But now came the risk of Jetta and Jaeia sharing their knowledge of Reht's situation with Triel. The sheer unpredictability of the twins' telepathic powers made erasing their memories far too risky, but their knowledge of the Sleeper program made them a liability. Somehow he would have to make the sisters understand the danger they would put themselves and Triel—and him—in if they told her the truth.

"There was an emergency Fleet meeting," he said, handing her the log. "I know it's not specific to your department, but I wanted you to have a look. I think Jetta has an idea about the type of weapon the Motti are using, and I wanted to run it past you."

Triel took it from him, her eyes growing wide as she read the record.

"What did she say?" Triel said in a hushed voice as she set down the file.

"That she wasn't sure, but she had to see it herself. She's heading out to investigate it with our new scanning parameters and see if she can pick anything up at a closer range."

"When is she leaving?" Triel said, standing up quickly, "I have to talk to her right away."

"Right now," the admiral said, pointing to the cosmos.

"No!" Triel shouted, running to the window. She banged her fists on the glass as the corvette navigated out of the docking bay, cleared the perimeter and initiated the jump cycle.

"What is it?" the admiral asked, grabbing her by the arm. "What's wrong?"

"I think I know what it is, too," she said, pulling away. Terror-stricken, her voice strangled by the gravity of her belief, she whispered: "Jetta won't be coming back."

***

Jetta's corvette had just jumped to the next site when Jaeia's ship was attacked.

"Report, ensign!" Jaeia shouted as she righted herself in her chair. Two more volleys followed and catapulted her onto the deck.

Smacking her hands down on the armrests, Jaeia pulled herself back into the command chair, adrenaline coursing through her systems. Smoke blasted down from the vents, making it almost impossible to breathe.

"Forward engines offline. Primary shield down to 10 percent and secondary to 20 percent!" the ensign manning the helm choked out.

Jaeia wiped her eyes, but something didn't feel right. Impulsively, she looked down at her hand. Blood, not sweat, slicked her palm and fingers. She touched her forehead and felt wet, gouged tissue.

Both stolen and previous experience told her that if she gave this a second thought, she would faint. Gritting her teeth, she gripped the armrests with all her strength. "Helm to my terminal!" she yelled.

The ensign relayed her manual control of the ship, and she quickly typed in a string of evasive maneuvers as several more missiles grazed their hull.

"*Mae dereke ni onanosk*," she prayed in Fiorahian as she tried to gain some distance from their attackers.

Jaeia counted four unidentified starcraft on the scanner readings on the right of the viewscreen, two of which hid from direct view behind a nebulous cloud of protoplasm.

"I can't stop this reaction—we're going to have to eject the engine core," the chief of engineering screamed over the internal explosions.

"Don't eject the core!" Jaeia shouted back. She crawled over to the engineering relay as the ship rocked starboard. "Ensign, fire everything we have, full spread!"

She didn't fault her engineer for not knowing the subroutine and execution of a manual coolant washout. That was a trick she had come up with after synthesizing what she had learned from one of the battle-tested chief technicians aboard the Dominion Core vessels and her uncle's experience with burnouts on deep core mining ships.

"Keep an eye on the secondary drives," Jaeia said to the engineer as she inputted new commands into the relay. "And instruct your crew to start dumping Phadion into the backup valves in case that happens again."

Saving the engines won't mean much if I don't solve the bigger problem, she thought, checking the scanners. Four starcraft surrounded their vessel, and her ship's failing shields and damaged reactors gave them little chance in a fight.

Even if we were up and running, the Rapture, *isn't outfitted for this kind of confrontation,* reason countered. *Warhawks are used for evasion and speed, and aren't suited for heavy fire.*

Stolen knowledge merged into her thoughts. *Someone must have known we were coming to be able to outclass us like this. They even waited for my sister's corvette to jump before revealing their position.*

"Commander Kyron," a voice called over the com. "Pathetic. And you're supposed to be the best?"

Urusous Li, she thought, clenching her jaw. His voice, just as snide and arrogant as it was all those months ago when they battled him for the right to command the Alliance Fleet, evoked a deep-seated anger she didn't know she carried.

Without breaking composure, Jaeia reached out to her sister for her insight. *I need you,* she called across the stars, but the connection felt murky and muted.

I can't have this now, she thought, but there was no time to investigate the psionic dissonance with Li on her heels.

"Send an emergency transmission to Central Command," Jaeia ordered.

"All network frequencies are jammed, Sir," the ensign said.

"Okay. Put him on," Jaeia said, moving to the center of the bridge.

Battle strategies from former commanders circulated through her mind as the crewman manning the com terminal converted Li's audio signal into a holographic projection: *Know your enemy. Who is he? What does he want? What are his weaknesses?*

Thinking back, Jaeia tried to recall as much information as she could about the former Alliance prodigy. *Li is a phenotypically Asiatic and Reamis, but genetically spliced with many other species.*

There were rumors about his origins—that he was human-hosted or that he was grown in a lab—but the Alliance claimed that many of his files were corrupted after his defection, not that they weren't already tight-lipped enough about their former prize officer.

Even though I've beaten him once, she thought, *I can't rely on old strategies to do it again. Li is cunning, and he didn't ascend the Alliance ranks by chance.*

Worst of all, she realized, unable to access more than wisps of his psionic presence. *He has apparently been perfecting his Rai Shar.*

"Don't even try your mind tricks, leech," Li said. "I'll end you right now."

The emotions of the crew leaked into her mind. *They're frightened,* she sensed, *but they still have confidence in me, even against impossible odds.*

But after squaring herself against Li, self-doubt ebbed away her aplomb. *They need Jetta, not me. I'm not that kind of strategist.*

"Rule number one," she remembered Jetta explaining after she'd tricked the leader of a child labor gang into giving up his food. "*Never let them know you're afraid.*"

Drawing in a deep breath, Jaeia continued to channel her sister. *Jetta would exploit Li's weakness. That's what I need to do to save the ship and crew.*

(But I can't do that—)

An old memory awakened at the thought.

"*We all do things we're not proud of,*" Jetta said, sharing her stolen bakken with blood-soaked hands. Jaeia remembered how defensive her sister sounded, but how hollow she felt inside, green eyes never meeting hers. "*We do these things because we have to survive.*"

Okay, Jaeia thought. *To save my crew...*

Jaeia cleared her mind and concentrated on Li's psionic frequency, hoping to find the chink in his armor, when it dawned on her why accessing his mind was so difficult. *Li isn't aboard any of the ships—he's commanding remotely,* she deduced, sensing a great distance to the source of his tune. *He thinks physical separation will give him an advantage.*

Thinking of his personality, she came up with an alternative explanation. *Or he doesn't want to risk actual confrontation.*

Realizing what she needed to do, Jaeia typed in a string of commands to the helmsmen and the engineer.

"What are you up to these days, Li? There are a lot of people interested in talking to you," she said, trying to buy some time. She eyed her other crewman, seeing that they picked up on the strategy as the helmsmen input the coordinates and relayed the secondary commands to each terminal.

"Ending the conflict you started," he sneered. "The Starways has no place for warmongers like you. My Republic will have peace and order."

"Your Republic? You mean *your* peace and order, *your* concept of morality, *your* ethical principles, right? That's called a dictatorship," Jaeia replied.

"It will be a Republic," he said, just below a shout. "One with a strong military and council. Not your weak-hearted fools like Chancellor Reamon and Minister Razar ruling over a corrupt line of inbred bureaucrats and terrorists."

"What's your plan then? Do you want to kill me and this crew? Capture us? Come on, Li—you're not that good. You got us with the surprise attack—I'll give you that. But where you've always failed," Jaeia said, standing up and nodding, "is sealing the deal."

Her crew snickered, eliciting the response she wanted from Li. Anger curled his lip and stiffened his posture.

"I wanted to see the look on your face before I eliminated you, just so I can tell your sister all about it before I eliminate her, too," he said. "Then the Starways will be free of you bloody leeches once and for all."

After catching the eye of her engineer, Jaeia saw the *command-ready* flashing on her console armrest. *Time to play my hand.*

She sat back down and steadied herself on the armrests of her chair. *I haven't gone all-out since I forced Jetta against Jahx... and I swore I would never use my talents like that again.*

(What are you doing?) her conscience screamed, reminding her of all the sleepless nights haunted by her brother's shriek and the sound of millions of voices blinking out into starless oblivion.

The only thing I know.

"Li, you're forgetting something," she said, driving back her fear with thoughts of her crew. Allowing her mind to extend away from herself, Jaeia homed in on the tiny thread of a connection between his voice and his body light years away. She reached back and in, through the dimensions folded into a spaceless void. *"You can't see me."*

Her second voice reverberated back at her, a driving force much stronger than she remembered. She cupped her ears, unable to withstand the noise of the aftershock.

"Your pathetic mind games are useless on me, leech!" he shouted, terminating their communications. Despite the severance, she felt her talent latch on, splintering his mind with the deception she had implanted.

"Release the module," she shouted as the enemy starcraft recharged their weapons. "Fire!"

Her crewman responded, catapulting the TX4-module filled with high-density gases and phasic neutrino fields. When the disrupter fire from her ship ignited the timing capsule, the compressed gas detonated, shooting out the smokescreen she needed for their cover. Still locked into the guidance system, she slammed on the primary engines as the module exploded, angling them away from the targeting arms of the enemy ships.

The synergy of the gases and the phasic neutrino fields overloaded the navigational systems and visual displays, but with their course laid in and executed prior to the TX4 explosion, the warhawk stayed on trajectory.

Blinded and dislocated by the generated anomaly, Jaeia had assumed that the ships trapped within the smokescreen would have anchored until the event dissipated, but she hadn't anticipated the impact her second voice would have on Li.

"Sir, they're firing on each other," the ensign reported.

Jaeia closed her eyes, the weight in her chest crushing her heart. Not wanting her crew to see her pain, she pushed the wave of emotion back as the vaporous cloud erupted with gunfire.

I didn't want Li to find us, but I didn't want this!

She heard her brother's voice in her head as clear as it had been years ago: *We can't control our talents, so we must never use them against others.*

And she heard her own voice admonishing Jetta from years past: *It's too dangerous—it isn't a gift, it's a curse.*

(Yet I've killed once again.)

As she watched the enemy ships destroy each other, she relived old nightmares: *Freshly gnawed, bloody stumps from the crazed junkie waving in her face, the sweet, beefy smell of his flesh twisting her stomach. The dead eyes, open and unseeing, of the boy she had tricked into finishing her job aboard the mining ship following her no matter where she ran.*

That was on Fiorah, she told herself, *I have more control now—*

Guilt dragged her forward in time, forcing her to see herself once more at Jetta's side in the medical bay: *Jaeia held her sister down as her twin's mind fractured against the truth of what she had done at the battle of the Homeworld Perimeter, sending her spiraling into a dark abyss.*

"Why?" *Jetta screamed as medics struggled to administer another round of sedatives.*

"Jetta, please—you'll hurt yourself," *Jaeia tried as Jetta grabbed at imaginary enemies.*

"You made me kill Jahx," *she hissed, turning her head to Jaeia. Green eyes, filled with rage, projected hellish visions.* "You are not my sister."

Even as she pulled away from the caustic repercussions of the memory, Jaeia could not help but hear her greatest pain spoken across the bounds of time: *(It was my voice that guided Jetta's deadly hand, and if it hadn't been for Triel, my talent would have not only killed Jahx but destroyed my sister...)*

Stop this, she told herself. *Focus.*

"Come about—mark 41.99.577," she said, voice barely above a whisper.

She watched in silence with the rest of the crew as the debris and wreckage from the ships drifted out of the cloud.

"Life signs?" she finally dared to ask.

"The anomaly is still too dense to scan, Sir," the helmsman answered, "but preliminary data suggests no survivors."

No, there wouldn't be, she thought, hope crumbling. Infected by her words, Urusous Li had commanded all four starcraft to fire, even though they were blind and their missile-locking system could potentially target each other.

(But I only intended to confuse Li!)

Stolen memories and sentiments from battle-worn officers surfaced. *(Death and sacrifice are a part of war.)*

Still, they did not assuage her pain. *If my talents lead to murder, then they are a curse,* she decided.

(What I am is unnatural, perverse.)

A terrible reminder surfaced to the forefront of her attention. Triel's voice, frightened and absolute: *Rion... Harbinger of Death and Destruction...*

Jaeia rubbed her hands along the armrest hard enough to abrade skin. "Any contact?" she asked, refocusing herself.

The crewman manning the com looked at her. "We've lost the transmission signal from Li, Sir."

Jaeia thought about it. "I bet it was hubbed into one of the starcraft."

"I can try and retrace the signal—"

"Don't bother," Jaeia said, pressing her fingertips against her temples. "He didn't want to be traced, so there won't be anything to find."

Slumping heavily in her chair, Jaeia reached out to her sister, but the same murkiness clouded the connection. Jaeia grimaced. *There shouldn't be interference if Jetta had made the jump as scheduled.*

"Any calls from the *Telluron?*" Jaeia asked, hoping that her sister had reported her position.

"Negative, Sir."

Jaeia touched the laceration on her forehead but quickly retracted her hand. *I can't forget my duty.*

"Are you still tracking a cargo ship near the asteroid belt?" she asked.

"Confirmed, Sir, and we have a visual on them, but no registry," the ops officer said. "It looks like '*Ultio*' is painted on the broadside."

"It's stolen. Its design is from Jue Hexron, Barrak district," she said, zooming in and flipping between the bow and stern, noting the crescent accents on the bowsprit. "They never travel out this far."

"They're altering their course; heading mark 28.44.929."

"Course correction—intercept that ship," she said. Silently, she called out to her sister. *Where are you?*

"Sir, our primary engines are shot; we're running on backups. If they decided to run, it'll be a short chase—and we'll be stranded," the engineer reported.

"Continue on course heading," she said. "We'll just make sure they don't run."

As soon as her orders left her tongue, an old, borrowed memory from over a hundred years ago reawakened:

Two old men, drunk and full of bitterness, were recalling the good ol' days of war in a gloomy underground bar. She settled behind the eyes of a retired admiral, one who was missing more than his leg.

A knobby finger poked her in the chest. "Remember the time you ordered the Fleet to engage the Tarkns at their starbase? Crazy bastard!"

"That's nothing!" *the other officer slurred, spilling his drink.* "Remember when you used that* chakking *sticky trap on the Musoditti? How many did you kill? Forty-thousand?"*

Their inebriated laughter faded away as she reemerged.

"A sticky trap…" she whispered, considering the maneuver.

Diving in again, Jaeia weaved back through time to the actual event. In a fraction of a second she relived the admiral's battle, witnessing his masterful tactic. She pinched herself, pulling out of the stolen lifetime.

Jaeia weighed the odds. *This is crazy—there's too much risk to my ship and crew.*

No, I can't be afraid, she reminded herself. *I'm always playing the conservative hand. What would Jetta think of me if I failed my mission?*

"Lieutenant," she said, making her way to the engineer's console. "You're too young, but do you remember the battle for the Seven Cities of Nareth from your studies?"

The Lieutenant looked at her blankly, then snapped his fingers. "Sticky trap."

"Sticky trap," Jaeia repeated, patting him on the back. "Make it happen."

"But Sir, those calculations—if I'm off by more than 0.0001 then we're all—"

Jaeia kept the confidence in her voice. "I have faith in your calculations, Lieutenant."

Still searching for her sister in the back of her mind, Jaeia watched as the cargo ship changed its course again, heading directly into the asteroid belt.

"Lieutenant, are you ready?"

The young man scrunched his hair in his hands as he checked over his work. "Just a minute, Sir."

"I need it now," Jaeia said, checking their relative position. *The warhawk is much larger than that cargo ship,* she thought, cycling through the area scans. *So they're betting that we won't follow them into the asteroid belt.*

Looking over at her pilot, she realized she would have to make a tough decision. *He's one of the best pilots in the Fleet, but he doesn't have this kind of experience.*

But as she prepared to rethink her strategy, she remembered someone else's experience. *Of course,* she thought, digging into the knowledge of fighter pilots she had gleaned off of during the Dominion Wars. *He might not, but I do.*

"Pilot?" Jaeia asked they approached the edge of the belt. "Ship to me."

The pilot turned around, stunned at her request. "Sir, I—"

"Ship to me," she repeated more firmly, taking a seat in her command chair.

"Yes, Sir," he said, relinquishing control of the ship to her position.

Blue and red spherical interfaces appeared on her armrests. Holding fast to the grafted memories of the fighter pilots, Jaeia positioned her fingers within the spheres.

"Ready with the trap, Commander," the engineer called as she steered the ship around the first obstacle.

"Hold for my signal," Jaeia said as she partially closed her left hand, pitching the ship to port.

Weaving in and out of the asteroids, Jaeia couldn't help but admire the enemy pilot with uncommon reflexes and deft maneuvers. *Whoever that is,* Jaeia thought, *they have exceptional skills.*

"Oh Gods," she muttered under her breath as her forward wing clipped the side of an asteroid. Sparks and more smoke poured onto the bridge. She coughed violently, shielding her nose and face with her uniform.

"Clear that now!" Jaeia shouted above the whine of the alarms.

"Ventilating systems offline!" the engineer shouted.

She couldn't see now, nor could she check the lieutenant's calculations. *I can't gamble like this—*

(Jetta wouldn't hesitate.)

"Fire the trap!" she said.

Sharp, wailing charges from the gravitational boosters followed the thunderous blast of the ion cannons.

"Trap deployed," the engineer announced.

Setting the ship to hover, she removed one hand from the spheres and fanned the smoke from her face. As they waited, the ship drifted amidst the ominous sounds of smaller asteroids striking the hull. *If this doesn't work, I'll have to abandon pursuit or I'll lose my ship.*

"Sir, the cargo ship is trapped in the Pull," the ops officer said.

Jaeia allowed herself a quiet exhalation of relief. *It's working; the cargo ship can't escape from the temporary gravitational pool.*

"Amazing," she heard the pilot mutter.

Not really, Jaeia thought, compulsively flexing and relaxing her hands. *I stole someone else's trick.*

"Status report," she said.

"I'm reading a massive amount of Sentient life signs," the ops officer replied. "Human, I think. Over five hundred."

"Over five hundred humans?" Jaeia repeated, pulling up the scans on her armrests. *The cargo ship isn't designed for that kind of transportation load,* she thought, losing count of all the points of light indicating a lifeform aboard the ship. *They must be packed shoulder-to-shoulder.*

"I want three boarding parties ready to go. Hail them," she commanded.

"Sir—look!" the ops officer said, pointing to the viewscreen.

Jaeia stood up, fanning the smoke from her face. In the corner of the viewscreen, a cruiser emerged from the cargo ship's launch doors, jump drives glowing orange with a full charge.

"Oh Gods, no—"

Breath caught in her chest, Jaeia shielded her eyes as white light exploded across the holographics and the viewscreen.

"Full reversal, now!" she shouted, lunging for her terminal as the rip in space-time tore apart the cargo ship.

"Sir, the cruiser's jump has triggered a massive chain reaction within the Pull," the ops officer said, clinging to his terminal as blast force and debris struck the ship.

Jaeia shouted commands, but nothing she did could counter the inverse reaction dragging the surrounding objects into the rift. Asteroids, smashing into one another, only strengthened the event.

We're being pulled in—

Crewmen screamed as asteroids crushed down on the ship from every side, fire and internal explosions rocketing the ship. Tapping into the steely concentration of a thousand years worth of close calls, Jaeia recalled the Alliance Central Starbase location, manually programming it in as the ship around her collapsed. She didn't know if the jump drives were operational anymore, but it wouldn't matter in a moment.

As she slammed the emergency jump button, the support beam for the viewscreen came crashing down, knocking her in the back of the head. She fell to the ground and rolled over, something warm trickling down her face. Thinking of her sister and her certain disappointment, her world came undone.

***

Agracia hated the Spillway, but it was Bossy's favorite Pit. Located in the mountainous region of the west, the fighting-ring capital was one of the hardest underground shelters to reach. It took her three days to travel there, selling whatever she had lifted from Scabbers, even hustling one out of his Rover.

This has been too easy, she thought, hanging a lazy hand over the steering wheel of the Rover as she depressed the accelerator to the floor. Scanning the burnt wasteland and cloud-covered skies, she saw nothing. No Necros or rival Jocks—not even a hint of trouble. *By now I should have been in about two or three fights, or at least a scramble before the city border. What gives?*

Agracia shook off the idea and thought of her friend. Bossy was pissed at her—and she got that—but a few drunken nights and a several good lays later, she was usually approachable.

But to go this far? Doesn't make sense. Still, Agracia had scoured the Dives and the surrounding subterranean networks. *The Spillway is the only other option.*

"*Chak,*" she muttered, momentarily overpowered by the compounding stench of the hazard suit she had stolen.

What was that assino *eating?* she lamented, cracking open her visor to try and blow away the rancid air. *It smells like fat man sweat and rat-sausage farts.*

Relieved to see the access hatch to the Spillway jutting out from a denuded hillside, Agracia swallowed her disgust and parked the Rover behind the remains of a fallen billboard. After accessing the Pit and getting down below dangerous radiation levels, she ripped off her helmet and cursed out the previous owner of the hazard suit under her breath. "Doesn't any *chakking* Jock ever shower?"

A few passerbys gave her distrustful looks, but otherwise left her alone as she walked the down the subcity blocks. However, the wayward glances from strangers and the occasional whisper alerted her more sharply than she had ever remembered reacting. Fear and anxiety quickened her pace. *Is that* assino *going to jump me?* she wondered with every step she took.

Hiking up her shoulders, she thanked the stars that her reputation wasn't as bad in the Spillway. Anybody who was anybody knew that she was a Jock, and a mean one, but she hadn't cheated too many folk in these parts. The townies gave her once-overs, but nobody said anything.

Chakking *Jetta Kyron,* she thought. *She did this to me. I was never scared like this before.*

Fake memories, real ones—Agracia didn't know what happened, but seeing a glimpse of a different life had done something to her, thrown her off her game. Now she questioned everything and everyone.

I'm not me anymore, she thought. *It's like a stranger jumped into my skin—*

(Or am I the stranger?)

Shaking off the thought, Agracia concentrated on what she did know: The stakes seemed higher now, and without Bossy, she would be targeted and vulnerable.

Better start in the markets, she thought. *Maybe someone will cough up some info.*

With a careful eye she perused the scene from the safety of an alleyway before making her entry. The Spillway's commerce came from selling scrap and recycled material from old garbage dumps and salvage operations from the ancient remnants of the metropolis above ground. Jocks hung around the cheaply constructed stalls, making deals with vendors for their next run or selling the idea of a surface tour to a stupid Tourist.

Agracia spied Eddie and Sven, two rival Jocks from other tribes, and slunk back into the shadows. A Meathead, still covered in dirt and blood from the fighting rings, lurked around a junkyard booth not far away from the two surface jockeys.

This isn't going to be easy, she thought. Meatheads, oversized musclemen with chemically-fueled tempers, were just as bad as rival Jocks. *And that steroid junkie might have connections back to the Dives and know about us pulling out of our contract.*

If things had played out the way she had wanted them to, Doctor Death would have had three more bouts and made them enough scratch to make a good run of things for a while. But since Jetta Kyron split, and they didn't show to the next fight, she and Bossy had a price tag on their heads.

"*Chak*," she mumbled under her breath, reaching for a smoke. Despite the strong craving, the voice inside her rebuked the idea.

(Smoking is unhealthy and dangerous.)

Confused, she chewed on her lip.

Wait—don't I like smoking?

The tease of mastication caused her stomach to growl, drawing her attention to the more pressing matter of her empty belly. *When was the last time I ate?*

Thinking back, it had been a least a day, and food was scarce in the Spillway. Stealing meant losing a hand, and even though she was fast, she didn't want to risk losing any body parts, especially since she didn't have backup.

"Agracia," said a voice behind her.

Agracia slowly stuck her head out of the shadow to see a familiar face emerge from the crowd. "Jade, what are you doing here?"

Scarves hid all but the left side of her face. Seeing her truculence, Agracia tried to make amends. "I didn't pay you. You got stiffed by your debts. Sorry."

"Sorry?" she said, grabbing Agracia and throwing her against a wall. "I had to leave the Dives or else I'd be in the rings. I've got nothing, and nobody'll pay for a tramp like me. I'm as good as dead."

"Looks like you're getting by well enough," Agracia said, freeing herself from Jade's grip. But then she realized what Jade was probably doing.

The Scabber in Agracia would have laughed in her face. Jade was too ugly and too deformed to sell her chit on the street, and even though she was an expert scavenger in the Dives, she would be lost in the vast and complicated network of the Spillway.

She probably brought some of her most valuable artifacts with her, but was forced to sell them to stay alive, Agracia deduced. *Jade, a caretaker, whose oath to preserve Earth's history transcends her own life, has forsaken her vow.*

Jade spat at her feet. "You're a spoiled *ratchakker*, Agracia."

Agracia's instincts split between extremes, one of survival and the other of a nature she didn't know she possessed.

(The old bag is done for. Just use her up and throw her out—)
(—help her.)

"*Chak,*" she muttered under breath, trying to distance herself from the inner battle. "Look, I've got nothing, but if you help me, I'll get you and me some grub."

"I don't need your charity—I have a meal ticket. Listen here, kid," Jade said, grabbing her collar and pulling her close. "If I had the money, I'd hire those Dogs to rip you to shreds."

With quick, nimble hands the Scabber Jock did what she did best. She didn't know what she grabbed from within the folds of the woman's clothing, but Jade didn't notice, and Agracia shoved whatever it was in her pocket before the woman even set her back down.

"Look, just 'cause we go way back, I'll get you money and you'll get back to the Dives," Agracia said coolly, breaking her hold of her. "Just keep your panties on and nose down. And don't *chakking* touch me again."

Agracia shoved off of her, ignoring the profanities spouting from Jade's mouth. As she merged with the market crowd, her fingers toyed with the rectangular piece inside her pocket until she felt safe enough to take a peek.

"What the hell?" she said, staring at the odd-looking datawand with some sort of adapter piece at the tip. From old jobs, Agracia recognized that the adapter was formatted to interface with the ancient computer models from the Last Great War.

I'll have to figure this out later, she thought, putting it back in her pocket.

A voice behind her made her snap to attention. "Where is she?"
Jimmy!

Agracia turned the corner, trying to put some distance between them. *This is way too coincidental to see both Jimmy and Jade in the Spillway. Something's up.*

(Something that will not turn out in my favor—)

"Hey!" Jimmy shouted, trying to get her to slow down.

Agracia picked up her pace, feeling for her weapons.

"Gracie Waychild." Eddie stepped in front of her, and his boys closed in from behind. "So good to see you. I thought you'd never show your ugly face in the Spillway again."

Without Bossy she didn't have the muscle to take on Eddie and his boys, but she played her hand as if she did. "Step off, Eddie, or I'll do to you what I did to Mexi."

The smile left Eddie's face. "Your little dog-friend, Bossy, did that. Mexi still eats from a tube, *ratchakker*. I think it'd only be far if we got one for Mexi."

"Back off, *assinos*."

Agracia turned to see Jimmy carrying a 9-VM assault rifle, something that couldn't be bought on Old Earth. The market crowd took notice, people scattering and screaming, vendors and storekeepers slamming shut their doors and windows.

"*Chak,* man—where'd you get that thing?" she said.

"Back the *chak* off, *assinos*," Jimmy said. He tried to sound intimidating, but Agracia heard the nerves in his voice. Fortunately, the 9-VM automatic did all the talking for him.

"I won't forget this," Eddie hissed as he took a step back.

"Thanks, man," Agracia said, trying to turn away.

"Don't go anywhere," he said, grabbing her arm. "Follow me."

"You're gonna wish you killed me, you *chakking* little *baech*!" Eddie shouted. The rest of his gang joined in, threatening to commit acts worse than murder as Jimmy and Agracia backed away.

"Gonna take your eye out and put it you-know-where!"

"We'll pull your guts out nice and slow and feed 'em to the Necros."

Once clear, the two sprinted down an abandoned street, winding their way down a flight of stairs and through another junction tunnel into a bustling thoroughfare.

"Straight ahead—the Watering Hole. Now," Jimmy said, not letting her slow down.

Still holding the 9-VM automatic under his jacket, Agracia did as she was told. She entered the bar, ignoring the surprised looks of the patrons as she and Jimmy headed to the back.

"*Chak* you, Jimmy," she said as he sat her down in a candle-lit booth.

"No, *chak* you, Agracia. You shorted me and Jade, and now it comes to this. Me and her been waiting for this for a long time."

Agracia snorted. "Come on, man—you're going to kill me? String me up? Sell me? Who gives a rat's *assino*?"

"I do."

Eyeglasses glinted in the shadows as a man emerged from the booth across from them. Agracia picked up the scent of his aftershave through the yellow haze of cigarettes and booze.

Gods, what is that? she thought, reminded of something old and debonair.

"Don't tell me you're working for a stiffie Tourist, Jimmy," she said, trying to force out a chuckle despite the hollow pit forming in her stomach. *Why is this old geezer making me nervous?*

"How I've wanted to meet you, Agracia Waychild," the man said, resting both hands on a black cane. "You're quite the legend on Earth."

She rolled her eyes. "Cut to the chase, alright? I don't have the time."

He smiled, but it didn't look natural. Squinting in the low light, Agracia tried to figure out what was wrong with his face as he took a seat across from her. *He looks human, but his skin is tight and shiny like plastic.* She guessed he was probably rich and had some heavy cosmetic work, but not very well done.

"Thank you for your time, Jimmy," the old man said, throwing him a purse. "Please give the other half to Jade."

"My pleasure. Though I'd off this little rat for free," Jimmy said.

Agracia laughed. "Come on, you nearly pissed yourself holding that 9-VM. And, jeezus, the *chakking* safety is still on. Good thing those thugs didn't know a *godich* thing."

Jimmy flushed, and his finger moved to the trigger, but the other man interceded, smacking his cane on the table between them.

"Enough. Thank you, Jimmy. Consider your debts and the debts of Jade finalized with Ms. Waychild."

"Alright," Jimmy grumbled.

"Later," Agracia said, waving at him as walked away. Mouthing an expletive or two, the ringside medic flipped her off before exiting the Watering Hole.

"*Chak*, old man—you don't need to take care of my business for me," she said.

Except for maybe his cane, she hadn't noticed any weapons on him, and he didn't appear to have any watchdogs. All the other patrons were minding their business, leaving her to wonder what the hell he would want from her, especially given her violent reputation.

"On the contrary," he said. He paused as he signaled the barkeep. "I assume you drink beer?"

"You assume correctly," she said, swiping the bottle before the barkeep even set it down. The new voice inside her piped up that it was stupid to consume alcohol during a deal—and an empty stomach—but she shut it up with a giant gulp. "So, 'on the contrary' what?"

"You're the best Jock on Earth, correct?"

She lifted an eyebrow, giving him her best *no gorsh-shit* expression.

"And you know the layouts of all the major cities around Ground Zero?"

"Duh," Agracia said, chugging the rest of her beer.

He smiled, revealing the diamond finish to his teeth. The thought occurred to her that she could probably get some money for his teeth and the other implants he probably had in his expensive-looking body, but she wanted to hear him out first, especially since he had gone to some trouble to hunt her down.

He used people I know and bought off my debt, she mused. *This is going to be good.*

"Well, you have a lot of enemies—too many to kill," the man said. "I had to buy most of them off. So you see, I'm a very trusting man, investing in you like this."

Agracia scoffed. "Ain't my problem."

"I beg your pardon?"

"You don't know Earth too well, or at least Jocks like me. I don't give a *chak* if you paid off my debts—that's your deal. I got my own *gorsh-shit* right now. Unless you have a pretty penny to shine for me, I'll thank you for the beer and be on my way."

The old man's smile didn't change. Agracia's stomach tightened. She kept up her vernacular and her usual act, but she was beginning to regret her decision. Somehow, some way, she felt like he could see right through her.

"You have a little sidekick, don't you?" he asked.

"Don't you worry your pretty face about that," Agracia said, smacking her lips.

The old man leaned forward, and Agracia caught a glimpse of his suit coat, another item that would fetch her at least a grand. She hadn't seen silk like that except on commercials.

"What's this?" Agracia said as the old man offered her a palm-sized portable viewer.

"Play it," he said, showing her the orientation.

Agracia eyed him and then pressed the top button.

"You *chakker!*"

The viewer showed an image of Bossy bound and gagged, her head bloodied and her eyes swollen shut.

"Ratchakkers!" Bossy rasped, her voice barely audible.

"Shove it," Agracia said, getting up to go.

"She'll be dead by tonight."

"*Chak* you," she said, turning to go again. She wanted to kill him as he sat there all smug, but she'd have to wait until he left the bar and drag him into the alley so the other patrons couldn't cash in on her kill.

"If her life isn't enough, then how about yours? How about I tell you the truth about your parents and brother?"

A strange and sudden pain spiked inside her skull, causing her to lose her balance and bump into a nearby table. Other patrons glanced at her but otherwise paid no attention to the presumably drunk young girl.

She went back down to the booth and stared at the old man, trying to understand what was happening to her. "Who are you and what the hell do you really want?"

"You aren't a Scabber, Agracia, and you aren't really human," he said. "You were meant for so much more than this. But first I need you to find something for me—something very important—and then I can help you."

Agracia massaged her forehead until the pain slowly dissipated. "You have my friend."

"I rescued her, too. She found her way into the fighting rings in the Spillway, but the bettors rigged her fight. I saved her, but she was quite brutal despite my hospitality. Those injuries you see were from before we got to her, but we did have to put her in restraints, lest she try to hurt me or my staff again."

"You said she'd be dead by tonight," Agracia said.

The old man folded his hands together, his eyes hidden behind the glare on his glasses. "She won't eat, drink or sleep—she's very weak."

I don't like the vibe of this old man, 'specially since he seems to know so much more about me than I know about him, she thought. *But I can't play into his hand, can I?*

No, this is gorsh-shit, she decided, angry with herself. *I have to save Bossy.*

"What do you want?" she said, keeping her tone even.

"I have a bet with an old friend that the very first space jump actually happened 1,128 years ago, right here, on this planet."

Agracia shook her head. "What?"

His lips upturned at some point between a sneer and a grimace, making the skin around cheeks crinkle. "I want you to get me the launch signature on a ship. The information is stored near Ground Zero, and you're reputed to be the only person ever to venture into those parts and live to tell about it."

Agracia shrugged her shoulders. "That's it?"

"Yes, that's it. And it comes with two tickets to the Mars colony and a month's pay."

Agracia bit her lip. It was a pretty good deal, but she didn't see the angle. "Why the hell would you want that *sycha*?"

"Because," he said, leaning forward again, "I want to give due credit to the man who revolutionized space flight."

"Whatever," Agracia said. "Look—you're gonna give me back my friend, and square with me about this 'family' of mine?"

The old man nodded, tapping his ringed fingers against his cane.

"And I want a year's pay. Nothin' short. Going out there in the wastelands ain't child's play."

The old man smiled again, his perfect teeth poised to bite into her. "Three months. Final offer."

Agracia wanted more, but she had no choice. If this man really had Bossy, and had enough money and power to pay off her debts, then she had to let it play out.

"So, what did you say your name was?" she asked as she watched him get up, his body making a queer crackling sound.

Leaning on his cane, the man gave her one last smile, the diamond-finish of his teeth sparkling through the cigarette haze. Her breath caught in her chest at the consuming black of his eyes. "You can call me Victor."

***

Jetta checked and rechecked her armrest display, keeping close tabs on the sensor readings. Even though she had hand-selected her pilot and navigations officer, she wanted to make sure they didn't fly too close to the border as the corvette approached the distortion field.

Making a fist, Jetta told herself to relax.

"You can never relinquish control, can you?" she imagined her sister saying.

This is the best I can do, she argued back.

After the Motti war she had been entrusted with command of the Special Missions Teams, and out of sheer necessity she had learned to trust and delegate dangerous operations to her team members. Now, surrounded by her most trusted soldiers and fellow officers from her SMT, she found herself regressing back into old habits.

This is different, she thought. Somehow, some way; she felt it in her bones.

Looking around at her crew, she realized why. *They're afraid, but they also know just how afraid I am.*

"Skucheka," she muttered, putting on her best face.

Determined to rein in the situation, Jetta flipped through the visual displays on her armrest.

The suspected Motti ship is nearing a remote outpost station, she observed. The site had been evacuated, but Erion, a planet home to billions of Sentients, was next in line. Even though the evacuation proceedings had begun, there was no way to move out the entire population of the planet before the ship came in range.

"Approaching the event horizon," her helmsmen reported.

Jetta zoomed in on the projection. She could see nothing abnormal, making it all the more disturbing. The stars shone innocuously in the background as Erion's outpost rotated on its axis, the distant, solitary sun reflecting off its tinted surface.

What's out there?

Chewing on the inside of her cheek, Jetta thought of Jahx and her sister, of Galm and Lohien, and Triel. She even thought of the people of Erion, remembering that they had been advocates of the telepaths.

I'm can't let my crew down, either, she reminded herself. Even though she had serious reservations about her superiors and governing bodies, she respected the men, women, and other Sentients that served alongside her.

As her inner conflict grew, she thought of her twin. *I wish Jaeia was here.*

At the same time, she was glad her twin wasn't. She didn't want Jaeia to be in harm's way, nor did she want her sister knowing what she was about to do.

Jetta pressed down on the intercom button. "Attention all hands—hold your positions."

"Lieutenant Ferraway," Jetta said, releasing the button and turning to her first officer. "I'm going to try and make contact. If anything happens… you know what to do."

Her first officer kept his voice low. "Sir, I implore you to utilize our medical staff to monitor your—"

"Lieutenant," Jetta said sharply, "Mind your post and remember the plan."

The first officer backed off and faced the front as the rest of the bridge fell into a hush. All eyes locked on the viewscreen where the mysterious ship lay hidden in the depths of space.

What am I doing?

Rational thought tried to intercede: *(This is insanity—a death wish.)*

But what other choice do I have? she countered.

Jetta remembered her last battle Motti, and the slick feeling of the demon that seduced her—

(*With eyes open, they burn*)

—and how a dark corner of her mind still hungered to be reunited, even though that thing had nearly cost her not only her own life, but those she held dearest.

No one is here to help me; I have to rely on my own abilities, she tried to tell herself even as the truth unfurled in her mind's eye: *Nightly dreams of the monster slipping back underneath her skin, one part of her reveling in its unimaginable powers as another wilted in terror. Dark yearnings giving rise to strange new appetites.*

Instead of feeling irritable, impetuous or indifferent in times of stress, finding herself unable to control the power sizzling at her fingertips.

That's how I ended up on Earth, she realized. Her inner voice finished the thought: *(And that's why I enjoyed the bout with Rigger Mortis, and attacked Agracia.)*

Is that why am I doing this? She looked down at her hands, not seeing her own pink skin but the flimsy outer covering an imposter. *(What am I becoming?)*

For the first time since she had recognized the dark pull inside her, she accepted another truth: *There's a reason I chose this mission—I am drawn to something on that Motti vessel.*

Even as the revelation struck fear in her heart, she couldn't bring herself to turn the ship around. *I can't go back now,* she told herself. *I have to do this—for my family.*

Concentrating on the dark space beyond the Erios station, Jetta relaxed her mind, reaching out. White noise, diffuse and static, gained volume and intensity.

"I hear you," she whispered, sliding out of her chair and onto her knees. Her first officer yelled something, but her vision telescoped away as she detached from her body.

Unlike the realm where she encountered Jahx and the demon, Jetta fell into a place of pure pain, concentrated and precise, shearing like a razor and gutting her from the inside out. Lipless screams echoed across the expanse, speaking of the minds fractured by an agony with immeasurable depth. She wanted nothing more than to run away, but at the same time, the voices, hypnotic in their torture, kept her from turning back.

Flecks of flesh peeled off from her body as she approached a rising halo of light. Its scorching brightness burned her eyes and skin, but she couldn't look away. Disembodied voices became clearer. She could distinguish language and their numbers, feeling their words—jarring and abrasive—within her bones:

"Ai-lĕ, ime, Ai-lĕ—nos k'etekμe imæ Ai-lĕ"

"Umnïero, Amaroka, f'ro ime nos wrli e"

"Dk'a ovŋĭl sh'dar'o"

Jetta reached out to shield her eyes, but her skin, stripped from her hands, left only melting bones and blood to drip down her arm. Nerves immersed in liquid fire, Jetta dragged herself towards the light, even as the pain surpassed any threshold she could have ever conceived.

Somewhere deep inside her, Jetta knew that there was only one explanation for this place, for the holocaust of pain and suffering she experienced. With everything she had left, Jetta fought to be heard.

(I know what you are,) *she screamed, thinking of Triel.* (It's not too late! I know how to save you—there is another.)

The pain intensified, driving her to her knees. She clutched her head with disintegrating hands as her psionic wall crumbled.

(This isn't real. Oh Gods, this can't be real—)

Jetta screamed as phantom roots slithered into her mind and dragged her into the burning light. Tasting madness and void, she lost sight of herself and any awareness of her life as the fire ate into her soul.

(Aelana *uxoris*,) *someone whispered,* (rise, be gone.)

A jolt of familiarity—Jaeia, Jahx—Triel. Her aunt and uncle. The Alliance. The Starways. Purpose.

Someone else in the flame, a presence apart from the pandemonium, rushed her away from the lure of the halo. She writhed and screamed as she shot back through the strata of hell.

(Jahx?) *she cried.*

Not Jahx.

(Who are you?)

Someone else.

Someone with the power of life and death.

***

A flurry of hands held Jetta down by her arms and legs. Someone shouted orders above her head in a fuzzy, jumbled confusion.

—*this isn't right!*—

The only thing that seemed real was the pain. It raged through her body in a torrent, the intensity spiking as she gained awareness.

"Drop the payload and jump us back, now!" she heard Ferraway say.

"No!" she screamed. Something sharp stabbed her thigh, and warm liquid seeped into tense muscle tissue. "Don't leave! I can stop the—"

(They're coming!)

Her words were cut short. The gravitational flux of the jump loosened the grip of the crewman, but she had already lost her drive to fight. All of her muscles relaxed, and anxieties dissipated in a comforting haze.

"We've got to stabilize her—"

Someone lifted her head and pressed an oxygen mask over her nose and mouth.

"I have to find her..." she mumbled, trying to stay conscience. "I have to tell her... we can't..."

Jetta's head rolled to the side. Her arms and legs felt like wet sand. As her eyes drifted downwards, she caught sight of the bloody, mangled mess that had been her hands. She tried to scream, but her mouth felt stuffed with cotton.

As she floated away, a demon with eyes like burning coals whispered from the shadows, telling her to come home.

CHAPTER VIII

Admiral Damon Unipoesa was on his second round of Old Earth vodka, staring at the picture of himself and the student class of '80 when his terminal buzzed.

This was taken a week prior to the selection of the final thirty candidates for the Command Development Program, he remembered. Urusous Li stood to his right and Tarsha Leone to his left.

Bitterness and spite overshadowed the memory. *Back when I could still care about my students.*

His terminal buzzed a second time.

"*Sycha,*" he muttered, putting the picture back under his desk where it would be safe. He scooted over in his chair to the terminal, pressing the button to receive the signal.

He didn't look at the screen, assuming it would be a status report from one of the operations, as he pulled on one of his boots.

"Damon Unipoesa."

The voice sent chills down his spine. He dropped his shoe and pushed aside his drink.

"Victor Paulstine. How did you get on this channel?" the admiral said, eyeing the alphanumeric code of the signal. Somehow Paulstine had breached the network and secured a direct line to him.

"I wrote the designs for your security system—you don't think I left a few backdoors?"

Unipoesa cocked his head. "Our defense system was designed by the Strader Corporation—"

Victor smiled. "I've gone by many names over many years to protect my investments. When I invented the flash transport device, I did so on Tralora, under a Narki title—Tt'ek So MeCaią. When I wrote the concept designs for the wave network, I had fourteen different identities, each one submitting different components to various military and investment corporations. And your security system—I *was* the Strader Corporation—all 111 employees."

The admiral laughed. "That is simply not possible. No human could possibly—"

Victor's face went cold. "You underestimate the human race. That was my mistake 1,100 years ago."

"Excuse me?" the admiral said as he typed in a tracking command. Unipoesa slammed his keypad, trying to understand the error message that kept appearing on his console.

"I'll save you the time—don't bother trying to track this conversation. And if you try and alert the staff outside your office, I'll terminate this link."

"What do you want?" the admiral asked, eyeing the door. If he could alert the guards stationed at his door, he could possibly get a remote terminal to track the conversation and maybe even the signal source.

"Your superiors pale to a man of your intellect. Razar and Reamon make a mockery of leadership. So I will tell you this: I am going to finish what I set out to do 1,100 years ago, and I want a man of your ilk at my side."

"And what was that?"

"To create peace."

The admiral leaned forward in his chair. "Of all the brazen—"

"Consider my offer," Victor said. "I already have the rest of your kin working for me. Why not make it a family affair? If you're ready to be something more than a pawn, meet me in the Holy Cities at the Temple of Zeitus in two hours. I will make my announcement then, and I want you at my side."

The transmission terminated, and the screen went blank.

Realizing his hands were shaking, Damon reached for the bottle of vodka but missed, spilling it all over his desk.

"*Chak!*" he said, trying to salvage what he could. Finally he stopped, sat back and remembered to breathe. Why the hell had Victor unnerved him so badly?

"My family…" Unipoesa said, thinking out loud. "What the hell did he mean?"

The Dominion Wars had killed most of his biological family, leaving him with only a few distant cousins on Arkana that worked the milling plants. His wife, Maria, from whom he had been separated for years, was vehemently anti-military, and would never associate with a man like Victor.

Just to make sure, Unipoesa pulled out his personal interface tablet and queried Maria's bio-signature. Even though it was illegal, an invasion of the privacy of a citizen, he could never stop himself when it came to her safety.

To his relief, he found her in her favorite location: her front yard, tending her field of wild roses and white Catheilia bushes. He quickly terminated the feed to save himself the hurt and returned to his earlier problem. *What family member would be of any value to Victor?*

Then he remembered the photo of the class of '80. He removed the picture from under the desk.

"Tarsha," he whispered, rubbing his thumb over her face to clear the smudges. She was like a daughter to him—as, at one time, Urusous had been like as son. But that was before he had to pit his prize students against each other, and abandon his own humanity.

Intelligence reports pointed toward a connection between Li and Victor, but Victor had implied the involvement of more than one family member. Unipoesa's other students were either dead or Sleeping, but if Victor could breach their security system, he could locate the ones who were still alive. *And if Victor is half the snake the reports make him out to be, it's plausible that he could coerce my former students into joining his cause.*

"Tarsha," he said again, taking the last swig of Old Earth vodka. He wouldn't allow himself to feel anything. Not guilt, not regret, not sorrow. Not for her.

Tarsha is dead, he reminded himself. *Only a crude, foul-mouthed Scabber remains.*

Other bits of the conversation with Victor reemerged. He pinched his eyes between his fingers, flabbergasted. *Did Victor really write the routines for their defense system?* He hurriedly rang in the Minister. "We've got trouble."

"Where have you been? I've sent the guards for you," the Minister said. "I need you on the bridge right now."

Unipoesa heard the guards shouting outside his door. "Victor Paulstine just contacted me through my private line. We've got even bigger problems. He claims he wrote our security system and left 'back doors.' I don't know if he's full of *gorsh-shit* or not, but our entire Fleet could be vulnerable."

The Minister scoffed. "That's ridiculous—he wrote an entire Fleet defense system?"

"That's what he claimed, and he did get through to me on a secured channel."

"That's plausible, Admiral, though close to impossible—messages can be piggybacked," the Minister said, shaking his head. "But writing the entire defense system is unheard of, especially for a human. Besides, I personally know the director of Strader. He's lying, pulling some angle."

"But Sir, wouldn't it be worth investigating—"

"Admiral, I've got mass causalities coming in from the *Rapture* and an emergency jump from the *Telluron*. I've also got Wren on the line saying that he's lost two battleships and that the distortion field has reached the first moon of Erion."

"I thought the *Telluron* was launching nukes?"

"Ineffective. We're facing the destruction of an entire cityworld."

Unipoesa's stomach dropped to his knees. "My Gods…"

"I need you to start coordinating the evacuation of the next planet."

"Where are Jetta and Jaeia?"

"Both Kyrons were critically injured during their missions," the Minister said.

Unipoesa gripped the lip of his desk. "You can't send Triel to medical if either Jetta or Jaeia are injured—I haven't discussed the Sleepers with them, or Triel's treatment."

"I can't afford to lose any of my top battle commanders right now. We'll have to sacrifice the Healer."

Unipoesa bolted from his chair, sending the bottle of vodka crashing to the floor. Ignoring the shouts of the guards outside his quarters, he jumped onto a moving lift and redirected its route.

"Come on, come on!" he said taking over the controls and accelerating the lift as fast as it would go. He took a corner too sharply, nearly beheading a line of soldiers marching down the corridor.

"Caution. Please slow down," the automated system warned.

Unipoesa jumped off the lift when they reached the medical ward, careening straight through the double doors and catching himself on the admissions desk.

"Where are they bringing in the casualties from the *Rapture* and the *Telluron*?" he said between breaths.

The befuddled attendant pointed him toward the secured ward down the white-tiled hallway.

Heart slamming up against his chest wall, Damon ran to the sectioned receiving area. Doctors and nurses ran every which way, monitors alerting in the background, bags of fluid and medication dangling from the ceiling. Injured soldiers moaned and screamed on medical tables, the smell of blood and burnt flesh singeing the air.

"Where's Triel?" he shouted above the clamor.

"Admiral!" Dr. Kaoto shouted, pushing his way through the crowd to him. "Over here!"

The admiral followed the doctor through the isolation corridor, back to the intensive care unit.

"Both commanders are critical," Kaoto said. "Jaeia has Class 5 head trauma and Jetta—well, I can't explain Jetta's wounds. They are completely off the charts."

The admiral looked down at the readings on the datafile. "This doesn't make sense to me."

"Those are Jaeia's intracranial pressure readings, and that's the analysis of the corrosive tissue damage Jetta sustained," the doctor explained. "But don't' worry, Triel's on her way—thank God she's back. I don't think they'd survive."

The admiral bowed his head. "This is a direct order, doctor. I want Triel to heal them, but as soon as she's finished, I want her tranquilized and secured in medical lockdown. I also want the twins sedated until I'm able to debrief them on the current situation."

"Sir?" the doctor said, astounded.

I'm doing it again, he thought, trying to keep his hands still. Right then he would have given anything for the burn that only vodka could give him. *I'm breaking promises in the name of the greater good.*

He looked the Kaoto dead in the eye. "It's for your safety—and mine."

***

"There is a history in this room that stretches back farther than you could imagine. And what transpires between you and I will determine more than you could ever conceive."

Victor stood over her, his plastic skin glinting in the light. Pinned down by an unseen force, Jaeia found herself unable to move as he turned her right arm outwards. With a smile that stretched across his face and distorted the shape of his eyes, he took a knife and cut into her flesh. She tried to scream, but her cries could not be heard above his chanting as he sliced away her tattoo.

"With eyes open, they burn."

Jaeia shot up, screaming and pawing at her right arm. Striking her head on an exam light, she dropped back onto the table, discombobulated and mumbling.

"Hold still," said a familiar voice. Triel's warm hand wrapped gently around her forearm. "It's okay. Let me finish."

Burning liquid flowed up her hand to her shoulder. She looked to the left and saw the intravenous line secured to her skin.

"I'm going to make another pass," she heard Triel say as her anxiety melted away and she drifted from corporeality.

The Healer's ethereal touch glided toward her core, dissipating pain and fear the further she traveled. As Triel repaired her injuries, aligning with her internal rhythms, Jaeia witnessed snippets of Triel's conversations, sensations, and feelings.

Surprise, delight. The smell of yingar root and karrin potatoes. Sensing Jetta's nervousness as she hands her a container full of traditional Algardrien food—

—"They don't exactly serve that in the mess hall."

Drawn away from her own discomforts, Jaeia reached back, taking shelter inside Triel's mind as the Healer stayed focused on restoration. Entire memories unfolded before her, vibrant and unguarded, until she encountered a barricade.

This feels wrong, *she thought, feeling the cold, hard exterior of the psionic wall encapsulating Triel's memories from the moments after the theft to her rescue on the* Mercury. ...Like an unwanted memory suppressed by pain.

Jaeia focused on the black surface, testing its icy smoothness. I've never felt anything like this, *she thought, unable to find the slightest crack or blemish.* Something horrible must have happened for this kind of blockade.

Concerned about her friend, she resorted to her second voice: (Let me in.)

At the sound of her talent, the barricade imploded, sucking her down and in. Before panic had a chance to gain hold, Jaeia stumbled into some sort of store piled high with books and ancient devices. The smell of preservatives and dust tickled her nose, reminding her of a museum.

What is this place? *she wondered as an elderly man behind a counter counted and hummed to himself.*

After looking around, she convinced herself that odd wares and a storeowner couldn't be the extent of the trapped memory. This doesn't explain Triel's pain; there has to be more.

Jaeia closed her eyes and reached back, rewinding through the disordered memories. When she opened her eyes again, a human woman, perhaps in her twenties or thirties, with fair coloring and light brown hair stood in front of her against a gray backdrop.

How do I know you? *Jaeia thought, trying to reconcile the familiarity of her serious expression. Staring into the woman's pale green eyes, she realized why.* I recognize that look.

The woman spoke in disjointed sentences: "There isn't... I was born on Earth in 2021... The most important thing... Earth, when it was green and full of life... but that day in 2052 changed... I can only hope that it isn't too late, that maybe my surviving... our surviving... mankind still has a chance."

As muted colors seeped into the gray backdrop, Jaeia reached out to the woman, but her touch sent ripples through the image.

It isn't real, *Jaeia realized.* That's why everything is choppy and skewed—like a bad copy of a copy. It must be part of a recording or impression that Triel accidentally gleaned.

"The man on fire knows... where... go next," *the woman said, her voice fading in and out.* "If you... look for... familiar sign. And when you find Charlie... answered."

The man on fire... *Jaeia remembered, thinking back to the mysterious message she had received not too long ago.* Is this woman the one who tried to contact me?

Back up again.

Jaeia gasped. She saw Reht in Triel's arms and a red-haired human officer in an Alliance uniform sneering at her. Immersing herself in the memory, Jaeia absorbed every moment as the red-haired officer told her about the Sleeper program and what was to be done to the crew of the Wraith.

Reht... *Jaeia thought, looking more closely at the dog-soldier captain. The unusual red and black-tipped coloring to his hair made it look like fire.* It's you—but why?

Piecing Triel's memories together with her own, Jaeia formed a disturbing theory: The Alliance couldn't make Triel a Sleeper because of her telepathic abilities, so they tried to erase her memories and stage an accident. However, whatever impression Triel had gleaned off of Reht was protected, and it consequently protected her, preventing the Alliance from completely wiping her memories.

Jaeia pushed further, listening to Triel's thought process about the memory stain and came to another conclusion: The woman who stained Reht must have also sent me the piggybacked message. I was supposed to find Reht but never reached him in time. Triel got to him first and picked up part of the message.

(Reht—the man on fire—he knows where to go next,) *Jaeia said aloud.*

Then it hit her. Who could perform a memory stain like that? What kind of telepath was capable of something that powerful? And why did the woman look so familiar?

Thoughts and images faded as Triel completed the restoration and withdrew. Jaeia fought to wake up, and when she finally opened her eyes, white-masked medics held her down as a doctor rushed over with a sedative in hand.

"No!" Jaeia screamed. "Stop! I just saw—I just saw—" she began, wrestling against their grip. She managed to free a leg and kick the medication out of the doctor's hands, but someone else got her from behind, jabbing something into her shoulder.

"I saw her…" Jaeia said, fighting the sedative's effects as her resolve washed away. She looked straight into the overhead light and laughed, tears streaming from her eyes. "I saw my mother."

***

Even as Jaeia's screams faded in the next room, Triel could afford no time to investigate. Jetta's wounds were serious enough that the Healer had sensed the fallen commander's injuries even before she had been transported to the critical care unit.

"Jetta," the Healer whispered as they pushed her stretcher under the exam light. "No…"

Her knees, suddenly weak, didn't feel like they could support her weight. Stomach churning, she looked again at Jetta and confirmed her greatest fear.

"What's your impression, Triel? What could have done this? None of the other crewmen were injured," Dr. Kaoto said, waving a bioscanner over Jetta's mangled body.

This is worse than I could have imagined.

The commander's hands were an ugly red, and suppurating blisters had broken open over the skin of her neck, chest and thighs. Ugly black streaks branched out from the fissures in her skin, and the smell—the acrid stench Triel had only encountered once in her lifetime—carved terror into her heart.

"No agent is registering on the bioscanner. However, I'm reading a systemic inflammatory response, necrosis of tissue, ketoacidosis," Kaoto remarked. "Thank the Gods they evaced in time."

Triel elevated the stretcher and stood at Jetta's head. Even unconscious, the commander's eyes stayed open, her pupils dilated with unseen horror.

"Triel, please—do you know what this is?" Kaoto asked.

The Healer knew, but she couldn't bring herself to answer the chief just yet. "I just have to make sure…" Triel said, resting her hands on Jetta's neck and falling in.

"Ai-lĕ, ime, Ai-lĕ—nos k'etekµe imœ Ai-lĕ"

"Dk'a ovŋĭl sh'dar'o"

—*her people's words—prayers she hadn't heard in so long—*

Triel relived Jetta's encounter as she foolishly tried to connect to the dark force harnessed by the Motti. A long time ago on Algar, Triel had experienced a similar dysphoria, but with her tribe—never alone like Jetta, and certainly never against a horde of the Fallen.

Jetta's pain assaulted the Healer as she was drawn into the malevolent web of the Dissembler mind, seduced by their caustic whispers, body and mind detached, mind eclipsed as the body dissolved from the inside out.

Then Triel heard his words: (Umnïero, Amaroka, f'ro ime nos wrli e)

— I give myself to the Great Mother so that she may wield my spirit—

(My Gods—) *Triel cried out.*

Just as the Dissemblers were about to deal Jetta the final blow, Triel felt him, *jarring her concentration. Bewildered, the Healer fell backwards but struggled to stay anchored, not wanting to lose his essence, even if it was only a memory. He shielded Jetta from the final onslaught, pushing her away from the halo of light, back to her body on the safety of her ship.*

(Please, no!) *Triel screamed, seeing his kind face in the blur of light before Jetta's memory faded away.*

"My Gods," Triel whispered as tears cascaded down her cheeks.

"What is it, Triel?" Dr. Kaoto asked, holding her by the shoulders.

"Dissemblers—it was Dissemblers that did this. And one of them—one of them," she said, stumbling backwards. "Was my…"

Father.

"We're losing her," one of the nurses shouted, the alarms shrieking.

Triel wiped the tears from her eyes with shaky hands and returned to Jetta's body.

"Are you well enough to—" Kaoto started.

"I'm fine. Everybody, please, stay back," Triel said as she laid her hands on the sides of Jetta's face.

With the commander's awareness buried beneath the lies of Dissembler, Triel couldn't forge the usual connection to bring her patient's mind and body into sync. The rest of Jetta's body, succumbing to the Dissembler-created illusion of disease, turned upon itself, ravaging every cell and structure.

If I don't act now, her body—and mind—will consume itself, she thought, not allowing herself to assess the true risk. She had done a full immersion on Jetta before, but never against the black tide of her peoples' dark power.

(Don't be afraid,) *Triel whispered, sinking deeper into Jetta's mind, trying to find her essence. She met with resistance—from the malignancy of the Dissemblers, but also from Jetta. Pushing harder, Triel fought through the infectious deceit, holding fast to her mission.*

(I can't let you see me,) *Jetta whispered back.*

Pride and fear swathed the commander's mind, preventing Triel from breaking through. (Jetta, you have to let me help you or you'll die. Do it for Jaeia, please!)

Reminding her of her twin usually worked, but not this time. Jetta resisted further, pulling away from Triel as cells erupted in a massive cascade effect. In the periphery of the Healer's mind, alarms blared and Dr. Kaoto frantically shouted for cardiac stabilizers.

(I can't let you,) *Jetta said again.*

Even though they never discussed their relationship, there had always been an inexplicable bond between them, deeper and more complex than most friendships. Because of their unusual ages and circumstances, Triel hadn't pursued anything further, especially given how closely Jetta shielded her feelings from others. But now, seeing Jetta's life bleeding away, she knew she would have to expose what had been left unspoken.

(Jetta... I care about you. Please, let me help you.)

Shame and terror pooled all around her, but Jetta's mind yielded just enough to allow Triel to slip inside. Layering herself against Jetta's psionic tune, she began the healing process, funneling Jetta's consciousness back into her body and guiding her mind back to her soul.

Submersed deeper inside a patient than she had ever gone before, Triel didn't grasp her place within her friend until she heard whispers sounding from an unseen source. Curious, Triel shifted her connection, illuminating the hidden realm within.

I shouldn't be here, *Triel realized, seeing the luminescent ghosts of Jetta's inner world act out dreams and yearnings. But as she thought to leave, she caught the edge of something buried in the farthest reaches of Jetta's subconscious.*

Held away from others, away from her sister—even away from herself—Jetta sheltered her greatest secret. Drenched in humiliation and bound by grief, her secret pulsated with the light of a thousand stars. Wounded and vulnerable, Jetta couldn't prevent her from seeing it, if only for a glimpse.

Triel gasped in disbelief.

(Jetta,) *Triel whispered.* (I didn't know—)

(Get out!) *Jetta screamed.*

With her remaining strength, Jetta lashed out, severing her connection to the Healer. Triel spun back and away, reeling as she reentered her own body.

"Grab her!"

Strong arms caught Triel as she fell backwards, gently guiding her to the floor as she regained her sight.

"Is she—?" the Healer forced through numb lips.

"Jetta's stabilized," Kaoto said. "Get her to the treatment room, now!"

"What?" Triel said. The hands that helped her now held her down in the confusion of movement all around her. Medics crowded around her, grabbing at her limbs.

"Stop!" the Healer shouted, sensing what was coming. "You don't know what you're doing—"

She fought until she couldn't move her arms anymore, until her legs felt heavier than cement. As the world faded to black, Triel listened as the voices above her discussed her fate.

***

"What did he say?" the Minister asked.

DeAnders checked his clipboard, flipping down the screen and putting his finger on the line. "Oh, here. 'His name is Josef Stein.' And that's all he said before we lost him."

"What do you mean, lost him?" the admiral asked, looking down at the motionless body of Jahx Kyron, formerly belonging to the Grand Oblin.

"He's showing minimal brain activity; nonresponsive to any of our therapies. If I can't have Triel on this case, then I'm afraid I'm out of options."

The Minister threw an indignant look at the admiral before speaking. "Keep him stabilized, Doctor. I'll consult with you after we secure the situation on Erion."

The admiral followed the Minister out of the Defense/Research lab and back to the quarantined area in the medical ward.

"Josef Stein—oh my Gods," the admiral said under his breath.

The Military Minister burst through the double doors to the critical care unit. "I want everyone out except you!"

Dr. Kaoto stayed by Jaeia's bedside while the rest of the team scattered behind the partition.

"Is the Healer secured?" Tidas asked.

"Yes, Sir," Kaoto said. "We put her in cryostasis."

"Cryostasis? I only ordered sedation," the admiral said.

"Yes, Sir," Kaoto said, looking to the Minister. "But Prodgy telepaths have the ability to maintain some degree of telepathic awareness even in sleep. Cryostasis is the only way to eliminate all telepathic functions."

"You overrode my order?" Damon asked, turning to Razar.

The Military Minister got in his face, enough so that Unipoesa could smell the antacids on his breath. "If you can't secure the situation with the Kyrons, I'm keeping the Healer on ice—indefinitely."

"But Jahx—" Damon started.

"That's my final decision," the Minister said, straightening his uniform top. "We've lost almost all of Erion, and we're about to lose its third moon, Tellemikas. I need the twins back on this situation, *now,* before that ship hits the perimeter."

The Minister said something quietly to Kaoto before turning back to the admiral. "I'm sending Wren to the front lines to try launching nukes again. But if you can't secure the twins and Wren is lost, then you're next in line for the big chair."

"Yes, Sir," the admiral said, barely rising above the voice screaming inside of him. *I can't command again—it was all a fluke—*

(I am a fluke.)

Quieting old demons with the promise of alcohol, the admiral watched the Military Minister exit the medical wing in a hurry to get back to Central Command.

Damon looked at the interface on his uniform sleeve. Blue holographics projected the latest estimated death toll on Erion at 4.5 billion.

I have to secure the twins.

(I can't take command again.)

After smoothing down his thinning hair, he addressed Kaoto. "Alright, I want both sisters awake—but keep a line in them just in case. No restraints, though."

Dr. Kaoto nodded. "I understand, Admiral," he said, signaling one of the nurses to wheel Jetta's stretcher next to Jaeia's "However, there's something else I need to tell you about them—there are some very strange findings."

"I don't have the time, doctor," the admiral said, rolling up his sleeves. "Get them awake."

"But these findings are very—"

"It will have to wait, doctor. Revive them."

Kaoto frowned, but drew up the yellow medication from the medport and administered the reversals in their intravenous lines. Within seconds, the twins came around.

"Admiral," Jaeia said, her voice dry and scratchy as she tried to sit up. "Is everything alright? Where's Jetta?"

Pupils pinpoint and unfocused, Jetta held her head in her hands in the adjacent bed. "I'm here. What just happened?"

"You're both fine. Jaeia, you sustained a head injury, and Jetta some systemic and localized tissue damage, both of which Triel was able to heal," Dr. Kaoto reported.

"Thank you, doctor. Now, if you don't mind…" the admiral said, pointing towards the door. Irritated but compliant, Kaoto left the room, positioning himself behind the observation station to continue to monitor the twins' physiological progress.

"Jaeia, Jetta—both of your missions were prematurely aborted," Damon said. "Triel saved your lives, and I came here to talk to you about saving hers."

Jetta held her head in her hands. "What the hell are you talking about?"

The admiral rolled a footstool between the stretchers. Assuming they already knew the details of her ordeal, he cut to the chase: "She doesn't know that we altered the memories of Reht and his crew, and she can't know. It's a potential trigger for her to Fall."

Jetta's face turned bright red. Still emerging from the sedation, he could tell by her tight jaw and creased forehead that she hadn't organized all her thoughts to give him hell just yet.

"Sleepers," Jaeia said, closing her eyes. "You made Reht and his crew into Sleepers."

Damon took a deep breath. *Full disclosure is the ultimate risk.* "It was the only option."

He saw them both mounting their arguments, tempers flaring—even Jaeia's—so he did something he promised he wouldn't. "Despite your friendship, I'm sure Reht has not shared with you his violent history."

"What do you mean?" Jaeia said.

"The destruction of Elia, for starters. Reht has betrayed all those who have trusted him. To the Alliance, he's an unknown quantity, making him dangerous to the Fleet and therefore the Starways. I will be honest with you: We're using him as a Sleeper to gain intelligence on a key figure that may be involved in the silent genocide that's happening across the Starways."

"You mean the disappearance of human colonies," Jaeia said.

"Yes. He's the only person who could possibly get close to our lead source. After that mission is complete, he can run his life the way he wants—playing his pirate games, screwing women, whatever."

"But you won't release him from the programming," Jaeia pointed out. "Even after you've risked his life."

The admiral shook his head. "We'll always keep tabs on him. He's too big a security risk."

A vein throbbed on Jetta's forehead. "What did you do to Triel? How could she possibly not know what happened to Reht?"

"It was taken care of," the admiral said.

"No, it wasn't," Jaeia whispered, sliding off the stretcher. Her legs wobbled at first, but she found her footing, using the assistance of a tray table. Slowly walking toward him, Jaeia kept her gray eyes pinned to his face, searching for something. "You tried to erase her memories, but it didn't work. And I found them. She'll remember now, if she tries."

"Is that so?" the admiral said.

"I'm certain of it. And I need her—we need her. She knows things about our past."

The admiral raised a brow. "What do you mean, Jaeia?"

"That's all I can say."

Damon didn't believe her, not with the resolute look in Jaeia's eyes or the way her sister's expression changed from anger to astonishment.

They're silently communicating, he realized, watching Jetta's blood pressure rise on the monitors. *Whatever Jaeia leeched form Triel is eliciting a strong reaction in Jetta.*

"We've deployed every single warship in the Fleet, so we need you two suited up and ready to ship out as soon as Dr. Kaoto clears you, is that understood?" he said, hardening his voice.

Jetta tipped her head back and laughed. "You can't fight what the Motti has."

"You confirmed it was a Motti ship?" he said.

"Oh yes," Jetta said, her laughter dying. "And nothing will stop them from killing us all. Not even with every warship in this galaxy and the greatest commander at her helm. They've harnessed pure malice."

"I get it now," Jaeia whispered, her eyes moving rapidly back and forth. "The ship *is* a giant communications dish—and it projects the telepathic vibrations of the Dissemblers."

"But we have weapons—" the admiral said.

"You don't get it," Jetta said, hoping off the stretcher. As she ripped the intravenous lines out of her hands, she passed around her sister to stand in front of the admiral. "We can't get close enough to launch an attack, and they'll have time to detect any traps we set."

How the hell is she walking—standing—on such swollen legs? he wondered, trying to keep his eyes from dropping to Jetta's red and weeping lower limbs. "Then what do you suggest, Commander?"

Blood dripped down Jetta's hands and onto the white-tiled floor. "We took the Motti to the brink of extinction after the war, but somehow some of them survived and are really, *really* pissed off. There's only one person who can get close enough to a Dissembler without being killed, and you're trying to screw her seven different ways."

"I don't know if—"

"She's the *only one* who can stop them," Jetta said with great emphasis.

"How do you know? How could you guarantee that?" the admiral asked, standing so she would stop towering over him.

Jetta closed her eyes and turned her head to one side. "Something—someone—in there pushed me out when I thought of Triel. It's the only reason I'm standing here. If her memory could do that much, then I know she could do much more."

"Look," Jetta said, tying her patient gown more securely around her waist as she headed for the door. "This military *gorsh-shit*, turning Sentients into Sleepers—that's your price to pay, not mine. You want to save the galaxy, you have to level with Triel."

"Excuse me," Dr. Kaoto said, rounding the corner, stopping Jetta from leaving. "I'm afraid I can't let you leave."

"Don't start with me, Doc. I've had a very bad day, and I want to see Triel and my brother *now*," Jetta said, trying to shove him aside.

The smaller, hybrid human stood his ground. "You can't—I still need to treat you."

"What for?" Jetta asked, arms on her hips. "I'm fine."

"I'm sorry to disagree with you, Commander," Kaoto said, giving a slight bow.

The admiral watched as Jetta's face, then Jaeia's, drain of all color.

"So... how long do we have?" Jaeia whispered.

"Doctor," the admiral said, grabbing Kaoto's arm. "What is this all about?"

"I tried to tell you earlier," he said, handing the admiral a datafile.

Even though the he felt pressure in the back of his mind as he read the datafile, the admiral didn't stop the twins from reading his thoughts.

"What does this mean?" Unipoesa asked, not understanding the complex prognosis.

Dr. Kaoto took the file back and faced the sisters. "Our latest scans have revealed marked endogenous and exogenous damage to your DNA. Have you been noticing any troublesome symptoms?"

"I thought it was stress," Jaeia said, fidgeting with her gown.

Jetta scoffed. "This is a joke, right? What are you saying? That we're dying?"

The room fell silent as Dr. Kaoto manually adjusted the artificial lens in his right eye. "Unless we find a pure source of your DNA, then the degradation will be irreversible and eventually your organs will fail."

"But Triel can heal anything," Jetta said, her voice carrying her concern.

Dr. Kaoto shook his head. "Her healing techniques rely on your DNA as a source code. Essentially, you're the blueprint, and she guides your cells to reconstruct themselves accordingly. But since your DNA is corrupted, her powers are limited."

"How did this happen?" the admiral asked. "Why didn't the biochips pick this up?"

"My best supposition would be that the alterations the Motti made to enhance their growth and strength corrupted their DNA, and that the mutations were initially miniscule enough that they went undetected by the biochips—and, incidentally, by Triel."

The admiral moved just in time as Jetta's hand came crashing down onto the nearby instrument cart, caving it in and scattering instruments across the unit. "That is a load of *gorsh-shit*!"

"He's not lying, Jetta," Jaeia said, leaning against the stretcher and covering her eyes. "You know it's true."

"Well, where the hell would we find a 'pure source' of our DNA?" Jetta said.

Dr. Kaoto shifted his feet. "That's where things become complicated."

"What about Fiorah? Have you looked in our old apartment?"

The admiral chose his words carefully. "We shared those intelligence reports with you. There was some sort of electrical fire in the community housing block you lived in shortly after you were taken by the Core. There wasn't anything to salvage."

"How much time do we have?" Jetta asked.

Dr. Kaoto looked at his datafile. "From the looks of these markers—a few months. Maybe less. It's hard to predict."

"Great," Jetta laughed. "All that's left for you to tell me is that Jahx is dead."

The admiral cleared his throat. "Drs. DeAnders and Kaoto had to induce coma again. His new body is too unstable."

Jetta's lips curled in as she transformed her hands into fists. "Fine," she said, looking for her belongings next to her stretcher. After finding her weapons belt and uniform, though bloodied and ripped, she began dressing herself.

The admiral and Dr. Kaoto turned away as she disrobed.

"My guess is that you put Triel on ice," Jetta said, pouring fire into every word. "That leaves my brother in a coma from which he may never emerge, my aunt and uncle missing but most likely dead, and my sister and I are toast. So—what's left, eh?"

"Jetta," the admiral said, approaching her with caution. "We still need you. The Starways still needs you. You and your sister are our best battle commanders."

Jetta ignored him, but Jaeia grabbed her arm and spun her around. Putting a hand on her sister's shoulder, Jaeia stared intently into Jetta's eyes while their bodies swayed back and forth in unison. The rapid exchange of information never failed to make his skin prickle. *I would give anything for that talent.*

"Commanders, what's going on?" the admiral demanded.

"I was just giving her a reason to stay," Jaeia said, holding up a hand to keep her sister quiet. "But the bottom line is, we still need each other, and we're going to have to have complete disclosure if we're going to continue this relationship."

"And Triel off ice," Jetta added vehemently.

(Oh Tarsha—what have I done?)

Pushing aside the thoughts of his former student, the admiral made a decision he knew he would later regret.

"I'll tell you the most important reason to stay," he said, checking his pockets for a smoke, even though he knew he was out. "1,128 years ago, there was a ship that disappeared during the Exodus from Earth. A very important man was on it—one who had the technology for biosphere resurrection. Until you two appeared, nobody thought there was any chance that he could have made it. But that tattoo on your arm and your unusual age—it may be the key."

"How so?" Jaeia asked.

"At the time it was customary for passengers to tattoo the symbol of their vessel crest on their arms. If we can find the name of your ship and match it to your tattoo… well, then there's hope that he could have survived, too."

"And then what?" Jetta said.

"All these dead planets—all the worlds destroyed by the Motti, even Earth—we can resurrect. We can find homes for all the refugees. The Starways will be reborn."

"Admiral," Kaoto whispered, shaking his head.

I know—I've just signed my own death warrant.

But even if the Minister had him killed for what he did, the twins knew the truth.

I finally did something right.

"What was this man's name?" Jetta asked.

"Kurt Stein."

The twins looked at him skeptically. Pressure built in the back of his mind, and he allowed his guard to fall.

(I am risking everything for this.)

The pressure ceased. Identical looks of satisfaction lit their eyes.

"But something troubles me," the admiral said as he watched Kaoto disappear behind the monitoring station to alert the Minister. *If only I could have seen Tarsha one more time.* "Your brother—the last thing he said before he went into a coma. He said, 'His name is Josef Stein.' Do you have any idea why?"

Jetta and Jaeia exchanged glances.

Believing them to be ignorant, he explained further: "He was the man who started the biological warfare that ended Earth. He's the notorious Doctor Death."

Jetta went pale. "Doctor Death?"

"And Kurt Stein was his son," the admiral added.

Jetta seemed troubled by the name. "Josef Stein… Doctor Death," she mumbled.

"It was your fighting name on Earth," Jaeia reminded her.

"N-no," Jetta stuttered, covering her mouth. "There's more. When he made the connection between Josef and Kurt… I felt something more."

A score of guards entered the critical care unit.

"You don't have much time," Jaeia said to the admiral as the guards filed into the unit.

"I know," Unipoesa said, adjusting his uniform and patting his hair down. *I never wanted it to end like this.*

With the ghosts of his former students by his side, he imparted what he could: "You're more than just battle commanders, Jetta, Jaeia. You're a chance at a new beginning; you can lead us to rebuilding our worlds. That's why the Minister has kept so much from you, and that's why you can't know your own importance."

"Admiral Unipoesa, you're under arrest for treason by order of Military Minister Razar," one of the guards announced.

The tip of a gun poked into his ribs, but he didn't go quietly. "Don't give up. Keep fighting. Believe in the Alliance," he shouted as the doors clamped shut behind him.

He'd never been electrocuted by a shockwand before, though he had ordered it numerous times on his students in the Command Development Program. As the blue arc snaked out of the wand and bit into his side, he thought only of Tarsha. *Will they ever let us wake up again?*

Body bucking and twisting, the admiral hit his head on the floor before his arms could cushion the blow.

***

Jetta thought she and her sister would be arrested and imprisoned after Admiral Unipoesa's disclosure. Instead, the Minister ordered them to be escorted to the Alliance flagship, the *Star Runner*, where he met them in the upper deck observatory. With CCO Wren at the helm, the ship rumbled and shook as every available weapon discharged in rapid fire.

"You *bendakca asjole!*" Jetta cursed, heading straight for the Minister as soon as the guards left. But before she could take more than a few steps, her sister's emotions defanged her attack.

"My Gods," Jaeia said, rushing to the two-story windows overlooking the battle. Erion, once a blue and green planet, had crusted over into a brown and black wasteland. Ships that couldn't escape the distortion field turned nose down, adrift, life support and backup drives failing within seconds. The Alliance starcraft synchronized their retreat, staying a good distance from the encroaching anomaly, setting traps and desperately firing weapons.

"I feel them..." Jaeia said, pressing her hands against the glass.

"No, Jaeia, don't—" Jetta said, trying to prevent her sister from opening up their telepathic channel.

Gasping, Jaeia fell to her knees, clutching her head in her hands. Jetta stood her ground the best she could, trying to block out the torment of the planet below. Billions of Sentient minds blasted their agony across the psionic plane, their suffering roiling through her with molten fury as the Dissemblers tore them apart.

—*save me, Gods*—

—*skin peeling away*—

—*blood spilling*—

—*my insides*—

—*on fire, I*—

—*pain and madness*—

—*burning lights of*—

—*Hell*—

"Make it stop," Jaeia whispered, crawling over and gripping her sister's pant leg.

Tipping her head back, Jetta struck out against the panic-filled interspace and pulled herself and her twin back into the safety of their own minds. As the two of them retreated as far as they could, the peripheral pains lessened to a dull ache that lapped against their skulls like waves against a shore.

After collecting herself, Jetta helped her sister off the ground, keeping her arm around her waist. "Why did you bring us here?" she said between breaths. "We can't do anything without Triel."

"The Healer would prove a liability right now. So, it is up to you," the Minister said, crossing his hands behind his back and positioning himself at the far window. "That ship will cross the border and into the Homeworlds in a few days. Trigos is only weeks away. We need you two back in command."

Jetta looked at her sister. *Is it worth it?*

Tears welled in her sister's eyes. The image of the woman Jaeia thought to be their mother flashed through Jetta's mind.

And what about Jahx—his impossible second chance at life? Jaeia added.

I know... Jetta thought, unable to dismiss the miracle.

A flash of bright light filled the observatory, then vanished. "Who the hell...?" the Minister exclaimed as the ship quaked in the aftermath. He rushed over an access terminal and punched into the secured com link to ring in the bridge. "Get me the CCO!"

"What's going on?" Jetta said, following the Minister's gaze out the window. Near the port side of the flagship appeared a rogue legion of starcraft. The ship designs represented many different factions, making it difficult to determine who was leading them or what they stood for.

Jaeia's eyes narrowed as she sucked in her breath. Jetta heard her thought before she said it out loud. "This is a trick..."

"Sir, they jumped within our ranks, but are not engaging us," Wren said over the com as two starfighters broke from the rogue legion and accelerated towards the distortion field. "They're heading straight for the event horizon."

"What is that?" the Minister said, pointing to the object in their tow.

I've never seen anything like that before, Jetta thought, trying to understand the iridescent tetrahedral object that rotated and spun impossibly, as if fluctuating between dimensions of space and time.

"It's an illusion," Jaeia replied.

This isn't right, Jetta said, sharing her sister's sentiment.

"Oh Gods—" the Minister said as the starfighters shot the tetrahedral object at the distortion field.

Stolen memories overshadowed her own reaction as shockwave rippled back toward the Alliance Fleet, obliterating starcraft in its wake.

(Never detonate a warhead so close to your Fleet—)

(We're all going to die!)

Sirens alarmed, but Jetta had no time to respond as the detonation wave struck the ship and flung them into the air. She racked her shoulder and chest against a support pillar, knocking the wind from her lungs. As she gasped for breath, she looked over to see Jaeia rolling onto her side, stunned from her crash-landing against the far wall. The Minister fared the worst, cracking his head open on the edge of the observatory relay station.

"All hands to battle stations," Wren shouted over the com. "Repeat, all hands to battle stations."

The second wave hit the *Star Runner*, this time catapulting Jetta against a bulkhead. Electrical wires fizzled out and dropped from the ceiling as a series of internal explosions rocked the ship. Jetta rolled out from beneath the live wires, ignoring the pain in her neck and shoulder, and grabbed her sister lying next to her. "Are you okay?" she asked, helping her sister up.

"I'm fine. The Minister—" Jaeia said, crawling over the overturned chairs. She kneeled next to him, careful not to move his body. "He doesn't have a pulse. I'm starting emergency resuscitation"

Jetta ran to the relay station but paused as she was about to hit the call button.

(Let him die.)

She went rigid, unable to move or think.

(Watch him die,) the voice hissed. *(Take what you will from him.)*

"Jetta?" Jaeia said. "What is it?"

Confused, Jetta shook her head. *No. That's wrong. I know that's wrong... isn't it?*

"Make the call!" Jaeia shouted.

Jetta snapped to attention. "I need the medical team to the observatory. The Minister is down," she yelled over the intercom.

Picking her way back to her sister and the Minister, Jetta minded her footing as the ship continued to rumble and quake. "Sorry, Jaeia. I just... I just don't know what I'm thinking sometimes."

"Get down here and help me," Jaeia said, pumping on the Minister's chest.

But Jetta couldn't. Something dark inside her unfurled, turning her limbs into cold wax. She stood transfixed, unable to move as her sister struggled to administer emergency treatment.

(He betrayed you. He hurt your friends.)

"Please, I need you—help me!" Jaeia pled as she started to fatigue.

Despite her sister's desperation saturating her mind, Jetta couldn't move. With her feet cemented to the floor and muscles rendered inert, she felt her mind exposed and vulnerable to the foul thing lurking in the sewers of her subconscious.

(He has always deceived you,) the incubus whispered in her ear. *(He will hurt everyone you love.)*

Jolted by a vicious impulse, Jetta lurched forward. *I have to make sure the Minister doesn't survive—at all costs.*

(If Jaeia gets in my way, I will hurt her, too.)

"Sorry, Commander," a medic said, coming up from behind them. "We've got injury reports coming in from all over the ship."

Broken from her thoughts, Jetta shuddered. *What is happening to me?* Ashamed and embarrassed, she stammered, "Jaeia, I'm so sorry—I don't know what came over me."

The look on Jaeia's face made her cringe. "We should get to the bridge," her sister said quietly, keeping her distance. "There's nothing we can do for him now."

Jetta watched as the medical team attached electrodes to the Minister's chest, unsure of what she was feeling and too afraid to put any thought to it.

"Come on," Jaeia said, pulling at her arm.

"Fine, let go," Jetta relented. Once she got her arm freed from her sister, Jetta retied her hair back, only to inadvertently pull out a handful.

Oh no.

Looking at her sister, Jetta saw more of the same disturbing signs. Jaeia's skin, paler than ever before, only served to exacerbate the dark bags beneath her eyes.

Don't think of that now, she told herself.

"Let's grab a lift," Jetta said as they entered the corridor.

"Maybe not," Jaeia remarked, fanning the smoke from her face. Inoperative lifts and shattered equipment formed various blockades across the walkways. "I guess we're running."

Soldiers, trapped beneath fallen beams and debris, cried out for help as they ran through the corridors and down the access shafts to the bridge. Before Jetta could even put her thoughts to words, Jaeia cut her off: "I know we can't help them right now."

Already too upset with herself to argue with her sister, Jetta swallowed her response as they squeezed through the broken doors leading to the bridge.

"Commanders," Wren acknowledged as he helped his helmsmen out from under a collapsed routing duct.

"How's the Fleet, Sir?" Jaeia asked, offering an extra hand.

"We've lost a warship close to the impact point," the CCO said, wiping the blood from his eyes. The cut above his brow looked deep, but none of his injuries appeared life-threatening. "I'm just getting the rest of the reports in now."

Jetta considered the options silently with her sister. "Lieutenant," she said, addressing the navigations officer. "What are the readings on the distortion field?"

The wounded officer crawled up to his terminal and punched in. When the numbers came up he blinked several times and got closer to the screen. "This can't be right."

"Report, lieutenant!" Wren said.

"Sir, these readings indicate that the distortion field is... receding."

"Chief, my sister and I can helm two warships and pursue," Jetta offered.

Before Wren could respond, the viewscreen fizzled and popped. An image oscillated across the projectors, and a high-frequency whine shrilled over the speakers.

"What is that?" Wren shouted as they all covered their ears. "Who's on the communications relay?"

"People of the Starways, I am Urusous Li, your loyal son, and I have returned."

"How is he doing this?" Wren said, running over to the communication relay.

Jetta took in her old enemy. Standing in front of a red and black flag bearing the symbol of a bird and prey, Li sported the same brazen smile and air of self-righteousness she remembered from their first encounter,

Something's different, she thought, trying understand her gut reaction.

Did he always have those scars? Jaeia responded, tapping into her sights.

Jetta zoned in on her sister's observation. Faint scars crisscrossed the skin around Li's right eye, and a new deformation partially closed his ear on the same side.

No, those are new.

"I think I've seen those kind of scars before, and that symbol," Jaeia whispered, forehead knitting.

Jetta tuned into her sister's thoughts, helping Jaeia search their collective memories for a connection to the red and black flag.

Fiorah—no. The Dominion Core? A borrowed memory—no. The Alliance? The old USC? A Contact mission—an SMT operation? Where have I seen it?

Heart thumping in her chest, Jetta felt a sense of dread looming over her as Li continued his speech.

Oh Gods—

Jetta saw it first as Jaeia replayed the memory: the flash of his ring as he saluted with his martini glass, his diamond-toothed smile making her heart stop in her chest.

The same symbol etched in black gold.

Victor.

"He's on every channel, Sir," a crewman said. "He's jammed the entire wave network. I don't know how he's doing it, but he's everywhere."

"I come to you with a promise," Li said. "The Alliance has failed to protect you from the threat of the Deadwalkers, and it has failed to secure the homelands. Under my banner, I promise peace—"

"What the hell?" Jetta exclaimed as her sleeve vibrated.

"I have it, too," Jaeia whispered.

Side by side, they accepted the alert.

Not much time, the message read. *Input this sequence or you all will perish at the right hand of the devil.*

A numerical sequence followed, as did a subroutine for a security lockout.

"What is this?" Jetta said.

"I don't know," Jaeia said, looking more closely. "But it looks like a defense patch for our systems."

"...pledge your allegiance to the Galactic Republic and be

promised life, liberty, and the pursuit of wealth—" Li proclaimed in the background.

"Can you turn that thing off?" Wren shouted to his crew.

"Right hand of the devil..." Jaeia muttered.

"Can we trust the source of this message? What if it is Victor—what if it's a trick?" Jetta said as Jaeia ran over to an open terminal.

After wiping the debris off the screen, her sister downloaded the patch from her sleeve. "I think it's her again," Jaeia said, concentration trained on the data transfer.

"You mean... our mother?"

"Yes."

"How can you be sure?" Jetta asked.

"I can't," Jaeia said, fingers racing across the keyboard. "It's just a feeling."

Li's voice boomed over the airwaves. "...and to prove to you the corruption and conspiracy that saturates our current governing body, I give you the Alliance's answer to their enemies: the Sleeper Program."

Jetta's attention snapped to the viewscreen as the gruesome footage of the surgical procedures used to make a Sleeper Agent played out. Awake but paralyzed, the subjects, children and adult alike, lay helplessly as drills bored into their skulls.

"Gods have mercy," Wren whispered.

Unable to look away, Jetta watched as tears streamed from the victims' eyes and pooled into the blood collecting around their heads. Next, robotic-assisted arms fed guidewires through the cranial hole, burrowing deep into the exposed gray matter. Smoke curled up to the lights as an overhead locking system unleashed an electrical current.

So many people, Jaeia said across their bond.

Faces of all the victims cycled through. Jetta didn't recognize any except for one.

Agracia—

"That last victim you saw was Admiral Unipoesa's own daughter, his own flesh and blood, whom he turned into a Sleeper because she failed to measure up to his standards," Li said. "Tell me, if your leaders can abandon and dispose of their own children, then what do you think will happen to the rest of you?"

He took on an even grander tone. "If you choose to remain with the Alliance, you align yourself with an impotent Fleet and sadistic, incompetent leadership. But if you choose life and liberty, the Galactic Republic welcomes you under her flag."

Stunned and horrified, Jetta could barely form the thoughts to share with her sister. *This is so much worse than I could have ever imagined.*

I know, Jaeia replied, steering all her efforts into the transfer on the terminal interface.

"Sir—we're being hailed," one of the crewman announced.

"Put it in," Wren said.

"Gaeshin Wren," Li said, sneering. "Another pathetic CCO. Oh—and look—the diabolical twins of the apocalypse. I'm not impressed."

Jetta peeked over at her sister. *Faster, Jaeia.*

Then stop pestering me, she said. *At least buy me some time.*

"Urusous Li, you're under arrest," Wren said. Jetta admired him for maintaining his composure. "Lay down your arms and—".

"Chief, I just saved your hides and this is the thanks I get?" Li said, acting hurt. "The Deadwalkers are retreating. You're safe—for now."

Just as she moved to position herself in front of the viewscreen to address Li, Jetta's breath hitched in her chest. A distant light in the back of her mind raced toward her, spearing into her with a thousand voices concentrated into just one. Her arms and legs exploded with electric current, invigorating her senses. *I know what we have to do.*

"Can you network that defense patch?" Jetta said, stumbling over to her sister, arms and legs tingling as the effect died down.

"I'm trying, but it's going to take some time," Jaeia said. "Whatever Li did to tap into the wave network and our communications systems has jammed our ship-to-ship transmission."

"I'm only going to say this one more time. Lay down your arms and prepare to be boarded," Wren asserted.

"Your warships are no match for my Fleet," Li said, goading the CCO.

What? Jetta thought, trying to understand Li's angle. *He's got nothing more than a handful of fighters and a few refurbished frigates from the pre-Dominion era.*

Stupefied, Wren pointed out what seemed obvious: "One of my

warliners could easily take down your 'Fleet,' Li, let alone my entire legion of warships."

A look of satisfaction crossed Li's face. "I have been waiting for this moment for a long time," he hissed just before his image winked out.

"I want him in the brig in less than an hour," Wren said calmly, taking a seat in the command chair. "Ready arms and target the lead frigate."

"Just one more second—" Jaeia said, hunching over the terminal.

But as the tactician targeted their armament, the lights dimmed, and Jaeia's console went dead.

"Status?" Wren said.

"All systems offline," the helmsmen announced. "We're running on backup life-support."

Jumping terminal to terminal, Jetta tried to reboot the interface. "What happened?"

Jaeia cursed under her breath, hands in her hair. "I thought I downloaded it in time."

A split second later, the power came back on, and the ship rumbled as the turrets fired.

"Systems back online, but shields are down to 20 percent," the helmsman said. "Recharging. Sir, the enemy has opened fire."

"The other warships—" Jaeia whispered.

Li's ships fired, targeting the main drives of the Alliance warships. With shields rendered inoperative and power down, most were destroyed with a single volley. More explosions rocked nearby battleships and destroyers, setting off a chain reaction.

"Why aren't their shields up? Why aren't they returning fire?" Wren shouted above the din.

"They've infiltrated our defense systems," Jaeia said.

"Why aren't we down?"

"Because I downloaded a patch. I don't know if anybody else in our network is protected."

"Concentrate all fire on their frigates," Wren said.

"Sir, my guidance system is offline," the tactical officer said.

Jetta pushed him aside and manually entered the coordinates to the frigate, relaying on her intuition for the numbers. "Firing."

No match for the weapons of the Alliance flagship, the lead

frigate went down on the first hit. The rest of the rogue fleet retreated behind Tellemikas, charging up their drives.

"Sir, the enemy ships have engaged their jump cycle," one of the crewman reported.

"Pursue and destroy!" Wren commanded.

"They're outside targetable range, and engines are still offline," the navigations officer replied.

"Send the fighters," Wren tried.

"Communications aren't up yet," Jetta said, working the console next to her sister.

The bridge crew watched helplessly as the rogue fleet jumped away in a flash of light.

"*Godich*," Wren said under his breath. Neither twin had ever seen him so emotional.

Jetta left her station to speak privately with the chief commanding officer. "Sir, the engines are offline, but the jump drive is still operational. Jaeia and I could take a fighter and manually upload the defense patch to the other remaining starcraft while the *Star Runner* returns to the Central Starbase and uploads it to the rest of the interior Fleet."

Wren pursed his lips. "Make it happen, Commander."

"How did things turn out like this?" Jetta asked, heading towards the lift shaft as Jaeia trailed behind.

Jaeia waited to answer until after they'd reached the docking bay. "I don't know."

The only ship undamaged by the initial impact was a two-man stealth fighter. As Jetta loaded up, Jaeia stopped her. "I'm afraid, Jetta. This doesn't feel right."

"I know, but we don't have any other choice. Come on, Jae," Jetta said, popping on her helmet. "Time is against us."

Jaeia zipped into a pilot's suit and jumped into the cockpit next to her sister, downloading the defense patch as Jetta ran through checks.

"You're not driving. You're a terrible driver," Jaeia said, trying to take over the controls as Jetta hit the ignition.

"Like hell you are," Jetta said, wrenching free and clipping the edge of the bay door. Sensing her sister holding back a chuckle, Jetta grumbled. "Don't you say a word."

Instead of responding with a jibe, Jaeia's face blanched.

"Hey, are you okay?" Jetta asked.

Her twin coughed violently, clutching her chest. "We're not doing so well, are we?" she wheezed.

"No, we aren't. Just like old times, though, right?" Jetta said, thinking of their last few months on Fiorah.

"Jetta," Jaeia started. She paused while she contacted the damaged warship stuck in the orbit around Tellemikas. "I don't want to give up. Not now. Not when there's a chance."

Jetta looked at her sister, and though she couldn't see her sister's eyes through her visor, she felt the longing in her heart. "I know."

The com screeched and whined. Jetta tapped the signature waiting approval, noting its foreign source.

"Track it?"

"On it," Jaeia said.

Jetta accepted the call, and the top right subscreen flickered to life.

"Warchild."

"Victor," Jaeia said.

His seamless pink face and unusual glass lenses took Jetta aback, though she wasn't sure why. As she tried to rein in her own fears, her sister's conflicted emotions boiled in the back of her mind, adding to her own growing discomfort.

"You've met the new commander of my military, yes?" he said.

"Urusous Li is commanding *your* military?"

"Well, of course. The balance of power in the Starways is changing. This is a time for real leadership."

"Who are you?" Jetta interrupted.

"No," Victor said, tilting his head, "The question is, who are you?"

Jetta looked at her twin. "What the hell do you want, Victor? Because once we're done with Li I'm coming after you."

Victor clicked his tongue and wagged his finger. "Another sowed you, your mother birthed you, but I gave you your soul."

Suddenly furious, Jetta extended herself, reaching out and into Victor, ready to devour him with her talent. Jaeia screamed, but it was too late.

Caught up in the black tide of his mind, Jetta was swept down and away, further and further from herself as reality splintered. Her mind crossed boundaries she didn't know existed, physical, psionic, and beyond any known realm, until she came to a place without time. The past fused with the present and future while voices in the background narrated the doom of the human race in a language she had never heard before, but implicitly understood.

Scenes from ancient times threaded together. Long spears and arrows flew through the air as swords clashed and axes cut into bone. Hollow eyes and a serpentine smile looked down upon the never-ending battle as the blood of forgotten men painted battlefields red. Weapons changed from stones to blades to guns and armored cars, winged fighters, and suborbital ships, but the dark force behind it did not, poisoning malleable minds with hatred.

Images shifted and reformed. Jetta saw a man tied to a post, tortured by gray, faceless assailants, pleading for death. Different people—men, women and children—suffered the same fate as centuries passed, the same atrocity committed over and over again until she lost count.

Jetta tried to turn away, but everywhere she looked were their pleading eyes, faces upturned as their tormentors cut away their flesh bit by bit.

Unable to catch her breath or slow the hammering of her heart, Jetta sank to her knees and covered her face, trying to separate herself from the serpentine smile that pervaded the dark realm. Even with her eyes closed, Jetta saw the dead eyes that masked its true identity and heard its silver tongue whispering untruths to the weak and wounded.

—kill or be killed—

—strip down your enemy—

—condemn them to Hell—

Why don't they see? *she wondered.*

Droves of ill-gotten memories pushed through her mind. Jetta witnessed men and women, blind and hobbled, submitting themselves to false Gods. Screaming and chanting on their knees, they called out to different deities over the ages, but the lord they sought had only one name.

(My name.)

Did she think that—or did someone whisper it to her? Jetta tried to pull back, but found herself stuck fast, unable to turn around or see her way out.

(With eyes open, they burn,) *rang out over and over again in her mind as she fought to right her senses.*

The final moments of Earth scorched her eyes, mushroom clouds and explosions marring the horizon. Panicked screams erupted as the sky turned black and the day to night, and the world ended in a blaze of fire.

Confused and disoriented, Jetta no longer understood her own feelings. Even though she felt repulsed and frightened by the breadth of death and destruction she had witnessed over the course of human existence, a poisonous undertow capsized her conscience.

There is such power here, *she realized, unable to surface from the timeless, inhuman well of Victor's mind. The nightmarish memory of the Deadwalker collective grazed her awareness, only to be dismissed. (This is a thousand fold of what they offered me.)*

Ambivalence wormed its way into her heart, awakening unpalatable needs as she kneeled upon the charred remains of Earth. (I want his power.)

Did she think that? Or was it some terrible thing inside her wanting to connect with the dark tethers of Victor's mind?

No, it isn't like that, *Jetta told herself.* I can take him. All of him. I am strong enough to bear his wickedness.

With Victor's knowledge and her talent, she could right the Sentient races of the Starways. The citizens of the Starways are weak, driven by vanity and desires of the flesh, *she decided.* I have the wisdom of a thousand ages. With me in control, there would be no more senseless violence; there would be strict order and peace.

Jetta dug her hands into the ashes of the Earth, squeezing until blood ran between her fingers. After all, it's always the same—one warring faction against the other, brutality ruling over the weak. But that will end with me.

She would take charge, and she alone would cast judgment. Needless death and destruction would cease. Punishment and fairness would be hers to decide. And should enemies arise, she would devour them, even if it meant hurting someone she loved.

(Jaeia. Jahx.) Unable to remember anything but the pain of Victor's world, Jetta closed off her heart. (They are ignorant, and if they can't see my way, then I will terrorize their minds with the bleak truth. The Starways needs a ruler, and I will be the one to rule.)

The ashes shifted and the ground rumbled. Knocked backwards by the jolt, Jetta tumbled down the heap of debris. Before she could right herself, shafts of light exploded from the ground.

Jetta covered her eyes, afraid of the light, but, sensing the warmth and radiance emanating from the source, dared a glance. From the ashes emerged an angel, a man with an immeasurable second shadow and an aura so bright that her heart sang. His eyes, kind and gentle, connected to a forgotten place within as the dark pull inside her yielded to his purifying light.

As he approached, he reached for her, luminescent skin shining in the dark of Victor's world. Jetta reached back, only to bear the horror of what she had become. Black, scaled and hideous, she didn't recognize her own skin. Terrified, she tried to stop herself as she sunk her claws into the man. His light faded and his skin eroded, transforming him into something inhuman.

(No!) *she cried, breaking free as M'ah Pae erupted from the fallen angel's skins.*

Jetta scrambled through the wastelands of Old Earth with the Motti Overlord in pursuit, his screeching voice tearing into her skull as his spidery feet cracked against the ground like thunder.

I have to get away from here. I have to get back to me—what I was before this. I have to get out of Victor's mind, *she thought, searching for a familiar connection within. Gray eyes flashed through her memory.* (My sister.)

(Jaeia, help me!) *she screamed, falling to her knees.*

The thing with the burning red eye grabbed her by the waist with its mechanical arms, hissing and cackling. "You are nothing!"

As M'ah Pae reared back to spear her with his pincers, Jaeia's presence breached the void and pulled vigorously at her mind, retracting her back across time, across the stars.

"I warned your sister about that," Victor said, tapping his head.

"You're not human," Jetta gasped, holding her head in her hands as she fell back into her own body. Her stomach stewed with sickness, but she did her best not to throw-up in her air-regulated helmet. "You're the devil."

Victor laughed. "The devil. What an antiquated idea."

"What the hell do you want?" Jaeia said, holding on to Jetta.

"I want you to join me. There are many that wish to control you, to cage your powers and your minds. But I do not. I will set you free. I will give you the answers you seek about your life, your family and your destiny."

"Destiny?" Jetta said, head still spinning.

"Warchild," Victor said, leaning into the subscreen. "I'll be waiting here, on Jue Hexron, for your arrival."

"Jetta," Jaeia whispered, her eyes growing wide in disbelief as the image of Victor panned out and two figures in the background came into focus. Galm's smile was the same, toothless and timid, though his hair was a little thinner and his posture more hunched. Lohien had also aged, but her sad expression remained unchanged. They held hands as they waved to the camera.

Victor kept his voice just above a whisper. "And so will your aunt and uncle."

"Jaeia..." Jetta said as the transmission ended. She looked at her gloved hands, but all she could see was the same black, scaly skin she had seen in Victor's mind. "I don't know who I am anymore. I don't know what I'm becoming," she said. "I feel like... I feel like something terrible inside me is trying to get out."

Jetta heard her sister's fear in the back of her mind: *The Abomination.*

"Hold on, Jetta," Jaeia said, inputting the coordinates for their course heading into the jumpdrive. "This isn't over yet."

Jetta surprised herself with the speed of her attack as she smacked her sister's helmet against the crossbeam. Mumbling, Jaeia slumped in her seat.

Unable to sense her twin, or even her own feelings, Jetta put the fighter into standby mode.

"I'm afraid it is for me," Jetta said, unbuckling her sister and hoisting her over her seat. With a grunt, she dragged Jaeia to the emergency booster pods in the secondary chamber. Jaeia tried to open her eyes, unintelligible words spilling from her mouth in slurs as Jetta clicked her into the booster.

"We both knew it would come to this," Jetta said, cinching herself on a safety line to a latch panel as she prepared to open the hatch and eject her sister from the fighter.

The medical frigate cast a shadow from above as it drifted by on its side, emergency power backups sputtering. Jetta released the locks, and her sister shot out of the fighter, skimming the belly of the frigate.

After repressurizing the secondary chamber, Jetta unhooked

from the safety line and returned to the cockpit. With a strange self-assuredness she inputted the jump coordinates, relying on more than her own intuition. A wave of nausea rose in her throat just before she hit the ignition, but she didn't hesitate.

I'm coming, Victor.

As the jumpdrive pulled apart the strings of space-time, she felt something wet on her face.

"Goodbye, Jaeia."

The saga continues...

    Jaeia lurched over the railing, but fell backwards onto the lift as if someone had kicked her in the gut.
    "Captain, are you okay?" one of the medics asked as another checked her vital signs.
    Jaeia reached out, trying to grasp at the connection that was no longer there.
    Jetta was dead.

—Triorion: Reborn

For more information go to: www.triorion.com

Acknowledgements

Once again, I couldn't have done this without the support of fans, friends, family, and a good editor. Special thanks to all my beta readers, but most of all to Paula Herrmann—you really went above and beyond. I can't tell you how much that means to me.

And to everyone else who helped, from the little bits of encouragement to the constant harassment for the second book in the series: thank you and enjoy.

About the Author

L. J. Hachmeister is a registered nurse from Denver, Colorado. When not writing novels, she enjoys everything from the arts to mountain climbing with friends, family, and her favorite canine companions.

Made in the USA
Middletown, DE
04 April 2017